A GATHERING OF EAGLES

ROBERT DIXON

PublishBritannica
London   Baltimore

© 2004 by Robert Dixon.
All rights reserved. No part of this book may be reproduced, stored in a retrieval system, or transmitted in any form or by any means without the prior written permission of the publishers, except by a reviewer who may quote brief passages in a review to be printed in a newspaper, magazine, or journal.

First printing

ISBN: 1-4137-3498-7
PUBLISHED BY PUBLISHBRITANNICA
www.publishbritannica.com
London   Baltimore

This book is dedicated to the memory of
Squadron Leader John Sample, DFC.,
whose short life provided information
and inspiration.

Acknowledgments

The production of a book such as this one relies on a great deal of, not only help, but also encouragement. This has come from a great number of various people and organizations. The incoming help can be divided into roughly two groups: Official and private. On the private side I am indebted to Nicholas Craig, who allowed me to pillage through his father's collection of documents and photographs. He was also a mine of information on his late father as well as 607 Squadron. Charles J. Sample also provided me with his uncle's photograph album to view at my discretion. The late William Whitty, former pilot on 607 Squadron, was also a mine of information on the squadron, in particular its early members in the early days.

The family Heppell, and in particular Philip Heppell, were a great help with piecing together the life of their late father, Philip W.E. Heppell. The late Kathleen Collier provided me with information and photographs of her late brother, Ralph V. Hogg. I would also like to thank William Ricalton for his input on Alan L. Ricalton; and Maurice W. Cottam for his help with his brother. Among the many others who deserve not only thanks, but praise are: Wentworth Appleby, S.H Ashurst, Miss B. Cracknell, Reg Charleton, Trevor Handley, George Hall, Sara O'Doherty, Douglas J. Ross, Derek J. Wilson and D.G. Mears. Behind all these people they are an even greater number to whom I am indebted and sadly, I know I have forgotten. I acknowledge their help and give them thanks, they know who they are.

Of the official help, I am deeply indebted to that fount of the Countries information, the PRO. Also the RAF Museum, The Spitfire And Hurricane Hall, Manston—who deserve special thanks, Tangmere Museum, Battle of Britain Museum, Hawkinge. The CWGC were always helpful as was the RAF Historical Branch. The Bundesarchive in Berlin and Achen were, as always, a mine of information on the Luftwaffe. The records office of Durham was always helpful, as were the records center in Newcastle upon Tyne and the records office of Northumberland at Melton Park, Gosforth, as well as the Records Centre Morpeth. Various libraries were also invaluable; among these were the libraries of The Guildhall, London, West Hartlepool, and the Newcastle upon Tyne City Library. Not to mention a great number of libraries up and down the Country. Also much deserving of help, but rarely getting any, are the various cemeteries and crematoria throughout the Country who have given help. No matter how small your contribution: thank you all.

My thanks to the publishers, PublishAmerica, for taking on the book in the first place. And, in particular, Melissa Crook, Loretta Burdette and Kerry J. Stanley for their help, and also the editorial team.

Thanks must also go to my wife, Shirley, for putting up with the inconvenience, as well as supplying endless meals and cups of tea. And the inconvenience that has lasted over a number of years.

Table of Contents

Introduction	9
William Armstrong	15
George Atkinson, DFM	19
Mathew Richard Atkinson	25
Wilkinson Barnes	27
Sidney Baxter	31
James Michael Bazin, DFC	35
Henry Albert Bolton	45
Harry Hutchinson Chalder	49
Hubert Weatherby Cottam	53
John Teesdale Craig, DFM	59
George Dudley Craig	69
Henry Peter Dixon	79
Charles Edward English	83
George Mathwin Forrester	89
Anthony Douglas Forster, DFC	93
Denys Edgar Gillam, AFC	99
John Nixon Glendinning	107
William Ernest Gore, DFC	113
Douglas Hastings	119
Phillip Whaley Ellis Heppell	127
Erik Lawson Hetherington	139
Ralph Vincent Hogg	145
Maurice Milne Irving	151
Michael Jebb	155
John Ferdinand Read Jones	159

Joseph Robert Kayll, DFC, DSO	163
Ronald Gustave Kellett, DFC, DSO	173
Neville Charles Langham-Hobart	181
John Lonsdale	185
Ernest Mayne	189
James Henry Gordon McArthur, DFC	197
John William McLaughlin	203
Joseph Pearson Morrison	207
George Charles Calder Palliser	213
Vincent Parker	219
William Albert Peacock	225
Oswald St John Pigg	229
Alan Leslie Ricalton	237
Marmaduke Ridley	243
Robert Durham Rutter	249
Stuart Nigel Rose	253
John Sample, DFC	259
Richard Smithson	271
Jack Stokoe	281
Sydney Stokoe	291
James Anderson Vick	295
Douglas Cyril Winter	299
Bibliography	305
Explanatory Notes	307
Ranks of RAF and Equivalent Luftwaffe Personnel	309

Introduction

The First World War brought about many changes to the face of modern warfare: the tank and trench warfare were only two of such changes. The aeroplane, still thought by many as a relatively new invention was yet another. It was soon found that the aeroplane could be used as an extended arm of the Army. In a reconnaissance role it could reach much further than the Army could see. Another adaptation was soon to follow; aeroplanes could be fitted with bombs, therefore extending the reach of the Army, for it could hit the enemy with more accuracy than the long-range guns. However, if an aeroplane could carry bombs it could also carry guns. If the enemy had aeroplanes that could carry bombs, then aeroplanes fitted with guns could destroy the bombers. A new fighting man was created from the ranks of the Royal Flying Corps, the fighter pilot.

With the end of hostilities and the end of the Royal Flying Corps, for it had in 1918 become the Royal Air Force; the need for fighting men in the sky was toned down. The pilots of the Royal Air Force were known universally as members of the world's largest flying club. It is not too great an exaggeration to claim that most pilots of the RAF knew everyone else in the inter-war years. Nothing stays the same and all was soon to change. It was during these inter war years that another arm of the RAF, the Auxiliary Air Force, came into being. Originally most of these Auxiliary Squadrons were light bomber units but many of them were to be transferred to Fighter Command. Where once pilots had been mainly professionals, in that they were full-time pilots, with the coming of the Auxiliary Air Force came the part-time pilots. Although still of the officer class they were mainly looked down upon by their more professional, full-time brothers.

Full-time pilots had gone through a long training programme; part of that training was to turn them not only into officers, but also gentlemen. The men of the Auxiliary Air Force were faced with a shorter and more leisurely training programme. For them training was to be two nights a week, along with the weekend. On qualifying as a pilot they automatically became of the officer class with the rank of Flight Lieutenant. Their shorter training had allowed them to jump the promotion queue, already they were to outrank some of their longer serving full-time brothers. Some of the full-time pilots are known not to have taken this situation lightly.[1] With the clouds of war already looming on the horizon, the RAF brought in another extension of their flying arm: the Volunteer Reserve.

As with the Auxiliary Air Force, the Volunteer Reserve pilots were to be trained on a part-time basis, some of this training being carried out by the Auxiliary Air Force. However, these were to be a different breed of men again. On completion of their training the men of the RAFVR became sergeant pilots. The RAF had always been class conscious; mainly this was to be seen between ground crew and aircrew. Now, even the flying arm itself had become class conscious later, especially in the early war years, this was to bring about more than a little friction over leadership of a squadron in the air. It was not uncommon for sergeant pilots to lead officers into battle, a situation not often met with in the other services.

It is during this almost twenty-year period that this book is set. Fledgling years that saw the Auxiliary Air Force come into being as well as the strengthening of the RAF.

In the form of the RAFVR as the world teetered towards all-out conflict, full-time pilots would fight alongside men who, until a short time before, had worked in the industries of the country. Manual workers alongside white-collar workers joined forces to fly and fight against the common foe, but it was at times an uneasy alliance.

The beginning of the war brought expectation that was soon to turn to boredom in what came to be known as the 'phoney war'. Soon this was to give way to the real battles. Firstly came the battle of France: many of the following stories have their roots there, while for others what was to be their first taste of battle was also to be their last. The final battle of this conflict was to be fought over the beaches around the area of Dunkirk. This episode of the war is thought by many to have been kind of victory; for others it was seen as a miracle but by most it was seen for what it was, a defeat. The next stage in the air fighting was to be fought over the British heartland itself: an air battle, unique in our history, which has been handed down as the Battle of Britain.

Battle of Britain: these words are used to describe a unique battle that occurred in our more recent past. However, for many these words cause confusion. It is truly amazing that a large number of people today are unsure of when exactly this battle was fought and what it was about. A further number are quite sure. It took place in the summer months of 1940. Most of the men named here fought in this battle, however, in no way is this a rewrite of that battle but in writing about these men various questions have to be addressed and these concern the battle that they fought in.

The official version states that the Battle of Britain began in July of 1940, finishing on the last day of October in that year. As with many 'official versions' it is fraught with its own problems. A battle of any kind is fought between opposing forces. That battle cannot be won, or lost, until one of the protagonists has left the field. If this simple rule is applied to the Battle of Britain, then that battle cannot have ended before May 1941. That was the date the German Air Force, the Luftwaffe, turned its attentions elsewhere. Early 1941 is becoming increasingly accepted by the historians, both British and German, as the end of the battle. In retrospect it is only common sense. Although this book does not set out to analyse the Battle of Britain, some of the myths—and there are many surrounding the conflict—have to be examined. Certainly one of these has to be the answer to 'who won'? The honest answer is no one. If the Luftwaffe had been so decisively beaten, as some would have us believe, how could that same Luftwaffe even think of fighting on the Russian front?

This battle, like countless others before it, could not be fought without one main ingredient: men. The following is an attempt to place these men where they should be, with their contemporaries. I am of a generation who were born during World War Two. We were brought up with the 'myth' of the Battle of Britain. In the last twenty or so years much more information has come to light on this unique battle. However, by some odd quirk, the Battle of Britain has become even less well known than it used to be. There are arguments as to why this has happened, but they are beyond the scope of this book. However, one reason must lie with the nostalgia brigade. Most battles have their own battlefields, note the numbers who visit the battlefields of the First World War. An air battle, however, is fleeting. As soon as it is over all sight of it is lost, apart from a few wrecks that may litter the ground, with its passing the sky once more is blue. Not a sign of a battle in sight and no battlefield to visit.

Over the years, beginning with the 1941 film; *First of The Few*, a stereotype has been put forward as to what a Battle of Britain pilot should be. At first this was a morale boosting exercise. Later with books and films, a public hungry for heroes gradually accepted that stereotype as the real thing. There was only one accent, what came to be known as the clipped BBC accent. No regional accents here. In fact no foreign ones either. It was Churchill himself who gave birth to the legend of 'The Few', a misnomer if ever there was one. Almost three thousand men of RAF Fighter Command contested the Battle of Britain, although not at the same time. A number, nevertheless, that hardly constitutes a 'Few'. A large number of these men originated from many different countries. If one thing should be made clear above all others, it is the fact that the men who took part in the Battle of Britain, like all battles before it, came from all walks of life and many different cultures. We were not, as the 'myth' would have us believe, standing alone.

What started out as an interest for me soon became a quest. Although many men who contested the Battle of Britain have become forgotten, indeed some were never known in the first place, an increasing number of men seem to have been all but forgotten. In fact, they have become almost wiped off the face of history. Literature on the Battle of Britain has also passed most of these men by.

In the following pages there will be found almost every type of person which, the 'myth' makers would have us believe, makes up the Battle of Britain pilot. There are 'aces', men who have been officially credited with at least five confirmed 'kills'. There are leaders of men, men who led the squadrons in this epic battle. For many, their career began in what came to be known as the battle of France; some were active even before that. There are also men who faced that living hell in the sky; trapped in a burning cockpit. Also numbered among these men are those who gave not only their life but that most basic of rights, a Christian burial. For these men who fought their last enemy out of sight of anyone else but their foe: for them, their last resting place remains unknown. There is no finality in their demise, no gravestone, no entry in a burial register; only a question mark to mark their passing. These men were posted 'missing'; today they remain so.

There will also be found, in the following pages men who, although they were forced out of the fighting, usually by enemy action, steadfastly refused to give up the fight. For them the war went on, albeit behind the prison camp wire. Often their lone fight behind the enemy lines was fraught with more danger than they had known in the skies, and that could be frightening enough. There are, of course, those men who just did not last long enough to begin any kind of career. These men are every bit as important as their more illustrious colleagues. They faced their final battle with courage against a dangerous and, more than likely, more experienced foe. This they did with the minimum of training. They were soon forgotten by their comrades who, for their own sanity, pushed the memory of their dead comrades aside so that they could continue their fight. In most cases these men have remained forgotten. At the other end of the table there are men who began their career long before the outbreak of hostilities. At the war's end they were still flying. The odds against these men surviving for so long and at such a pace was long indeed.

Many of those mentioned here, if their name was mentioned to any but the most knowledgeable, would bring forth the reply; who? However, they have one uniting bond—they did their job without seeking to gain glory from it. When an aircraft was shot from under them, they did what was asked of them; they got into another one and carried on the fight. In many cases they went much further than the call of duty. These men should never be forgotten.

INTRODUCTION NOTES
Peter Townsend: *Time And Chance*, P 95. Townsend was to describe this new intake of men in the late 1930s as '…parvenu pilots'. He was later to change his views after he had fought alongside them in the heavy fighting of the Battle of Britain.

WILLIAM ARMSTRONG, 41812
PILOT OFFICER

William Armstrong was born in 1922. He was the son of William and Jessie Armstrong, who made their family home in Darlington, County Durham. As an eighteen-year old, William Armstrong applied to join the RAF. He was accepted on a short service commission. Flying training began in January of 1939. After the completion of which, it is thought that Armstrong was posted to 54 Squadron. At that time, 54 Squadron was a Spitfire unit, having converted from the Gloster Gladiator shortly before the outbreak of war. Armstrong also had a period at Number 4 Ferry Pilot Pool before being posted on to Number 7 Operational Training Unit (OTU) at Hawarden, in North Wales. Armstrong arrived there on September 3, 1940. Presumably this was for further training.

October 28 saw Armstrong posted to his first fighter squadron. This was Number 74 Squadron, the famous 'Tigers'. At this time 74 Squadron were based at Biggin Hill in Kent. Having just returned from a 'rest' at Coltishall, 74 Squadron had arrived at Biggin Hill on October 15. With the end of October, the main daylight attacks by the Luftwaffe had, in the main, deceased. Large raids had been mostly cut. The main thrusts of the Luftwaffe were now to be carried out during the hours of darkness. However, this was not to say that the Luftwaffe was defeated or inactive. Number 74 Squadron were in action on November 14. A mass raid was detected over the Channel making an attempt to bomb a convoy. This raid consisted in the main of Junkers Ju 87 dive-bombers, numbering around fifty. A large formation of Messerschmitt Me 109s were acting as escort. The German fighter escort was made up of Me 109s of Jagdgeschwader 26 (JG 26) and three Gruppe III/JG 5.

At 1.30 P.M., 74 Squadron were scrambled along with 66 Squadron. 'Sailor' Malan on this occasion was away on leave and Pilot Officer J.C. Mungo Park was at the head of the 'Tigers'. Arriving on the scene, 74 Squadron was faced with heavy opposition from the fighter escort as it attempted to get at the Ju87s. Armstrong was flying Spitfire P 7386. Wynn states that this Spitfire was P 7836. However, this Spitfire did not fly until 1941.[1] P 7386 was a Mk 2 Spitfire from the second batch built by Vickers Armstrong at their factory at Castle Bromwich. Taken on charge by Number 38 Maintenance Unit (MU), it was passed on to 74 Squadron on October 24. When Armstrong took possession of it, P 7386 was relatively new.

Heavy though the fighter escort was, 74 Squadron fell on the Ju 87s. These aircraft had been shown to been to be one of the weaknesses in the Luftwaffe. This had especially come to light during the Battle of Britain. Armstrong singled out a Ju 87 and began his attack. As the Spitfire closed on its target, the German pilot jettisoned his bomb load and tried to make good his escape. The rear gunner did his best to foil Armstrong's attack, firing short bursts from his gun. However, his aim was reported as not being good. Armstrong now pressed home further attacks.

With further bursts from the Spitfire's guns finding their target, the Ju 87 finally succumbed to the attack. Rolling over onto its back, it carried out its final dive... into the Channel. Armstrong immediately singled out another Ju 87 and once more carried out his attack. By now the air fighting had neared the English coast. Unfortunately for Armstrong, this gave the ground defences the chance to join in the fighting. Heavy AA fire was aimed at the Ju 87 with little thought for the pursuing Spitfire. Armstrong was frustrated in his attempt to harry the Ju 87. Deciding discretion was better than valour on this occasion. He could only claim the Ju 87 as a probable.

With the fight now over and the surviving Ju 87s on their way back to their bases in France. Armstrong turned to form up with other Spitfires of 74 Squadron. As he did so, his Spitfire was hit in the engine at least once. Cossey,[2] states that a stray shell hit Armstrong's Spitfire. However, it would appear that it was more than likely that

Armstrong had been bounced by Me 109s. Both Major Adolf Galland, Geschwader Kommodore of JG 26, and Oberleutnant Joachim Muncheberg, Staffel Kapitan of the 7th Staffel JG 26, made claims for a Spitfire destroyed. A multi-claim was not unusual in the heat of the battle. One aircraft would carry out an attack. As the aircraft fell, another would make an attack on the same target. Both would think that they had a legitimate claim. It would seem that one of the above carried out the attack on Armstrong. In this fight only one Spitfire was reported lost, Spitfire P 7386 flown by Armstrong. The engine of Armstrong's Spitfire then blew up, forcing its pilot to take to his parachute. He landed unhurt near Tilmanstone in Kent. From there he made his way back to Biggin Hill.

A quiet period was to follow and we do not hear of Armstrong again until February 5, 1941. On patrol, in the area of Dover, Armstrong was among those who attacked a Dornier Do 17. This aircraft was also described as a Do 215. Armstrong was only awarded a share with three others.

Sporadic raids by the Luftwaffe kept 74 Squadron's pilots on their toes during their stay at Biggin Hill. With the beginning of May came a move to Gravesend. This was a small, bleak airfield, which guarded the eastern approaches to London. On the downside, the airfield was the cause of many accidents due to its short, bumpy runway. However, on the plus side, accommodation for the pilots was in Cobham Hall, an Elizabethan Mansion. During this time Armstrong was to successfully attack an Me 109 while on patrol on May 9, 1941. Most of the time, however, the Me 109s attacked the airfield at low-level and were gone as quickly as they appeared.

On October 23, 1941, Armstrong was promoted to the rank of Flight Lieutenant. He does not appear in the records again until February 18, 1943. At this time he was attached to the Ferry Pilots Pool at Gibraltar when he was killed. Armstrong was buried in the Dely Ibrahim War Cemetery in Algeria in grave 3. G. 15. The war cemetery lies in hilly country about six miles south west of Algiers along the road to Blida.

Armstrong Notes
1. Morgan and Shacklady: *Spitfire: The History*, P 111.
2. Cossey: *Tigers: The Story of No 74 Fighter Squadron*, P 83.

George Atkinson, DFM, 47413
Sergeant Pilot

The coastal town of Blyth in Northumberland was the birthplace of George Atkinson. Born June 16, 1915, George was the youngest son of Robert Smith Atkinson and his wife Isabella. At the time of his birth, the family home for the Atkinson family was Number 16 on the High Street of Blyth. Atkinson senior worked as a joiner. In later years, the family were to make the move to Hambledon Street. It was here that Isabella kept a confectioners shop. A well-known haunt for the local children.

Like a large number of the children from the area, the young George Atkinson, was educated to a standard deemed good enough to earn him a place within the industry of the area. This education was carried out courtesy of Blyth Secondary School. Like a growing number of the young hopefuls within the area, George Atkinson had different ideas. For him, the way ahead lay in the RAF. There was an apprenticeship with a secure job ahead of it. It also offered him travel and security. Therefore, George Atkinson, after the tests and examinations, found himself at the Number 1 School of Technical Training at RAF Halton, Buckinghamshire. George had become one of those, affectionately referred to, as 'Trenchard's Brats'. For the next three years, Halton was to be the home of George Atkinson, 565476, as he trained to become a metal rigger.

It can safely be assumed that the training went well. On August 16, 1934, George Atkinson passed out of Halton a fully trained metal rigger. Immediately, he was posted onto the staff at the RAF College Cranwell,

Lincolnshire. This was followed by an overseas posting, which took George Atkinson toNnumber 4 Aircraft Park at Atbara. Atkinson arrived at Atbara on September 4, 1935. He was not destined for a lengthy stay as he was soon reposted to 47 Squadron based at Khartoum.

During this period, 47 Squadron flying Fairey 111 Fs and their later version, the Fairey Gordon. These aircraft were flown in the light bomber role. The squadron used two types of these aircraft; one with wheels and the other with floats. The latter were flown from the Nile. Being a two-seat aircraft, there was often the opportunity for non-flying members of the squadron to fly. It may have been on one of these flights that George Atkinson had his desire to fly kindled. What is known for sure is that, while based at Khartoum, George Atkinson volunteered for pilot training. With his successful application, George Atkinson was posted back to England. His new life as a pilot was to begin at Number 1 Depot at Uxbridge.

Atkinson's flying training was begun at Number 8 Elementary and Reserve Flying Training School (E&RFTS) at Woodley, near Reading. His training began at Woodley on September 26, lasting just over two months; it ended on November 29, 1937. Moving via Uxbridge once more, Atkinson's next move was to Number 3 Flying Training School (FTS) at South Cerney, Gloucestershire, beginning his training there on December 11. July 7, 1938 saw Atkinson pass out of Number 3 (FTS) a fully trained pilot. His next posting was to Eastchurch on the Isle of Sheppy as a staff pilot. September 3, 1939 saw Atkinson's dream fulfilled as he was posted to his first fighter squadron, Number 151.

When Atkinson joined 151 Squadron it was based at North Weald, Kent. The squadron had been equipped with the Hawker Hurricane since November 1938. Only three days after Atkinson joined the squadron, it was involved in what came to be known as the 'Battle of Barking Creek'. During the time of what came to be known as the 'Phoney War', many mistakes were made as the RAF attempted to get itself ready for the forthcoming war. The above involved faulty controlling in which fighters of 74 Squadron shot down two Hurricanes of 56 Squadron. Although 151 Squadron were only onlookers, morale was dented, not only within the squadron but, throughout Fighter Command. It must also have affected the new boy on the squadron, George Atkinson.

The squadron was fortunate to have as its commanding officer, squadron leader Edward Mortlock (Teddy) Donaldson. Donaldson was one of the old school who insisted on practice and more practice. Mainly, the practices involved scrambles, air drills, formation flying and most of all, air-firing practice. It became a matter of honour between the two resident squadrons of North Weald, 151 and 56, which did the most practice and which did it better. While with 151 Squadron, Atkinson was given plenty of practice and plenty of air firing time.

On the morning of May 12, 1940, three Hurricanes of 151 Squadrons Blue Section set course for an offensive patrol in the area of the Hook of Holland. The three Hurricanes, Flight Lieutenant Freddie Ives, Flying officer Derek Ward and Atkinson flew first from North Weald to Martlesham Heath then on to the Hook of Holland. Atkinson, on this occasion, was flying Hurricane L 1654. They formatted with a section of Blenheim bombers before taking a closer look at the Hook of Holland. On the ground they noticed a number of discarded parachutes, while only a short distance to the southwest, a small aerodrome showed evidence of the remains of some burnt out Ju 52s. No further movement was witnessed and, as there was no enemy air activity, the section returned to Martlesham Heath.

The real war for Atkinson was to begin on the morning of May 17, 1940. On this day a number of Hurricanes were ordered to France to reinforce the Air Component. The Hurricanes flew out from Manston to Abbeville. Once in France action was soon to follow. While on patrol later in the day, a number of Ju 87s were spotted. Squadron Leader Donaldson called for a number one attack. Atkinson following Flt Lt Freddie Ives attacked one of the Ju 87s. Atkinson opened fire on the Ju 87 at a range of 150 yards then again at 80 yards. The Ju 87 was not seen to carry out any evasive tactics.

The following day nine Hurricanes flew into Vitry at around 3.00 P.M. Blue and Yellow Sections, along with two Hurricanes from 56 Squadron, were immediately ordered off. Three He 111s were intercepted near Vitry and the Hurricanes began their attack. Atkinson delivered a two-seconds burst into an He 111 before breaking away from his attack. On pulling away, Atkinson saw a further three He 111s and proceeded to attack along the port side of the formation. Flames and black smoke was seen to issue from the port engine of one He 111 as it dived away. Atkinson was to make a claim for a 'probable'.[1]

Separated for a short while from the others, Atkinson eventually joined Yellow Section and joined in as they attacked a formation of twelve Me 110s. Picking out his target, Atkinson fired an eight-second burst into an Me 110 without any noticeable result. Atkinson appears at this time to be lost. He states that he flew northwest looking for an aerodrome: 'I hit the coast near LeTouquet and landed.'[2]

Atkinson was once more on patrol, May 21, when an unidentified aircraft was spotted in the distance. Blue Section was ordered to take a closer look. The aircraft turned out to be an He 126 of 1 (H)/14 PZ which was apparently doing a bit of spotting. Atkinson, flying Hurricane P 3315 attacked the He 126, giving it a four-second burst. Mortally wounded, the He 126 blew up and crashed.

July 29, 1940 saw the squadron at full strength scrambled to patrol the English Channel. There they found some forty plus Me 110s of Erprobungsgruppe 210 and ZG 26. Although battle was joined over the convoy, the outcome remained inconclusive. Both sides were to leave the scene unscathed.

August 13 was the day designated as 'Adler Tag' by the Germans. The day was to start early for 151 Squadron when they were scrambled from North Weald at 5.00 AM. A formation of enemy bombers was briefed to attack shipping in the Thames Estuary. The Dornier Do 17s of KG 2 were without their usual fighter escort and had already suffered at the hands of 74 Squadron. On this occasion Flt Lt Roddick Smith, the 'B' Flight commander, led 151 Squadron into the attack. This attack was to be a first as Flt Lt Smith was flying one of the first cannon-armed Hurricanes. Knowing that about half of his pilots were 'raw' he told them to fly through the enemy formation, dive hard and head for the clouds below. Mistakenly Smith thought that the aircraft at the rear of the formation were the fighter escort. In effect they turned out to be more Do 17s rather than the Me 110s that he had expected.

Atkinson was flying Hurricane P 3310. This was one of a production batch of five hundred aircraft built by Hawker Aircraft Ltd in March/April of 1940. These aircraft had the Mk 3 Merlin engine and metal-covered wings as opposed to the fabric-covered wings of earlier aircraft. While carrying out an attack on a Do 17, Atkinson came under heavy crossfire from other Do 17s in the formation. His Hurricane severely damaged, Atkinson baled out of his aircraft and descended into the sea off Margate. Atkinson was rescued by the

Margate lifeboat and taken to hospital near Maidstone. Atkinson was diagnosed as suffering from shock. His Hurricane was last seen diving into the sea off Christchurch.

Although listed as suffering from shock, the severity of the shock must have been a bit more than can be imagined. Atkinson was not to return to North Weald for some three weeks. On his return, it was to find that 151 Squadron had departed to Digby in Lincolnshire. Atkinson was to spend most of his time ferrying spare parts and equipment from North Weald to Digby in the squadron's Magister. He was also to deliver the spare aircraft as they became serviceable.

It was not until September 24 that Atkinson was passed officially as fit to fly. For Atkinson, however, the Battle of Britain was over. Neither he nor 151 Squadron took any further part. Only the occasional skirmish off the Lincolnshire coast gave the squadron any taste of action. March 7, 1940 saw Atkinson awarded the DFM for courage and devotion to duty. The duties of 151 Squadron had by now changed. Though still flying the Hurricane, the squadron had become a night fighter unit. Atkinson was to remain on the squadron until October of 1941.

October 31, 1941 saw Atkinson depart the squadron and take up his new post of flying instructor. This was to be with Number 60 Operational Training Unit (OTU) at East Fortune in southeast Scotland. November 24 saw Atkinson commissioned. It was as Pilot Officer Atkinson that he began training pilots on the Boulton Paul Defiant. After his period of 'resting' at the OTU, Atkinson was posted to 96 Squadron, a night fighter unit, on March 26, 1942. Number 96 Squadron were at the time based at Wrexham from where they formed part of the night defence of Liverpool. Atkinson was not to stay long with 96 Squadron. He was posted back to his old squadron, Number 151, now based at Wittering in Cambridge. Atkinson was later promoted to the rank of Flying Officer.

In 1943, Atkinson was posted back to further instructional duties. This time he was posted to Canada. Atkinson took up his post as instructor on October 15, 1943, at Number 36 OTU based at Greenwood, Nova Scotia. Promoted to the rank of Flight Lieutenant on November 24, 1943, Atkinson was posted across the airfield on July 1, 1944. Number 8 OTU shared the same airfield as Number 36 OTU. Atkinson was to remain with this unit until he was posted back to the UK on December 31, 1944.

On his return to England, Atkinson was posted to Number 54 OTU at Charter Hall, Berwickshire taking up his duties from January 1945. On this unit, Atkinson was to instruct on the Mosquito. No doubt after his stay in Canada, Atkinson found his posting to Charter Hall conveniently near his home. Only a few days after his last visit home, Atkinson was killed in a flying accident on March 1. Mosquito NF Mk 2, HJ 569, attempted to carry out two unauthorized slow rolls while on a demonstration flight. The Mosquito spun into the ground at around 3.00 PM, some five hundred yards from the front of Pallinsburn House. Eyewitness, Mr John Porteous said, '...it fell in a spin, like a falling leaf. It crashed and exploded in a field in front of Pallinsburn house which, at that time, was a convalescent hospital.' Pallinsburn House is situated some five miles east of the border town of Coldstream. Both crewmen, Flt Lt Atkinson and student pilot F/O A.T.R. Cleave (160943) were killed in the accident. It is not clear who was actually flying the Mosquito at the time of the accident.[3]

The local press covered the story of Atkinson's death. The Blyth News, March 8, 1945, reported under the heading; 'Funeral of Blyth Flight Lieutenant.' A short biography is given which notes that Atkinson left a widow, Pat Dore, and a two-year-old son, Geoffrey. Flt Lt George Atkinson was buried in Blyth cemetery, on the Links road, to the south of the town of Blyth. At this time, the family were living at Number 40, Beatrice Street in the Newsham area of Blyth. Today the cemetery on the Links road is well kept, as is the grave of Flt Lt Atkinson. The grave bears a CWGC headstone. On the base of the headstone is the legend, 'One of the few.'

ATKINSON NOTES
1. Cull: *Twelve Days In May*, states that only one He 111 was lost during this action, the He 111 of 9/KG 54 flown by Uffz Otto Elinghaus.
2. Combat fighter report George Atkinson. Cull: *Twelve Days In May* states that Atkinson's Hurricane was damaged by an Me 110 of 11/ZG 76 and force-landed near Vitry with the pilot unhurt. Appendices Lists.
3. Local aviation history sources claim that only one pilot was in this aircraft: F/O A.T.R. Cleave. RAF Historical Branch clearly state that two pilots were in this crash; F/O Cleave and Flt Lt Atkinson.

Mathew Richard Atkinson. 39364
Flight Lieutenant Pilot

Mathew Richard Atkinson was born circa the first quarter of 1916. It is thought that he was born in the Gosforth area, a mere mile or so to the north of the City of Newcastle upon Tyne. On joining the RAF Atkinson was accepted on a short service commission. His training in elementary flying began in November of 1936. Number 11 Flying Training School (FTS) at Wittering, Cambridgeshire was next. Atkinson arrived there on February 6, 1937. Training over, Atkinson was posted to Number 52 Squadron at Upwood, Huntingdonshire. When Atkinson arrived on the squadron, September 4, 1937, it was to find that the squadron was equipped with the Hawker Audax and its brother the Hart. These aircraft were flown in the light bomber role.

In 1939, 52 Squadron moved on to the more modern era of aviation in the form of the Fairey Battle. A single engine three-seat light bomber. This aircraft was later to become known as the 'flying coffin'. Another 'Battle' plot, Sqdn Ldr D.H. Clark DFC, was later to describe the Fairey Battle as being; '...born too late; it died early—but not early enough.'

In April of 1940, 52 Squadron were disbanded. Atkinson then volunteered for Fighter Command. Presumably he was then sent on a short conversion course to convert to the Hawker Hurricane. September 3, 1940 saw Atkinson promoted to the rank of Flight Lieutenant. On September 20, Atkinson was posted to 43 Squadron, the 'Fighting Cocks'. However, the 'Fighting Cocks' had been in a fight at this time and had taken a beating at the hands of the

Jagdwaffe. The squadron had suffered many losses and had lost many of its best pilots while based at Tangmere. Early September saw the squadron on rest period. The squadron having arrived at Usworth in County Durham on September 8. It was during their stay at Usworth that 43 Squadron were joined by Atkinson.

Number 43 Squadron had been stripped to a bare minimum of experienced pilots. The experienced pilots left on the squadron were there for training purposes. By now 43 Squadron was classed as a 'C' class squadron. Tucked away in the more secluded areas of the northern part of Fighter Command, their job was to train other pilots, like Atkinson, in the finer art of aerial combat. It is not known how long Atkinson stayed with the 'Fighting Cocks'; probably no more than a couple of weeks. Atkinson does not merit a mention in the squadron's history.

Although classed as 'resting', 43 Squadron had to take its turn on the convoy patrols as well as chasing the occasional lone raider. It was probably during this time that Atkinson saw the action that qualified him as being an operational pilot during the Battle of Britain. Atkinson appears to have taken no further part in the Battle of Britain.

December1, 1941 saw Atkinson promoted to the rank of Squadron Leader. It is thought that at about this time, Atkinson transferred to Bomber Command. Certainly, by June of 1942, Atkinson was the Commanding Officer of 1418 Flight of Bomber Command. It was while flying in this role, June 26, 1942, that Atkinson was killed in action. Atkinson's body was never recovered. Today, along with all the other aircrew posted as 'missing', Flt Lt Mathew Richard Atkinson is remembered on the Runnymede Memorial, panel 65.

WILKINSON BARNES. 90294
FLYING OFFICER

Wilkinson Barnes was born in Sunderland on July 13, 1913. Education for the young Barnes was firstly at Tunstall Boys School, on the south side of Sunderland. Later he was to move to Durham School. In 1931 Barnes began his career as an estate agent. Firstly he was articled to William Milburn in Sunderland. At a later date he was to move to the family business of Barnes, Welch and Barnes. Subsequently, Barnes, Jr was made a partner in this firm during 1937. In early 1938, Barnes was to join the Auxiliary Air Force. Becoming a member of 607 (County of Durham) Squadron.

Gazetted as Pilot Officer Barnes, August 2, 1938. However, Barnes was not feted to stay long with 607 Squadron. With the beginning of hostilities, Barnes was mobilized into the RAF. Not yet fully trained, he was shipped off to Number 7 Flying Training School (FTS) at Peterborough. Flying training for Barnes was to last until early 1940. Barnes was then posted to his first fighter squadron, Number 504.

March 1940 saw Wilkinson Barnes take up his duties with 504 (County of Nottingham) Squadron. During this period 504 Squadron were based at Debden in Essex. The stay at Debden was to be a short one. Number 504 Squadron were hurriedly moved to France to reinforce the Air Component there. May 12, 1940 saw 504 leave Debden for Tangmere. After a short stop the squadron made the short cross-Channel flight Lille. The squadron was then split into two sections. 'A' Flight was moved to Bepaume while 'B' Flight took up station at Vitry. Wilkinson Barnes did not fly out with the squadron initially but followed on arriving in France on May 16. He was one of at least four replacement pilots. The squadron, only four days in France, had already suffered losses.

For Wilkinson Barnes and 504 Squadron, the French campaign came to an end on May 22, 1940. After ten days facing increasingly high numbers of enemy aircraft both in the air and on the ground, as well as high numbers of casualties, 504 Squadron were to return home. Constantly on the move, 504 Squadron had fought hard. Their bases constantly under attack and often overrun, the ground crews had fought a losing battle to keep the aircraft in the air. The remains of 504 Squadron were withdrawn back to England. Not all the members of the squadron had the luxury of flying home however. Wilkinson Barnes was obliged to take the slower route. This was by way of a boat from Boulogne. Weight being at a premium, Barnes left his kit, and with it his log book, in Boulogne harbour.

The next posting for Barnes was to Wick in Caithness, Scotland. Number 504 Squadron were to be reformed and trained up under its new commanding officer, Flt Lt John Sample. A man known to Barnes from his days with 607 Squadron. The squadron were later to move even further north as they took up station at Castletown. From where the squadron could cover the air defence of Scapa Flow.

Castletown was a newly completed airfield. In fact it was still partially under construction when the squadron arrived. The squadron flew into the new airfield in sections. First in was Sgt R.T. Holmes. The second Hurricane in was flown by Flg Off K.V. Wendel. This aircraft was suffer a brake malfunction and came to a stop on a mound of rubble. Wilkinson Barnes, flying Hurricane P 2725, coded TM-B suffered a similar fate when it ended up alongside the Hurricane of Wendel. Hurricane P 2725 was to end its days in a London street in September of 1940. Flown at the time by Sgt Holmes, this aircraft had rammed a Dornier bomber over London. However, after a bad start at Castletown things were not to remain so for Barnes. Wilkinson Barnes was promoted to the rank of Flying Officer on August 2.

Number 504 Squadron were next posted south to Hendon. Departing from Castletown September 4, 1940. The first stop was Catterick, to take on fuel, before continuing to Hendon where they arrived September 5. The squadron was involved in the heavy fighting almost as soon as it arrived. Although Barnes hardly gets a mention, the squadron was to suffer heavy casualties during the fighting of September. With the Luftwaffe scoring some success against the aircraft factories in the West country, 504 Squadron were moved to Filton, near Bristol, to provide the necessary air cover. A further move took the squadron to Exeter. This being more convenient for cross-channel offensive patrols.

With the end of the Battle of Britain, 504 were to carry out offensive patrols against targets in France. July 29, 1941 saw the squadron split into two sections. On this occasion, 'A' flight was renumbered Number 81 Squadron and were equipped with the Hurricane 2B, subsequently they were sent to Russia as part of 151 Wing. 'B' flight on the other hand was posted to Aldergrove in Northern Ireland. Wilkinson Barnes, now a flight commander, was to help reform 504 Squadron from 'B' flight.

During December 1941, Wilkinson Barnes was posted away from 504 Squadron to become a flying instructor. He took up his new post with Number 55 Operational Training Unit (OUT) at Crosby-on-Eden. Barnes was mentioned in despatches in January 1942. In April of the same year he was promoted to the rank of Acting Squadron Leader. Later he was to become commanding officer of RAF, Brunton in Northumberland. Barnes was not to remain at Brunton very long. He was next posted to Wittering, Cambridge, where he was with Number 1592 Bat Flight on a beam approach course.

The day of October 28, 1942 was dull and misty. Barnes was detailed to fly as number two in a Miles Master, AZ 803. His instructor was to be Pilot Officer Hay. In the fog, the beam was taken away as it was needed to guide a bomber which was in distress. The result was that the Miles Master crashed in the fog. This was probably due to disorientation due to flying in the fog. For some reason, Plt Off Hay was not strapped into the cockpit of the Master. When the aircraft crashed, Hay was thrown clear of the aircraft which resulted in his death. Wilkinson Barnes was suffered severe injuries which resulted in his admission to the RAF hospital at Ely. Barnes was to remain in hospital until June 1943. He was then sent to a rehabilitation unit at Loughborough before being moved to another unit at Newcastle. March 1944 saw Wilkinson Barnes invalided out of the RAF, retaining the rank of Flight Lieutenant.

On leaving the RAF, Wilkinson Barnes returned to his peacetime occupation of estate agent. Joining the family firm of A.S. Bowes and Barnes. In 1961 this firm was amalgamated with another to form Charles Bell Sons and Barnes. Wilkinson Barnes retired in 1978 but was to act as consultant until March of 1980. Wilkinson Barnes died May 19, 1980 in his hometown of Sunderland.

SIDNEY BAXTER, 566388
SERGEANT PILOT

The son of Edward Robinson and Jessie Baxter, Sidney Baxter was born at Birtley, County Durham in the second quarter of 1916. Education was by way of the nearby Chester-le-Street Secondary School. Joining the RAF as an apprentice, his training was carried out at RAF Halton. With the completion of his training I in 1935, came the trade of fitter. This was followed for a while, but the idea of flying seemed to offer that something extra. With this in mind Sidney Baxter volunteered for flying training and was accepted. Nothing appears to be known of Baxter's flying training or his early flying career. We first hear of him in the early part of the Battle of Britain. At this time he was serving with 222 Squadron and for some reason had gained the nickname 'Sludge'. During this period, 222 Squadron were based at Kirton-in-Lindsey, a few miles to the south of Scunthorpe. The squadron had recently converted from the Blenheim to the more agile Spitfire.

August 29, 1940 saw 222 Squadron take up their duties at Hornchurch, releasing 65 Squadron for a rest period. Next day, August 30, the air fighting was to begin in earnest for 222 Squadron. As a relatively fresh squadron in the Battle of Britain, 222 Squadron had not learned much in the way of air fighting tactics. Many of the squadrons were flying loose formations that allowed for better all-round vision as well as increased manoeuvrability if they came under attack. Number 222 Squadron were still flying in the pre-war tight formation with a weaver to protect their rear.

The first action of the day saw the squadron on patrol in the area of Gravesend. Shortly before 11.20 AM the squadron were badly bounced by a formation of ten Messerschmitt Me 109s. The Me 109s caught 222 Squadron unprepared and, from high altitude, tore straight through 'B' flight, causing utter mayhem. Luckily for 222 Squadron only one of their Spitfires was severely damaged. Its pilot, Sgt L Hutchinson, was only slightly wounded.

During the afternoon the squadron were again action. On this occasion their opponents were the Me 110s of 2 Staffel Zerstoerergeschwader 2 (2/ZG 2). Along with them was the fighter escort of Me 109s. It would appear that nothing had been learned from the earlier encounter. Once more the squadron was bounced. Three of their aircraft going down in quick succession shortly after 3 PM. One of those that fell was Sergeant Baxter in Spitfire P 9325.

This Spitfire had first flown on February 3, 1940. It then passed through Number 6 Maintenance Unit (6 MU) before arriving on 222 Squadron March 16. Although severely damaged in the fighting of August 30, it was to continue flying until struck off charge October 15, 1944.[1] Baxter returned to his unit unscathed. However, in one days fighting—the squadron's first—they had lost a total of eight aircraft with one pilot killed and three more wounded. Number 222 Squadron had been thrown in at the deep end. The lessons had come hard and swift at the hands of the Luftwaffe. They had paid a high price.

There was little flying over the next couple of days; enough, however, for the squadron to lose a further three aircraft. September 2 saw the squadron in action again. A raid had been plotted to the south of Calais as it built up, 222 Squadron were airborne by 8.35 AM. The raid was now on its way to the airfields of the south and 222 Squadron had taken up a patrol line in the path of the oncoming bombers. The raid turned out to be some forty plus bombers with a fighter escort of around sixty Me 109s. As the raiding force was about to pass over the Kent coast in the vicinity of Dover, 222 Squadron were on patrol in the area of Chatham, Hawkinge and Manston. By the time the enemy formation passed over Hornchurch 222 Squadron were in a position to attack. Baxter was to report that he attacked the Me 110s of the fighter escort making a claim for one destroyed and another damaged. However, none of these aircraft are traceable.

September 4, 1940 saw the squadron lose a further three aircraft with the loss of two pilots. A third pilot was lucky when he was blown clear of his aircraft by the 'friendly' fire of the AA defences around Dover. A further Spitfire of 222 Squadron was lost to the same defences on the following day. With the loss of a further two aircraft September 9, 222 Squadron were beginning to feel the pinch.

The afternoon of September 11 saw a large raid building up in the vicinity of Calais. Crossing the Channel, the bomber force escorted by some two hundred fighters turned over the Thames Estuary and set course for its main target, London. The Me 110s of the fighter escort turned to the south of London where they took up their station in defensive circles, and awaited the bomber force to escort it home. Attempting to get at the bombers, the defending fighters became increasingly frustrated. Every move was beaten off by the Me 109s.

However, the resulting dogfights and the fact that the fighters had to stay with their charges, caused the Me 109s to use their precious fuel. With the fuel warning lights blinking, they were forced to break off the engagements and return home. The bombers were now left under the protection of the Me 110s, rendezvousing with them to the south of London. Number 222 Squadron were one of the fighter squadrons which now moved in to the attack, the bombers by now almost defenceless. Attacking the bombers of 1&2/KG 26, Baxter singled out an He 111 and harried the bomber with a number of attacks.

The He 111 picked out by Baxter was 5680 coded (1H+CB). This aircraft was finally forced down at Burmarsh in Kent shortly after 4.00 PM. The He 111 was able to make a reasonable forced landing. However, the area was covered in ant-invasion poles. Hitting some of these, the He 111 burst into flames. The crew of Feldwebel's Friedrich and George, Unteroffizier's Hoffmann, Dreyer and Stirnemann were all captured. Due to a press photographer being on the scene it was captured forever. The resulting photograph became one of those used to depict the Battle of Britain. The photograph appears in the book 'Battle of Britain Then And Now', pages 314–315. The low flying Spitfire is believed to be that of Sgt Baxter as he made a fly-by. Baxter also made a claim for a Junkers Ju 88 damaged. This was a shared claim with Flg Off Brian Van Mentz. However, no Ju 88s appear to have been on this raid and it can be assumed that the pilots mistook an Me 110 for a Ju 88.

On the afternoon of September 14, 1940, the Luftwaffe launched three attacks in quick succession against London. These aircraft crossed the coast of Kent in the area between Deal and Dungeness. The attacks each followed their own separate corridor towards the main target of London. One took the route directly over Kent while the other took the northerly route that saw it approach from the Thames Estuary. Shortly after 3.00 PM, 222 Squadron were airborne and attempting to engage the Me 110s of the fighter escort. A task they found increasingly difficult due to the Me 110s forming defensive circles as they tried to protect themselves. Me 109s were also engaged in the dogfights as they tried to pick off targets otherwise engaged by the Me 110s. It was during this time that Baxter came under attack from an Me 110.

During the attack, Baxter's Spitfire sustained damage which rendered a landing as soon as possible. Baxter withdrew to the north in an attempt to make a forced-landing in the area of Rochford, Essex. For some reason the attempt failed. The Spitfire crashed and burst into flames leaving Baxter fatally injured. On his last flight, Baxter was flying Spitfire X 4275. This was an almost new Spitfire having first flown August 26, 1940. Passing through Number 6 (MU) on August 29 it arrived on 222 Squadron on the last day of the month. Spitfire X 4275 had lasted only two short weeks on 222 Squadron before it was destroyed. An all too often occurrence in the summer of 1940. The remains of Sgt Sidney Baxter were transported north to his home in Birtley. From there they were taken to the crematorium on the West Road, Newcastle. His ashes were scattered on the garden of remembrance and the name of Sgt Sidney Baxter is remembered on panel one.[2]

Baxter Notes

1. Morgan and Shacklady: *Spitfire: The History*, P 83.
2. Correspondence form Tyne & Wear Archive Service.

James Michael Bazin, DFC, 90281
Flight Lieutenant

To have survived the battle of France was no mean achievement. To have survived the Battle of Britain as well was even more of an achievement. To have survived World War Two, and still be flying at the end of it was an achievement afforded to only a rare few. One of these rarities was James Michael Bazin. Apart from a 'rest' here and there, Bazin had flown throughout the whole of the war, almost six years of it. To have survived so long under such conditions needs a fair amount of luck. It also needs a large amount of skill and a great deal of courage. Jim Bazin had all of these. Today, however, he is one of the not so well known men of the Battle of Britain. Outside the environs of the RAF squadrons in which he served, Bazin is almost unknown — some would say forgotten.

Jim Bazin was born in Kashmir and later brought up in Newcastle upon Tyne. Those who knew him consider him a Newcastle man. As a young man, Bazin leaned towards the mechanical. It was no surprise that he saw his future in engineering. Prior to the outbreak of World War Two, Bazin trained as an engineer with Armstrong Whitworth Engineering before moving on to a large electrical engineering company. It is also thought, that at one time, he was also a director of a local chemical works. Bazin had never shown any real inclination to fly. However, like a great many of his contemporaries in pre-war Britain, Bazin decided to learn to fly in his spare time. This he did with his local Auxiliary Squadron. It was not out of an act of patriotism or any willingness to save his country, that Bazin joined the 'colours'. His reason was simple. Many of his friends had already joined.

Jim Bazin therefore, in May of 1935, found himself as a member of 607 (County of Durham) Auxiliary Squadron. The spirit of adventure, in all probability, being more of a spur than the approach of a possible war. During this period, 607 Squadron was a light bomber unit flying the Westland Wapiti. However, for Bazin his first taste of flying would have been in the squadrons Avro Tutor.

In November of 1935, Bazin carried out his first solo. The ninth of the following month saw Bazin gazetted when he was commissioned as a Pilot Officer in the Auxiliary Air Force. Bazin's knowledge of the squadron's aircraft, the Wapiti, was to be short lived. The following year, 607 Squadron became a fighter squadron when it took on charge variants of the Hawker Hart. This included the Hawker Demon, an aircraft that became the main equipment of the squadron. Life took on a more purposeful role at this time for Bazin. Summer camps brought the squadron into contact with other Auxiliary squadrons as well as with the full time squadrons of the RAF. Summer camps were held at such places as Rochford, Warmwell and Abbotsinch. From these bases many more airfields were visited giving the Auxiliary squadrons, and their pilots, a glimpse at airfields which many would come to know under more demanding circumstances in the years ahead.

December of 1938 was to bring further change to 607 Squadron. The Gloster Gladiator was to replace the Hawker Demon as the main compliment of the squadron. Having been promoted to Flying Officer on June 9, 1937, Bazin was now in 'B' flight which was led by Flight Lieutenant John Sample. Taking part in the summer camp of 1939, that year at Abbotsinch near Glasgow, the squadron was hurriedly returned to its base at Usworth in County Durham. From there it was informed that it had been embodied into the RAF, as was Bazin, on August 28. The squadron was to remain at Usworth on its war station until October 10, 1939. On that date the squadron moved north, temporarily, to take up station at RAF Acklington in Northumberland. The reason for the move north was to allow the laying of runways at Usworth. Number 607 Squadron was to share the station with 152 and 609 Squadrons. The former were none operational while the latter were only operational during the hours of daylight. The brunt of air defence patrols fell to 607 Squadron. During this period Bazin had amassed a total of 173 hours on Demons and 129 hours on the Gladiator. Eleven of these hours were experience in night flying on Gladiators.

The shooting war came to 607 Squadron only seven days after taking up station at Acklington. Led by Flt Lt John Sample, a section of three aircraft were in combat against a Dornier Do 18 flying boat. At 1.30 PM a second section consisting of Flg Offs Thompson and R.E.W. Pumphrey and led by Bazin left Acklington. As far as spotting the enemy was concerned, this section outdid Sample's section. They spotted four Do 18 flying Boats and attacked the formation. Although various bits were seen to fall off the enemy aircraft, none could be claimed. After numerous attacks, the section had to return to Acklington after running out of ammunition.

What had been seen as a temporary move to Acklington came to an end on November 15. On this date the squadron began a move that would ultimately take them to France. What must have looked a motley fleet, a mixture of Gladiators, Ensigns, Dominies, a Fokker F 36 (formerly of KLM Airlines) and a Miles Magister made their way south. After a stop at Croydon, due to weather conditions, the formation eventually landed at Merville. Number 607 Squadron had made the trip in the company of 615 Squadron. The formation brought forth the description from Churchill that they were, '...two of the worst equipped fighter squadrons...' The statement was meant to be taken as complimentary rather than a true description.

Although France was a war-zone, there was little action. Patrols and training missions were the staple diet of the day. The only real change to routine came with the move from one base to another. Merville, because of the constant use and bad weather, became a virtual bog. December 15 saw the squadron move to Vitry-en-Artoise. Patrols were mounted from there as well as from the satellite field of St Inglevert. The biggest challenge came in the way of frozen potholes, lumps and bumps which became the cause of many accidents on the airfield.

Confidence on the squadron rose in April 1940. The squadron was to be re-equipped with the more powerful and up to date Hawker Hurricane. Bazin began his association with the Hurricane when he flew his new Hurricane from Abbeville on April 14. With the new aircraft, patrols increased, as did the training programme. Many of the pilots were still 'training' on the new aircraft when, on May 10, the Germans mounted the 'Blitzkrieg'. The element of surprise came in the early hours, which caught out 607 Squadron. The airfield was just beginning to come alive when the Luftwaffe hit it. Through falling bombs and low flying Messerschmitt Me 109s, 607 Squadron managed to get at least some of its aircraft into the air.

Bazin was soon in the thick of the fighting. On this, the first day of the real war, Bazin attacked a Heinkel He 111 to the north of Douai. His attack was successful and Bazin claimed the He 111 as his first kill. This was followed by the destruction of another He 111 near Brussels, followed by a Dornier Do 17 on the following day. The air fighting at this time had moved up a few gears. As the fighting became ever more intense, 607 Squadron took more than a few casualties. One of these was Bazin. Concentrating on shooting down the bombers, Bazin was caught by the Me 109s of the fighter escort. His Hurricane shot from beneath him, Bazin took to his parachute successfully. However, he was not so lucky in choosing his landing spot. Bazin had landed behind the enemy lines. Taking the imitative and with more than a little confusion amongst the advancing Germans, Bazin made it back to his own side of the lines and eventually back to base.

May 18 saw 607 Squadron begin its withdrawal from France. The squadron had taken more than a few casualties in their time and the time had come to pack up and leave. This was effected on May 20, with the final elements of the squadron leaving by any means that they could find. Reforming at Croydon, the squadron was next moved on to their home base of Usworth. The squadron had lost almost everything during their final days in France. The aircraft that were not destroyed in the air fighting were destroyed in the bombing attacks. Many more, the lame ducks, were destroyed by the ground personnel who had kept them flying through thick and thin. Only a small number of the Hurricane compliment made it back to England. The majority of the squadron's paperwork, as well as the pilots personal papers, was also lost making any accurate assessment of aircraft lost very difficult.

Re-equipment of the squadron was carried out at Usworth. Bazin was equipped with Hurricane P 3668. One of Bazin's duties, back at Usworth, was to carry out 'pip squeak' (Identification Friend or Foe—

IFF) tests. Another of his duties was the training of new pilots. More than a few new pilots were posted to 607 Squadron in order to strengthen the squadron. Most of these pilots were 'raw' and had to be taught the basics of aerial combat. Bazin, as an experienced 'battle hardened' pilot was one of the pilots allotted this task.

The next real action for Bazin was to come on August 15, 1940. The Luftwaffe chose this day to mount an attack against the North East area of England. Luftflotte Five launched its attack on the 'Northern Flank' from its base in Stavanger, Norway. Scrambled from Usworth, 607 Squadron were vectored to various parts of County Durham before finally engaging the enemy in the area of St Mary's Lighthouse, Whitley Bay. Bazin was leading Blue Section consisting of Plt Off S.B Parnall and Sgt G.A. Hewett. Neither man made a claim for aircraft destroyed that day. The squadron, however, was to make an optimistic claim for eight enemy aircraft destroyed. The logbook of Bazin merely mentions that he flew two sorties that day.

With their experience and confidence now rebuilt, 607 Squadron were posted south to Tangmere in early September. Perhaps they were overconfident. After a quick familiarization with the area, 607 Squadron were thrown in at the deep end on September 9, 1940. Bazin was once more leading Blue Section when, high over Mayfield, the squadron was badly bounced by Me 109s thought to be of Jagdgeschwader 27 (JG 27). During this engagement 607 Squadron was to suffer severely. Six of the squadron's aircraft were downed in this engagement alone, a high price to pay at such an early stage.

September 11 saw Bazin once more in action. On this occasion he was flying Hurricane P 2617, his usual Hurricane P 3668 having suffered damage, probably in the fighting of September 9. Hurricane P 2617 had been part of the compliment of 607 Squadron during the French campaign and was not feted to bring Bazin much luck, at least as far as shooting down enemy aircraft was concerned; Bazin was to make no claims on this day. Hurricane P 2617, however, was to outlast most, even Bazin himself, as today it resides in the Battle of Britain Hall within the RAF Museum at Hendon.

September 15, 1940, the day marked out in posterity as 'Battle of Britain Day' saw 607 Squadron scrambled on no less than four occasions. On the first two patrols the squadron saw nothing. Scrambled again at 2.15 PM, 607 Squadron were vectored to the Biggin

Hill—Kenley area. At around 15,000 feet, the squadron was faced with a large formation that was stretched out over a ten-mile front. Bazin attacked two aircraft on this occasion, claiming one Dornier Do 17 destroyed and another damaged. Shortly after 5.30 PM, the alarms went again and 607 Squadron were back in action. The squadron was to patrol their home base at first, however, the order was soon amended, and the squadron was vectored in a southerly direction. Over Poole, the squadron made contact with an enemy formation at around 15,000 feet. Attempting to attack the bombers from the rear, 607 Squadron were continually frustrated in their efforts by the ever-present Me 109s of the fighter escort.

September 30 saw Bazin in action against another bomber formation. On this occasion he was to make a claim for a Junkers Ju 88 destroyed and another Ju 88 damaged. Bazin does not appear to have been in action again until October 5. The squadron was brought to readiness in the afternoon and later scrambled. Vectored to the area of Swanage, 607 Squadron were met by a formation of Me 109s. On this occasion Bazin was not to be so lucky. Bounced by an Me 109 who came from under Bazin's rear, his Hurricane was severely damaged in the engine compartment. Bazin was forced to take action to force-land his damaged Hurricane. Hurricane P 3668 was left in a field near Hurn.

The Battle of Britain, for 607 Squadron, was now at an end. The squadron had taken heavy losses and were to be rotated to the north for a 'rest' period. October 10 saw the squadron leave on its flight north, staying only overnight at its traditional base of Usworth. The squadron moved on next day to Turnhouse before reaching the eventual destination of Drem. Bazin was awarded the DFC October 25, 1940. His citation reported that he had destroyed no less than ten enemy aircraft, many of these being in the battle of France.

From the beginning of 1941 Bazin was deemed as being in need of a 'rest'. To this end he was posted to the operations room of 13 Fighter Group at Inverness. Serving as a controller, Bazin was to keep his hand in during this posting, flying himself around 13 Fighter Group. This he did in a number of differing aircraft as he chauffeured his way around the various bases in Scotland and the north of England.

The year 1943 was to see Bazin back on official flying duties as he volunteered for Bomber Command. A refresher course followed with a beam approach training course. From Spring of 1944 Bazin was flying the Short Stirling, a four engine bomber, with 1660 Heavy Conversion Unit (HCU) prior to moving to Number 5 Lancaster Finishing School. With his courses and training over, Bazin was now posted onto an operational squadron. This was 49 Squadron then based at Fiskerton, a mere three miles from what came to be known as the 'Bomber Town' of Lincoln. The posting to 49 Squadron came in time for Bazin to play his part in the D-Day landings. On the night of June 5/6, 1944, Bazin was to take part in sorties against the gun sites at La Parnelle, while on June 6; he carried out raids against bridges in Caen to cut off any German retreat.

A further posting came at the end of June. This time his move was to Number 9 Squadron, then based at Bardney, Lincolnshire. One of the first targets to be assigned to Bazin on his new squadron was Rilly-La-Montage, a storage base for the V1 rockets. Number 9 Squadron were accompanied on this occasion by 617 Squadron of 'Dam Buster' fame. An arrangement that was to become more frequent during what was left of the war.

September 11, 1944 saw the beginning of a series of three attacks on what was, at that time, regarded as the most important target for the RAF, the battleship *Tirpitz*, which lay in Alten Fjord, Norway. Although rarely used in its premier role as a battleship, its mere presence was seen as a constant threat to the convoys that sailed between Britain and Russia. The attack on the battleship was once more a combined effort between Number 9 and 617 Squadrons. The difference this time was that the raid had to be launched from Russia. From Lossiemouth the Lancaster bombers flew to their forward base of Yagodnik.[1]

In the actual raid, Bazin was sixth in line as they lined up for the target. At 11.04 AM, September 12, Bazin released his specially modified 'Tallboy' bomb against *Tirpitz*. Although hits were recorded, the mighty battleship refused to be sunk. Still it remained a threat to the North Sea convoys. October 29, 1944 saw the second raid against the mighty leviathan get under way. To increase the range of the Lancaster bombers on this occasion, the mid-upper gun turret and its heavy armour had been removed. This increased the fuel capacity of the bombers. The bombers had already seen an increase in the engine power when newer, more powerful versions of the Merlin engines were fitted. The plan was to make this a round trip rather than launch the attack from Russia. The round trip involved over eleven hours of flying. Bazin recorded that he dropped his 'Tallboy' at 07.45 AM. Once again, however, the *Tirpitz*, although hit, refused to sink.[2]

A further raid against *Tirpitz* was to be carried out a few weeks later, November 12, 1944. Once again the bombers of Number 9 and 617 Squadrons flew north to Lossiemouth to launch their attack. After this attack, the Tirpitz was seen to roll over, leaving her unsinkable hull exposed. Many of the crew were to die, as rescuers could not penetrate the hull quick enough to release the crew trapped there. Unfortunately for Bazin, he did not take any part in this last raid. When the Lancasters were started up, the engines of Bazin's aircraft refused to fire up. They had simply fallen victim to the Scottish cold weather.

Between the attacks on the *Tirpitz*, Bazin had led a raid against the Sorpe Dam, October 15. Once again the flight was lengthy, some five hours. Each aircraft armed with a 'Tallboy' bomb. All bombs were reported to have hit their target and Bazin led his men home safely. A further dam-busting attack was to be carried out December 11; this time the target was to be the Urft Dam. Bazin was to lead his bombers once more against a premier target. This was to be a daylight attack carried out April 24, 1945. Once more the target was to be a precision attack involving a lengthy flight of over eight hours, most of it across Germany. The target was to be Berchtesgarten. Known to the RAF as Hitler's country estate, it was the German leaders mountain retreat in Bavaria more commonly known as the Eagles Nest.

Bazin was released from the RAF with the rank of Wing Commander in May 1945. As recognition for his courage in flying some twenty-five sorties with RAF Bomber Command, Bazin was awarded the DSO, September 21, 1945. Bazin was to return to the Jesmond area of Newcastle where he resumed his career as an engineer. Flying, it would seem, still had a place in Bazin's life as he re-joined his old Squadron, 607. As a member of the Royal Auxiliary Air Force, Bazin's rank now became Flight Lieutenant.

In 1949, Bazin took command of 607 Squadron. The squadron was now based at Ouston in Northumberland. Saturday, September 17, 1949 saw 607 Squadron taking part in their open day to mark the anniversary of the Battle of Britain. The highlight of the day was the flypast. At the head of the squadron were two of its most eligible pilots, Jim Bazin and Joe Kayll. However, the RAF and with it the RAAF, were changing. New advances in aviation meant the end for piston engine aircraft; its place now taken by the newer jet engine. In 1951 Jim Bazin finally hung up his flying helmet. In later years, with his retirement, Jim Bazin moved to the south where he died in 1985. His ashes were scattered over the airfield of Tangmere, from where he had taken off so many times to engage the bomber forces during the Battle of Britain. Of the many pilots from the North East, the career of Jim Bazin stands out as illustrious. He had fought the German war-machine from the mud covered airfields of France to Hitler's 'country house' Berchtesgarten.

BAZIN NOTES

1. Fred Whitfield DFM, an air gunner on Number 9 Squadron: privately published book; *We Sat Alone*.
2. John Sweetman: *Tirpitz: Hunting The Beast: Air attacks on The German Battleship 1940–44*.

Henry A. Bolton.

HENRY ALBERT BOLTON, 754530
SERGEANT PILOT

Henry Albert Bolton was one of a number of plots born in Hartlepool, Cleveland. Henry Albert Bolton was born in the first quarter of 1919. He was the only son of Herbert S. and Margaret, formerly Bainbridge, Bolton. In 1940 the family home was situated at 14, 'Sunnymead', Eldon Grove in West Hartlepool. The young Bolton must have had a technical career in mind as he attended the West Hartlepool Technical College. This was later followed by a spell at Pocklington School. With his studies behind him Bolton moved on to the family business. During this period his paternal grandfather and his uncle, under the name Bainbridge and Son, were running the family business.

Like many other young aspiring pilots, Bolton was a keen shot with a rifle. Much of his spare time being spent at the local Hartlepool Rifle Club. Also at this time, with war looming, Bolton must have seen his duties lying with the RAF. July of 1939 saw Bolton joining his local branch of the RAFVR, learning to fly during his spare time as an airman under training as a pilot. Approaching hostilities brought his part-time training to an end. September 1, 1939, Bolton was mobilized into the RAF. After a period of square bashing, Bolton was posted to Number 2 Flying Training School (FTS), based at RAF Digby, there he would complete his training. Training was carried out on the Tiger Moth and was to advance through to the Miles Master, the first piece of modern technology Bolton got his hands on. This was followed by a period at the OTU where Bolton was to get the feel of the much more advanced Hawker Hurricane. Training for Bolton came to an end July 11, 1940. His next posting was to 79 Squadron.

Number 79 Squadron was one of the newer squadrons in the RAF. Formed from a nucleus of 'B' flight of 32 Squadron, it had flown the Gloster Gauntlet. Number 79 Squadron received their new complement of Hawker Hurricanes in November, 1938. After the Blitzkrieg of May 10, 1940, 79 Squadron were sent to France. With their withdrawal from France 79 Squadron were based at Biggin Hill. It was from there they fought in the early skirmishes of July over the English Channel. Deemed to be in need of a 'rest', after the early fighting, 79 Squadron departed north to take up residence at Acklington.

While 'resting' at Acklington, 79 Squadron was one of the squadrons that took part in the defence of the North East on August 15, 1940. This was the day that the Luftwaffe launched its one and only massed attack against the North East. In the ensuing encounter, 79 Squadron was the only squadron to receive casualties during this action. One of its Hurricanes being slightly damaged by return fire from the bombers. No doubt the squadron was still flushed with its success when, two days later, a new pilot named Bolton turned up at Acklington to take up his duties. Bolton was posted to 79 Squadron for further training, especially in the art of air fighting. In the more quiet backwaters of the North East this training could be carried out without intrusion from the Luftwaffe. The training was much needed. Nine days later, the squadron was posted back to the south where they arrived at Biggin Hill, August 27.

Little time was available for the squadron to adjust and resettle at Biggin Hill. August 28 saw them in action. A formation estimated as being over one hundred enemy aircraft, most of them fighters, were plotted in the vicinity of Cap Gris Nez and heading for the coast of Kent. Subsequently, the formation split into two major sections over Deal. One section turned towards Eastchurch while the other turned towards Rochford. Number 79 Squadron, already in the air as they moved to their advance base of Hawkinge, managed to make a sighting report. The squadron then dived into the attack. Attempting to get at the bombers, 79 Squadron were continually frustrated by the Me 109s of the fighter escort. After much jousting with the Me 109s, 79 Squadron at last landed at Hawkinge feeling extremely lucky that they had come through the encounter without loss. The afternoon of August 31 saw 79 Squadron scrambled to intercept a formation of enemy aircraft in the area of Dungeness. This turned out to be a large force of a hundred plus aircraft. As in previous attacks, the force split itself into two sections; one section attacked Biggin Hill while the other attacked Croydon. During the air fighting it is thought that Bolton's Hurricane came under attack from the Me 109s of the fighter escort. His Hurricane seriously damaged and, maybe even the pilot wounded, he made an attempt to make a forced-landing at Haliloo Farm near Warlington, Kent. The Hurricane crashed and killed its pilot at 4.00PM. The Hurricane of Bolton, V 7200, was the first aircraft built in the fourth production batch of five hundred built by Hawker Aircraft Ltd.

An odd, even relatively bizarre photograph of this crashed Hurricane exists. The photograph was taken on the day following the crash. It shows soldiers, obviously there to guard the crashed Hurricane. In a happy, if somewhat callus mood, they are skipping for the camera a belt of ammunition from one of the machine guns is being used as a skipping rope. A report of the time states that Bolton was shot in the back. If this was so, then Bolton must have been very seriously wounded when his Hurricane crashed.[1]

The remains of Henry Albert Bolton were returned to his home in Hartlepool. There, they were buried in the family plot, September 12, within Stranton cemetery. A small entry in the *Northern Daily Mail*, September 11, gives some details of Bolton's brief career under the heading; 'Killed in action'. The last resting place of Henry Albert Bolton is numbered, Con 10a 258 and carries a CWGC headstone. In all, Sergeant Henry Albert Bolton had been on an operational squadron a mere thirteen days. In action against the enemy, he had lasted four short days. Today, like so many of his contemporaries, Bolton is almost a forgotten man of the Battle of Britain.

Bolton Notes
1. Ramsey: *The Battle of Britain Then And Now*. A photograph of the crashed Hurricane appears on page Xii, while a photograph of Bolton and his last resting place appears on P 398.

H.H. Chalder.

Harry Hutchinson Chalder, 43691
Pilot Officer

Harry Hutchinson Chalder was born in the first quarter of 1915. He was the son of Thomas Chalder and his wife Sarah, formerly Russell. The Chalder family lived at 114 Cedar Street, a modest house in the Fenham area of the west end of Newcastle. Thomas was well known in the city, having been employed as a traffic superintendent with Newcastle Corporation Tramways between the years 1902 and 1935, retiring during the latter year. Thomas Chalder was to die without knowledge of the Second World War, dying before its outbreak.

Little is known of the early life of Harry Chalder. It is known that he attended the Royal Grammar School in Newcastle and that he was later to join the RAF in 1935 under the direct entry scheme, as an airman under training as a pilot. Of his training there is nothing known. We first hear of him in 1940. April 1, 1940 was the day on which Chalder received his commission and was posted to 266 Squadron.

At this time, 266 (Rhodesia) Squadron was based at Wittering on the Cambridge border. The squadron had only been formed in late 1939 and was one of the newer squadrons in the RAF. Having been equipped with the Spitfire, it was working up on the aircraft at about the time Chalder joined the squadron. The only action that the squadron had during this time was patrols and night-flying duties, the latter giving the squadron its fair share of accidents. In early August the squadron had moved south into the Tangmere sector.

Flying was carried out from Eastchurch from August 12. The following day Eastchurch was paid a visit by the Luftwaffe. August 13 brought a surprise attack between 7.20 and 7.50 AM. The attack was carried out by fifteen Dornier Do 17s of Kamfgeschwader 2 (KG2). Although without their escort fighters, the bombers of KG2 managed to penetrate the defences and drop over a hundred bombs across the airfield. Much damage and confusion was caused with some of the airmen's quarters hit, killing sixteen. Also hit were some of the hangars and sundry equipment. However, more important, six Spitfires of 266 Squadron had suffered various degrees of damage. Among the injured was Chalder who had been hit in the foot by shrapnel from an exploding bomb.

By September 15, 1940, Chalder was back to his normal fitness and, after a spell of sick leave, had found himself posted to 41 Squadron, then based at Hornchurch. Two days later, September 17, a multi wave raid of Me 109s were briefed to engage the RAF defences. In particular, the Me 109s were to lure the fighters of the RAF into an aerial fight. This formation crossed the south coast of Kent between 3.00 and 4.00PM. The group consisting of mainly I and II Gruppen of Jagdgeschwader 53 (JG 53). The forces of Me 109s were first engaged by the Hurricanes of 501 Squadron. A short time later they tangled with the Spitfires of 41 Squadron. The attack soon developed into a running dogfight over the Dover area. Number 41 Squadron, in the thick of the fighting, lost one Spitfire with three others severely damaged. Among those damaged was Spitfire N 3266 flown by Chalder.[1] Spitfire N 3266 had first flown December 29, 1939. Compared with contemporary aircraft, it had lasted a while. It was to go on and have a lengthy career. It flew with at least one other squadron as well as a couple of Operational Training Units (OTUs). Its days finally came to an end November 19, 1943 when flying with 57 (OTU) based at Eshott in Northumberland. It was involved in a mid-air collision over Long Witton, Northumberland, killing its pilot.[2]

September 20, 1940 saw 41 Squadron in action again. Flying in company with 72, 92 and 222 Squadrons, they were bounced by the Me 109s of JG 3 (Udet) and counted themselves lucky to get away with only one aircraft damaged. They were not to be so fortunate in their next combat. Tangling once more with Me 109s, September 27,

41 Squadron lost three of its aircraft in the vicinity of West Malling.

September 28 saw a change in the tactics of the Luftwaffe. Due to their recent high losses, the Luftwaffe resorted to using their faster bombers. The raids were smaller in number and made up mostly of Junkers Ju 88s and Me 110s, both aircraft flying in the role of fast bombers. Fighter escort was much heavier than normal with the Me 109s flying at a more economical speed. This, of course allowed the Me 109s a little more time over England. The object of the exercise appeared to be to lure the fighters of the RAF into a dogfight. The numbers of escorting Me 109s, instead of some forty or fifty, was a whole Geschwader—some two hundred fighters in all.

The attacking bombers, smaller in numbers than usual, failed to get to their target of London. However, RAF Fighter Command were to pay heavily for their defence. In all the RAF lost sixteen aircraft and nine pilots in this engagement. The Luftwaffe were to lose thirteen of their attacking aircraft but only three of these fell in actual combat. On this occasion Chalder was flying Spitfire X 4409. This was a relatively new aircraft having been first flown September 9, 1940. It then passed on to 41 Squadron three days later. After being damaged in the air fighting of September 17, it had been force-landed by its pilot P/O H.C. Baker. After repairs on site, the Spitfire then passed into the hands of Chalder. The luck of this aircraft was not to change with its new pilot. At around 10.10 AM, Me 109s got the advantage of 41 Squadron in the area north of Ashford, Kent. Chalder's Spitfire was severely damaged and set on fire. Chalder manage to extricate himself from the doomed Spitfire and take to his parachute. At 10.30 AM his Spitfire exploded when it crashed into the ground at East Stour Farm, Chilham.[3]

Chalder was to land at Garlinge Green severely wounded and was removed to Chartham Hospital. So severe were his wounds, presumably burns as well as others, that he fought for his life for over four weeks. October 10, 1940 Chalder finally succumbed to his wounds and died. His remains were transported north to his native Newcastle. There he was buried in the family plot at St Nicholas' Cemetery, only a short walk from his home at Cedar Road. Chalder is buried in section 'W' grave number 300. There is no CWGC headstone. The grey headstone merely gives the names of the family buried there. It does not give any service details of the serviceman buried there.

A local newspaper of the day gave a brief account of Chalder and noted that he was a married man. He left behind a widow, Ann Chalder.[4]

CHALDER NOTES

1. Ramsey: *The Battle of Britain Then And Now*, P 458.
2. Morgan and Shacklady: *Spitfire: The History*, P 82.
3. Ramsey: P 480. A photograph of Chalder's grave appears on P 481. This photograph was taken in the eighties and has changed slightly over the years. The kerbstones have now gone, removed by the City Council mainly to facilitate ground maintenance.
4. The Newcastle Journal issue November 14, 1940.

Hubert Weatherby Cottam, 77790
Pilot Officer

Hubert Weatherby Cottam was born in the third quarter of 1919. He was the first son of Edmund Samuel Cottam, a brush manufacturer, and his wife Margaret Annie Weatherby. His mother's maiden name was gifted to the young Hubert as a second Christian name. The family during this time had set up home at Number 30, Worm Hill Terrace in Biddick near Chester-le-Street County Durham. At a later date, probably attracted by the industry found in larger towns, the family moved from Biddick to the town of Sunderland. There, the family settled at Number 13 Hillside.

Education for the young Cottam was firstly by way of Barnes School in Sunderland and later at the Bede Grammar School. During this period, the name Hubert was shortened to Bert, the name he became known by. Cottam was a keen pupil at both the Barnes School and the Bede Grammar, becoming a deputy head boy at the latter. This keenness boiled over into life outside school when Cottam took up Scouting. As keen in the Boy Scouts as he had been at school, Cottam became the Assistant Scoutmaster of the Bede troop. At the end of his school days, Cottam matriculated in the Oxford School Certificate. On leaving school Cottam took to the 'white collar' employment of insurance. Cottam worked in the offices of the Newcastle Company of Northern Assurance.

Working as a clerk in an office was fine for the wages. However, Cottam had already shown his liking of a more adventurous existence. Like many of his age, this was to come in the form of the

Hubert Cottam. Photo: Maurice Cottam.

local Auxiliary Air Force unit. Not far from his home was the RAF station of Usworth. Here, was the base of 607 (County of Durham) Auxiliary Squadron. Cottam applied in 1938 and was accepted as an aircraft hand. In this capacity, Number 807327 Cottam probably flew as one of the air gunners on the squadron. However, his career as an aircraft hand was put under threat at the end of 1938. Number 607 Squadron were to re-equip with the Gloster Gladiator, a single seat fighter. The days of the air gunners on the squadron were over. However, as a serving member of the squadron, Cottam, along with the other air gunners and aircraft hands, was given a choice. Move to another squadron, more than likely Bomber or Coastal Command, as an air gunner or stay with the squadron and re-train as a pilot. Cottam, determined to become a fighter pilot, chose the latter.

However, Cottam's stay with the squadron was once more placed in doubt in the latter part of 1939. On this occasion it was the fault of the Germans. Number 607 Squadron was embodied into the RAF in September 1939. The trainee pilots on the squadron were transferred to training units within the RAF. For Cottam, now remustered in the RAFVR as Number 77790, his training was to continue at Number 7 Flying Training School (FTS) at Peterborough. Training, for Cottam, beginning there in October of 1939. From Peterborough, Cottam moved on to Cranwell before his training came to an end in March of 1940.[1]

At the end of his basic training in March, Cottam was commissioned, March 21, 1940. His next posting was to Number 6 Operational Training Unit (OTU) at Sutton Bridge in early May. At Sutton Bridge, Cottam came into contact with his first fighter, the Hawker Hurricane. In the latter part of May, Cottam finished converting onto the Hawker Hurricane and was posted to his first fighter squadron. This was to be Number 213 Squadron, and Cottam arrived on the squadron May 25, 1940. The squadron had formerly been based at Wittering. The day after Cottam joined 213 Squadron, it was moved south to Biggin Hill.

Number 213 Squadron had been formed at RAF Northolt in March of 1937. They flew the Gloster Gauntlet before they were re-equipped with the Hurricane in January 1939. On May 26, Number 213 Squadron flew into Biggin Hill. Along with 242 and 229 Squadrons, they took over from 32 and 79 Squadrons. While 229 Squadron took up home defence, 213 and 242 Squadrons were at Biggin Hill to take part in operation 'Dynamo', the air defence for the evacuation of Dunkirk.

Action was not long in coming to 213 Squadron. The squadron was airborne at 5 AM on the morning of May 28. Initially 213 Squadron was to act as escort for a formation of Blenheim bombers who were to bomb targets in the area of St Omer. With their escort duties completed, 213 Squadron were to continue on a patrol line between Gravelines and Nieuport. During the patrol, 213 Squadron encountered a formation of He 111s. In the ensuing encounter 213 Squadron brought down one He 111. In return, they lost two Hurricanes with their pilots. However, one of those pilots was to return to base later.

After their first encounter with the enemy, 213 Squadron were down to ten serviceable Hurricanes. These were put into action shortly after breakfast. The squadron was ordered to the area of Dunkirk. Approaching Dunkirk, 213 Squadron encountered a large formation of enemy bombers. This consisted of He 111s and Ju 88s that were in the act of bombing the beaches. With the bomber force was a large fighter escort of Me 110s and Me 109s. Number 213 Squadron attacked the fighter escort destroying one Me 110 and two Me 109s without loss. A further patrol was carried out in the afternoon but, as often happens, nothing was encountered.

The squadron's 'B' Flight, temporarily based at Merville in France, was returned to Biggin Hill where it rejoined 'A' Flight May 26. The squadron was to remain at Biggin Hill until June 18, 1940. On that date the squadron moved to Exeter, a move which effectively removed the squadron from the main fighting of the Battle of Britain.

On August 11, after a feint attack towards Dover, the Luftwaffe launched an attack against Portland. Squadron Leader Hector D. McGregor led eight Hurricanes off from Exeter and attacked the Ju 88s. The attack was to break up the formation but 213 Squadron were to pay for the privilege. Six Hurricanes were forced down during the attack, with two of the pilots killed. During raids on Portland and Portsmouth the following day, 213 Squadron were to fare little better. The squadron clashed with the Me 110s of the fighter escort over the Isle of Wight. Cottam engaged an Me 110 and claimed it as destroyed, the Luftwaffe lost a number of Me 110s in this area during the action.

However, 213 Squadron were once again to suffer casualties, with three Hurricanes lost and two of their pilots killed.

With the weather affecting 'Adler Tag' in the east on the 13th, the Luftwaffe launched an attack against the Southampton area. This attack curving in from the direction of Jersey. Number 213 Squadron attacked the fighter escort of V/LG1[2], Number 213 Squadron on this occasion managing to lose only one Hurricane with its pilot. The following day had a similar pattern while on the 15th the Luftwaffe launched a heavy attack against the area of Hampshire. The heavy force numbering around two-hundred and fifty aircraft were met over the Isle of Wight. Number 213 Squadron, along with 87 Squadron, engaged the Stuka dive-bombers of 11/StG1 as well as the fighter escort of Me 110s. Heavily outnumbered, 213 Squadron were repeatedly frustrated by the Me 110s defensive manoeuvres of forming a circle. Rising above the defensive circle, in order to attack from above, the Hurricanes were immediately attacked by the ever-present Me 109s of JGs 27 and 53 that prowled above. Once again Cottam was to make a claim for an Me 110 destroyed when 213 Squadron attacked the fighter escort. Number 234 Squadron, flying Spitfires, were making heavy weather of defending against the Me 109s. This was the same engagement in which fellow North East pilot P/O 'Bush' Parker was to be shot down.

September 7, 1940 brought a change of base for 213 Squadron. On this date the squadron moved to Tangmere where they shared the base with Cottam's old squadron, Number 607. It must have been around this time that Cottam was to suffer a slight leg wound. Cottam's Hurricane was riddled with bullet holes, while he was wounded. After having his wounds dressed, Cottam was sent home on leave. Exhausted, he fell asleep in the chair when he got home. On waking once more it was to find a telegram ordering him back to Tangmere. A quick meal was followed by his return to the railway station and the trip back to Tangmere.[3]

With the Battle of Britain over, Cottam was sent home on leave once more. His brother Maurice described his appearance at the time as 'Looking like a ghost'. He was later sent on an instructor's course. Nothing is known of where he then went. However, he was sent, sometime during 1941, to Southern Rhodesia. There, he continued instructing with Number 23 SFTS at Heany. At this time it is thought that he was instructing on the Oxford, a twin engined aircraft. An Oxford in which 'Bertie' Cottam was flying crashed and Cottam was killed. The body of 'Bertie' Cottam was never to return to England. He was buried in Bulawayo Athlone Cemetery, Zimbabwe in grave number 25

Cottam Notes
1. Personal correspondence with Cottam's brother, Maurice W. Cottam.
2. Mason *Battle over Britain*. At least one of those Me 110s shot down was Me 110D. Known as the *Dora* this was the long range version of the Me 110, used mainly in Norway where its long range was much needed.
3. Personal correspondence with Maurice W. Cottam.

JOHN TEESDALE CRAIG, DFM, 564573
SERGEANT PILOT

John Teesdale Craig was born in the second quarter of 1914 in the City of Newcastle. However, his family were not native to the City of Newcastle. Craig's parents were Robert William Craig, a stationmaster of Wolsingham and Elizabeth, formerly Teesdale, Craig. His mother gifting the young Craig with her maiden name of Teesdale. The family home was at Whitton -Le-Wear high in the Weardale area of west Durham.[1] Education for the young Craig was via Woolsingham Grammar School, a short distance up the Dale. On leaving school, Craig was to pick a career in the RAF joining the service in January 1930.

To the young Craig, like so many more who picked the RAF for their apprenticeship, home for the next couple of years was to be RAF Halton, Buckinghamshire. Hugh, later Lord Trenchard, created Halton in 1920 for the training of the future technicians of the 'third service'. Hence, these young men were to become known by the affectionate nickname of 'Trenchard's Brats'. These young men were to become the true bedrock of the RAF throughout peacetime and into wartime. Many of these 'Brats' held the boyhood ambition to fly, and a great number of their ranks were achieve their ambition, flying as aircrew in all the RAF Commands. It was from Halton that many aspired to the greatest of these ambitions, to become a fighter pilot. One of these was John Teesdale Craig.

It is not known if the work of a tradesman did not live up to the expectations of Craig, or if it was his ulterior motive, on joining the

RAF to become a fighter pilot. Either way, Craig had volunteered for pilot training and had passed out as such with suitable abilities for training as a fighter pilot. He then passed on to an OTU where he was converted to the Hawker Hurricane. His first squadron posting was to 111 Squadron.

Number 111 Squadron were the first squadron to be equipped with this new-age fighter. As such the squadron was to gain much publicity in the years before the war; some of it welcomed and some of it not. The Hawker Hurricane was the first of its type in service with the RAF. Many looked at its sleek shape with awe, looked at its eight guns enclosed in its wings, its wide retractable undercarriage, its speed and versatility. It had broken records, flying from Turnhouse near Edinburgh to Northolt near London in record-breaking time. This record was to earn its pilot, Squadron Leader John Gillan, Commanding Officer of 111 Squadron, the eternal nickname of 'Downwind Gillan'. The Hurricane also broke pilots, or so the press of the day would have us believe. This publicity was to give the Hurricane pilots almost 'superman' status; taming this beast. No doubt the Hurricane pilots were to encourage the attention more than a little.

With the outbreak of war in September 1939, 111 Squadron was moved from its cosy Northolt base to what the squadron pilots must have viewed as a wilderness—RAF Acklington in Northumberland. If the pilots thought that things could not get any worse, along came their next posting first to Drem in East Lothian, then on to Wick in Caithness. With the battle of France beginning to hot up the squadron was moved hastily back to Northolt. From May 13, 111 Squadron was to provide extra air cover for the British Expeditionary Force (BEF) in France.

Six Hurricanes of 'A' flight were sent to France. The aircraft being based at Lille/Marcq from May 13, 1940. At 3.25 PM of the first afternoon, 'A' flight was in action and Craig was one of those on patrol. Craig, flying Hurricane L 1607, spotted a Messerschmitt Me 110 on a converging course, flying at about the same altitude as himself. The Me 110 turned away from Craig who gave it a burst from around one hundred yards. Craig noticed hits along the belly of the Me 110. The twin-engine fighter then dropped to the right in an uncontrollable state. While watching the first Me 110, Craig came under attack from a second. As fire passed close, Craig took avoiding action. On turning, Craig saw the Me 110 shot down by another Hurricane. Craig went on to carry out an attack on another Me 110, giving it two short bursts but without effect.

The flight commander recalled the flight to return to Lille/Marcq. Craig noticed yet another Me 110 flying below and silhouetted against the clouds. A target too good to miss in the heat of the battle. Manoeuvring into position, Craig noticed that his Hurricane began to vibrate. This was a legacy of his earlier encounter; Craig's Hurricane had been hit in the engine. Worse was to come. The Hurricane's cockpit began to fill with smoke and fumes, forcing Craig to get his crippled aircraft down to safety. Craig managed to force-land his Hurricane in a field on the northern side of Vimy.

In the adjoining field was the wreckage of a Heinkel He 111, the victim of some earlier encounter. Craig took the time to give the enemy aircraft a quick inspection and noted that all the crew were dead. It is presumed that someone else was on the site, as Craig stated that French soldiers had shot one of the German airmen, the others had been killed in the crash. Craig then set off on foot in the general direction of St Omer. In the French town sergeant G. North of 32 Squadron joined Craig. He had also been shot down. On their travels towards the French coast, the pair met P/O John Southwell of 615 Squadron. The group of three now moved on to Mezieres. There they were provided with transport, which delivered them to Calais. Boarding a Royal Naval drifter, the trio were landed safely in Dover the following day.

With their return to England 111 Squadron were posted on to Digby, Lincolnshire. The stay was to be short-lived however. By May 30, 1940, the squadron had been relocated to North Weald from where it could fly patrols over Dunkirk. Craig celebrated his return to the fighting with the shooting down of an Me 109 on May 31.[2] With the end of the Dunkirk campaign, the squadron was once more on the move. On this occasion their new base was to be Croydon, the pre-war civil air terminal that now lay in the Kenley sector. June 10 saw Craig still adding to his score when he claimed two Dornier Do 17s as damaged. The squadron now found itself on convoy patrols that were later to lead to the first skirmishes of the Battle of Britain.

The squadron lost four of its aircraft in combat during July 10. At least one of these aircraft fell when it collided with a Do 17. At this time the main tactic adopted by 111 Squadron was the head-on attack. 111 Squadron was one of the few squadrons to adopt this tactic. This form of attack demanded great courage from the pilots involved. With squadron numbers diminishing, the new pilots were not experienced enough to carry out such an attack. The squadron was, therefore, forced to abandon this form of attack, due mainly to lack of experience of some of the pilots but also for safety reasons due to high losses. Most of the losses on the squadron during this period were not due to enemy action as such, but collisions with the enemy aircraft due to misjudgement caused by lack of experience.

On July 10, the squadron was ordered from Croydon to take up position at their forward base of Hawkinge. Take off was at 1.00 PM. With the aircraft still climbing, they were immediately diverted to the Dover-Folkestone area. A convoy had come under attack by Do 17s of 1/KG2. Craig, on this occasion flying as Red 2, picked out his target, a Do 17, and carried out an attack. Pulling away from the first target, he attacked another.[3] Noticing another Hurricane under attack from an Me 109, Craig decided to join in. His attack caused the enemy fighter to retreat. The skirmish had been a short one, but it was the squadron's first in the Battle of Britain.

A lull in the fighting now developed. The only action for the squadron was the daily moving back and forth from Croydon to Hawkinge. On July 25, the squadron had just returned from Croydon at 1.30 PM and were placed on fifteen-minutes readiness. At 2.50 PM the scramble bell rang and the Hurricanes were off yet again. Climbing hard, they were vectored towards a formation of Me 109s at around 17,000 feet over Dover. However, due to a mistake in recognition, the squadron was jumped and attacked by a formation of Spitfires, not once but several times. The commanding officer, Squadron Leader John M. Thompson, was himself attacked twice by these 'friendly' fighters. In the melee only two pilots actually made any contact with the enemy formation. One of these was Craig. Flying as Yellow 3, Craig came under attack from two Me 109s. Flying in line astern the two fighters approached Craig head-on. The leading aircraft overshot his target and left his number two to attack Craig. Both aircraft approached each other at high speed, firing as they went. Neither giving way, the combat was declared as indecisive.

Craig could only report that he thought his fire had hit the enemy before he broke away. On return to Hawkinge the squadron had more patrols without result before eventually returning to Croydon at 9.20 PM.

A further lull developed with some brief skirmishes on July 31. Nine of the squadron's aircraft had been scrambled and attacked a Junkers Ju 88 in mid-channel at 07.35 AM. This attack was to end with inconclusive results. Increasing activity over the Thames Estuary led to the squadron being scrambled shortly after mid-day on the afternoon of August 11. A force of forty plus Do 17s accompanied by small number of Ju 87s and the ever-present escort of Me 109s were attacking a convoy. Although the squadron made no confirmed kills, they lost five of their Hurricanes to the escorting Me 109s. Four of these pilots were killed.

August 13 dawned and was due to be recorded in history as 'Adler Tag'. The first day of what the Germans called the 'Attack of the Eagles'. The weather, however, was against the Luftwaffe. Do 17s of KG2 were briefed to attack targets in the area of the Isle of Sheppy. Unknown to the bomber force, the raid was called off due to bad weather after they had got under way. The fighter escort had heard the recall and obeyed it; the bombers were left from that point on their own and without escort. Twelve Hurricanes of 111 Squadron were scrambled at 05.50 AM. Leaving their Croydon base, they set course to patrol the area of Hawkinge below cloud base. Enemy aircraft were spotted at 3,000 feet and Yellow Section led by sergeant William L. Dymond initiated a head-on attack in an attempt to break up the bomber formation.

Flying as Yellow 3, Craig opened fire at about 500 yards range, closing to 100 yards before breaking away in a sharp downward turn. Turning in again swiftly, Yellow Section closed for an attack from the rear. One of the bombers was seen to break away and was pursued by Craig and Dymond. Both were to carry out two further attacks. With smoke pouring from one engine of the bomber, Dymond broke away, leaving Craig to finish off the wounded bomber. After a further attack by Craig, one member of the bomber's crew was seen to evacuate the aircraft. Craig pulled back to allow further members of the crew to leave. Seeing no further evidence of the rest of the crew vacating the stricken aircraft, Craig closed in once more and gave the aircraft a lengthy burst, after which the Do 17 rolled over and crashed onto the mud flats at Seasalter, Whitstable. This aircraft has been identified as U5+DS of 7/KG 2. Of the crew, Oberfw Langer was killed while Oblt Morch and Fw Hansgen were taken prisoner. Craig's Hurricane, P 3888, was also damaged in the conflict by return fire from the Do 17. With his fuel low, Craig returned to base.

At 2.45 PM, August 15, 111 Squadron were scrambled, with Craig once more flying as Yellow 3. Originally the squadron was detailed to attack the fighter escort, however, in trying to engage the high-flying Me 109s, the squadron became split. Rather than be placed at a numerical disadvantage, the squadron attacked the bomber formation that was flying much lower. Yellow Section carried out a head-on attack in order to break up the formation. After breaking up the formation, the Hurricanes picked their own individual targets. Craig picked out a Do 17 and delivered a lengthy ten-second burst. The effect was immediate; smoke began to pour from one of its engines. Deciding it was finished, Craig turned his attentions to an Me 109 which was in the process of attacking another Hurricane. The Me 109 made off without Craig causing it any damage. Turning back to the bomber force once more, Craig attacked two Do 17s, delivering short bursts into each, however, he could only claim both as damaged.

Returning to base, the Hurricanes had barely time to refuel and rearm before they were once again scrambled. A large formation of Junkers Ju 88s and Me 110s with an escort of Me 109s acting as top cover, were heading in the direction of Thorney Island. Flying at around 16,000, feet the enemy force was intercepted in the area of Thorney Island. On this occasion, due to unserviceability and losses, 111 Squadron were able to muster only ten Hurricanes. This was further reduced to nine when the C.O., Sqdn Ldr J.M. Thompson, was hit by engine trouble. Craig was now at the head of Red Section and, seeing the enemy, decided to use the sun to his advantage. Two Ju 88s, having become detached from the rest of the formation, now came under attack from Craig. Giving one of the Ju 88s a lengthy ten-second burst, he watched as the bomber rolled onto its back and spiralled into the ground. Swiftly he turned his attention to the other Ju 88 and delivered a successful attack sending it down with one engine on fire. Looking around for more trouble, Craig singled out another Ju 88. On this occasion he delivered a beam attack, using up the rest of his ammunition in the process. Craig noted the tracer seeming to pass through the bomber cockpit before the hapless bomber rolled onto its back and dived down, disappearing beneath Craig's Hurricane.

Back at Croydon the aircraft were speedily refuelled and rearmed. As earlier, the job was barely carried out when the air-raid sirens began to wail. Without waiting for further instruction, 111 Squadron scrambled itself. Even so, the squadron was almost caught on the ground. The raid that materialized was a low-level one carried out by the Me 110s of Erprobungs Gruppe 210. This unit was an experimental one specializing in low-level precision attacks, and was led by the one-legged Hpt Walter Rubensdoerffer.

Most of the Hurricanes were still climbing away from Croydon as the Me 110s forced home their attack. One of the last Hurricanes into the air was that of Craig. As he looked across the airfield he noticed one of the Me 110s about to make its attack. Craig was in a good position to carry out a head-on attack from slightly below. As the Me 110 pulled up, Craig gave it a lengthy burst, seeing pieces fall away from the Me 110 as he did so. Ground-crew watching the action, which was being carried out over their heads, from various vantage points around the airfield, later reported that an Me 110 crashed just to the west of the airfield. Mason states in *Battle Over Britain*, that this aircraft was Me 110, S9+BB flown by Oblt Fiedler, Gruppen Adjutant of the Stab Flight Erprobungs Gruppe 210. This aircraft crashing at Redhill airfield at 7.10 PM. Opposing this, 'Battle of Britain Then and Now', credits this aircraft to sergeant Dymond of 111 Squadron and sergeant Pearce of 32 Squadron. It also states that the Me 110 crashed at Nutfield aerodrome at 7.15 PM.[4] Judging by the directions of the ground crew, and that they were eyewitnesses to the event, Mason appears to be the better choice.

The Me 110s, after their surprise attack on Croydon, had been surprised by the counter attack of RAF Fighter Command. The Me 110s had made a slight navigational error that led them to carry out an attack against Croydon rather than their intended target of Kenley. With the surprise gone, the Me 110s had to fall back on their usual defensive tactic, forming a circle. Craig was one of those who attempted to break the circle. Craig carried out two attacks from below, firing deflection shots, but gave up the pointless exercise, as he was having no success. As he disengaged from attacking the Me 110s, Craig was immediately pounced on by six of the ever-present Me 109s which had formed the escort. The move by the Me 109s caused Craig to take some violent evasive action in order to escape his attackers and return safely to base.

The following day was to bring little reprieve for 111 Squadron. At 9.00 AM the squadron was ordered to its advance base at Hawkinge. Shortly after their arrival, a large formation was plotted approaching the coast in the area of Dover. The squadron was well fanned out, as they had been scrambled with enough time to get in position. Red, Blue and Yellow Sections located a large formation of Do 17s and carried out their normal head-on attack. Craig, however, was unable to get into position to carry out a favourable attack. Breaking away to the right, he came up the left side of the bomber formation and delivered three beam attacks. During one of these attacks Craig noticed the crew of a Do 17 bale out. Before Craig could carry out any further attacks on the bombers, he became a target for the Me 109s. Taking avoiding action to evade the Me 109s, Craig lost sight of the battle as he fell into the mist.

At 1.05 PM, August 18, 111 Squadron were scrambled and ordered to patrol base at 20,000 feet. However, the raid that developed was a low-level one. The squadron was brought down to 5,000, then 3,000 feet. However, they were still far too high, as the raid was being carried out at by Do 17s of 9/KG 76 at only fifty feet. This raid making its way towards the sector station of Kenley. Craig, flying as Red 2 was the only pilot in his section to engage the bombers—the other two pilots were unable to pick out the bombers against the dark backdrop of the ground. As Craig attempted to carry out his attack on the bombers, his Hurricane came under fire from the over zealous ground defences. Later it was found that 111 Squadron had lost six aircraft during this sortie. At least one of these was lost to the anti-aircraft defences. Craig later found a lone bomber en-route to Biggin Hill. He moved into the attack and noticed his fire striking home. However, the bomber put up a fight and Craig was hit by return fire that forced him to back off. The enemy bomber lived to fight another day, as it avoided the persistent attacks by Craig who, by now, had run out of ammunition and was forced to return to Croydon.

August 30, 1940 was to prove an unlucky day for Craig. Having been ordered to Manston, 111 Squadron were scrambled at 5.10 PM to meet an incoming formation. This turned out to be a formation of Do 17s with an escort of some forty plus Me 110s. Flying as Yellow 3, Craig engaged an Me 110 and gave it a hefty burst of seven seconds. Overshooting his target, he dived away fast to avoid becoming a target. His manoeuvre proved a little too much. By the time Craig turned to re-engage the enemy he was too far away and had insufficient speed to regain the altitude he had lost.

Dawn of August 31 saw 111 Squadron at readiness. At 8.10 AM the squadron were on patrol and were investigating a raid that had been plotted approaching the area of Duxford. This turned out to be a formation of Do 17s with a heavy escort of Me 110s. The fighters of twelve group had not been brought to readiness. It was up to 111 Squadron to make the interception. Finding themselves in a favourable position, 111 Squadron carried out a head-on attack over Hildersham, some eight miles to the north of Debden. During the resulting dogfight, Craig's Hurricane P 2888 was hit by gunfire from an Me 110. The damage caused Craig to abandon his Hurricane. Fortunately, his parachute landed Craig alongside a first aid post in the village of Harlow. Shortly after, an ARP ambulance conveyed the wounded Craig to St Margaret's Hospital, Epping, where some shrapnel was removed from a wound in his leg. Craig's terminally damaged Hurricane crashed on the Hertfordshire side of the border, where it burned itself out.[5]

On September 6, 1940, Craig was awarded the DFM, the citation for which reads: 'His magnificent spirit has been of high order, and he his ably upheld the fine work of his squadron'.

It is presumed that Craig returned to 111 Squadron. By the end of September, the squadron had been posted to Drem for a rest. Later the squadron was to re-equip with the Spitfire. In the first half of 1941, Craig was posted on to Sutton Bridge, Lincolnshire, there to take up instructing duties with 56 (OTU). Craig was flying Hurricane W 9114, an aircraft from his old unit of 111 Squadron, on the afternoon of June 2, 1941. For some reason his Hurricane dived out of the sky and crashed at Terrington near Sutton Bridge. One explanation for the crash, put forward by the RAF Historical Branch, is that Craig's Hurricane collided with Hurricane P 3162 of former Battle of Britain pilot and fellow instructor, Flight Sergeant I.K.J. Bidgood. Evidence for this theory being that, both aircraft crashed in the same vicinity, at the same time. Sadly both pilots lost their lives in the accident.

The remains of Sergeant Craig were transported back to his home in Weardale. There, they were buried at the Crook and Willington Cemetery, some three miles north of his home at Witton-Le-Wear. Wynn, mistakenly states that Craig was buried in the Isle of Man. Sergeant Craig was, and remains, a Weardale man from County Durham. He is also one of the forgotten 'Few' as well as one of those granted the status 'ace'.

J.T. CRAIG NOTES

1. Shores: *Aces High* 1994 edition, mistakenly states that Craig lived in the Isle of Man and, was also buried there. This was later corrected in Vol 2 of 1999.
2. This aircraft was shot down a few miles to the northwest of Dunkirk.
3. Craig was credited with two 'damaged'.
4. Ramsey: *The Battle of Britain Then and Now*, P 571.
5. Rayner: *One Hurricane One Raid*, P 113.

George Dudley Craig, 90285
Flight Lieutenant

George Dudley Craig was born September 13, 1914 in Bangkok, Thailand. He was the only son of R.D. Craig and his wife, Sarah Louise, formerly Wilkinson. Craig senior had arrived in Bangkok as part of the Diplomatic Corps; later he was to become a legal adviser to the Thai King. Education for the young Craig was to be carried out in England. Aysgarth Public School, in the Pennine Chain area of northwest Yorkshire, was followed by Winchester and then Pembroke College, Cambridge. While at Cambridge, Craig became a soccer blue and gained his degree as well as his M.A in Law studies. This pre-war period saw an increase in the expansion of the Auxiliary Air Force. One of those who looked with interest on this arm of the Air Force was George Dudley Craig, at that time working in a solicitor's office.

Craig was to join 607 (County of Durham) Auxiliary Air Force Squadron in the latter half of 1936. A main criterion at this time for joining such a squadron was eagerness. Armed with this eagerness, an interview was arranged with the C.O. Walter Runciman, later the Rt Hon, M.P. Also at the interview was the squadron adjutant Flt Lt G.A.L. 'Minnie' Manton, a regular RAF officer acting as adjutant as well as flying instructor. After the interview came a trial flight with 'Minnie' Manton. If the candidate was still keen and eager, as well as performing well during the interview, then he was declared suitable for training. Craig was obviously one of those thought to be suitable, as he records his first flight November 1, 1936. This flight was made

Dudley Craig as a POW. Photo: Nicholas Craig.

in Hawker Hart K 6482. In control was Flt Lt 'Minnie' Manton. Craig's first real flight was not to come until May 1, 1937. On this day Craig made his first dual flight in Avro Tutor K 2364. Once again it was Flt L Manton who was to fly in the other seat. This was the standard trainer of the day. Craig was to fly his first solo in this aircraft April 26, 1937.

Number 607 Squadron was originally a light bomber squadron. In 1937, after some reorganization, 607 Squadron became a fighter squadron. Two Hawker Hart trainers were to arrive at Usworth soon after the squadron was re-designated. These were followed by the first of the Hawker Demons, the squadron's new equipment. November 13, 1937, was a momentous day for Craig. After a flight in Hawker Hart K 6482, he finally gained his 'wings', the much-coveted flying badge of RAF pilots. Craig was to take part in various activities attached to a fighter squadron over the next few months. Cross-country flights, formation flying and aerobatics were all undertaken. Of interest at this time were the flight with a passenger and also the battle-climb with a passenger. On both occasions Craig was accompanied by the then-aircraftsman Charles Edward English. English was to become a regular crewman to Craig until the end of 1938. At this time crewmen were to be dispensed with when the squadron took on its single-seat aircraft. English went on to become an accomplished pilot in his own right and his story is told separately.

Craig's flying abilities were not to be classed as outstanding. His rating at the end of his first year shows that he was below average ability in flying, while he was average in aerial gunnery. August 1, 1938 saw a new kind of aeroplane on the squadron. This was the squadron's new equipment, the Gloster Gladiator. At the end of the year the number of Gladiators on the squadron was five. Getting a seat in this new fighter was, therefore, at a premium. It was not until January 8 of the following year that Craig was to get his hands on this fighter for the first time. On that day, Craig flew Gladiator K 8030, on a series of circuits and bumps. At the Empire Flying Day that year, Craig flew Gladiator K 7999 in the dive-bombing exercise. Recalled from the Summer Camp of that year, 607 Squadron was embodied into the RAF, as were its pilots. Craig received his form 1445 September 27, 1939, informing him that he was now a pilot in the RAF. The squadron was to be temporarily moved north to Acklington to allow for runways to be laid at Usworth. The squadron arrived at its new base October 10, 1939.

The squadron was now under the command of Squadron Leader Lance E. Smith, having taken over from Sqdn Ldr Walter Runciman. Flight Lieutenant Joe Kayll was in command of 'A' flight with Flight Lieutenant John Sample in command of 'B' flight. The squadron was now prepared for war, and this was to prove not long in coming. The afternoon of October 17, 1939 saw Blue Section, Craig and F/O W.H.R. 'Nits' Whitty led by Flt Lt John Sample, scrambled from Acklington in search of enemy seaplanes. One was found some thirty miles out to sea. This was duly attacked, the three aircraft diving from 8,000 feet and attacking from astern. However, ammunition soon ran out. With fuel also at the critical level the threesome turned for home, leaving the Dornier Do 18 still limping further out to sea. Later the three pilots were to learn that the Do 18, coded M7+YK, of Kustenfliegergruppe (Ku Fl Gr) 806, had made a forced landing alongside the destroyer *HMS Juno*. The crew were taken prisoner, the aircraft subsequently destroyed by naval gunfire and Blue Section had gained the first kill of the war for 607 Squadron. Bill Whitty was later to state that he had seen damage in the Do 18's wing, causing fuel loss.[1] Dudley Craig was to note; 'Johnnie's work' referring to the leadership of Flt Lt John Sample.

Routine patrols took up the squadron's time over the next month. Things were to change on November 13. On this day the squadron were to leave their temporary home and head, not back to Usworth, but south to France. Two days were spent at Croydon due to bad weather. On November 15, the squadron took its leave of Croydon and departed across the Channel to France. There they were to take up residence as part of the Advanced Air Striking Force (AASF) in support of the British Expeditionary Force (BEF). For the rest of the year the routine was simple. Patrols and more patrols. Among these were the 'Blighty' patrols, escorting ships taking servicemen home on leave. During this, one of the worst winters on record, Merville became a sea of mud. This was to make flying difficult. A move was soon under way which took the squadron to Vitry-en-Artoise, where things were not much better. The mud had frozen into potholes, which was equally dangerous for aircraft, and more than a few accidents resulted from the bumps and holes.

Craig, taking off on February 7, 1940, in Gladiator 'Z', had a bit of a mishap. Having just reached flying speed, the engine cut out. The aircraft force-landed in a field, leaving its disgruntled pilot to walk away from his aircraft, which was to be written off. With April a further change was to come for the squadron's complement. This was the Hawker Hurricane. Craig recording his first flight April 18, in Hurricane 'M', from Abbeville. To get used to the new aircraft, patrols, formation flying—both night and day—were interspersed with air tests and gunnery practices, the latter at a floating target.

With the fall of Belgium and Holland and the Blitzkrieg attack on France, May 10, the war stepped up a gear.

Craig was detailed to fly as escort to a flight of three Fairey Battles of 88 Squadron. Their mission was to attack a target in the area of Maastricht. On the flight from Vitry to Maasstricht the Hurricanes were put under attack by a formation of Junkers Ju 87s. The Hurricanes decided to meet the challenge and carried out their own attack. Craig carried out a head-on attack and was later to write; 'Three bursts and the enemy was seen to dive in a steep spiral as if in trouble. Enemy formation broke up. No return fire.' Flying Hurricane 'L', Craig saw pieces flying off the 'Stuka' and he later made a claim for a 'probable'. However, the ground defences opened fire and brought an end to any further attacks.

Craig tangled with the Luftwaffe again on May 16. On this occasion he made a claim for one 'floored'. The following day Craig attacked a Dornier Do 17, leaving it falling in flames. This was followed by a Heinkel He 111. On his own admission, Craig never fired a shot at this aircraft. However, as it fell when he was about to attack it, he claimed it as destroyed. Many of the Hurricanes had by now become unserviceable. Mainly this was due to the constant pressure of flying under battle conditions as well as moving from base to base as the enemy advanced. The squadron was ordered to depart from France. Craig was not to fly home in his trusty Hurricane on this occasion. He flew as a passenger in a 'Douglas', this aircraft being flown by an unknown Belgian pilot. The Douglas and its fleeing twosome made a landing at Hendon.

After a period of leave, Craig was returned to 607 Squadron once more. The squadron was now back at its traditional home of Usworth. However, it was a squadron with almost no aircraft, most of these having been left in France. New aircraft arrived in July and training of new pilots also got under way. August 15, 1940 saw the North East brought into the Battle of Britain when the Luftwaffe carried out its one and only massed attack against the area.

Luftflotte Five launched its attack from Stavanger, Norway. Other fighter squadrons had already savaged the force further north before 607 Squadron were to join in. At around 1.15 PM 607 Squadron were scrambled from Usworth, at their head was Flt Lt W.F. Blackadder, the squadron was first directed to the Seaham Harbour area. This order was rescinded and the squadron was ordered back to the area over their base before once more being directed towards the mouth of the Tyne. Here, at last, 607 Squadron caught up with the Luftwaffe over the area of Tynemouth. Craig, flying in Hurricane 'L' with Green Section, made a claim for two enemy aircraft. However, his Hurricane on this occasion was not on 'song' and he later experienced oil pressure trouble some fifty miles out to sea, eventually making it back to Usworth to hear that the squadron had made a rather optimistic claim for nine enemy aircraft destroyed and a further six probables.

After the action of August 15, 607 Squadron were geared up for the fighting that was going on in the south. The rumours became reality when the squadron was ordered south to Tangmere. There, they took over from a rather battered 43 Squadron on September 8. This coincided with a tactics change by the Luftwaffe. No longer were the airfields the prime targets. The main target was to be London. Soon after landing, 607 Squadron were ordered into action, however, no contact with the enemy was made. The following day, September 9, was to prove different. The pilots of 607 Squadron were still full of confidence and exuberance. At 5.00 PM the squadron was scrambled to intercept a raid. In the area of Mayfield, the Luftwaffe put their lack of experience to the test. Number 607 Squadron was severely bounced by Me 109s. In the resulting melee, 607 Squadron were to lose six aircraft, with three of their pilots killed and a further two wounded. The confidence on the squadron had been given a nasty shock. The pilots of 607 Squadron had been still flying in the old close formations, which they had been trained in prior to the war. The Luftwaffe had shown up this lack of experience and 607 Squadron had paid for it

The rest of September was to pass relatively quietly. Many patrols were flown with little contact with the enemy reported. September 14 saw Craig giving chase to an He 111. Although bits were seen flying off, the He 111 made its escape into cloud cover and Craig could only claim it as damaged. Craig was on patrol over London, September 24, however, his logbook records his frustration: '…with nothing seen all day'. Although the action during this period seemed to be infrequent, 607 Squadron had suffered many losses in its ranks. Being an Auxiliary Squadron, with most of the pilots coming from the same area, this must have had a severe effect on morale. A pilot lost was like a family member lost. In early October, 607 Squadron was ordered north to Turnhouse. They arrived in the Scottish capital October 10. There, they could rest and rebuild the squadron. A short while later, Craig was one of the experienced pilots posted away from 607 Squadron. However, his move was not to be far. He remained at Turnhouse as a controller.

Number 607 Squadron were based at Skitten, near Wick when they gained a new C.O. in March of 1941. A new commander, but old squadron member: the new C.O. was to be Dudley Craig. The squadron was reported as to be going onto the offensive. Rumours grew into truth as the squadron moved south, taking up station at Martlesham Heath, Suffolk. There, the Hurricanes, now Mk IIs, were modernized to carry bombs. The end results being that 607 Squadron was to be the first 'Hurri-bomber' squadron in the RAF. At first the Hurricanes took over Operation Channel Stop, an operation flown originally by Bomber Command to keep German shipping under control. It was for low-level attacks on the Continent that the 'Hurri-bomber' had been envisaged. With this in mind the squadron was moved to Manston.

First results for the new 'Hurri-bomber' were seen as a success. October 30, 1941, was the first day of action for the new aircraft. This was a low-level raid known as a 'Rhubarb' on the power transformer near Tingry. Craig, who was accompanied by Sergeant Lees led the raid. Other targets to be picked during this period ranged from railway yards and airfields to coastal shipping. Anything was a fair target. Churchill himself was to state that Europe '...was to be set ablaze'. Number 607 Squadron were to put that into practice.

Success was to be followed by bad luck for Craig. November 4, 1941 saw Craig leading a low-level attack on the airfield at LeTouquet. Hurricane 'L' was hit by light anti-aircraft fire as it crossed the airfield. With the controls of the Hurricane almost fully jammed, the aircraft was forced to fly through the tops of some trees in an attempt to escape. Struggling to make flying speed, Craig attempted to get his Hurricane home. However, flying speed could no longer be maintained and Craig was forced to ditch his aircraft in the shallow water just off the French coast. With no chance of escape, Craig was taken prisoner. Dudley Craig's flying days were over, however, his fighting days were not.

Originally Craig was sent to Dulag Luft, the holding camp at Oberosel near Frankfurt Main. Some of the more trusted (by the Germans) prisoners were formed into a 'permanent staff'. Their job was to ease the new intake of prisoners into the way of life of a POW camp. A way of life that they were to endure over the next few years. Craig was not to be at Dulag Luft for long. His next home was to be Stalag Luft 1.

Stalag Luft 1 was a fairly new POW camp at Barth on the Baltic coast. It was at Barth that the escape committee, later known as the 'X' organization, came into being. After clearing his plan with the escape committee, Craig was to make an attempt at escaping on the night of January 15, 1942. The plan was simple. After the guards had made their nightly inspection, Craig, along with former 607 Squadron pilot Willie Turner, would walk out of the camp dressed as German guards. The homemade uniforms would have just about passed muster on a dark, winter's night. However, the German guards were a bit more vigilant and the pair was stopped at the gate. Although their heads were covered with balaclava helmets, the fact was that Craig, at this time, sported not only a moustache but also a beard. German guards did not have facial hair. A term in the 'cooler' followed. This was meant to dampen any enthusiasm for escaping.

As further punishment, Craig along with a couple of hundred other POWs, were to be sent to another, new camp. The new camp was to be Stalag Luft 3. A camp for Air Force personnel run by their German counterparts, the Luftwaffe. This new camp was at Sagan in what was known as the 'dust bowl' area of Silesia in Germany. It represented a place about as far away from Britain as it was possible to get. With little to do, Craig became an intelligence officer with the escape committee. During the summer of 1942, Craig was one of those who took exercise over a homemade vaulting horse. The exercise was a cover for other prisoners to escape by way of a tunnel. This escape came to be known as the 'Wooden Horse' escape. By way of the tunnel, two prisoners were to escape and make a home run back to England.

At the end of October, 1942, Craig and other known escapees, were purged to Offlag XX1 B. This camp was at Schubin near the Polish town of Bromberg. The Germans had tried to put an end to escape activities. However, their efforts were in vain. Even on the train to Schubin, more than one prisoner had attempted to make good his escape through the floor of the train. Within a week of their arrival at Schubin, October 28, a tunnel was underway. This tunnel had its origins beneath a lavatory. Its ending was just outside the camp wire: a distance of a mere hundred and fifty feet. Unlike Sagan, the tunnel was only five feet deep due to water.

Thirty-three men were to make good their escape by this tunnel. Craig was one of those, escaping with Wing Commander Harry 'Wings' Day'. Although it was the following day before the escape was discovered, Craig did not get far. He was to remain on the run for only two days. The original Big 'X', leader of the escape committee, Jimmy Buckley was also to break out during this escape attempt. Escaping with another officer, Buckley was never seen or heard of again. The place of Buckley as Big 'X' was taken by another officer who had been on the run more than once, Squadron Leader Roger Bushell.

The short stay at Schubin had reunited Craig with two other former 607 Squadron pilots; Joe Kayll and Bobby Pumphrey. Along with other determined escapees, Craig was sent back to Stalag Luft 3. However, this was not the old camp. April of 1943 had seen the opening of the new north compound. This was to be Craig's new home. The escaping, of course, went on. Craig once more was to become an intelligence officer, this time working on what came to be known as 'The Great Escape'. A mass breakout from which fifty officers, Sqdn Ldr Bushell amongst them, were to be shot by the Gestapo. The perils of escaping are shown in the photograph album of Craig. A photo of a comrade bears the caption of only one word; 'shot'.

Although escaping was to take up much of Craig's, and other prisoners, time, there were other ways of filling in the time. One of these was study. Craig finally took his law finals courtesy of the Red Cross and the Luftwaffe, while he was a 'guest' of the Germans.[3] It is interesting to note some of the many gifts requested by the prisoners during this time. High on their list was 'black bullets'; a North East mint flavoured boiled sweet, and Edinburgh Rock. It is hoped that the prisoners had access to a good dentist.

With the Russian advance, the prisoners were forced to march away from the fighting. Craig found himself marched to Luckenwalde near Potsdam before being handed over to the Allies. In May of 1945 Craig was returned to England where he was eventually released from the RAF. For his efforts against the enemy while a prisoner, Craig was awarded the OBE as well as being mentioned in despatches.

Craig was to return to take his place in a law practice working from Newcastle. He was to rejoin the now Royal Auxiliary Air Force. However, this was mainly in an administrative capacity. Although he kept in touch with his former squadron, he was to work mainly in the control branch from RAF Newcastle. He did, however, travel to the summer camps at places such as Lubeck in Germany. Craig came across Hurricane P 2617 when it was on parade in Durham City. This aircraft he recognized as having flown with 607 Squadron during the battle of France as well as the Battle of Britain. Craig attempted to obtain this aircraft as a permanent memorial to the members of 607 Squadron. However, he was informed that it had been earmarked for a museum: and so it was. Today it resides in the Battle of Britain Hall within the RAF Museum at Hendon. George Dudley Craig fighter pilot and POW escapee died in 1974.

G. D. Craig Notes
1. Personal correspondence with William Whitty.
2. Pilots log book of Dudley Craig.
3. Personal correspondence of Dudley Craig.

Henry Peter Dixon, 90283
Pilot Officer

Henry Peter Dixon, known as Peter, was born in the first quarter of 1915. He was the son of John Reginald and Elsie Margaret Dixon. The family home at this time was in Heighington, near Darlington, County Durham. Education for Peter Dixon came by way of Marlborough College and Sidney College, Cambridge. Peter Dixon was to graduate in engineering from Cambridge. It is also thought that Dixon's first flying ambitions were realized while at Cambridge when he flew with the University Air Squadron.[1]

After graduating from Cambridge Dixon returned north and found employment with the Cleveland Bridge Engineering Company. To maintain his interest in flying, Dixon joined the Auxiliary Air Force, becoming a member of 607 (County Durham) Squadron based at Usworth. Dixon joined the squadron in 1935 gaining his 'A' Licence and being gazetted December 20, 1936. At this time 607 Squadron was still a fairly new squadron and Dixon became one of the original squadron members.

Life on an Auxiliary Air Force Squadron, particularly in the pre-war years, was almost family orientated. The members of the squadron were mostly recruited from the surrounding area of Sunderland and north Durham. Therefore, almost everyone knew everyone else, as well as their background. As such, lifelong friendships were formed. The members of the squadron met two nights per week as well as weekends. Some of their families became intermarried and when it came to holidays, they often went together.

Left Peter Dixon, Right Joe Kayll. Probably in France: Kayll still wears his 607 Squadron flying suit. Photo: Dixon Family via Simon Muggleton.

One of the latter was to Scotland with Dixon driving some of the others in his big, open top tourer.[2] Summer Camps were the order of the day. These were to give the part-time pilots a taste of service life on an operational airfield. Dixon appears in the official squadron photographs of 1937 and 1939. He is missing from the photograph of 1938.

During the latter part of 1937 Dixon spent some time overseas spending a period in Calcutta. Dixon was with the engineering staff of Cleveland Bridge Company as they built the foundations of Howrah Bridge. This explains why he does not appear in the official 607 Squadron photograph of 1938. Dixon was back in time to rejoin 607 Squadron as it went on its Summer Camp to Abbotsinch, Glasgow. In August, along with the rest of 607 Squadron, Dixon was called to full-time service. The squadron was first to move to Acklington, then on to France. First landfall in France was Merville the latter becoming the squadron's base for a short while.

Number 607 Squadron were to fly regular patrols from Merville. The surface was not ideal, however. As the winter set in Merville was left in a sea of mud sometimes as much as a foot deep. A much-needed move was carried out, December 13, 1939. This was to take the squadron to Vitry. The move to Vitry was for the better. Although always operational, 607 Squadron had been frequently bogged down with the mud at Merville. Now at Vitry, the surface was firm and dry. Flights were detached to St Inglevert, making it easier to patrol the Channel area. Number 607 Squadron provided 'Blighty' patrols which covered the ships carrying men on leave back and forward between England and France. However, as the winter began to bite more severely 607 Squadron began to suffer. Burst tyres and broken undercarriage legs being regular occurrences that left the squadron hard pushed to maintain serviceability.

Patrols were carried out throughout the winter months. Dixon was one of six pilots detailed to carry out a continuous patrol of over thirteen hours, February 11, 1940. The patrols flown were regularly hampered by the heavy snowfalls. In April of 1940, 607 Squadron was equipped with the Hawker Hurricane at Abbeville. These came none to soon, as the German Blitzkrieg broke through May 10.

The afternoon of May 11 saw Dixon flying as Red 2 to Flying Officer Francis Blackadder. Nothing was to be seen until an He 111 was spotted some way off. After an exchange of fire, the He 111 was shot down and was seen to fall, on what was believed to be an empty house. Returning to their patrol line Dixon, in Hurricane P 2573, AF-A, spotted some other enemy aircraft that turned out to be a formation of He 111s. Two of the bombers were noticed to be straggling, Blackadder and Dixon picked out one each. Dixon carried out his attack and noticed smoke issuing from the bomber, however, it refused to go down. Dixon kept up his attacks until he ran out of ammunition. By this time he was also beyond range of his base. Looking for a convenient field, Dixon noticed a deserted airfield. This turned out to be Tirlemont. On landing he was surrounded by Belgian soldiers who demanded that he identify himself. After they were satisfied, Dixon tried to find some fuel. On his return to Tirlemont it was to find that the Luftwaffe had attacked it leaving his Hurricane in charred pieces. Dixon was left to find his own way home.[3]

On the afternoon of May 15, Dixon was part of a section of three returning from an uneventful patrol in the area of Villeneuve. Returning via Reims a staffel of He 111s was spotted. The section went into the attack and Dixon was to make a claim for two shared.

One of the He 111s made an attempt at escape by trying to out-climb the Hurricane. Dixon in Hurricane P 2536 coded 'R' kept up his attacks. Still attacking as his Hurricane passed through 17,000 feet, his oxygen ran out making breathing difficult. Although the shortage of oxygen was making life difficult for Dixon, he still pressed home his attacks until he was forced to break off due to hits on his aircraft from heavy return fire. On return to Vitry Dixon was forced to land at a high speed, the flaps on his Hurricane had been damaged by the return fire from the He 111. Exhausted after the fight, Dixon was forced to admit that if this situation had occurred during peacetime he would '...have radioed for the fire engine and the ambulance...'

Dixon was once more in action during the afternoon of May 16. He was again flying Hurricane P 2536, 'R' as part of a section that encountered five Do 17s. The bombers were flying so close that the fighters were forced to attack in line astern only. This had little effect on the bomber formation. The fighters were forced to break off after the first attack, as their leader had used all of this ammunition in one lengthy burst. The following day, shortly after 7.30 AM, Dixon was one of a few pilots who returned to England for a short leave. The pilots were to make the trip sitting on the floor of an Ensign. Dixon was not to return to 607 Squadron. At the end of his two days of leave, he was posted to Number 145 Squadron.

Number 145 Squadron had only recently moved to Tangmere to carry out operations over France. Dixon was on patrol over Dunkirk, June 1, when his Hurricane N 2952 was shot down in flames. Dixon managed to get out of his aircraft making a landing by parachute near Dunkirk. He was taken to the 'Mole' where his wounds were tended to before being put on a ship to England. Two days after his landing in France, Dixon was on a ship for England. However, the ship was bombed and sunk, June 3, off Dunkirk. Dixon was among the dead. The remains of Henry Peter Dixon were buried in Dunkirk Town Cemetery. Dixon is buried in plot 2, row 13, grave number 16.

Dixon Notes
1. Shores, *Aces High, Vol 2*.
2. Personal correspondence and papers of G.D. Craig.
3. Cull, Lander and Weiss: *Twelve Days In May*.

CHARLES EDWARD ENGLISH, 77791
PILOT OFFICER

Charles Edward English was born in 1912, the eldest of three children born to Joseph and Bertha E. English. The family home being at Number 37, Grosvenor Place in the Jesmond area of Newcastle. This was an area that could be described as typical Jesmond, Grosvenor Place lying within reach of both the tennis club and the cricket club and not far from the picturesque Jesmond Dean, a haunt favoured by artists and photographers alike. Of English, not much is known of his early life. The children were known to be of a competitive nature. This may account for the fact that both sons were to be fighter pilots.

Prior to the outbreak of World War Two, English worked in an office of a local brewery. Like many young men of the day, English had a longing to fly. It is thought that his early flying career began at the nearby Newcastle Aero Club, then based at Woolsington, later to become Newcastle Airport. Wynn has English joining 607 (County of Durham) Auxiliary Squadron in 1938. However, English was a member prior to this. According to the logbook of George Dudley Craig, a pilot on 607 Squadron, English flew as his passenger—air gunner from November 1937. This early flight of English being recorded on November 21, 1937.[1] This flight was made in Hawker Demon K 8193. As Craig had been a qualified pilot for only a week, it is possible that English had been on the squadron longer than this.

When 607 Squadron took on its new equipment, the Gloster Gladiator in 1938, English, as with many others, was given the chance to stay with the squadron and be trained as a pilot. However, the outbreak of the war in September 1939 brought his training with 607 Squadron to an end. English was posted to 7 FTS at Peterborough as from October 7, 1939. English had completed his training by March 7, 1940. He was then commissioned and posted to 6 OTU at Sutton Bridge, Lincolnshire. English was now converted onto the Hurricane. Although he had been taught to fly the Hurricane, he had not been taught to use its potential as a fighting machine. This was to come later as part of his advanced training, if he had time. Luckily English was posted to 85 Squadron. Number 85 Squadron were at that time based at Debden. The squadron at this time, having recently returned from France, was resting as well as retraining with its new pilots.

Number 85 Squadron had suffered severely while in France. Many experienced pilots had been lost, as well as aircraft. They were down to three Hurricanes when they arrived at Debden. Also lost was their C.O. Their new Commanding Officer was the redoubtable Squadron Leader Peter Townsend. In his own efficient way Townsend, a pre-war career officer, set about rebuilding the squadron, with the help of some squadron veterans, into an efficient fighting machine. Many of the new pilots had little training on the Hurricane and most had no air fighting experience at all. Among these new pilots was Pilot Officer English, who for some long lost reason, was to gain the nickname 'Honk'.[2]

Throughout June and into early July Townsend trained his new squadron religiously. Passing on all the knowledge he had gained over the years. Always keep a lookout, keep watching the sky, your instruments, back to the sky—keep a lookout at all times. He sent them to Sutton Bridge so that they could fire their guns in anger. Then came the endless convoy patrols. Townsend was to consider these as a good training ground. At last the day came when 85 Squadron was considered fit to enter the battleground. The squadron was sent to Martlesham Heath, arriving there July 10, just in time for the first phase of the Battle of Britain that was about to begin.

Throughout July and into August, 85 Squadron had frequently met with the enemy. Embarrassingly for Townsend, after all his teaching, he was the first squadron member to be shot down. To double his embarrassment, he was shot down by return fire from a Do 17 and, taking to his parachute, was rescued by the Navy.

A GATHERING OF EAGLES

August 18, 1940 was the first encounter that 85 Squadron had at full squadron strength: some thirteen Hurricanes. Some ten miles east of Foulness Point at around 5.50 PM, 85 Squadron became entangled in a dog-fight with Me 110s of ZG 26. On this occasion English was flying as Red 2, to the right of Townsend. In the resulting melee, English spotted an Me 110 which crossed his nose. Giving it a lengthy burst he noticed hits along the wings. At this point the rear gunner ceased to return fire — obviously hit by the gunfire from the Hurricane of English. With the rear gunner gone, the Me 110 was defenceless from the rear: English took advantage of the fact and pressed home another attack giving the Me 110 a lengthy burst from a range of 200–300 yards. However, another Me 110 came to the rescue of his comrade and English found himself driven away from his target. With his ammunition now expended English returned to Debden a little disappointed that he had not claimed a kill but could only record the Me 110 as damaged.

August 30 saw the Luftwaffe launch a strong raid against the sector stations of Kent and Surrey. After being brought to readiness, eleven Hurricanes of 85 Squadron were scrambled and in the air by 10.36 AM. Townsend climbed his fighters into the sun and keeping them in that position, out of sight from the bomber force, watched and waited for the right moment to carry out his attack. The bomber formation was flying at around 16,000 feet. The escorting fighters, a mixture of Me 110s and Me 109s were stepped up to 20,000 feet. Still keeping his fighters up-sun, Townsend stalked the bomber force before carrying out one of his favourite manoeuvres, the head-on attack to break up the enemy formation.

'Sammy' Allard was leading Red Section on this occasion with 'Honk' English as his number two. As the fighters rushed in to the head-on attack English did not get a good shot at the bombers. He could only manage a short burst at one of the bombers at the rear of the formation before breaking away downwards. Pulling up again he closed for another attack on an He 111 at the rear of the formation. He gave the bomber a short burst from close range — in fact he almost overdid it. So close was the range that English was forced to take severe avoiding action in order to avoid ramming the bomber. However, fortune came out of his mistake, English found himself in a good position to carry out an attack on an Me 110. Giving the Me 110 a lengthy six-second burst, English was once more frustrated by yet another Me 110, which forced him to abort his attack. However, English was not in a mood to be put off once more. He avoided the attacking Me 110 by breaking away in a hard turn, outmanoeuvring the heavier Me 110. As English turned away he noticed his original target Me 110 descending in a 'crabwise' motion, its two engines leaving a trail of black smoke. However, another Hurricane was on its tail so he looked around for another target. English next picked out an He 111, once more delivering only a short burst before being driven off by the ever-present Me 110s. English easily avoided his pursuers once more with a descending series of tight turns. Wynn credits English with the destruction of an Me 110 on this day. However, this aircraft remains unidentified.

Having been in the thick of the heaviest fighting for some time, 85 Squadron were stood down the following day, August 31. The squadron was not due to be on readiness until 1.00 PM. However, the Luftwaffe picked the lunch break period to launch an attack against Croydon. The attack brought about a hasty end to lunch for 85 Squadron. Townsend, annoyed at having his lunch break interrupted, led twelve Hurricanes off amid the bomb blasts that were erupting across the airfield. Managing to gain height rapidly on full power, Townsend led his squadron into the attack against the Me 110s of the fighter escort, mistakenly thinking that they had been responsible for the actual bombing. Townsend admits that he was a bit 'irate' at the time. This is not the best frame of mind to be in when facing the enemy in a dog-fight. Perhaps Townsend had lost a bit of his 'edge' due to the increased activity over the preceding weeks. Before Townsend could get into a position to carry out his attack, the squadron were well and truly 'bounced' by the Me 109s proving the fighter escort. The squadron were to lose three aircraft during this action. Among those shot down was Townsend, who was wounded in the foot.

September 1 saw 85 Squadron scrambled at 1.55 PM. The squadron had already been on patrol, some of the aircraft still being refuelled when the scramble was called. An incoming raid of about 150 bombers escorted by Me 110s and Me109s had been plotted. With Townsend out of action due to his wounds, 'Sammy' Allard was leading the eleven Hurricanes that answered the scramble. Where

Townsend had favoured the more dangerous but effective head-on attack, Allard put his faith in the beam attack and, ignoring the fighter escort, went straight for the bombers. English was flying in his usual position of Red 2. However, for some unspecified reason he was unable to keep up with his leader and fell behind. English then joined P/O A.G. Lewis who was attacking the second wave of Do 17s. Carrying out his first run successfully, English broke away to carry out a second run. As he did so he became a target for a group of Me 110s. Evading the group, English found himself almost immediately put under attack by a further group of fighters, on this occasion they were Me 109s. Once more English was to make good his escape with the use of some handy cloud cover.

Descending from the cloud cover, English was faced with the target of a lone Do 17. This he proceeded to attack. Two lengthy burst from the rear stopped one of the Do 17s engines. English watched as his victim began to lose height and eventually force land between Ham Street and Hythe. Two of the bombers crew were seen to emerge from the aircraft that had crashed into a field. Once again, Battle of Britain literature has failed to identify this aircraft. However, it is known that Luftwaffe reports from the period are missing. The Do 17 is stated as having crashed, as above, in the squadron diaries.[3] The day had not gone too well for 85 Squadron; they had lost some seven aircraft in the fighting. Allard's aircraft, although counted in the total, was actually destroyed while on the ground.

September 2, therefore, was not a good day; the squadron could only muster six aircraft in all. The following day 85 Squadron were withdrawn from the battle zone, moving first to Castle Camps, then on to Church Fenton two days later. However, as well as some pilots needing a rest, experienced pilots were also needed by other squadrons. Squadrons needing a rest or not, English was now an experienced pilot. Other squadrons needed the pilots with that experience. Rather than being rested, English was posted on to another squadron.

So it was that English found himself back on an Auxiliary Air Force squadron. On this occasion it was 605 (County of Warwick) Squadron. This squadron had only recently moved south from Drem. Moving to Croydon they were joined there by English. Unfortunately for the eager pilots, their move south coincided with the weather closing in. Action for the squadron was, therefore, few and far between. Even the Luftwaffe stayed at home most of the time. There was some activity on October 4, even though the day was dogged by rain, mist, low cloud and generally bad weather. On this day it is recorded that a Hurricane force landed near Keymer to the north of Brighton. During an inconclusive combat the Hurricane of English is thought to have suffered some damage. English attempted to land his aircraft in a field at Pitchfont Farm at around 4.55 PM. The Hurricane V 6784, UP-E sustained some minor damage and English was unscathed in the accident.

With the brighter weather of October 7, the Luftwaffe resumed their attacks in strength. Number 605 Squadron were in the air shortly after 1.00 PM, joining in combat with a large number of Me 109s shortly after. In the resulting melee, Hurricane P 3677 was shot down by Me 109s over Westerham at 1.20 PM. The Hurricane of English crashed onto land at Park Farm, Brasted, where it burned itself out. English was killed and his victor was probably a pilot of JG 27. The local press revealed that English had been expected home on leave the following week. Perhaps he too, like Townsend, had lost a bit of his 'fighting edge' especially after the force-landing of only a few days before, only with differing results.

The body of English was brought back to the North East there to be buried in St Andrew's and Jesmond Cemetery only a short distance from his home. The grave is in a family plot but also bears a CWGC headstone. This shows that Charles Edward English shares the grave with his brother Robin who was also to lose his life as a pilot with Number 3 Squadron in 1941. Today, the cemetery is not the best-kept cemetery, even by Newcastle's standards and looks fairly neglected.

English Notes
1. Log Book of G.D. Craig.
2. Peter Townsend: *Duel of Eagles*.
3. A.J. Brookes, *Fighter Squadron At War* states that this aircraft was a Do 215.

George Mathwin Forrester, 81369
Pilot Officer

George Mathwin Forrester was born in the City of Newcastle upon Tyne February 17, 1914. His mother gifted the young George with her maiden name of Mathwin as a second Christian name. Apart from that, little is known of this area of Forrester's life. While Forrester was still young, it would appear that the Forrester family moved to the south of the country severing their connections with the North East.

Wynn states that Forrester attended Haileybury College from 1927 to 1930.[1] Later he was to move into business in the Portsmouth area. While there he became an active sportsman, mainly in rugby and rowing. In later years Forrester was to move again. This time it was to Oxford. It was while living in Oxford that Forrester became an airman. He joined the RAFVR as an airman under training as a pilot. Part-time training came to an end in September of 1939. Forrester was called to full-time service with the RAF on the first of the month. Training was continued at 12 Flying Training School (FTS) In Grantham, Lincolnshire. His basic training completed, Forrester was commissioned, July 6, 1940, and posted to 6 Operational Training Unit (OTU) at Sutton Bridge, also in Lincolnshire. Training and conversion onto the Hawker Hurricane was completed in three weeks. Forrester was then posted to his first fighter squadron, Number 605 (County of Warwick) Squadron, an Auxiliary Air Force unit, then based at Drem, a few miles to the east of Haddington, East Lothian in Scotland.

Number 605 Squadron had already seen service in the south of the country. Based at Hawkinge, they were to fly from there to cover the evacuation of Dunkirk. With their work in the south done, 605 Squadron were next posted to Drem, arriving there May 27, for a rest period. While flying from Drem, 605 Squadron were responsible for the air defence of Edinburgh and the Firth of Forth. The squadron was once more declared operational July 31. A short while later, 605 Squadron was one of the squadrons in action August 15. A large formation of enemy aircraft of Luftflotte Five based in Norway, attempted to attack targets in the North East. Forrester was not among those flying on that day. Of the squadron, only 'B' flight was to make contact with the enemy. September 7, 1940, brought the news that for 605 Squadron, their rest period had come to an end. The squadron was to move south and take up station at Croydon in the Kenley sector.

There was not to enough time to get used to the area around Croydon either. The morning of September 8 saw 605 Squadron in the air. Number 605 Squadron had been scrambled along with 253 Squadron towards the area of Maidstone. Arriving in the area over Maidstone and Rochester, the squadrons were to find that they had missed the main bomber force. In their place was another formation. This consisted of Dornier Do 17s escorted by a number of Me 110s. Stacked up above this formation was another formation of Me 109s. On this occasion the escorting Me 109s were flying too high to give adequate protection to their charges. The result was that some of the bombers were heading earthwards before the fighter escort could intervene in the fighting. A few more Do 17s were to suffer various amounts of damage before the Me 109s joined in the fighting, which was taking place over Tunbridge Wells. In the resulting dogfighting, Number 605 Squadron were to consider themselves lucky to get away with only one casualty. This was P/O J. Fleming who was to suffer serious burns.

The following afternoon saw 605 Squadron once more in action. An incoming raid consisting of Heinkel He 111s of KG 53 were making a westerly flight with their escort of Me 110s. Having flown up the coast of Kent, the formation turned to make an attack on Farnborough. The formation had to make a detour around London and in doing so had to run the gauntlet of Ground defences and fighter squadrons alike. The Me 110s had been taken by surprise at the ferocity of the defence put up by the fighter squadrons of RAF Fighter Command. To defend themselves they had formed defensive circles. As the raid was to progress, the bombers were left without their fighter escort. On this occasion, however, they made a good attempt at defending themselves. Flying in close formation and coordinating their fire power, the bombers put up a formidable crossfire.

In attacking the He 111s, Forrester was to witness some of this crossfire. Forrester's Hurricane, L 2059 was caught in the murderous crossfire and severely, if not terminally, damaged. The Hurricane then fell away from the battle. Falling down through the raging battle, Forrester's Hurricane was to collide with another He 111. This was He 111 *werke* Number 2630 coded, A1+ZD. This aircraft was of the Stab Flight of KG 53 that was flying at a lower level. Both Hurricane and He 111, in a last embrace of death, fell earthwards, the Hurricane having lost its starboard wing in the collision. Both aircraft were to fall near Alton in Hampshire at 5.30 PM. Forrester, presumably thrown from his doomed Hurricane, fell dead at South Field Farm. Of the bombers crew, Fw's Doering, Endorf and Wenninger were all killed. Oblt Meinecke and Fw Broderich managed to bail out and were taken prisoner. It had been Forrester's second day of action against the enemy. Unfortunately, the first enemy aircraft that he can be credited with destroying also destroyed him.[2]

Mason was to state that this He 111 was in collision with the Hurricane of F/O J.E. Boulton. The later having already been in collision with the Hurricane of Flt Lt G.L. Sinclair, both pilots of 310 Squadron. Boulton's Hurricane then, according to *The Battle of Britain Then and Now*, collided with a Do 215. Wynn states that Boulton's Hurricane collided firstly with Sinclair then with an Me 110. With the benefit of hindsight, it would appear that Boulton's Hurricane had its second collision with an He 111 of KG 53. These were the aircraft carrying out the raid. The Do 215 was a reconnaissance aircraft and as such would not be used on a bombing raid. The position of these two collisions, Boulton—Sinclair and the He 111, was over the area of Croydon at around 5.35 PM. The collision between Forrester and the He 111 was further west and timed at around 5.30 PM. Although the gap in time was only five minutes between the collisions, in distance it was almost forty miles.

George Mathwin Forrester was buried in Odiham Cemetery, Hampshire. He is buried on the north side of the cemetery in grave number 425. The cemetery is only a short distance from where Forrester fell. Forrester's squadron, 605, had been operational for just over a month. During that time their total time in action was just two days in the south. It was only the second engagement that Forrester had taken part in. Although Forrester had converted to the Hurricane at 6 OTU, he would have been shown how to fly it only. There was no time to be shown how to fire the guns. Neither was there any time to be taught aerial tactics. This training was only passed on when Forrester joined 605 Squadron, even then it would be a short training period. At the time of his death, George Mathwin Forrester was a resident of Upper Bassett in Southampton, having lived there with his wife Frances.

FORRESTER NOTES
1. Wynn: *Men of The Battle of Britain*, P 169
2. Ramsey: *Battle of Britain Then And Now*, P 440.

Anthony Douglas Forster, DFC, 90290
Flying Officer

Anthony Douglas Forster was born in the County Durham town of Bishop Middleham. Education for the young Forster was by way of Durham School; Forster was a Kings Scholar there. In later years Forster was to work in Newcastle upon Tyne for a well-known brewery company.[1] In 1938 Forster was to come into contact with the local squadron of the Auxiliary Air Force, joining 607 (County of Durham) Squadron in March of that year. Forster was gazetted May 31, 1938 and was called for full-time service August 24, 1939.

At first 607 Squadron was based at Acklington, Northumberland from October 1939. While there the squadron was ordered to France as part of the air component. The squadron arrived in Mereville November 15 before moving on to Vitry-en-Artois as a result of bad conditions on the surface of the airfield. Flights were mainly training as well as flying escort to the 'Blighty' ships carrying servicemen to and from France on leave. During April, 607 Squadron began to convert to the Hurricane at Abbeville. This move made an increase in the training schedule, most of the pilots of 607 Squadron never having flown a monoplane before. By the time that the Germans launched their Blitzkrieg in the early hours of May 10, 1940, 607 Squadron was still not fully operational on the Hurricane. Mixed patrols of Gladiators and Hurricanes were still common.

Action began for 'Bunny' Forster at 11.30 AM May 10. Flying with Yellow Section to the east of Mons, five Heinkel He 111s were spotted. Attacking the German formation at around 10,000 feet,

Forster was to make a claim for one He 111 destroyed and another as probable. Later the same day the squadron were scrambled again. This came at 1.30 PM. Some fifteen minutes later Forster, again flying with Yellow Section, attacked a formation of He 111s. On this occasion Forster; flying Hurricane P 2573, coded AF-A was to make a claim for one He 111 destroyed.

Returning to base, the squadron were rearmed and refuelled just in time to be scrambled again at 2.30 PM. Nine Hurricanes made up the formation that got airborne and flew to the area of St Quentin. Yellow Section, on this occasion led by F/O Will Gore, encountered three He 111s. The threesome attacked the enemy formation. Following Gore closely, Forster witnessed hits on the He111 attacked by Gore. Forster then initiated his own attack on one of the He 111s. Firing at the He 111, Forster witnessed his fire striking the bomber that eventually began to trail black smoke from its starboard engine. However, as its demise was not witnessed, Forster was allowed only a probable.

May 11 saw Forster in action again. Once more Forster was flying in company with Will Gore when the pair encountered two Junkers Ju 88s in the area of Ath. Initially both aircraft carried out attacks on the Ju 88s. However, the guns of Gore's Hurricane jammed, leaving Forster as the lone hunter. The two Ju 88s managed to make good their escape, however, and Forster could only claim the pair as both damaged. May 13, with the action still hot and furious, Forster was the pilot of one of three Hurricanes airborne from Vitry. The patrol was carried out in the area of Louvain. While looking for the enemy, the Hurricanes were bounced by Messerschmitt Me 109s. A turning dogfight was carried out but the outcome was indecisive; no kills were made by either side, and the Hurricanes returned to Vitry with slight, but repairable damage. By now 607 Squadron had taken more than its share of losses and the squadron was ordered back to Britain. In the early hours of the morning of May 17, Forster made his return to Britain minus his Hurricane. Transport on this occasion was the bare floor of an Ensign of the Air Transport Auxiliary that deposited Forster, and some of the other pilots, at Hendon.

Number 607 Squadron was more than slightly battered on its return to Britain. Some of the pilots had been killed and others were missing. The squadron's aircraft was almost non-existent. After a spot of leave, many of the pilots were to return to 607 Squadron to help rebuild it. For others, their future lay with other squadrons. One of the latter was Forster, who found himself posted to 151 Squadron in June, then based at Martlesham Heath in the North Weald sector. With the opening of the early stages of the Battle of Britain, 151 Squadron were soon in the action. July 9 saw 'A' flight scrambled at 1.36 PM. A raid was reported developing in the area over the Thames Estuary. Tagging along at the back was Wing Commander Victor Beamish, the station commander. Having heard the directions given over the tannoy system, and frustrated by the lack of action, Beamish joined up with 'A' flight where he flew as number two. Scattered cloud lay over the area and the controller's direction were not encouraging, bringing no immediate results and only frustration for the pilots. After all, they wanted to be seen to perform properly in front of the station commander. However, breaking through some cloud cover, 151 Squadron were immediately confronted with a large formation of enemy aircraft.

The enemy formation was on course to attack a northern-bound convoy that was about to leave the Thames Estuary. The bombers, a mixture of He 111s and Ju 88s, were flying at around 12,000 feet. To the rear and stepped up, was the fighter escort of Me 110s and 109s. 'A' Flight immediately split itself into two sections as the Hurricanes attempted to take on the one hundred plus enemy aircraft. One section turned towards the bombers while the second section of Beamish, Forster and P/O J.R. Hamar turned towards the fighter escort. In the ensuing dogfight none of the Hurricanes got within firing distance of the bombers, the fighter escort being far too strong. The second section managed to elude most of the fighter escort and, during the action, managed to corner an Me 110. Persistent attacks were carried out by all three Hurricanes that resulted in the Me 110 being shot down. The Me 110 was of 3 Gruppen ZG 26. This aircraft was seen to fall into the Thames Estuary; its crew were never found. The kill was shared by the three pilots.

July 30, 1940 was the day that Forster was awarded the DFC. This was in recognition for his actions in both France and the early part of the Battle of Britain. The citation appearing in the London Gazette, July 30, 1940, reads;

'This officer has displayed great courage and devotion to duty in participating in all patrols recently undertaken by his squadron, during which he has destroyed at least two enemy aircraft. Previously he has been involved in intensive flying operations in France, where he destroyed four enemy aircraft'.

With a total of six confirmed kills under his belt, Forster had gained the status of 'ace'.

Forster's days with 151 Squadron were soon to end. August 24 saw Forster back with his old squadron, Number 607. Not only his old squadron but also his old base for 607 Squadron was at this time based at Usworth. Having already met the Luftwaffe in action over the North East, August 15, 607 Squadron felt confident of returning to the fray in the south. They had not long to wait, September 8 saw 607 Squadron posted south to Tangmere. No sooner had they landed than they were scrambled into action. However, this was without result.

Still inexperienced, though full of eagerness and confidence, the squadron was scrambled the next day. In the late afternoon, 607 Squadron, having been scrambled were in the area of Mayfield when they were bounced by Me 109s. Six of the squadrons Hurricanes were shot down in this action. Their victors on this occasion were probably the Me 109s of JG3 who were flying as part of the high escort. Number 607 Squadron were to carry out a head-on attack against an enemy formation, September 14. Forster was credited with damaging a Ju 88 in this attack. However, the Battle of Britain had come to an end for Forster. Five days later he was to be taken off flying duties for medical reasons. He did not return to 607 Squadron until well into November of 1940.

Forster was promoted to the rank of Flight Lieutenant November 30, 1940. His stay with 607 Squadron was to come to an end again, December 15. On this date Forster was to the Central Flying School (CFS) at Upavon where he took a flying instructors course. Later, Forster was to join the staff of Number Ten Flying Training School (FTS) at Tern Hill, remaining there until December of 1942. Forster was next sent on a course at the Empire CFS at Hullavington, on completion of the course Forster was posted to Canada where he became a Chief Flying Instructor. Forster was to remain in Canada as an instructor until May 1945. After this date he returned to England and was released from the RAF. In June of 1946, Forster was to rejoin the RAF with a permanent commission. For the rest of his career Forster was to hold a number of staff appointments before eventually retiring from the service, April 24, 1962. On his retirement Forster held the rank of Wing Commander.

Forster Notes
1. Personal correspondence with W.H.R. Whitty.

Denys Gillam 1940.

Denys Edgar Gillam, AFC, 37167
Flight Lieutenant

Denys Edgar Gillam was born in Tynemouth, November 18, 1915. However, he does not appear to have stayed in the area for very long. His education was gained at schools in Yorkshire. Gillam attended Scarborough Grammar School before moving on to Bramcote School, Scarborough and then Wrekin College, Shropshire. His interest in flying dates from the time he attended the aviation camp for public schoolboys, which were held at Norwich, Norfolk. While a member, Gillam obtained his 'A' licence, September 12, 1934. It would appear natural that Gillam would decide on a career in aviation. This he did by applying to join the RAF. His application was accepted and Gillam joined the service on a short service commission. His career with the RAF began in February of 1935.

Service flying training began for Gillam at Netheravon on Salisbury Plain, Wiltshire. Gillam's training was to include flying on various types of aircraft including the Tiger Moth and the variants of the Hawker Hart. The flights would be on navigation exercises and cross-country flights as well as formation flying and aerobatics. With his training over, Gillam was posted to 29 Squadron at North Weald. Arriving there March 6, 1936, Gillam was to fly the more powerful Hawker Demon. After nine months of squadron service Gillam was posted on to the Meteorological Flight, the 'Met Flight' then based at Aldergrove near Belfast in Northern Ireland.

The Met Flight was a small compact unit. Its purpose was mainly to record the upper air temperatures. By definition, flying with the

Met Flight was, to say the least, demanding. The pilots of the Met Flight, to gain their information, had to fly in all weathers. This meant flying every day, even to the extent of flying when other pilots could not. This type of flying called for a pilot of above average flying ability.

On occasion the pilots of the Met Flight were called upon to fly even more demanding flights. Gillam's experience was to prove invaluable when Rathlin Island, to the north of Ballycastle, Northern Ireland, became cut off due to severe storms. Rathlin Island had been cut off and isolated for some three weeks. The people on the island were beginning to reach desperation point as far as food and supplies were concerned. It sighed with relief, therefore, when an aeroplane descended on the island from out of the storms.

Flying a Westland Wallace, Denys Gillam was to make the perilous journey to Rathlin Island on two occasions, each time carrying vital supplies to the islanders. For his courage and ability in carrying out these flights, Gillam was awarded the AFC, July 9, 1938.

July of 1939 saw the Auxiliary Air Force embodied into the RAF. In September of that year, Gillam was posted onto 616 (South Yorkshire) Squadron Auxiliary Air Force. Gillam was posted onto 616 as one of a batch of experienced pilots to reinforce the numbers of experienced pilots on the squadron. At that time, the pilots of 616 Squadron were still relatively inexperienced as a fighter squadron. Allied to this inexperience was the fact that the squadron had just been equipped with a new type of aircraft: the Spitfire. In January of 1940, Gillam became a flight commander on the squadron. In the following May, 616 Squadron now fully operational, was posted south. Arriving at Rochford May 26, 616 Squadron was to add its strength to the air defence over the beaches of Dunkirk. Although flying its share of patrols over the beachhead, 616 Squadron had little encounter with the enemy. June 1, 1940, 616 Squadron was ordered on to patrol over Dunkirk. On this day Gillam was leading the squadron. The squadron did get caught up in the air fighting during this day. Gillam was the only pilot to make any claim. This was for a Ju 88 damaged.

With its duties over Dunkirk filled, 616 Squadron returned to Leconfield. There, to take on its duties in the defence of Yorkshire as well as rest and rebuild the squadron. Only the occasional raider was to transgress the area until August 15, 1940. The radar station at

Staxton Wold picked up a plot over the North Sea and scrambled 616 Squadron to investigate. High over Flamborough Head 616 Squadron spotted the incoming raiders.

Some fifty Ju 88s of KG 30 had flown from their base at Aalbourg in Denmark. Now they were en route to bomb Leconfield: or so it was thought. The Ju 88s were roughly divided half and half—bombers and fighter escort. From their vantage point at around 20,000 feet, 616 Squadron dived into the attack, this first attack having the effect of splitting up the formation. At this point the Ju 88s turned onto a course for their true target, the airfield of Driffield. Number 616 Squadron were to make a claim for at least eight aircraft destroyed. Gillam, flying his usual Spitfire, N 3093 coded W-QJ, was to attack one of the Ju 88s and claim it as destroyed.

Within a few days of the attack on the North East, 616 Squadron were returned to the south. The squadron was to be based at Kenley. Just before 11.30 AM, August 26, 'A' flight were scrambled with only seven serviceable aircraft. Immediately they were directed towards of Dungeness. Arriving there they found they had missed the bomber force. Instead they were vectored to the area of Dover, presumably to investigate an errant barrage balloon. Gillam had ordered the second section home. However, over Dover, the section was bounced by around fifty Me 109s. The four Spitfires were forced to fly in a defensive circle. Gillam called for help. The second section returned while at the same time 'B' flight was scrambled. On this occasion 616 Squadron were to pay a heavy price. No less than six of their aircraft went down to the overwhelming number of Me 109s. Gillam was the only pilot to come out of the fray with any success, claiming an Me 109 as destroyed.

Gillam was to claim further success on the August 29, attacking an Me 110. It made a desperate bid for freedom diving headlong for the coast of France. In its wake was an equally desperate Gillam determined that the Me 110 was not going to make it home. Chasing the Me 110 to within five miles of the French coast, attacking it all the while, Gilam saw the Me 110 crash into the sea.

August 30 saw 616 Squadron defending their own airfield against attack. During the late afternoon a raid was plotted over the Thames Estuary. This raid fanned out and made simultaneous attacks on North Weald, Kenley and Biggin Hill. Number 616 Squadron was to tangle with the fighter escort of Me 109s. Gillam singled out an Me 109 and delivered a successful attack, the Me 109 crashing at Walderslade at 4.45 PM. This Me 109 was an E4 of 2 Gruppen JG 2, the (Richthofen Geschwader). It's pilot, Fw Harbauer was killed in the action.[1] Mason attributes this Me 109 to Sgt J. Hopewell, also of 616 Squadron, but states that this Me 109 crashed at Eastchurch. These two places are almost thirty miles apart. Gillam was to make a further claim for an Me 109 destroyed August 31.

September 1 saw Gillam once more in the thick of the fighting. He claimed a Do 17 destroyed and another Do 17 as a probable. He was also to claim as probable, an Me 109 and another Do 17. The following day was to bring a further increase in his score. Large raids had been plotted throughout the day. Mid-afternoon was to bring no respite. On this occasion it was a large raid approaching the southern coast of Kent that began to build up. Once more the targets appeared to be Kenley, Biggin Hill and Hornchurch. Many of the RAF pilots on this day were to find that, as they attempted to attack the bombers and their close escort, they in turn were bounced by Me 109s of the high escort.

Gillam immediately set about attacking an Me 110, seeing it destroyed by his gunfire. No sooner than he had accomplished this task than he became a target, probably put under attack by an Me 110. Gillam was forced to bale out of his Spitfire. His Spitfire, X 4181 buried itself deep in a field on Brook Farm, Capel. By now, 616 Squadron after taking heavy and sustained losses, was deemed in need of a rest. Number 616 Squadron were sent to Coltishall in Norfolk. However, the RAF had other plans for Gillam. He was posted to 312 (Czek) Squadron, then based at Speke, Liverpool. He was to take up the duties of Flight Commander.

In comparison to the south, life at Speke was fairly quiet. However, raids did occur, if rather infrequently. One of these was to occur October 8, 1940. Three Hurricanes of Yellow Section were lined up on the runway ready to take off. Leading Yellow Section was Gillam. To either side were P/O Alois Vasatko and Sergeant Joseph Stehlik. The three Hurricanes roared down the runway and lifted off to begin their climb. The attention of the three pilots was drawn to AA fire off to their right. Immediately a Junkers Ju 88 shot across their path. The enemy bomber, on seeing the British fighters, attempted to make a run for nearby cloud cover. The three Hurricanes, their undercarriage still not fully retracted, opened fire as one.

In the brief encounter the Ju 88 crash-landed with both engines smoking and its pilot dead. The three Hurricanes made a full circle of the airfield and landed to the cheers of their ground crews. From take off to landing had taken all of eleven minutes. In between they had managed to shoot down a Ju 88. This feat is still recognized as the fastest ever confirmed kill. All three Hurricanes were found to be damaged to some degree, the Hurricane of Gillam having a shattered windscreen. A painting of this event was executed by the well-known aviation artist Robert Taylor.[2] The painting leans heavily on artistic licence and only Gillam's Hurricane is shown. However, all three pilots were in the action and all three were credited with a share in the kill.

Gillam was awarded the DFC, November 12, 1940. The citation for this award reads;

> 'This officer has been responsible for the destruction of seven enemy aircraft and probably four more and has damaged six. On one occasion during a combat with a large force of Me 110s, he shot one down and his own aircraft caught fire. He descended by parachute and returned to his station in time to lead the next patrol. On another occasion Flt Lt Gillam shot down a Junkers 88 and landed within eleven minutes from the time he took off'.

Before the year was out Gillam was posted again in December. His new posting was to take Gillam to Tern Hill where he took command of 306 (Polish) Squadron. He was not to stay long and moved to HQ group, arriving there March 2, 1941. After a period of 'rest', Gillam was to return to operations in July, 1941 as the Commanding Officer of 615 Squadron. Leading this squadron, he was to carry out offensive patrols over Europe. One such raid, carried out October 9, 1941, Gillam led 615 Squadron in an attack on surface targets along the Belgian coast. Two targets attacked were a 1,500-ton vessel and an enemy AA post. Pilots of 615 Squadron carried out the attack on the latter in order to allow Gillam to fly unhindered into the Nouveau Basin, Ostend. There, Gillam attacked and destroyed two He 59s and their adjacent hangar. In honour of such achievements as above, Gillam was awarded a bar to his DFC, October 21, 1941.

Gillam was leading his squadron, November 23, when they attacked a distillery in the vicinity of Dunkirk. Gillam carried out the attack successfully, even though he had been wounded, both in the arms and legs, by light AA fire. His Spitfire did not fare so well, being badly damaged. Gillam eventually evacuated his stricken aircraft and landed in the sea where he took to his dinghy. The Spitfires from his squadron continually circled overhead providing protection until the RAF Air-Sea Rescue launch arrived on the scene, other Spitfires showing the way. Gillam was safely returned to Ramsgate Harbour. For this, and his continual bravery in action, Gillam was awarded the DSO, December 12, 1941.

The year 1942 was to bring new challenges for Gillam, starting with a tour of the USA. There, Gillam gave a series of lectures to American pilots. After a period in the USA, Gillam returned to England and took command of the first Typhoon Wing, then based at Duxford, arriving there in March 1942. Keeping on the move, Gillam was to take on a number of Staff appointments. These were to vary in range from the RAF Staff College between October 1942 and February 1943, to HQ 12 Group were he stayed for six months. Following this, Gillam was once more posted to the USA. On this occasion it was to the General Staff School at Fort Leavenworth where he took command.

In December of 1943 Gillam was once more to return to England. Moving once more onto operations, Gillam took command 146 Wing. A further move in April of 1944 saw Gillam take command of 20 Sector of the second Tactical Air Force (TAF). A bar to his DSO was awarded August 11, 1944. In command of 146 Wing once more, Gillam led them on a low-level attack on a building in Dordrecht. This was thought to be acting as a conference centre for a group of high-ranking German officers. This low-level attack resulted in two German Generals and seventeen senior officers dead as well as fifty other officers who were also killed in the attack.

Denys Gillam was released from the RAF October 1945, with the rank of Wing Commander. He returned to his civilian occupation in a carpet firm in the Halifax area of Yorkshire. He later became a director of the firm. With the reformation of the Auxiliary Air Force, now with the prefix, 'Royal', June 2, 1946. Gillam returned to 616 Squadron with the reduced rank of Flight Lieutenant. Denys Gillam died in September 1991.

Gillam Notes
1. Ramsey: *Battle of Britain Then And Now*, P 607. No Mention is made of Gillam as the victor.
2. F. K. Mason: *Battle Over Britain.* Aston Publications. 1990.
3. Robert Taylor: *Robert Taylor Air Combat Paintings, Vol 2*, P 66. Painting titled 'Fastest Victory'.

John N. Glendinning.

John Nixon Glendinning, 740032
Sergeant

John Nixon Glendinning was born in the tiny hamlet of Benfieldside near Shotley Bridge, County Durham. John Nixon Glendinning was born the only son of Maria Kegia Glendinning, July 7, 1912, their place of abode at that time being Morden Cottage in Benfieldside. The entry of baptism in the parish register of St Cuthbert gives no father's name. Little is known of the early years of Glendinning junior. The first we hear of him is that he joined the RAFVR, July 25, 1937 at the age of twenty-five. Glendinning was classed as an airman under training as a pilot. Just under one year later Glendinning was to receive his 'A' licence, March 18, 1938. September of 1939 saw Glendinning called to full-time service. Glendinning was despatched to Sealand, Clwyd and arrived there October 7, 1939.

Training at Sealand was mainly for assessment purposes, training him to service level prior to sending him out to a squadron. This training was to last some two months. Glendinning was next posted to Number Nine Bombing and Gunnery School (BGS) at Penrhos in Wales. The (BGS) had only been in operation for two months, the unit having been formerly the Air Observers School (AOS). Glendinning was on the staff there as a pilot, his duties being to fly the trainees in the bombing and gunnery courses in a range of aircraft from the Harrow to the Fairey Battle.

With the Battle of Britain taking priority on the new pilots of the RAF, Glendinning volunteered for fighter pilot training. The next posting for Glendinning was, therefore, Hawarden in North Wales: the home of Number 7 Operational Training Unit (OTU). Hawerden was the base used to convert pilots to the Spitfire. Glendinning was to spend the next two weeks getting to grips with the little fighter. On completion of his training at Hawerden Glendinning was posted to 54 Squadron. The squadron being at that time posted as 'resting' at Catterick.

Number 54 Squadron was a Spitfire unit until September 2, 1940, the squadron had been in the thick of the fighting in the south of the country flying from Hornchurch. Like many other squadrons during this time, 54 Squadron had taken its share of casualties in both men and machines. Number 54 Squadron were posted to Catterick for a 'rest' period arriving there September 3. Life had taken on a less hectic mode than had been the normal during the last few weeks. However, although classed as 'resting' 54 Squadron had to maintain a flight at readiness. The readiness flight was based at Greatham, West Hartlepool and was a result of the Luftwaffe attack on the North East August 15.

However, since their arrival at Catterick things were to change drastically for 54 Squadron. Many of the experienced pilots had been posted on to other squadrons. If this was not bad enough, the squadron had its status reduced to that of a 'C' class squadron. In other words it was to become a training squadron. This was much to the chagrin of the existing pilots, who were none too pleased at the thought of having to train 'rookies'. In particular, one of the squadron's pilots was to make his feelings clear. F/O Al Deere, in his book, *Nine Lives* was to state: 'That 54 Squadron should be singled out to suffer such an ignoble fate, seemed to us a peculiar form of gratitude'.[1] It was at this time, when 54 Squadron were feeling at their lowest, that Glendinning joined the squadron.

Glendinning was a pilot not without experience, as far as flying goes. However, he had no experience of fighting with the Spitfire. This was where 54 Squadron, as a 'C' class squadron came in. F/Os Deere and George Gribble, both experienced pilots in the art of aerial fighting, worked on a syllabus for the training of new pilots. This was based on their air fighting techniques that had come to them through hard experience. Reflector gun-sights were to be always switched on. Flying in formation was to be used only to test a pilot's ability to do so and not to be used when going into battle. At all times they were encouraged to be aggressive, even to the point where they were flying behind other aircraft in formation, they had to keep the other aircraft in their sights as if he were the enemy. Much of the course was around cine-gun exercises. Later they would be watched, assessed and mistakes pointed out.

Continually impressed on the pilots was the fact that the Spitfire was in effect, a gun carrier. It was designed for air fighting and that was the only way to use it. It was left to the discretion of 54 Squadron to say when their charges were fit enough to be sent to the operational squadrons in the south. Many tests had to be passed along the way. The final test was to be carried out in company with the flight commander or his deputy. This would result in a mock combat in which the commander would take on role of an enemy fighter. Only when a certain level of achievement was reached were the pilots to be passed as operational. For Glendinning this training was to last a month. He was then posted to his first fighter squadron, Number 74.

Number 74 Squadron; the 'Tigers' were based at Biggin Hill during this time. The squadron having arrived there October 15, fresh from a 'rest' period, which had been spent at Coltishall. Glendinning arrived at Biggin Hill October 21, possibly as a replacement for fellow North East pilot F/O A.L. Ricalton who had been killed October 17. At this time the Battle of Britain was winding down, the Luftwaffe restricting most of its attacks to the hours of darkness. Mainly this was due to the losses it had sustained during the previous weeks but also due to the fact that the days were now shorter, autumn being well on its way. The 'Tigers' had been in action but it is not known if Glendinning had been on any patrols. At this time, 74 Squadron was led by 'Sailor' Malan, a man known throughout RAF Fighter Command for his knowledge of fighter tactics and, also as a man who would not put his men at risk needlessly. Glendinning would still be classed as a 'rookie'.

November 14 saw the Luftwaffe launch another massed attack against London. Shortly after 1.30 PM 74 Squadron were scrambled along with 66 Squadron. A force of Ju 87s, numbering around fifty, with a large number of Me 109s as the fighter escort, was carrying out the massed attack. Both squadrons were to attack from above the bomber formation, 66 Squadron were to attack down the starboard side while 74 Squadron, on this occasion led by F/O Mungo Park, were to attack down the port side. After the initial attack, Glendinning carried out a head-on attack against the leading Ju 87 of a formation of three. Seeing the hapless bomber burst into flames, Glendinning turned his attention to another. Carrying out an attack on the second Ju 87, Glendinning got in some bursts of deflection shooting. Glendinning saw bits begin to fly off before the Ju 87 fell earthwards in its last dive, disintegrating as it went. The fighting on this occasion, had been made much more difficult due to the 'friendly' AA fire which served the purpose of breaking up the fight. The squadron commander was to complain bitterly about this on their return. Not so disgruntled was Glendinning. He had managed to claim two Ju 87s as destroyed with another as damaged.

Glendinning was on patrol the following day, November 15, when he came across an Me 109. A dogfight followed with Glendinning managing to shoot down the Me 109. This aircraft, Me 109 E4, was of the fourth Staffel JG 2, (Richthofen). The Me 109, *werke* Number 5049 coded White 10, fell into shallow water at Felpham on the east side of Bognor Regis and was destroyed. Its pilot Uffz R. Miese was taken prisoner.[2]

November 16 saw 74 Squadron once more on patrol, on this occasion in company with 92 Squadron. Arriving on the scene too late, the squadrons found themselves at a height disadvantage. Caught off guard, they were bounced by around twenty Me 109s. After the initial attack the inevitable dogfight developed. Glendinning saw four Me 109s attacking a Spitfire, probably the aircraft of Sgt L.E. Freese. However, Glendinning could not get in range and was forced to give up the pointless chase. At around 18,000 feet a lone Me 109 crossed the nose of Glendinning's Spitfire. Delivering a beam attack, Glendinning noticed his fire striking home as the Me 109 rolled over on to its back. A further attack followed with the Me 109 falling away in a series of rolls, Glendinning following him down. Pressing home further attacks, Glendinning was satisfied of his victory when the tail unit of the Me 109 broke away. Glendinning reported that the Me 109 crashed into the sea off Bognor Regis.

Number 74 Squadron were scrambled at around 11.30 AM, December 2, 1940. Once more 74 Squadron were in company with 66

Squadron. However, on this occasion, as they were vectored towards the area of Dungeness, the squadrons became split. Shortly after this, 74 Squadron was attacked almost head-on by a series of small groups of Me 109s. A dogfight broke out with 74 Squadron claiming at least five of the enemy as destroyed. One of these fell to the guns of Glendinning. Attacking the Me 109 from the rear, Glendinning closed until the German fighter filled his gun sight. Opening fire, Glendinning saw his fire hitting the Me 109 around the engine cowling. Black smoke and engine coolant streamed back before the Me 109 snapped into a spin before it fell into the sea below. The squadron by now had its tail well up after its victories and attempted to reform at 20,000 feet. However, a large formation of Me 109s was spotted high above and in a good position to attack 74. Short of fuel and ammunition, 74 Squadron decided discretion was better than valour and decided to depart the scene while they were still ahead.

At this time, the official part of the Battle of Britain was over. Although 74 Squadron were still carrying out daytime patrols. However, no enemy were even sighted after December 5, 1940. RAF Fighter Command now moved over from the defensive to the offensive, taking the fight to the enemy in their own backyard of France. The main emphasis was to carry the fight to the enemy. To help meet this end, 74 Squadron were moved from Biggin Hill to Manston. The enemy were now only five short minutes flying time away. Ground targets in France were well in the range of the low-flying Spitfires. Regular fighter sweeps were carried out over France as 74 Squadron beat up the ground targets and tangled with the fighters of the Luftwaffe over their own bases. On one of these fighter sweeps, Glendinning accounted for one Me 109, March 1, 1941.

Another fighter sweep at squadron strength was set to take place March 12. Glendinning was flying in the unenviable position of 'Tail End Charlie'. His job was the prevention of the squadron being bounced from the rear. On this day, 74 Squadron had been either followed back across the Channel or their opponents were lying in wait somewhere along the line. Either way, 74 Squadron were bounced by Me 109s of JG 51, in the area north east of Dungeness and only a few miles from their own base. In the resulting dogfight, Glendinning's Spitfire P 7506, was shot down and crashed near Ivychurch, Kent. The victor over Glendinning was none other than

Major Werner Molders, Geschwaderkommadore of JG 51 and arguably the top German 'ace' at that time. Spitfire P 7506 was a relatively new aircraft, having been taken on charge by 74 Squadron October 24, 1940. When it crashed, March 12, it had clocked up only ninety-four flying hours.

Glendinning had been flying for some time and rest may have been long overdue. The result being that he may have lost his fighting edge. It may also be suggested that Glendinning was suffering from a dose of overconfidence. A fellow pilot, Sgt R.H. 'Peter' May, was later to write of Glendinning;

> 'I can well remember talking to him whilst he was placing a photograph of his wife and children on the mantelpiece. I said that after only twenty hours on Spitfires and one hundred and fifty hours in all I found it difficult to cope. 'Be patient' he said, 'Once you have mastered it its as easy as flying a Tiger Moth'! We all had a soft spot for Glendinning for he was always endeavouring to bolster our spirits although perhaps he was becoming a little over confident himself'.[3]

The remains of Glendinning were transported back to the North East. March 19, 1941, John Nixon Glendinning was cremated at the West Road Crematorium, Newcastle upon Tyne. The applicant was his wife Dorothy who lived at the family home in West Stanley, County Durham. The records state that Glendinning was killed on active service at old Romney near Folkestone. His ashes were scattered in the crematorium and his name appears on the memorial panel four. In his short time with 74 Squadron, Glendinning had achieved the status of 'ace'.

GLENDINNING NOTES
1. A.C. Deere: *Nine Lives*, P 158 paperback version.
2. Ramsey: *The Blitz Then And Now*, Vol 2, P 276.
3. The diary of R.H. 'Peter' May.

WILLIAM ERNEST GORE, DFC, 90279
FLIGHT LIEUTENANT

William Ernest Gore was one of three sons born to George Ernest, a works manager at an engineering works and Edith Gore née Bond, of Middlesborough. William Ernest was born during the third quarter of 1915. Education for the young Gore was by way of Rossal School at St Bees. He later gained a BSc from Durham University. After education, the young Gore followed the tradition by becoming an apprentice that led him on to a career as an electrical engineer. Gore also had some interest in aviation and joined his local Auxiliary Air Force Squadron in 1934. Gore became a member of 607 (County of Durham) Squadron in early 1934 and was gazetted June 18 of that year. Gore became F/O Gore December 8, 1935.

Number 607 Squadron was still in its infancy when Gore joined its ranks. Flying the Westland Wapiti, 607 Squadron was a light bomber squadron. Gore obviously had one of the main essentials of the Auxiliary Air Force; his keenness. He had a great distance to travel, by the standards of the day, just to show up at Usworth, the home base of 607 Squadron in County Durham. Photographs of the squadron, at work and play, invariably show Gore somewhere, often the only man with his uniform on. Obviously, he took great pride in wearing it. He also took great pride in his flying abilities. The squadron moved on from the Wapiti to the Hawker Demon. It was in these aircraft that 607 Squadron flew at their Empire Day during 1938. A formation of three was to form a formation flypast. Gore was one of the three pilots in the formation and flew as wingman on the right side.

Moving on from the Hawker Demon, 607 Squadron began to fly the Gloster Gladiator in the autumn of 1938. Number 607 Squadron being the first squadron in the Auxiliary Air Force to fly the relatively new biplane. In 1939 the squadron departed from Usworth to move to their summer camp for that year which was held at Abbotsinch, Glasgow. Hastily the squadron was brought back to Usworth and the squadron found itself embodied into the RAF. Gore receiving his call-up August 14, 1939. The squadron continued to practice in its defence of the north flying from Usworth until it moved north to Acklington in Northumberland. After a relatively short stay, 607 Squadron found itself ordered to France to provide air cover for the British Expeditionary Force (BEF). The squadron had to make a stop at Croydon and found themselves stuck there for two days due to bad weather. Along with 615 Squadron, and a variety of transport aircraft, 607 Squadron made the last hop across the Channel to France. These men, because of their Auxiliary background, were more like a family than the usual RAF squadrons. Going to war, these two squadrons were described by Winston Churchill as; 'The worst equipped units in fighter Command'. Far from being derogatory the statement was meant as a term of admiration.

In this period of what became known as the 'phoney war', monotony was the order of the day. Although patrols were constantly mounted, most of the time they saw nothing. As winter turned to spring in 1940, 607 Squadron was re-equipped with the more advanced Hawker Hurricane, taking charge of their first Hurricane in April. At least most of the squadron had the new aircraft. There was a period when mixed patrols of Gladiators and Hurricanes were flown. With the new fighter came more practices as the pilots struggled to get to grips with the new fighter and fly patrols at the same time. Conversion to the Hurricane came just in time for the launch of the German Blitzkrieg that began in the early hours May 10.

One of the first squadron to be caught up in the action of May 10, was 607 Squadron. Shortly after 5.00 AM Green Section were in the air. These were followed by Yellow Section at 5.15 AM. To the northeast of Douai a formation of He 111s were spotted and intercepted. Will Gore in Hurricane P 2573, AF-A, attacked an He 111 of 2/KG1. He noted in his report; 'When attacked, e/a turned into sun and remained so.

Defensive fire from dustbin put out of action in third attack'. Pressing home further attacks, Gore broke off his action when he noticed both of the Heinkel's engines were pouring out oil. Gore was credited with the confirmed kill.

Later in the day, Gore was in one of nine Hurricanes that were scrambled at 2.30 PM. The nine Hurricanes encountered seven He 111s in the vicinity of St Quentin. On this occasion Gore was flying Hurricane P 3448 AF-H and leading Yellow Section. The three Hurricanes made an attack on the outside aircraft first. As smoke issued from the He 111 Gore instructed the other Hurricanes to follow him into the attack on the leader of the enemy formation. This He 111 was attacked with the same results as the first, Gore being credited with a third of a kill for each. The following day saw Gore once more in action when, in company with P/Os Trevor Jay and Peter Parrott they destroyed an He 111. Gore once more being credited with a third of a kill.

The following day, Gore flying with 'Bunny' Forster, attacked a pair of Ju 88s, near Ath. However, luck was not with Gore on this occasion. The guns of his Hurricane failed to work and all the attacking was, thereafter, left to Forster. This was all to the benefit of the Ju 88s, as they both escaped, although one had minor damage. Later in the day, Gore was flying in Yellow Section when they attacked a lone He 111 between Douai and Derain. The aircraft was last seen heading earthwards trailing black smoke and flame.[1]

As dawn broke May 12, Gore led a section of Hurricanes away from Vitry. Soon after they encountered three He 111s of 4/LG 1. In the ensuing encounter, all three pilots were to make claims for a kill, as all three He 111s were sent down in smoke. However, Gore was not so lucky on this occasion. During the encounter with the He 111s, Gore's Hurricane P 2572 AF-B, was caught in the returning crossfire from the He 111s. Gore's Hurricane burst into flames. Gore managed to extricate himself and take to his parachute; however, he suffered burns as well as shock and some bruising. Gore landed near Lille and was taken by allied troops to a nearby field Hospital. After a short stay at Lille, Gore was returned to England May 17 and admitted to Torquay Hospital. May 31, Gore was awarded the DFC for his actions in France.[2]

The citation for Gore's award of the DFC was to appear in the

London Gazette, May 31, and reads;

> 'This officer, whilst leading his section in May, 1940, on a dawn patrol, intercepted a formation of three Heinkel He 111s aircraft. Due to his good leadership a determined attack was delivered with the result that all three enemy aircraft were shot down. Flying Officer Gore's aircraft burst into flames immediately after the attack, but in spite of this he escaped successfully by parachute. This officer has for a long period shown great keenness and devotion to duty deserving of the greatest of praise'.

Although it is accepted as fact that all three He 111s were destroyed, to be fair to the memory of Will Gore, only one pilot from this section returned to Vitry. F/O Bob Weatherill was forced to land at Lille, due to damage caused in the attack, Gore was in hospital near at Lille, which left only P/O Gordon Stewart to land back at Vitry to tell the tale from his point of view. It is also accepted that, due to the heavy fighting during this period, the constant moving of squadrons from one base to another and, the fact that Hurricanes did not always return to their home base on the same day, the story may have been related a day or so later. To 'muddy' the waters further, it is also acknowledged that a lot of paperwork was lost at this time, mainly due to the squadron's hurried departure from France. This is not to say that the claim was not true. However, another query enters the equation. It is recorded that 4/LG 1, the unit that Gore's section attacked, did, in fact lose three He 111s on that day and in that area. However, one of those He 111s was claimed by P/O John Cock of 87 Squadron.

Little is known of Gore until we hear of him again in August of 1940. Obviously he would spend some time in hospital at Torquay and, no doubt this would be followed by a spell of leave. August 6, 1940 was the day that Gore joined 54 Squadron. Number 54 Squadron had been 'resting' and reequipping at Catterick and had been acting as a training squadron. Gore was to join the squadron on the day that they moved back to the south, being posted to Hornchurch. As 54 Squadron was a Spitfire unit, Gore would also need a little time to get used to the new—to him—fighter. Although based at Hornchurch, most of the flying by 54 Squadron was carried out from Manston, their forward airfield.

In being posted to 54 Squadron, Gore was to miss out on his former squadron's role in the attack, by the Luftwaffe, on the North East. However, 54 found themselves in the thick of some of the heavy fighting in the south. Gore must have taken part in many of the patrols during this time. He also proved that he was a survivor. Number 54 Squadron was to suffer severe losses during this period, their second in the Battle of Britain, before once more being withdrawn from the battle, September 3, and 'rested'. Gore, however, was not to be 'rested'; there was to be more action for him with a more familiar background. He was promoted to the rank of Flight Lieutenant and posted back to his old squadron, Number 607. Gore was to join 607 Squadron at their new base at Tangmere. The squadron having just moved back to the south on September 7, 1940.

Now at Tangmere, 607 Squadron found itself once more in the front line of the battle. However, 607 Squadron had precious little time to become accustomed to their surroundings before being thrust into the heat of the battle which was being fought around them. The Luftwaffe had changed its tactics by September 7. The airfields, once the Luftwaffe's prime targets, although raided sporadically were now mainly left alone. London was now the main area of attack. A large raid materialized on the afternoon of September 9. Shortly after 5.00 PM 607 Squadron were in action against an enemy force. However, they became a victim of yet another change of tactics by the Luftwaffe. The escorting Me 109s were now flying higher in an effort to lure the defending fighters into battle. Number 607 Squadron were the victim of a bad bounce on this occasion. Six of their Hurricanes were to go down, killing three pilots with another two wounded.

The scrambles and patrols were to continue. With the result of most being nothing seen. September 28 was to prove different. The Luftwaffe made another change in their tactics. With losses mounting, the bombers were to be fewer, yet faster. More emphasis was to be made on fast and low-level attacks from many different angles. However, while the bombers were fewer in number, the fighter groups were larger. Such was the case on the afternoon of September 28. A force of some fifty plus Me 110s with a large fighter escort approached the Portsmouth area.

According to one pilot, new controllers were being trained on this day. Number 607 Squadron found itself put at a disadvantage by the controllers, with the result being that the squadron was badly bounced.[3] While the bombers were denied their targets; the fighters became embroiled in a running dogfight down the coast. Although 607 Squadron were to lose only two of their aircraft in the fighting, they also lost two of their most experienced pilots. These were Gore and Flt Lt M.M. Irving.

While Gore and Irving were almost the last of the squadron's original compliment of pilots, they must also remain together forever in the history of the Battle of Britain. They worked together and that was the way that they died. Their loss would be felt deeply in the Auxiliary Squadron. Gore and Irving were both shot down in the area of Selsy Bill. Their Hurricanes shot down at around 2.50 PM. William Ernest Gore, the likeable flight commander, is one of the pilots of the Battle of Britain who remains 'missing'. He is commemorated on the Runnymede Memorial, panel 5. On his last flight Gore was flying Hurricane P 3108. This aircraft came from the first production batch of five hundred aircraft built by Gloster Aircraft Co Ltd at their Brockworth factory in late 1939 early 1940.

Gore Notes

1. Cull: *Twelve Days In May*, P 71.
2. Cull: *Twelve Days in May*, P 90.
3. Personal correspondence with W.H.R. Whitty.

Douglas Hastings, 42406
Pilot Officer

Douglas Hastings was born in Barrow-in-Furness, Cumberland during the fourth quarter of 1915. His parents, Francis and Mary Ann, formerly Scorer, were not native of that town. The family originated from Hartlepool. It is believed that the Hastings family moved from Hartlepool due to the German attacks on that port, one by the German fleet and sporadic attacks by Zeppelins. The family, therefore, moved west out of range of the Germans. With the end of the First World War, the Hastings family returned to the eastern coast. Probably this move was firstly back to Hartlepool, but later they were to move north to North Shields, on the banks of the Tyne. Francis Hastings was believed to have worked in the fish industry. Douglas Hastings was one of two sons, his brother Frank was also to die in World War Two while serving in the Merchant Navy.

In June of 1939, Hastings applied to join the RAF as was accepted on a short service commission. After basic training Hastings was posted to Number 6 Operational Training Unit (OTU) at Sutton Bridge arriving there April 28, 1940. While at Sutton Bridge Hastings was converted to the Hawker Hurricane. On completion of his training, May 15, Hastings was posted to Uxbridge to await further posting, possibly to France. However, this was not to be. Hastings with his experience on Hurricanes, albeit short, was posted to 74 Squadron, a Spitfire unit then based at Hornchurch. Hastings was with the squadron at the end of May.

Number 74 Squadron was at this time heavily engaged in the air operation that was covering the evacuation of Dunkirk. It is not known if Hastings took much part, if any, during these early battles. Having no experience in flying Spitfires, the air over Dunkirk was not the best place to learn air fighting. Numbers 74 Squadron took a number of casualties during this period and were ordered north to Leconfield to rebuild their strength. By June Number 74 Squadron were deemed fit to return to the fray. Once more they were posted to Hornchurch with detachments also being flown from Rochford and Manston.

The fighting was not long in coming to 74 Squadron. July 19, the squadron was scrambled at squadron strength in the afternoon. A large raid had been plotted moving towards the area of Dover. However, by the time 74 Squadron arrived on the scene, the bombers had dropped their bombs and departed. The squadron had managed two 'probables' when they encountered some straggling Me 109s.

It is not until the evening of July 24 that we first hear of Hastings. Ordered off from Manston, flights were patrolling the Channel. Within a short period 'A' flight were vectored onto a raid in the area of Dover. This turned out to be three Do 17s making a low-level flight almost at sea level. On seeing the Spitfires, the Do 17s jettisoned their bomb loads and attempted to make a run for France. At least one of the German gunners opened fire at the Spitfires. However, as the range was around two thousand yards, it was more an act of defiance than aggression. Chasing the bombers hard, 'A' flight held their fire until they were within three hundred yards. All three Spitfires reported getting in some good bursts of fire before the Do 17s disappeared into cloud near Gravelines. At least one of the bombers was last seen trailing smoke.

Over the first ten days of August there was little enemy activity, due mainly to the weather conditions. However, 74 Squadron were kept busy. From their bases at Hornchurch and Manston, they flew an average seventy sorties per day. August 8 saw one of the squadrons flight commanders, Flt Lt A.G. 'Sailor' Malan, take over command of 74 Squadron. With the weather greatly improved, the Luftwaffe launched a series of probing attacks on August 11. The first of these attacks turned for home then turned again towards Dover. The purpose of these attacks appears to have been an attempt to draw up the fighters of RAF Fighter Command so that they could be engaged by the prowling Me 109s.

In answer to these probing attacks, 74 Squadron were in the air by 7.49 AM and patrolling the area above Dover. The wily 'Sailor' Malan, always mindful of the safety to his pilots, turned the squadron away from the fight. Climbing hard up to twenty thousand feet, keeping the sun always at his back, ever mindful of the saying; 'Beware the Hun in the sun'. A formation of Me 109s was soon spotted. With no further fighters above them, 'Sailor' Malan led the squadron in for a perfect bounce. Records show that on this occasion the enemy were the Me 109s of JG 2 (Richthofen). Hasting, flying as Red three, noticed a Spitfire under attack from an Me 109. Turning from the formation Hastings lined up the Me 109. With the German fighter square in his sights Hastings opened fire at three hundred yards. Closing in, firing all the while, Hastings attack forced the Me 109 to break away.

Hastings pulled around hard and once more placed the Me 109 under attack. On this occasion Hastings noticed his fire strike home and white smoke began to stream back from the engine. Concentrating hard on his target, Hastings failed to notice that another Me 109 was about to place him under attack. This caused Hasting to take some drastic evasive action. Making a steep climbing turn to the right, engine on full power, Hastings forced the Me 109 to overshoot its target. In the attacks of this day, four in all, Hastings had one confirmed kill and made a claim for another as damaged. The squadron had scored twenty-three kills, which earned them a telegram from Air Chief Marshal Dowding, which read; 'A magnificent day's fighting… this is the way to keep the measure of the Boche, Mannock[1] started it and you keep it up'.

There was no flying for the squadron on August 12. Inclement weather being the cause. Time was used by the ground crews to patch up the Spitfires, which had gained more than a few bullet holes in the last few days. August 13 was known to the Germans as 'Adler Tag', the day of the eagles. The raids were to open early. A force of some seventy plus Do 17s appeared on the radar screens shortly after 5.30 AM, moving towards the coast of east Kent. Due to the still bad weather, the bombers were without their usual fighter escort. The fighters were recalled without the bombers hearing the order to return. Without their escort the bombers would be at the mercy of any attacking fighter.

At around 5.55 AM, twelve Spitfires of 74 Squadron were

scrambled, 'Sailor' Malan at their head. A formation of forty plus Do 17s were soon spotted in the area of Whitstable at around three thousand feet. These turned out to be Do 17s of KG 2. After an initial attack, the Spitfires broke up to attack individually. Hastings singled out a leader of a vic of three. Approaching, he began firing at three hundred yards. However, he failed to get much closer. The Do 17s were putting up a heavy defensive return fire. Even so, Hastings saw bits and pieces flying off the leading bomber. Breaking away from this aircraft, Hastings now turned his attention to the number three bombers in the formation. As this Do 17 came under attack from Hastings, it jettisoned its bomb load in order to make good its escape. However, the gunners on the Do 17 could not keep Hastings back from his attack. Repeatedly Hastings attacked the Do 17 until it began to fall. Even then he followed it down to witness its demise. The Do 17 crashed into the ground some four miles west of Manston. The Do 17 is not identified in any of the available sources.

The following day, August 14, saw yet another lull in the fighting due to bad weather. It also brought the temporary end to 74 Squadron's actions in the Battle of Britain. The squadron was deemed in need of a 'rest' and was withdrawn to Wittering. Having been on a roll for the last few weeks, the squadron found the pace of life somewhat slower. Morale also took a knock when the squadron was later to learn that it had missed some of the heaviest fighting so far. The move for the squadron had caught them on the hop. The same can be said for Wittering, which had not been expecting them. The squadron was next ordered to Kirton-in-Lindsey before making another move, this time to Coltishall in Norfolk where it arrived September 9. During its stay at Coltishall, the squadron operated occasionally from Duxford. One or two flights being carried out with Douglas Bader's 'big wing'.

September 11 saw 74 Squadron taking its place in Bader's 'big wing'. Eight Spitfires, led by 'Sailor' Malan, took off from Duxford. Malan had to keep his eight Spitfires to the rear of the formation, flying behind 19 and 611 Squadrons, their main task being to attack the bombers in the formation. At around 4.30 PM the formation intercepted the enemy some twenty thousand feet over the London docks. Initially, 'Sailor' Malan had called for a head-on attack against the bomber force. However, the ever-cautious 'Sailor' saw Me 109s coming in from above and altered his attack to approach from the beam. Hastings, flying as Red two to Malan, followed his leader into the attack against the bombers.

As Hastings broke away from this first attack, he noticed an Me 110 and turned to deliver his attack. Attacking from the rear, Hastings saw his fire strike home with the resulting issue of smoke pouring away from the fighter. In the resulting dogfight, Hastings was attacked by two Me 109s. Turning hard into the attacking Me 109s, he forced them both to overshoot. Regaining momentum, height and direction once more, Hastings realized that his original target Me 110 had disappeared, as had most of the rest. Hastings could only make a claim for one damaged.

There now followed a lull in the engagements with the enemy. However, 'Sailor' Malan was known to keep his men in fighting trim, keeping to a strict regime of training. 'Sailor' Malan knew that his squadron would be called upon again, probably at any time, to return to the battle being fought further south. His training regime had to be as realistic as possible, for ground crews as well as pilots. New pilots on the squadron had to be given as realistic training as possible and this meant air combat training. One of these new pilots was P/O F.W. Buckland who had joined 74 Squadron as recently as September 28. With very few flying hours on Spitfires and virtually no combat experience at all, he was paired off with Hastings to give him some combat training.

On the afternoon of October 8, Hastings and Buckland departed from Coltishall. The purpose of the flight being to carry out dogfighting tactics to the south of the airfield. On this occasion Hastings was flying Spitfire Mk 2 P 7329. The squadron having only recently been equipped with the Mk2 to replace their ageing Mk 1s. Hastings' Spitfire was an almost brand new machine, passing through Number 8 Maintenance Unit (MU) August 17. P 7329 was taken on charge by 74 Squadron, September 13, its first squadron. The two Spitfires climbed away from Coltishall airfield and began their air fighting practice some twenty miles to the south.

The two fighters, attempting to make the training as realistic as possible, came too close to each other and collided, both aircraft coming down on farm land in the area to the north of Beccles, Norfolk. As time has moved on there appears to be some confusion as to exactly where the Spitfires came down. Ramsey[2] states that it was Green Farm and Ivy House Farm both at Gillingham. Other sources place the debris site at Hill Farm, Beccles[3]. Cossey[4] places the accident site at Beccles but names no farms.

Either way, all note that the two aircraft fell in a spin, one crashing on hard ground and disintegrating, throwing debris over a wide area. The other, Buckland, fell minus its tail unit but, apart from that, relatively intact, and crashed onto the ground inverted. Its pilot still trapped in the cockpit. A farm worker, who was working nearby, was first on the scene but noted the pilot, presumably Buckland, was still in the cockpit. The above shows that training could be as deadly as actual combat. Hasting was an experienced battle hardened pilot. P/O Buckland was a raw novice receiving combat training.

The remains of Hastings were transferred back to his home in North Shields. Hastings was buried October 12 in the large Preston Cemetery at North Shields. His grave lies in unconsecrated ground section 'C', grave number 12984. The plot is a family one and there is no CWGC headstone.[5] However, the large grey headstone, apart from the names of those buried therein, carries the badge of the RAF at its top. Under Hastings' name is the proud legend; 'Tiger Squadron'. Today the gravesite is kept tidy by an efficient ground staff. The site is shared by Hastings father, Francis and his brother Frank, a Merchant Seaman killed in 1942. Douglas Hastings left a wife, Willamena Hails (Nindy) and a daughter Linda.

In the late nineteen seventies, a list of men killed in the Battle of Britain was produced for the Battle of Britain Museum at Hendon by Sqdn Ldr F.E. Dymond.[6] This list was based on a former list compiled by Flt Lt John Holloway. The difference being, the above Sqdn Ldr Dymond removed pilots killed by accident, five of them, from the original list. One of those removed from the original list was Douglas Hastings. Hastings was still on active service. He had already fought in the early part of the Battle of Britain. At the time of his accident he was on training duties but 74 Squadron were still called upon to fight occasionally, in Douglas Bader's 'big wing'. To strike off a pilot for such a reason is bureaucracy gone one step too far. To make matters worse, this decision was carried out with the knowledge of the surviving 'few': the comrades of Douglas Hastings.

Hastings Notes

1. Major Edward 'Mick' Mannock VC, DSO (2 Bars), MC (I Bar), flew with 74 Squadron during the First World War. An Irishman by birth he became Britain's top air ace of the First World War. Mannock was killed July 18, 1918 while flying as C.O. of 85 Squadron.
2. *The Battle of Britain Then and Now*, P 498, states Spitfire of Hastings crashed south of Green Farm, Gillingham. That of Buckland crashed at Ivy House Farm, Gillingham.
3. Personal correspondence, R.G. Turner, P. Sayer: both eyewitnesses. Mr R.T.T Bramley who farms Hill Farm, Beccles. States that both aircraft fell on his land, 1.5 miles south of Beccles.
4. Cossey states in Tigers; '…both aircraft crashed near Beccles'.
5. Information Office, Preston Cemetery, North Shields.
6. *The Battle of Britain Then and Now*, P 258.

Whaley E. Heppell At Ta Kali, Malta 1941. Photo: Philip Heppell.

Phillip Whaley Ellis Heppell, 86370
Pilot Officer

Phillip Whaley Ellis Heppell was born January 24 1921. He was the only son of Phillip Forsythe and Dorothy, formerly Fryer, Heppell. The family home then being situated in Kenton Road in the Gosforth area of Newcastle upon Tyne. Phillip senior was a chartered surveyor. He had also flown in the First World War as a fighter pilot in the RFC. Flying in the air battles over the Somme, Heppell senior had been shot down and taken prisoner. Between the wars, he was to become one of the founder members of the Newcastle Aero Club. In the Second World War, he was again called on to use his flying skills. This time as a flying instructor in Canada. The daughter of the family, Rhoda, was also involved in flying during the Second World War. She flew as a ferry pilot. It is little wonder then that the local press were to dub the family, 'The Flying Heppell's'.

Education for Phillip junior was by way of Newcastle Prep School. This was followed by a period at Uppingham School, in what was then, the smallest county in England, Rutland. At the end of his schooling, war was looming fast on the horizons of the young Heppell. With his family background there seemed only one route to travel, and that lay with flying. Heppell junior joined the RAFVR at his local depot in Newcastle, June 24, 1939. Flying training was to begin at nearby Woolsington airfield with Number 43 Elementary and Reserve Flying Training School, (E&RFTS). While there Heppell was to build up almost sixteen flying hours on the Tiger Moth. Eventually he was to go solo, July 17, 1939 in DH 82 N 6601.

September 2 saw Heppell's training take a different turn. What had been part-time now became official as Heppell was called to full-time service. November saw Heppell posted south to Hastings. There he became part of Number 3 Initial Training Wing (ITW), his square bashing being carried out along the Hastings sea front.

The next move for Heppell came May 9, 1940. On that date he was posted to Brough near Hull. During his stay at Brough, Heppell's flying training resumed on the Blackburn B2. After amassing a total of fifty-six flying hours, Heppell was moved to the RAF College at Cranwell. Flying training was to continue on the Hawker Hart at Cranwell, before moving on to the Hawker Hind. Although classed as advanced training at the time, it is worthy of note that Heppell's flying training still revolved around the First World War technology of the biplane. After almost a year in year in flying training, apart from a flight in a Fairey Battle, Heppell still had not flown a modern era fighter. However, while at Cranwell, Heppell amassed another one hundred and thirty six flying hours. His overall total now standing at one hundred and ninety eight hours. Heppell was to finish his training at Cranwell with the rating of above average. September 21, along with his 'wings', Heppell was commissioned and posted to his next base, Hawarden.

At Hawarden there was a first for Heppell. He flew his first modern generation aeroplane, the Miles Master. Not the swiftest of modern-day aeroplanes but at least it had a retractable undercarriage. Next in line was a quantum leap. As the next aeroplane in line was to be the Spitfire. Heppell was to take his first flight in the Spitfire October 5, 1940. It is worth noting another pilot's views on training at Hawarden at around this time. Johnnie Johnson was to make his observations, on his training at Hawarden [1]. 'Our time at Hawarden was spent learning how to fly the Spitfire; during my days there I never fired the eight guns or took part in any tactical training. This would come later, if there was time'. It is also worth a mention that Johnnie Johnson made a mess of his first flight in a Spitfire. On his second flight he crashed. Many a raw pilot was to end up on an operational fighter squadron and never find that vital piece of 'time'. It is also worthy of note, that Heppell's log book shows that he got the chance to fire the Spitfires guns on at least two occasions. Once at an airborne target and, on another occasion, into the sea.

Heppell was next posted to his first fighter squadron. This was to be 616 (South Yorkshire) Squadron, an Auxiliary Air Force unit, the squadron at that time being based at Kirton-in-Lindsey. The squadron had taken part in Douglas Bader's 'Big Wing' in the latter part of September. However, it was reduced, at the time Heppell joined it, to a category 'C' squadron. A training squadron. This was probably why Heppell was posted to it. The squadron at that time consisting of around five experienced pilots. At least Heppell was to benefit from the experience of battle-trained pilots. Heppell was to take to the air, in one of the squadrons Spitfires, for the first time, October 24, 1940. This flight being made in Spitfire X 4186.

Not all of Heppell's flights were to go without incident. Heppell, who had by now acquired the nickname, 'Nip', was flying on a short thirty-minute flight from Caistor when, for some reason best known to himself, he decided to land his Spitfire downwind. The Spitfire overshot the runway and overturned at 1.30 PM. 'Nip' Heppell was unhurt. However, his pride must have taken a bashing as the accident was found to be the fault of the pilot. Heppell's log book is adorned with the comments from the Wing Commander at Kirton-in-Lindsey to the effect that Heppell's accident, '... was due the gross carelessness...' Mason states that this Spitfire was destroyed. However, Ramsey states that the aircraft was repairable. The Spitfire was X 4330: a Spitfire that was gaining a reputation on the squadron.[2]

Heppell himself was to state that his first operational flight was carried out in November of 1940. Official the Battle of Britain was over on the last day of October 1940. Therefore, by official standards, Heppell did not take part in the Battle of Britain. Other sources claim that the Battle of Britain did not finish until a much later date. Simply, a battle cannot finish until the protagonist has left the field. The Luftwaffe did not give up on the offensive until May 1941. 'Nip' Heppell therefore, has every right to appear here alongside his comrades.

Number 616 Squadron were carrying out convoy patrols in the latter part of 1940. A task they appear to have been doing throughout the winter months. In February of 1941, the squadron became operational once more. When the squadron moved south to its new base at Tangmere, Heppell was one of those who moved with it. From February, 616 Squadron became part of the Tangmere wing led by Douglas Bader. The Tangmere wing continually carried out offensive patrols as they harried the Luftwaffe over their French bases. Heppell was to see action on the morning of July 2, 1941. Bader was in his usual place, at the head of 616 Squadron within the Tangmere wing. Heppell, flying in 'Dogsbody Section', (call sign for Bader's section), attacked an Me 109F to the southwest of Lille. A few bursts of gunfire and the pilot was seen to jump clear of his aircraft. Bader was later to write in his combat report: '...one was shot down by Heppell'.

July 10 saw Heppell flying as 'Dogsbody' four on a 'circus', (an offensive patrol escorting bombers). The wing left Westhampnett at 11.38 AM and set course for the area around Calais. As the section turned above Calais o their way back to Tangmere, A section of three Me 109s was spotted travelling in the opposite direction, some 1,000 feet below. The section, now reduced to three Spitfires, half rolled and dived at full speed reaching some four hundred MPH in the dive. Heppell, flying as number two to Flt Lt H.S.L. Dundas was on the right. Opening fire in the turn, at a range of about two hundred yards, Heppell closed fast and broke away under his quarry. The Me 109 was seen to enter a shallow dive with coolant streaming from its engine. However, no one witnessed the demise of the Me 109. Heppell could only make a claim for one damaged. Although there was a surplus of pilots on the wing at this time, the majority were to fly the standard convoy patrols. A hard core of about seven to nine pilots were handpicked by Bader to fly the offensive patrols: an inner sanctum of pilots. 'Nip' Heppell was one of those handpicked.

An offensive patrol was organized to fly over to St Omer, July 12, 1941. In the area between St Omer and Bethune, a heartland for the fighters of the Luftwaffe, the wing was to clash with some fifteen Me 109s at 20,000 feet. Heppell was to claim one damaged on this sweep. Two fighter sweeps were ordered for July 21. The first airborne at 07.42 AM headed into the area of Dunkirk. Flying as Red one on this occasion, Heppell spotted four me 109s at 09.00 AM flying at around 10,000 feet. Flying in a left-hand turn, Heppell ordered his number two into line astern and gave chase to one of the Me109s. The Me 109 was to evade Heppell's attention by turning hard into him while making a quick descent and running for home. Heppell squeezed off a burst at some four hundred yards, more in frustration than hope. Somehow he had lost sight of his number two in the pursuit.

Another attack was then initiated on two Me 109s. This time

Heppell was flying alongside a Hurricane that had appeared from somewhere. However, the result was to be the same as previous. The Me 109s departing without a fight. Hepppell now flew with the bombers but was soon put under attack from the rear by a further two Me 109s. As he turned to defend himself, Heppell noticed another two Me 109s about to join in the fight. A furious dogfight then broke out and Heppell was forced to use some drastic evasive action to try and extricate himself. Turning hard, an Me 109 passed through the sights of Heppell's Spitfire. Heppell just managed to give him a burst before taking avoiding action in order not to collide with the Me 109. He noticed the latter falling away trailing smoke and claimed it as a probable. It took a little longer to shake the other three off before he could return home. Even then he was not home safely. Only four miles from Dover Heppell was attacked by another Me 109. Low on fuel and ammunition, Heppell could only manage a short burst before he had to make a run for home.

Later the same day Heppell was to take part in another offensive patrol. Flying as 'Dogsbody' four Heppell shared an Me 109, as a probable, with Red one, Johnnie Johnson. Heppell's combat report describes the scene;

> 'While on patrol over the target area our section was flying in an easterly direction when about six Me 109s were sighted travelling to the south and about a thousand feet below us. Our section did a step turn diving slightly. I took the e/a on the extreme right, diving slightly below him until I was in range. I then pulled up getting my sights onto him and giving him a burst with cannons and machine guns from dead astern (250 to 150 yards, 4 seconds burst) then someone called over the r/t telling us to break as there were more e/as behind us. Just before I broke I saw glycol start to stream from the 109 and his nose dropped slowly and he went into a steep dive. I then lost sight of the e/a in my turn and Red 1 (P/O Johnson) gave him a squirt. When I had turned around and seen there was nothing close behind me, I looked down and saw the e/a was about five to ten thousand feet below still in the same attitude, pouring out glycol and black smoke. I then joined up with some other Spitfires who were shooting at some other Me 109s, who were diving for the ground'.

Heppell then joined up with Johnnie Johnson near Boulogne and the pair returned to Tangmere. It is of interest to note that Heppell was using a Spitfire with both cannons and machine guns. There was mixture of MkVAs and VBs on the squadron. Bader was known to show preference for the machine-gunned Mk VA.

An escort as high cover, for a bomber raid on Bethune, was to be flown August 9, 1941. Things went wrong from the very start. Bader lost his ASI shortly after take off. Accurate navigation relied on accurate air speed. Flt Lt Dundas therefore took over the navigating until they were across the French coast. Number 41 Squadron, detailed to fly with them, failed to turn up. At some 26,000 feet an attack was carried out on twelve Me 109s. The timing was misjudged, for whatever cause, causing confusion and delay. Yellow Section managed to carry out an attack down the right side. Heppell, Yellow three, claimed an Me 109 as destroyed. A vicious dogfight was to break out. Bader somehow misjudged his approach speed, overshot the target, and found himself alone. Observing two Me 109s, he turned into the attack but was himself put under attack by other Me 109s. For some reason he broke away from them rather than into them. The result was that he presented himself as a target and was duly shot down. His victor is generally acknowledged as being Obfw Max Meyer of the sixth staffel JG 26. The wing returned to Tangmere more than a bit dejected. As well as their leader, they had also lost Flt Lt L.H. 'Buck' Casson.

In the afternoon, 'A' flight of 616 Squadron left Tangmere. Their mission was a convoy patrol. However, this convoy patrol was flown, by what was described as, Bader's closest associates. Dundas, Heppell, Johnson and West. The foursome flew at low-level, up and down the French coast, hoping to find evidence of their leader. Unknown to them, Bader was already in German hands. August 19, 1941, was to bring forth a special patrol. Heppell was one of the pilots called to fly escort to six Bristol Blenheims. Their official mission was to attack targets in the St Omer area. Their unofficial mission was to drop Bader's spare false leg.

The award of the DFC came to Heppell, September 30. The squadron was also ordered north to their old base at Kirton-in-Lindsey for a 'rest'. Heppell became a flight commander, November 24, but was not to remain with the squadron much longer. The Motor

Vessel Cape Hawk was ordered to set sail for Gibraltar. Aboard M.V. Cape Hawk was sixteen crated Spitfires destined for the defence of Malta. On reaching Gibraltar, the Spitfires, now assembled, were transferred to HMS Eagle, which then set sail for the area off the North African coast. Early on March 7, fifteen of those Spitfires lined up on the flight deck and left Eagle for Malta. Flying one of those Spitfires was 'Nip' Heppell and his new squadron was 249.

On landing at Malta, the Spitfires quickly had their long-range fuel tanks removed. The ground crew even had the new squadron letters painted 'GN' onto the sides of the aircraft, albeit in white rather than the standard light grey. March 10 saw the squadron in action as seven Spitfires were scrambled from Ta Kali. An incoming raid having been plotted. Heppell was leading a section of four and was first to spot the enemy formation of Ju 88s. Leading his section into the fray, Heppell bounced the Me 109s of the fighter escort. Heppell fired a long burst into an Me 109 that was seen to fall into the sea. This was later confirmed as being Black 11 of 8/JG53. Its pilot, Fwb Heinz Rhalmeir was killed in the action. Heppell's kill was the one-hundredth confirmed kill by the squadron.

Heppell was leading Red Section, March 17. The section had been scrambled shortly after coming to readiness shortly after 6.30 AM. Although the pilots in Heppell's section were still classed as 'green', the section had sorted itself well and found itself well placed to carry out an attack on the enemy formation. Heppell dived his section from 20,000 feet down to 10,000 feet in order to engage the bombers. However, a number of Me 109s had other ideas and Heppell found himself continually frustrated in trying to penetrate the fighter screen. On return to base, Heppell's section was once more scrambled at 9.55 AM. However, the end result on this occasion was no better. Heppell's section had been scrambled far too late. The result was that the Spitfires could not get into any position to give them an advantage over the enemy. In fact they failed to get anywhere near the enemy. In the end they were forced to make a rapid departure for home in order to avoid being bounced by the Me 109s.

In the early afternoon, April 8, Heppell was at the head of a section scrambled at 1.30 PM. Making contact with the enemy formation, Heppell opened fire on one of the bombers and noted his fire striking along its wings. As he broke off his attack, another bomber drifted through his gun sight. Heppell gave it a burst and saw his fire hit home along the fuselage, cockpit and starboard engine. The latter issued heavy black smoke. Heppell again pressed home a further attack, giving the bomber a six-second burst before breaking away once more. At this point another fighter began attacking the same target, presumably from a different angle. Heppell saw the bomber crash into the sea but was only allowed to claim a share in the kill. A Hurricane pilot also making a claim for the kill.

A further raid was plotted at around 3.00 PM, heading towards Grand Harbour. This force was made up of a mixture of almost sixty Ju 88s with twenty-six Ju 87s. The whole bomber force being under the protection of a number of Me 109s. Heppell was leading the section in Spitfire AB 346, GN-K. Behind him was his section of three Spitfires accompanied by nine Hurricanes. At around 8,000 feet over Grand Harbour his section attacked the enemy. Lining up one of the Ju 88s, Heppell opened fire and immediately saw the effect as his gunfire struck home. However, on this occasion, things were not to go his way.

Later he was to write of the event;

> 'I recall registering strikes in the wing roots and the tail unit of the Ju 88... and the next thing I can remember was falling head first towards the harbour sans aircraft. When my parachute opened it seemed that I was on some kind of sky-hook, and not apparently losing any height, with the bombs falling past, ack ack exploding all around and a continuous rattle of machine guns all round. I crashed into a bomb hole, still conscious but unable to move. I was given a shot of morphine by a M.O. and taken to Mtarfa Hospital. Shortly afterwards I was on the operating table about to have the gashes in my head sewn up'.

At first it was thought that Heppell had collided with an aerial mine. However, later it was found that Heppell had been shot down by the 'friendly' fire of the anti aircraft defences. The direct hit blew Heppell clear of the cockpit of his Spitfire. Later the Spitfire was found to have crashed into a cemetery near Sliena. His victim, the Ju 88, was later confirmed as having crashed onto Comiso airfield while attempting to land.

Heppell was to remain in hospital until his release May 1, 1942. On this date Heppell left Malta bound for Cairo, there to join the AFDU Ferry Unit. June 20 saw Heppell on the move once more. On this occasion it was to Port Sadon where he was to carry out some work as a test pilot. Heppell was not to return to operational flying until December of 1942. He returned once more to Malta. His new posting was to 1435 Squadron as a flight commander. While with this squadron, Heppell was to carry out sweeps over Sicily making 'train busting' missions as well as some 'Spit bombing'. These were low fast bombing attacks against enemy positions, usually airfields, with bombs mounted under the Spitfire's wings. While carrying out one of these missions, January 30, 1943, Heppell almost came unstuck. His 'Spit bomber' had one of its bombs 'hang-up'. An arm that connected the bomb was hanging down making any landing suicidal. Heppell, therefore, had no choice but to evacuate his Spitfire. Landing in the sea off Calafrana, Heppell was picked up in a matter of minutes by a launch.

In April 1943, Heppell was promoted to the rank of Squadron Leader and posted to 229 Squadron to take command. With his new fighter squadron, Heppell was once more engaged in fighter sweeps across Sicily. Along with the fighter sweeps came various escort duties. During one of these, Heppell was providing air cover for some destroyers of the Royal Navy. An encounter with the enemy took place over the destroyer force. Heppell managed to shoot down a Ju 88 before he became involved in a turning dogfight with a Fw 190. During the ensuing dogfight Heppell was wounded in the thigh and was once more admitted to hospital. Heppell was returned to the UK May 10, 1943, where he was admitted to the RAF Hospital at Halton. On leaving hospital, Heppell managed to get in some flights to keep his hand in. One of these occurred May 29 when he took part in a sweep across France, acting as number two to his old friend Johnnie Johnson. Johnson was later to write of Heppell; 'Whaley... handles his Spitfire with masterly panache and always keeps his cool in a maul'.[3]

Heppell was next posted to a staff post at 13 Fighter Group in Inverness, arriving there in July 1943. While there he was in charge of tactics. At the end of 1943 Heppell made a comeback to operational flying. This time he became supernumery Squadron Leader of both 222 and 129 squadrons before moving on once more to take command of 118 Squadron. Heppell arrived at his new base of Castletown, January 18, 1944. Two days later the squadron was to move south to Detling.

Number 118 Squadron was now equipped with the Spitfire IX and Heppell was to lead this squadron on a number of bomber escort duties. A momentous day for Heppell was to come September 11, 1944. On this day Heppell recorded his first flight over the German mainland. On this occasion Heppell's squadron was providing fighter escort for some two hundred Lancaster and Halifax bombers. Six days later, September 17, 118 Squadron, Heppell at its head, was providing escort for some six-hundred gliders and four-hundred parachute aircraft to the area of Eindhoven, Nijmegen and Arnhem as operation 'Market Garden' got under way. Only two days later, September 19, Heppell was to lead his fighters back to the same area. Their brief, to cover airborne reinforcements. However, Heppell was to write in his logbook; 'Dicing with death! Weather bloody awful'. As a result of the conditions, the mission was called off, with many of the gliders falling into the sea. The following day was only marginally better but Heppell was left with no choice. The supplies carried in sixty-seven Stirlings, had to get through at all costs. The emphasis on the urgency is echoed in Heppell's logbook; 'Informed by planning that the supplies had to get through even if all the Stirlings and the Westhampnett wing were lost in the attempt'.

During December of 1944 the Spitfires were relinquished for the North American Mustang, the move bringing Heppell's long association with the Spitfire to an end. The first operational mission for Heppell in the Mustang came on February 14, 1945. Heppell led his squadron on an escort to eighteen Lancaster bombers that were to bomb Paderborn viaduct. The round trip took over four hours and Heppell was to record; 'An enjoyable first trip on Mustangs—but not quite long enough!!!!!'[4]

March of 1945 saw Heppell's operational flying days come to an end. Heppell was next moved to a staff appointment on the General Staff at HQ 11 Group. While there, Heppell was to fly more sedate aeroplanes such as the Oxford and the Procter as he ferried various officers around the Group. In April, Heppell was awarded a bar to his DFC as well as the French Croix de Guere with three palms. Later Heppell was to leave the RAF.

At the end of World War Two Heppell returned to his civilian employment of being a Chartered Surveyor, working from Newcastle upon Tyne. He still flew, just to keep his hand in, from the local airfield at Woolsington (Newcastle Airport). Many of these flights were in company with his sister, Rhoda. The pair carrying out aerobatic displays. Heppell's total amount of flying hours amounted to 1,547. A thousand of those flying hours were on Spitfires. Although Shores[5] credits Heppell with five kills, Heppell's personal tally amounts to some fourteen enemy aircraft destroyed or damaged along with eleven locomotives. 'Nip' Heppell died while on holiday in 1987.

Heppell Notes

1. Johnnie Johnson: *Wing Leader,* P 29.
2. Spitfire X 4330 is represented in a well-known photograph. Often it is described as flying with 92 Squadron. Mason P148, Shacklady P118; Hunt P399, Jackson P49. This Spitfire had suffered an undercarriage collapse October 14, 1940, when flown by R.V. Hogg. Crash and movement cards for this Spitfire have been lost.
3. Johnson and Lucas, p 65.
4. Flying Log Book of Whaley Heppell.
5. Shores: *Aces High,* P 179.

Erik Lawson Hetherington, 102091
Sergeant

Erik Lawson Hetherington was born in Hartlepool during the first quarter of 1918. He was the son of Thomas L. and Hilda M. Hetherington. At some later date the family moved north, taking up residence in the Northumberland village of Haltwhistle. Almost nothing is known of Hetherington's early life. At the age of twenty-one Hetherington joined the RAFVR and was called to full-time service in September of 1939. Training was carried out at Number 7 Elementary Flying Training School (E & FTS) at Peterborough. Hetherington then moved on to Number 10 Flying Training School (FTS) at Ternhill. With the basics over, Hetherington moved on to Sutton Bridge arriving there August 17, 1940.

After the completion of his conversion course onto the Hawker Hurricane, Hetherington was posted to his first squadron, Number 601 (County of London) Squadron, an Auxiliary Air force Squadron. The squadron at that time was based at Exeter. Number 601 Squadron had only arrived at Exeter on September 7, having been posted from its previous base of Debden, Essex. Number 611 Squadron was to take little part in the rest of the Battle of Britain, apart from chasing the odd sporadic raider.

However, the squadron was in action on September 25 over the area of Plymouth. Further action came on October 7 over Portland. This raid had been aimed at the Westland Aero factory and saw 601 taking credit for the destruction of three Me 110s. All three of these aircraft belonged to ZG 76. With the end of the official version of the

Battle of Britain, 601 Squadron were to take on offensive patrols over France.

Hetherington was still with 601 Squadron when it took on charge its new aircraft. In June of 1941, 601 Squadron were equipped with the new Bell Airacobra., a rather unconvential aeroplane for its day. Instead of a tail wheel, it had a nose wheel, with a long spindly leg. Unconventiality did not stop there, however. The engine, rather than being mounted in the front was mounted in the centre. As with all unconvential aeroplanes, the Airacobra was to suffer many accidents, some fatal, as its pilots tried to master it as best they could. Even the ground crew seemed to be having difficulty. Unserviceability was high on the agenda and the squadron rarely had more than four aeroplanes serviceable at the same time. However, while based at their new base of Matlaske, Norfolk, the squadron was to have little success. Hetherington had been commissioned in July of 1941.

In the following Autumn, Hetherington was posted to 611 Squadron and was probably well pleased as 611 Squadron was equipped with more conventional aeroplanes. In this case the Spitfire. Patrols were once again offensive patrols against ground targets, mainly across the Channel in France.

In April of 1942, Hetherington was given an overseas posting. Having not been told his destination, Hetherington must have wondered where it would be as he boarded the aircraft carrier *USS Wasp*. The destination of the Spitfires aboard the *USS Wasp* was to be Malta. Flying his Spitfire from the deck of the *USS Wasp*, Hetherington was one of ten new pilots to join 249 Squadron at Ta Kali, Arriving on the island in May. May 10 saw 249 Squadron scrambled at 5.40 AM. On this occasion it was an attack by the Regia Aronautica (Italian Air Force). The raid consisted of Z 1007s with a fighter escort of Macchi Mc 202s and Reggiane Re 2001s. Hetherington was to attack the fighter escort and he was to claim one of the fighters as a probable.

Hetherington was forced to make an emergency landing on July 7. Hetherington had attacked a Ju 88 that had put up some heavy return fire. This was to cause Hetherington's Spitfire BR 347, T-Z, some slight damage. Better luck was to come Hetherington's way two days later. On July 9, Hetherington was leading his flight when they attacked a formation of Ju 88s along with their escort of Me109s. The

Me 109s being of 1/JG 77 and had a small number of Mc 202s with them. Attacking the Macchis, Hetherington saw one fall to his guns. This was later confirmed by P/O Berkley-Hill who was last heard confirming the kill. 'I saw it Hether old boy'! Apparently these were the last words spoken by Berkley-Hill; he was shot down into the sea shortly afterwards. Hetherington and Sgt Beurling were to make a special search for Berkley-Hill, but no trace of pilot or aircraft was ever found.

Bad luck was once more to come the way of Hetherington on July 13. A group of some eighteen Ju 88s of 11/KG 77 carried out an early morning raid on Luqa. Numbers 249 Squadron managed to scramble eight Spitfires but were too late to engage the bombers, who were already departing the scene. Instead, 249 Squadron attacked the fighter escort of Macchis of 20 Gruppo. However, Hetherington was hit by accurate return fire and once more found himself obliged to force-land his Spitfire, BR 379 T-V, at Hal Far.

Eight Spitfires of 249 Squadron were scrambled into action at midday, July 23. A force of Ju 88s along with their fighter escort of Me 109Fs were approaching Luqa at 15,000 feet. Hetherington attacked the bombers from out of the sun. After his initial attack, smoke was observed issuing from the bombers starboard engine.

Hetherington, along with P/O Beurling, now commissioned, was sent on an offensive patrol along the southern coast of Sicily on August 9. It had been reported that an enemy Motor Torpedo Boat (MTB) flotilla was at work in the area. However, both returned without having seen any action. Another offensive patrol was organized for August 25. Ten Spitfires of 249 Squadron were to fly to Sicily in company with a further nine Spitfires of 229 Squadron. During this offensive patrol, Hetherington was one of the pilots to carry out a ground strafing attacking against Gala airbase. Many enemy aircraft were destroyed during this attack, with Hetherington making a claim for one Me109F damaged. On another offensive patrol, September 16, a patrol of eight Me 109s were encountered. A dogfight broke out which was to last for almost an hour as the fighters jousted with each other. Hetherington was again to make a claim for one Me 109 damaged.

The pace slowed down for Hetherington during the next month. However, October 13 saw Hetherington in action once more. On this occasion, eight Spitfires of 249 and a further eight Spitfires from 185 Squadron, Hetherington at their head, were scrambled at 6.35 AM. A formation of seven Ju 88s of 11/LG 1 with an escort of upwards of thirty Me 109s were inbound. In the attack, Hetherington was to make a claim for one Me 109 as damaged. The next few days saw Hetherington leading formations against the bomber attacks. Claiming one Me 109 damaged in a head-on attack October 16 with another confirmed kill over an Me 109 on the following day. Two days later Hetherington was awarded the DFC for his actions during the defence of Malta.

The defences of Malta were boosted on October 26, 1942, when the new replacement pilots arrived. Most of the pilots of 249 Squadron could now be sent home on leave. One of those was Hetherington. Some thirty-four passengers, two of them children, embarked on a Liberator transport aircraft. Al 516, on the evening of October 31. Their destination was England after a routine fuel stop on Gibraltar. Among the passengers were twenty-four pilots returning to England on a spell of leave. On the approach to Gibraltar a violent storm had erupted but the Liberator crew pressed ahead with their landing. However, the landing approach was mis-timed and the Liberator overshot the runway. Unable to regain any flying speed the Liberator flopped into the sea about a hundred and ten yards off shore. The resulting shock broke the back of the aircraft and, although not in deep water, it sank like a stone.

One of the wings of the Liberator stuck up out of the water like a guiding hand to those who came to the rescue. At least two reports stated that Hetherington was in the rear of the aircraft and that he drowned there. However, Cull states that; 'Hetherington was seen to be conscious and apparently not in difficulty when rescuers arrived, and even suggested they help others first, but seconds later he died, presumably from internal injuries and or shock'.[1]

When the dead were counted eight civilians and five pilots were found to have died in the accident. Among the injured was P/O Beurling who had a broken leg. One of the dead was Erik Lawson Hetherington DFC, Battle of Britain pilot and veteran of the air defence of Malta. Hetherington became one of those pilots granted the status of 'ace'[2]. Oddly, it is not clear where Hetherington is buried. It is known that he is remembered on the Gibraltar Memorial at North

Front cemetery but, it does not say that he was buried there.[3] The Commonwealth War Graves Commission Roll of Honour also acknowledges his presence on the war memorial but equally fails to mention where he is buried.

Hetherington Notes

1. Brian Cull, 249 Squadron At War, P 154–155. Shores and Williams, *Aces High*, merely state that Hetherington drowned while trapped in the rear of the aircraft, P 180.
2. Shores and Williams: *Aces High*, give Hetherington five confirmed kills and one third of a share, P 180.
3. The information from the Commonwealth War Graves Commission, concerning the Gibraltar Memorial states; 'The Memorial commemorates, by name, 91 airmen and soldiers who died during the 1939–45 war who were buried at sea'. If this information is correct, then Hetherington, who died, according to the evidence, only a hundred or so yards from land, is buried at sea.

Middle row 3rd right—Ralph V. Hogg. Front row 4th Right—George C.C. Palliser. Photo: Kathleen Collier.

Ralph Vincent Hogg, 754794
Sergeant

Ralph Vincent Hogg was born April 18, 1916 in the town of Hartlepool. Ralph Vincent Hogg was the eldest in an eventual family of five, three sons and two daughters, born to James William and Mary Catherine Hogg, formerly Keely. James William was a pharmacist working in a local chemist. The family home was situated at Number 18 Percy Street, Hartlepool. The house was to remain in the family until recent years. Education for the young Ralph Hogg was courtesy of Hartlepool Grammar School. On leaving school, Ralph Hogg went to work in a local paper mill.

The young Ralph appears to have had an adventurous nature; being the type who would volunteer for anything.[1] One day flying beckoned and Ralph Hogg joined the RAFVR in July of 1939. Training in his spare time. Flying training began with the Tiger Moth flying from nearby Greatham, his local airfield. Ralph took great pleasure in making flights over his own house. On returning home he would ask his mother if she had seen him fly over.[2]

September 1, 1939, was a momentous day for Ralph Hogg. His training at Greatham came to an end, cut short by the advance of war. From this day, Ralph Hogg would be in the RAF full-time. This must have caused a wrench on both the young Ralph Hogg as well as his family. His father had died some years before, therefore, Ralph had considered himself as the head of the family: a job which he took seriously.

Training was resumed for Hogg at Number 3 Initial Training

Wing (ITW) based at Hastings, the training lasting until November. It is thought that further training resumed in Scotland. With his basic training behind him, Hogg was next posted to Number 7 Operational Training Unit (OTU) at Hawarden, North Wales, arriving there in September of 1940. Hogg was converted onto the Spitfire. Passing out of Hawarden, Hogg was posted to his first fighter squadron, this was to be 616 (South Yorkshire) Squadron, an Auxiliary Air Force squadron. Number 616 Squadron was at that time based at Kirton-in-Lindsey, to the south of Scunthorpe. After suffering some heavy losses during the Battle of Britain, 616 Squadron were posted to Kirton-in-Lindsey for a 'rest'. The squadron also had to re-build itself, train new pilots, some of which were partly experienced others had just passed out of training wings. To meet this end, one flight was posted to Ringway, Manchester. The other flight remained was to remain at Kirton-in-Lindsey. One of seven new pilots, straight from the training wings, was Ralph Hogg, who arrived at Kirton-in-Lindsey on October 6, 1940.

Training on a fighter squadron was more demanding, and at times more dangerous, than anything experienced on a training unit. Hogg was to experience danger at first hand, October 14. On this occasion Hogg was flying Spitfire X 4330, coded, QJ-G. This Spitfire, being quite new had its first flight, August 13, 1940. A brief period was to be spent at Number 58 OTU before being handed over to 616 Squadron. Once there it came into the hands of Ralph Hogg. October 14, Hogg took off on a routine training flight. This appeared to be carried out without difficulty. Only the landing lay ahead. Spitfires were a handful when landing to anyone but the experienced. It was the landing that proved to be Hogg's undoing. Hogg either forgot to lower the undercarriage, not uncommon at this time, or it was not locked down properly or it was a genuine mechanical fault. Either way, the undercarriage on X 4330 collapsed on landing and the Spitfire was reported as crash-landed on the airfield.[3] The Spitfire received slight damage. Apart from a slight mishap a couple of weeks later, no further record of its career has been found. As for Hogg, he suffered only dented pride. A landing photograph of this Spitfire is commonly used in books on the subject. Confusion has arisen over its identity, mainly due to the fact that 616 Squadron used the code letters QJ. Spitfires of 92 Squadron also carried these same letters during the same period.[4]

A GATHERING OF EAGLES

Qualification for the Battle of Britain clasp states that a pilot must have flown on one of the recognized operational fighter squadrons during the recognized period of the campaign. The Ministry of Defence quotes that the Battle of Britain came to an official end on the last day of October 1940. It must have been while on 616 Squadron that Hogg flew on an operational flight. The squadron were at this time occupied mainly with convoy patrols. On occasion they did come across a lone raider. It is presumed that Hogg flew on one of these flights: hence he was active in the Battle of Britain.

For Hogg, the next move was to come on November 4, 1940. On this date he was posted to the south, to Hornchurch, where he was to join Number 41 Squadron. The official version of the Battle of Britain was now over. Reality, however, was a different story, 41 Squadron were still frequently scrambled to intercept raiders. One Spitfire had to force-land, November 9, due to enemy action, while on November 17, the squadron was to lose two of its aircraft in combat with the enemy. Two days later, November 19, aircraft of 41 Squadron were again scrambled. This was presumably to intercept 'hit and run' raiders who were using the bad weather to their advantage. Hogg was flying Spitfire P 7322, a not too mature Spitfire, having first flown in August 1940. A short stay with 611 Squadron was followed by a move to 41 Squadron. In the ensuing scramble, Hogg's Spitfire somehow managed to crash. How is not made clear. The Spitfire suffered only minor damage and Hogg managed to walk away. A photograph exists of 41 Squadron at around this period. It shows a handful of pilots grouped around Squadron Leader Finlay, the commanding officer; he holds a propeller blade on which appear the names of the pilots of the squadron. Ralph Hogg's name appears eighth from the bottom although he is missing from the photograph.

It is known that 41 Squadron were in action on November 27. On this occasion, Squadron Leader D.O. Finlay was leading his formation into a pack of Me 109s over Maidstone. The squadron were to chase the Me 109s back across the coast and were eventually to make a claim for a total of eight destroyed. This may well be an exaggerated number. They were on patrol again, December 12. Number 41 Squadron took off at 3.35 PM, Hogg flying Spitfire P 7326. This Spitfire had first flown in August of 1940 and had flown with 611 Squadron prior to being passed on to 41 Squadron.

What actually happened on this patrol appears, at first glance, to be uncertain. The facts that remain are that 41 Squadron returned to Hornchurch without Ralph Hogg. Evidence states that Hogg 'disappeared'. One source[5] states that Hogg went 'missing' while on patrol December 12. Foreman states in 'Battle of Britain—The Forgotten Months', that Hogg 'disappeared on December 10. To muddy the waters further, he goes on to state that Hogg's body was recovered from the wreck of his Spitfire. To even further muddy the water, another source[6] goes on to state that Spitfire P 7326 (Hogg's Spitfire) went missing on December 10 while on charge to 611 Squadron, the pilot of which was un-named. Number 611 Squadron were not in the area at that time.

That Hogg went missing on December 12 there is no doubt. An unofficial letter was sent to the Hogg family. This letter was from F/O A.D.J. Lovell, a flight commander on 41 Squadron. The letter states that a short while before he went 'missing' Hogg, who had been acting as a 'scout', had been ordered to ascend. It would appear that Hogg had been flying in the unenviable position of 'tail end Charlie' to the squadron on December 12. This was often the position delegated to inexperienced pilots. More often than not, they were to pay a high price for it, as they fell an easy prey to any stalking enemy fighter. There was heavy cloud at the time, giving plenty of cover to any enemy fighter stalking the squadron. Hogg appears to have been shot down while momentarily out of sight of the squadron. In all probability, he never saw his victor. His Spitfire was last seen to dive into the sea.

The official letter to the family arrived some time later. It merely states that Hogg was 'missing'. Today that is still the case. The body of Ralph Hogg was never recovered, either from his Spitfire or anywhere else, Ralph Hogg remains officially 'missing'. He is remembered on the Runnymede Memorial, panel 15. A small ceremony was held on June 16, 2000, at Hartlepool College, Hogg's former school. During the ceremony a plaque was presented to the college by Mrs Kathleen Collier, the pilot's only surviving sister, to mark the memory of her brother. A photograph is also displayed alongside. It has taken sixty years but Ralph Vincent Hogg is now remembered in Hartlepool as one of the 'few'.

HOGG NOTES
1. Personal correspondence with the pilot's sister Mrs Kathleen Collier.
2. Same as above.
3. Shacklady, *Spitfire the History*, P 90.
4. See also note on Heppell.
5. Wynn: *Men of The Battle of Britain*, P 237.
6. Shacklady: *Spitfire the History*, P 109.

MAURICE MILNE IRVING, 90277
FLYING OFFICER

Maurice Milne Irving was born in 1911. He was one of two sons born to Benjamin and Katherine Irving. Very little is known about Irving's life at this time. However, ex-607 Squadron pilot, Squadron Leader W.H.R Whitty states that Irving worked at the (Locomotive Division) of the Armstrong Whitworth Engineering Works in Newcastle.[1] Although it is thought that the family of Irving were probably not indigenous to the Jesmond area of Newcastle upon Tyne. The family were residing there by 1934. Home at this time for the Irving family being at Number Eight Osborne Villas. These dwellings being on the southern edge of Jesmond, overlooking the County Cricket Ground and only a short distance from the centre of the City of Newcastle.

It was in 1934 that the young Irving decided to join the Auxiliary Air Force. He was to join the newly formed 607 (County of Durham) Squadron. Irving became only the fifth man to join the squadron. It can be assumed that he was looked upon with awe by the other pilots; Irving had already gained his 'A' licence, and, had been gazetted, March 10, 1934. He was, therefore, already a qualified pilot. Main complement of the squadron at this time was the Westland Wapiti, a light bomber, the squadron being a light bomber unit. Just over a year later, Irving was promoted to Flying Officer rank, September 10, 1935. Later the squadron were to fly the Hawker Demon, a two-seat fighter. It is in front of one of these aeroplanes, that the squadron's pilots posed for the group photo of 1937. This was taken on April 25 and shows Irving, sitting, front, third from the right. The photograph being taken during the inspection by Air Commodore J.C. Quinnel.

The photographs of the squadron's activities are about the only place that Irving can be seen. The summer camp of 1937, like others that were to come, depended as much on the social life as on the more serious side, the flying. Sports days were held and, in one of these we see Irving standing with the other pilots as they watch some sporting activity. He stands fifth from the right in the photograph taken at the 1938 Summer Camp, that year held at Warmwell. However, he does not appear on the group photograph taken at the 1939 Summer Camp at Abbotsinch. For some reason Irving had left the squadron and moved south[2]. In fact Irving had moved to Slough. It is believed that the locomotive division, in which Irving worked, was closed at this date. In the last quarter of 1938, Irving had married Shelia Rose at Westminster. This may have had something else to do with his move.

On July 10, 1939, Irving was transferred to Reserve class 'A'. With the impending war, Irving was recalled from the reserve, September 9, 1940, and found himself posted once more to 607 Squadron. The squadron was now equipped with the Gloster Gladiator. A bit of movement for the squadron now took place. Firstly it was moved to Acklington in Northumberland then, November 13, the squadron was moved on to France. Flying by way of Sunderland, for a last flypast to their hometown and Digby for a fuel stop. The squadron moved on to Croydon. Stranded there for two days due to the weather, they at last made the hop across the Channel to land at Merville.

December 12 and 13, 1939 saw 607 Squadron move to Vitry. Merville had become almost bogged with the constant rain causing many accidents on the squadron. For Irving, however, the move was not to bring much luck. Only two days after arriving at Vitry Irving flew his Gladiator to Douai for some routine maintenance. Irving miscalculated his approach and overshot the runway. His flight came to an end in a dugout with his Gladiator on its nose, the propeller damaged. Little else is known of Irving's activities while in France.

Irving was the acting squadron Adjutant from March 14, 1940 and was flying with 'B' flight. In April of 1940, 607 Squadron began to take possession of its new compliment of aircraft, the Hawker Hurricane. Number 607 Squadron was to take heavy casualties during the battle of France, losing two of its commanding officers in quick succession. The squadron was to return from France with only three Hurricanes, their nose bloodied but their head unbowed.

After a short stay at Usworth, during which 607 Squadron took part in the defence of the North East, 15 August, 1940, 607 Squadron were to move south to Tangmere. A photograph of Irving exists from around this time[3]. He stands alongside Flt Lt W.F. Blackadder, two of the originals from the County of Durham Squadron. Although both Gore and Craig were also still on the squadron.

On the afternoon of September 28, a large formation of enemy aircraft were detected approaching the south coast. Number 607 Squadron was one of a number of squadrons scrambled into action. It had been observed by the Luftwaffe, that recent attacks on their formations were centred on the bomber force. On this occasion the bomber force was less in number and concentrated on a number of faster, lighter bombers, Me 110s loaded with bombs as well as a number of Ju 88s. This gave their attack a bit more momentum. The fighter escort, on this occasion numbering around two hundred, were not held back so much, as they had been on previous attacks when escorting the slower He 111s and Do 17s. Now they had the fuel to fly higher and further.

The defending Hurricanes of 607 Squadron had thought they were about to attack a large number of Bombers. In the ensuing fight, 607 Squadron did just that. Irving is credited with a 'share' in a Ju 88. However, as 607 Squadron was setting about the bomber force, they were severely bounced by the Me 109s of the high flying escort.[4] This caused utter confusion among the Hurricane pilots of 607 Squadron. Two of their number was to fall in the ensuing attack. These were Irving and Gore. Both Hurricanes were to crash into the sea off Selsey Bill. Irving had been flying Hurricane R 4189, a relatively new aeroplane, having been built in 1940. It was one of a batch of one hundred Hurricanes built by Gloster Aircraft Ltd at their Brockworth works. Hurricane R 4189 crashed into the sea around 2.50 PM. The body of Irving was never recovered.

Today F/O Maurice Milne Irving, always known by his middle name, Milne, survives only in a few faded photographs, mainly group shots dating from the pre-war days. As he was posted 'missing' on September 28, 1940, his name is remembered on the

Runnymede Memorial, panel 4. Over sixty years after the events that led to his death, Irving is still classed as 'missing'. His name is not remembered on the local war memorials, as bureaucracy does not accept that he is officially dead. Irving remains one of the forgotten 'few' of the Battle of Britain.

Irving Notes
1. Personal correspondence with Sqdn Ldr W.H.R. Whitty: the only surviving member of the original squadron.
2. Personal correspondence with Sqdn Ldr W.H.R. Whitty: the only surviving member of the original squadron.
3. Ramsey: *Battle of Britain Then and Now, Mk V ed*, P 485.
4. See notes on Gore.

Michael Jebb, 72449
Flying Officer

Michael Jebb was not a North Easterner by birth. He was born in the second quarter of 1918 in the town of Chester, Cheshire. He was the younger son of a soldier, Brigadier General G.D. Jebb. In later years the family of Jebb were to move north to Hexham in Northumberland. Education for the young Jebb was by way of Stowe School followed by Trinity College, Cambridge where he studied languages. It is believed that Jebb got a taste for flying courtesy of the University Air Squadron. On September 13, 1938, Michael Jebb decided to join the RAFVR. He was commissioned at a later date. September 1, 1939 saw Jebb called to full-time service.

After completion of conversion training, which saw Jebb converted to the Hawker Hurricane, Jebb was posted to 504 (County of Nottingham) Squadron, An Auxiliary Air Force Squadron. Wynn[1] has Jebb joining 504 Squadron in July of 1940. However, this cannot be true. Jebb must have joined the squadron in the early part of 1940. Certainly he was on the squadron strength in May of 1940 and had probably joined 504 Squadron as early as April of that year.

May 20, 1940, Sdn Ldr Joe Kayll was to lead a formation of fighters, drawn from three squadrons, 615, 607 and 504 Squadrons. The intention of the attack was in answer to a request from the army, this was for an air attack to delay a German advance that was taking place along the Cambrai-Arras road. This attack was carried out with the loss of three Hurricanes. One of these was caught in a heavy crossfire from ground defences; Hurricane P 3586 was severely hit by this ground-fire and forced to crash-land. Its pilot was wounded in the attack, either by the gunfire or by the crash-landing, his name was Michael Jebb. His Hurricane made its forced-landing near Cambrai. Jebb managed to make good his escape. Coming across some allied soldiers Jebb was admitted to a field hospital. He was to leave France a short time later making the last ship out of Dieppe. After his recovery, Jebb was to rejoin 504 Squadron then based at Wick, Scotland.

While based at Wick, 504 Squadron were responsible for the air defence of the naval base at Scapa Flow. As well as the standing patrols, 504 squadron had their share of convoy patrols as well as their endless practice. On August 12, 1940, Michael Jebb was flying Hurricane L 1999 on an air firing practice in the vicinity of the Black Isle. His Hurricane was struck with oil trouble that necessitated a forced landing. Jebb's Hurricane returned to terra firma in a belly landing near Evanton in Easter Ross. Luckily no harm befell the pilot. Later the squadron was to move on to Castletown before hearing the news they had been waiting for. The squadron was to move south. Flying into Hendon on September 5, the squadron was given a rest the following day before going into action on September 7. The squadron managed to destroy two enemy bombers on that day. September 12 to 14 were relatively quiet days, while on September 15, they fought in some of the heaviest fighting so far seen in the Battle of Britain.

Number 504 Squadron were in action high over London. In the ensuing action, they were to lose three aircraft with another damaged. Michael Jebb was flying in Hurricane N 2705 when he was shot down during this action. Attacking the Dornier Do 17s, Jebb's Hurricane was caught in the crossfire from the bombers, his Hurricane set on fire. Jebb managed to make good his evacuation of the doomed Hurricane and take to his parachute. Both Jebb and his Hurricane were to land at Dartford to the east of London at around 2.45 PM. Jebb was later admitted to Dartford Hospital with grievous burns. Hunt[2] states that Jebb '... died the same evening'. However, this was not so. Michael Jebb was to fight for his life for another four days before succumbing to his injuries September 19, as stated by Ramsey as well as Wynn[3].

Michael Jebb was cremated at the local crematorium at Hendon.

His name was inscribed on the panel of the screen wall next to the cross of sacrifice, panel 5. Another pilot of 504 Squadron, killed in the same action, was P/O John V. Gurteen. He is also commemorated on the same memorial. With uniforms having to be paid for from their own pockets this often put a strain on the finances of pilots. Uniforms, often worn while in flight, were often damaged in the fighting. Michael Jebb's parents were to make a present of their son's dress uniform to fellow squadron pilot Ray Holmes.

JEBB NOTES
1. Wynn: *Men of the Battle of Britain,* P 263.
2. Hunt: *Twenty-One Squadrons,* P 285.
3. Wynn: *Men of the Battle of Britain,* P 263.
4. Ramsey: *The Battle of Britain Then and Now,* P 455.

JOHN FERDINAND READ JONES, 128559
SERGEANT

John Ferdinand Read Jones was born in South Shields, County Durham, October 28, 1918. He was to inherit his mother's maiden name of Read as one of his Christian names. Education for Jones came by way of Rippon Grammar School. On leaving Rippon Grammar, Jones gained an apprenticeship with Armstrong Whitworth Aviation, beginning his association with aeroplanes. In 1938, Jones decided to join his local RAFVR. He became an airman under training as a pilot on January 22 of that year. Flying training was to begin at Number 9 Elementary and Reserve Flying Training School (E&RFTS) at Ansty. Called to full time service in September of 1939, training for Jones was to continue at Number 11 Flying Training School (FTS) at Shawbury. Jones arrived there September 21, 1939, and on completion of his training Jones was posted to Number 601 Squadron.

Number 601 (County of London) Squadron was an Auxiliary Air Force squadron. The squadron was known, unofficially, as the 'Millionaires Squadron'. Jones was to join the squadron when it was based at Biggin Hill. Flying from the Kent airfield, 601 Squadron was equipped with the Bristol Blenheim a twin-engine fighter. Within three weeks of Jones joining the squadron it was in action. Six of the squadron's Blenheims were involved in the first action of the war. Flying with another six aircraft from 25 Squadron, they attacked the Luftwaffe Seaplane base at Borkum. The raid was deemed a success. As Jones was a new pilot on the squadron and with almost no experience, he was forced to sit out the action. A fellow pilot on the squadron during this time was Flt Lt Roger Bushell. Later, as a squadron Leader, Bushell was to gain immortal fame as a prison escapee after being shot down over Dunkirk. He was later shot by the Gestapo after his escape from Stalag Luft III.

Jones' stay with 601 Squadron was to be a relatively short one. During February of 1940, 601 Squadron began to replace its compliment of Blenheims with the single seat Hurricane. Jones, staying with the Blenheim, was posted to Number 25 Squadron then based at north Weald. As what came to be known as the 'phoney war' gave way to the real thing, the Blenheim was relegated to the night fighting role. For Jones, therefore, the Battle of Britain was to be fought in the night skies over Britain.

Although the night skies could be seen as more of a cat and mouse pursuit of the enemy, and usually a bit more quiet than it was for their daytime counterparts, it also had its own hidden dangers. The night of September 4, 1940, 25 Squadron had one of its aircraft hit by 'friendly' AA fire. However, this was not as bad as what had happened the previous day. After a raid had developed, three Blenheims had been scrambled in an effort to attack any stragglers in the enemy formation. As they were returning to their base, Hurricanes of 46 Squadron in turn attacked them. The latter mistaking the Blenheims for Ju 88s. The Hurricanes managed to shoot down two Blenheims and damage a third. In the confusion, the Hurricane pilots were to claim the destruction of two Ju 88s.

On September 21, 1940, Jones was involved in an air crash at Hendon. This occurred during part of a routine training flight. Jones was not to return to flying again until March 27, 1942. At this time Jones was posted to 54 Operational Training Unit (OTU) at Church Fenton. The period at Church Fenton being spent converting to the Bristol Beaufighter, a more potent and powerful beast than its old stable mate the Blenheim. Jones was to receive his commission on July 25, 1942. On completion of his conversion course, Jones was once more reunited with his old squadron Number 25. This unit also being based at Church Fenton. Jones was then to go onto a beam approach course followed by a course at 1489 Gunnery School.

October 27, 1943 saw Jones complete his second operational tour on fighters. Following this he was posted to 62 OTU at Ouston in

Northumberland. There he remained until early 1944. Jones was to embark on his operational tour on fighters beginning April 27, 1944. Once again Jones was to make a return to 25 Squadron. Although by now it was stationed at Coltishall, Norfolk. With the third tour completed, Jones was posted to the Empire Air Navigation School at Shawbury, arriving there July 29, 1945. Three months later, Jones was posted to HQ 11 Group at Uxbridge.

Jones was released from the RAF in January of 1946. He had twice been mentioned in Despatches during his operational career and left the RAF with the rank of Flight Lieutenant. Remaining in aviation as a career, Jones joined British South American Airways, later transferring to British Overseas Airways when the two merged on October 1, 1949. In October of 1973, Jones retired from the airline, and from flying, with the rank of Senior Captain. John Ferdinand Read Jones died in 1997.

JOSEPH ROBERT KAYLL, DFC, DSO, 90276
SQUADRON LEADER

Joseph Robert Kayll was born in Sunderland, April 12, 1914. He was the son of Joseph P. and Kathleen Kayll. The family made their home in the residential area on the south side of the town of Sunderland. The family home being Number Two, the Elms. Education for the young Kayll was by way of Aysgarth School in the secluded north Yorkshire Pennine district. Aysgarth was to be followed by a period at Stowe School. With the academic part of his life over, Joe Kayll was to begin work at the Sunderland timber business of Joseph Thompson. Like most young men, Kayll was always on the lookout for some other challenge: something to get the excitement going. The forces were to offer plenty opportunities during this period. The RAF, being the youngest service, appealed to many who longed for a bit of 'dash'. What was to be the most appealing, however, was the Auxiliary Air Force. Membership and training could be carried out from home. Flying training was at the expence of the government. When members were qualified, they were granted officer rank.

In the latter part of 1933, Joe Kayll joined his local Auxiliary squadron. This was 607 (County of Durham) Auxiliary Squadron. The squadron, conveniently for Kayll, was based along the road at nearby Usworth. He was the fourth member pilot to join the squadron and completed his 'A' licence and was gazetted, March 9, 1934. Number 607 Squadron was a light bomber squadron during this period, flying the Westland Wapiti. Before Kayll got his hands on one of these he worked his way through other, less demanding aeroplanes including the squadron's Gypsy Moth and the Avro 504. Kayll was promoted to Flying Officer, September 9, 1935. Being the only Auxiliary Air Force Squadron in the northern counties, north of Yorkshire, 607 Squadron was a tightly knit squadron, building up its membership mainly from the Durham area as well as Northumberland. Although there were a few members from other parts of the country as well. Comradeship was, therefore, close. Not only did these men fly together, they also spent much of their spare time, as well as holidays together. The photographs that have been left behind evidence this. Young men training for war on holiday in Scotland and Austria. Walking, skiing and climbing, always together.

Number 607 Squadron were to change their role in mid 1937. From that date they became a fighter squadron. The compliment of the squadron was changed to the Hawker Demon; in turn this was to change into the single seat Gloster Gladiator in December of 1938. The following year brought change for Joe Kayll. He was promoted to the rank of Flight Lieutenant as from July 1, 1939. As further promotion, Joe Kayll became commanding officer of 'A' flight. A photograph of Kayll[1] exists from this time. Taken at the annual camp at Abbotsinch, Glasgow, it shows Kayll, in a group photograph of the squadron. Kayll sits to the right of the squadron commander surrounded by 'A' flight. This was to be the last official photograph before the hostilities of World War Two began. The men of 607 Squadron were hastily ordered back to Usworth.

As from August 24, 1939, Joe Kayll was embodied into the RAF. The Gladiators were repainted in their wartime camouflage and, after a short stay at Usworth, were moved north to Acklington in Northumberland. Patrols were flown from Acklington with detachments flying from Drem. November 13 saw 607 Squadron depart from Acklington to take up its post in Merville, France as part of the Air Component of the Advanced Air Striking Force. The squadron was to move again. On this occasion from Merville to Vitry-en-Artois. There it was to stay throughout, what was to become the worst winter on record. However, things were once again on the change for Joe Kayll. In March of 1940, Kayll was posted to 615 (County of Surrey), also known as 'Churchill's Own' Squadron, the Auxiliary Squadron that had flown to France in company with 607

A GATHERING OF EAGLES

Squadron. Now Kayll was to be its commanding officer. Soon after the arrival of Kayll, 615 Squadron began to convert to the Hawker Hurricane. Conversion was to take place at Abbeville.

Conversion came none too soon, the German 'Blitzkrieg' breaking through the allied lines in the early hours of May 10. However, the German advance was not without stiff opposition. In the forefront of the defence was 615 Squadron. On May 15, 615 Squadron clashed with the fighters of the Luftwaffe. On this occasion Kayll was to make a claim for two Me 110s destroyed. This was followed up by further claims on the 20th of the month. Kayll was detailed to lead a formation of Hurricanes drawn from 615, 607 and 504 Squadrons. This was as a direct request from the Army. The German advance had to be delayed and this attack was to be carried out along the Cambrai-Arras road. Kayll's formation drew some heavy return fire from the ground defences, three of the Hurricanes being lost in the action. Kayll was to claim an He 111 as destroyed, along with a further unidentified aircraft. Two days later Kayll was to make claims for two He 111s. The first as destroyed with the second as damaged. In action during May 30, Kayll was to claim an Me 109 as destroyed with a further Me 109 as a probable. May came to an end with a high point for Joe Kayll. On the last day of the month he learned that he had been awarded not only the DFC but the DSO as well. Number 615 Squadron were then withdrawn from France and re-mustered at Kenley.

Although based in England, Kayll still led his squadron on attacks over France. After one such patrol, June 27, Kayll had led his squadron over France as they flew as escort to a photographic mission. On his return from this patrol, Kayll found that none other than the King was visiting the station.

The King was there to present with both the DFC and the DSO. Photographs of this event are often used. The still photographs appear in many books. The event was also filmed and shown in a recent documentary film.[2] The citation for the DFC reads;

> 'This officer has shown courage and skill in shooting down four enemy patrols' While the citation for the DSO reads; 'Owing to his inspiring training and leadership this officers squadron has destroyed 32 enemy aircraft. The squadron

responded to every call made and, in particular, made several important and dangerous reconnaissances for the Army. Squadron Leader Kayll combined flying leadership and administration in an exemplary manner throughout, and destroyed five enemy aircraft, bringing his total to nine'.

An uneventful patrol was carried out, July 27, 1940. The squadron had returned and were about to land at Hawkinge. The squadron was then diverted to the area of Dover to investigate a suspected raid. However, all that could be found was a lonely He 59 floatplane. The war cabinet had previously posted orders about these aircraft. These orders stated that all enemy aircraft carrying red crosses and thought to be 'spotting' for the long range guns had to be shot down. This order, on this occasion, was duly carried out. The He 59 of Seenotflug Kommando 3, an air-sea rescue unit, was shot down at 6.50 PM, some ten miles northeast of Dover. Oblt Chudziak and another three were missing.[3] However, all sources do not seem to agree. This kill was awarded to Sgt James Robinson of 111 Squadron, who is credited with shooting this aircraft down on the following day, July 28, by another source.[4] Kayll was to make another claim, August 16, for an He 111 as a probable. Number 615 Squadron having encountered an incoming raid in the area of Brighton.

On August 18, 1940, Kenley came under heavy attack from the Luftwaffe. Number 615 Squadron were to lose six of its Hurricanes to the low-flying Do 17s. Other aircraft from the squadron had been in action over Biggin Hill and had managed to attack the bombers that had been flying at a higher altitude. However, they in turn were engaged by the Me 109s of the fighter escort and a furious dogfight broke out. Kayll managed to claim one Me 109 as damaged. The rest of the squadron were to pay severely, however, as two of the Hurricanes were shot down and a third severely damaged.

The weather on August 20 was described as 'Autumnal' and helped to cut back the attacks if only for a short while. Shortly after 2.00 PM a raid was reported in the vicinity of the Thames Estuary. This raid consisted of some twenty-seven Do 17s with an escort of thirty plus Me 109s, the latter being of 1/JG51. The defences had been well alerted due in part to the earlier reconnaissance flights that normally preceded enemy operations. As a result, six squadrons were scrambled and well placed to meet the coming attack. Joe Kayll's 615 Squadron was the first squadron to encounter the action. Kayll led his squadron into the attack against the bombers while 65 Squadron's Spitfires took on the fighter escort. Two Do 17s were to fall to 615 Squadron and Kayll was to share a kill with P/O C.R. Young. Their victim was a Do 17 of 9/KG 3. This aircraft was to crash near Eastchurch, the target for its bombs, at 3.09 PM.

On August 24, the Luftwaffe stepped up its attack. In the afternoon 11 Group found themselves facing the ensuing attacks with all their available aircraft in the air. Neighbouring 12 Group were asked for assistance. Kayll led his fighters into the attack over the Thames Estuary. Singling out an He 111 of KG 53, Kayll successfully attacked the bomber in company with P/O J.A.P. McClintock. The two pilots were to share the kill. This He 111 eventually crashed at Clay Tye Hill, Bulphan at 3.50 PM. The crew of He 111, A1+KT, Lt Willi Luttigen, Fw Alfred Fraas, Uffz Oscar Lackner, Uffz Karl Platzer and Uffz Herbert Hermans were all captured. However, the luck of the squadron was in for a change two days later. A raid on the afternoon of August 26, was launched against Hornchurch. This raid consisted of 40 plus Do 17s with around the same number of Me 109s and 110s. Number 615 Squadron was reduced, due to unservicabilty, to nine Hurricanes in the air. The Hurricanes of 615 Squadron waded in to the attack against the Me 109s of the fighter escort over Rochford. As a result, 615 Squadron lost four of its Hurricanes to the Me 109s. P/O McClintock, Kayll's partner on August 24, was shot down but unhurt. P/O D.H. Hone was shot down for the second time in two days, on this occasion he was wounded. Joe Kayll was to make claims for an He 111 destroyed and an Me 109 as damaged.

August 28 saw 615 Squadron again in action and still they were reduced to nine Hurricanes serviceable. A raid approached the south coast, splitting into a two-pronged attack over Deal, one group turned towards Eastchurch while the other turned towards Rochford. Kayll attacked a Do 17 severely damaging it. This Do 17 was eventually to crash near Marche, Oblt Graf von Platen-Hallermund and one NCO was killed in the resulting crash. A further two NCOs were wounded. Not all sources were to agree on the demise of this bomber.[5] In the resulting combat 615 Squadron lost one Hurricane. This was to mark the end of the Battle of Britain, for the time being, for 615 Squadron. The squadron was deemed as to be desperately in need of a rest. To this end the squadron was posted north to Prestwick in Scotland. After leading 615 Squadron for so long, Kayll was promoted to the rank of Squadron Leader.

During its stay at Prestwick, 615 Squadron trained its new pilots. Some of the pilots being posted on to other squadrons, while others were destined to stay with the squadron. On October 10, 1940, 615 Squadron was once more posted to the south, Kayll leading his men to Northolt before moving on once more, three days later, to Heathrow. It was from the latter that Kayll led patrols at Wing strength of three squadrons. However, by now, raids had become much less frequent due to the bad weather and losses suffered by the Luftwaffe.

The morning of October 28 brought marginally better weather conditions. Mist and fog restricted the Luftwaffe to nuisance raids. The afternoon brought finer weather and with it the Luftwaffe, although raids were mainly against shipping in the Channel one or two were aimed against London. Kayll led 615 Squadron into action against the Me 109s of the fighter escort. In this action Joe Kayll was to make his last claim before the official end of the Battle of Britain. This was to claim an Me 109 as damaged. In December of 1940, Joe Kayll was taken off flying and posted to HQ Fighter Command.

After a suitable period of rest, Joe Kayll was appointed Wing Leader at Hornchurch from June 2, 1941. While with the Hornchurch Wing Kayll led a number of fighter sweeps across the Channel. However, things were not always straightforward. There may have been more than a little disenchantment in the camp according to some authors. Smith suggests there was some discord over who was to actually lead the Hornchurch Wing.[6] Later, Kayll was to state that he was going to lead a raid on Lille when Group Captain Harry Broadhurst, station commander at Hornchurch, made it known that he would lead the raid. Kayll was asked to lead another squadron but refused to do so.[7] This escort of three Halifaxes was carried out on July 25. As the Hornchurch Wing turned for home, Broadhurst decided to have another look around. Turning his section back over France. Climbing into the sun, the section was bounced by Me 109s. Two pilots were killed and Joe Kayll was forced to crash-land. The only man from the section to return to Hornchurch was Broadhurst.

Obviously, Kayll would be none too happy with the events of the day.

Kayll's Spitfire landed in a field near St Omer where he became a target for German soldiers. Kayll was none too pleased at not being dined by the Luftwaffe, a practice that was usually carried out for RAF senior officers who found themselves as 'guests' of the Luftwaffe. Home for Kayll was to be Dulag Luft where he was processed before being sent on to Spangenberg Castle then later to Oflag VIB at Wartberg. It was from Wartberg that Kayll made one of his escape attempts. As part of a mass-breakout Kayll attempted to walk to Switzerland. Kayll was on the run for a week. Hiding in a clearing within a wood, he was captured by a gamekeeper and returned to the Germans.

Kayll was one of a number of prisoners purged to Schubin in Poland. Although it is common knowledge that all cameras were strictly banned from prisoners, photographs that exist appear to deny this. Certainly at Schubin, cameras were pretty much in evidence. As was the old Auxiliary Air Force spirit. One photograph shows four pilots of 607 Squadron while another shows eight pilots who were all Auxiliaries. Kayll is on both of these.[8] Kayll was also to make an escape bid from Schubin. This was via a tunnel from beneath a lavatory.

Kayll, like many others, was considered a nuisance and an escape risk. He was, therefore, sent to Stalag Luft III. While there he worked on the intelligence side of the escape committee. Like others he took his turn in the jumping queue as they jumped over a vaulting horse. A screen for what became known as the 'Wooden Horse' escape. At a later date Kayll along with a large number of other officers was transferred to the new North Camp. While at Stalag Luft III Kayll was to remain in charge of the intelligence section working on what came to be known as the 'Great Escape'. However, although escaping had to remain as part of a captured officers duty, thoughts of escape were to die down after it became known that fifty of their comrades had been shot by the Gestapo.

With the Russian advance, Kayll and the other prisoners were force-marched for about three weeks in an attempt to get the prisoners away from the Russian advance. Many of the prisoners thought that they were to be used as a human shield or a bargaining device. Eventually they reached a farm in Lubeck that was run by

Russian women. It was from here that they were repatriated by the Russians in May 1945 and flown back to England in Dakotas. Kayll was released from the RAF with the rank of Wing Commander in 1945. For his work behind the wire, Joe Kayll was mentioned in Despatches, December 28, 1945 and became an OBE on July 26, 1946. On returning to civilian life, Joe Kayll resumed his work in the timber business in his hometown of Sunderland.

The RAF may have finished with Joe Kayll but Kayll had not finished with service flying. May 10, 1946 was the day that 607 Squadron was re-born. The prefix 'Royal' was added to the title of Auxiliary Air Force on December 16, 1947. Among the first to re-join the squadron was Joe Kayll. He was also awarded the honour of being the squadron's first post-war Commanding Officer.

The first aircraft were soon on the squadron's strength. These were two Harvards for training purposes. The end of the year brought the squadron its first operational aircraft, the Spitfire. The squadron held its first post-war Battle of Britain Day on September 17, 1949. This took place at the squadron's new home of Ouston, Northumberland. The flypast at the Air Day was led by two of the original members of 607 Squadron, Joe Kayll and Jim Bazin. Summer camps were still on the agenda and one of the most popular was at Lubeck. The nearest RAF station to the Russian border. The official photograph of the summer camp at Lubeck in 1948, shows a much more gaunt Kayll sitting centre front.[9] With the coming of the jet age many of the older pilots were to retire, among them was Joe Kayll who eventually retired in 1951.Early in the year 2,000 Joe Kayll DFC, DSO, OBE fighter pilot and prison escapee died.

KAYLL NOTES

1. Group photograph of 607 Squadron taken at Summer Camp at Abbotsinch, Glasgow, 1939.
2. A documentary film and accompanying book, *Their Finest Hour*. People who had lived through the Battle of Britain.
3. Mason, *Battle Over Britain*, pages 195–196; Shores, *Aces High*; and Wynn, *Men of the Battle of Britain* all state that Kayll shot down this aircraft.
4. Ramsey: *The Battle of Britain Then and Now* awards this aircraft to Sgt Robinson of 111 Squadron.

5. Mason, P 315 states that this aircraft was damaged by Hurricanes led by Kayll.
6. Ramsey, P 604 states of the crash, 'Cause not stated'.
7. Smith R.G.: *Hornchurch Offensive, Vol 2*, P 17. However, further evidence can be seen in Johnson and Lucas' *Winged Victory*, P 45–46. The authors state; 'A few days after his (Kayll's) arrival, the Wing Leader had harsh words with his Station Commander about who would lead the Wing on a Circus over France. As usual rank prevailed and Broadhurst led with Kayll flying as his number two'.
8. Max Arthur: *There Shall Be Wings*, P 260.
9. Photograph from personal collection of Sqdn Ldr George Dudley Craig.
10. Photograph from personal collection of Sqdn Ldr George Dudley Craig.

Ronald Gustave Kellett, DFC, DSO, 90082
Squadron Leader

Ronald Gustave Kellett was born November 13, 1909, the fifth son of Mr and Mrs M.H. Kellett, at Bishop Auckland in County Durham. The family later moved north to Biddick Hall near Chester-Le-Street on the edge of the Durham mining field. Mr Kellett senior was a mining engineer and coalmine owner. Education for the young Kellett was by way of Rossal School in the Lancashire town of Fleetwood. The young Kellett showed signs of having a political career in mind, or at least the aspirations, for he stood as the Conservative candidate for Chester-Le-Street. He was later to seek a career in the city and became a member of the stock exchange where he began his career with Messers Lawrence, Keen and Gardener.

With the emergence of the Auxiliary Air Force, Kellett decided that he would like to fly. To meet this end, Kellett joined 600 (City of London) Auxiliary Air Force Squadron, the squadron then being based at Hendon. Kellett was commissioned to the rank of Pilot Officer (Aux AF) on March 20, 1934. At the summer camp, held that year at Sutton Bridge, the Auxiliaries were to claim 96.3 per cent in air firing. This score was higher than the regular RAF squadrons and Kellett was among those who performed well.

Working in London and flying during his spare time, his promotion within the Auxiliary Air Force was to follow him. Kellett was promoted to the rank of F/O (Aux AF) September 20, 1935 and then Flt Lt (Aux AF) September 20. 1938. It is possible that shortly after this date Kellett made the move north to Yorkshire. Shores[1] was to make the claim that Kellett was from Tadcaster, a small town between York and Leeds. What is known for sure is that Kellett was transferred to 616 (South Yorkshire) Squadron. The squadron was at that time based at Doncaster. Kellett was to make this move on January 30, 1939. Number 616 Squadron had only come into existence the previous November. Experienced pilots were posted in to 616 Squadron at this time both to help train the pilots on their new aeroplane, the Spitfire and, to give experienced strength to the squadron. Kellett was to take up the post of Flight Commander.

Kellett was called to full-time service on August 25, 1939. He was now a Flight Lieutenant in the RAF. Kellett was soon on the move again when he was posted from 616 to 249 Squadron. Kellett was once more to help with the building of a new squadron, Number 249, as he took up his post of Flight Commander. Number 249 was being formed at Church Fenton and Kellett, along with F/O J.R.C. Young, were the first two pilots to join the squadron arriving there, in a Fairey Battle (N 2027), in early May of 1940. Kellett, by this time having somehow gained the nickname (Boozy), was to command 'A' flight.

The squadron still had no operational aircraft at this time but were to be equipped with the Hawker Hurricane. The first two Hurricanes were flown in to Church Fenton on May 16, having been collected from 19 Maintenance Unit (MU) at St Athen. However, some confusion got into the works at this time. Only two days later, a signal was received by the squadron, stating that it had to move to nearby Leconfield. They were to leave their new Hurricanes at Church Fenton and take over the Spitfires at Leconfield. The new Hurricanes were finally transferred to 242 Squadron. Confusion was to follow on 249 Squadron; however, the squadron received a further signal, June 11, stating that they were once more to become a Hurricane squadron. Kellett was now promoted to the rank of Squadron Leader and, the squadron now equipped with their new Hurricanes once more, were ready to go to war.

Kellett was known throughout the squadron as being a fairly wealthy man. He was variously described as being rather stout and shy, patient, irascible, charming and abominably rude. He was also known for his eccentricities. He went about his daily duties chauffeuring himself in his yellow Rolls Royce. This car was also loaned out to the squadron as the squadron transport. Neither was Kellett known for his mechanical 'feel'. Part of the flight commander's tasks was the training of 'rookie' plots on the squadron. Training on the Hurricane was carried out on one of the Miles Masters. Kellett, in the back seat, would give great bursts of engine in his normal heavy-handed style, knocking the throttle back and forth. Many of the squadrons' junior pilots were given this treatment. One of these, P/O Thomas Francis Neil, was to describe such a flight;[2] '... springing about like a demented gazelle with the engine howling in agonised protest'.

Kellett was to remain with 249 Squadron only until they had worked up into a fighting unit. Before 249 Squadron moved south, Kellett had been posted July 19, 1940. Once more Kellett's finesse was needed in the forming of a new squadron. However, it was to be a much more serious challenge. The squadron was 303 (Warsaw Kosciusco) Squadron: its pilots all being Polish, it was to be the first Polish squadron in the RAF. Although Kellett was the RAF leader of the squadron, leadership was shared with his polish counterpart, Squadron Leader Z. Krasnodebski. So far in the fighting, the Poles had been kept away from the action and were held in reserve. The reasoning behind this move being, according to some, they had lost their chance in the early part of the war. They had lost the air fight for their own country, how could they defend ours? However, other reasoning points to the fact that few of the Poles could speak English. With the constant RAF 'banter' over the radio, they ran the risk of not being understood. This may well have put not only themselves in danger but, also their comrades. By August attitudes had changed. These pilots were much needed by the RAF. New pilots coming on to the operational squadrons were mostly 'raw' and untrained. What was not generally accepted during this period was that the Poles were fully trained fighter pilots before they came to England.

August 30, 1940, was to prove a momentous day for Kellett and 303 Squadron. Kellett was leading 303 Squadron on a training sortie. After leaving Northolt at 4.15 PM, 303 Squadron were to rendezvous with a formation of Blenheim bombers, the purpose being to carry out practice attacks on the bombers. On nearing the rendezvous point a formation of upwards of sixty Do 17s crossed their path. Above and behind them the ever-present fighter escort of Me 109s were stacked and waiting. One of the Polish pilots, Ludwig 'Paszko' Paszkiewicz saw the enemy formation and called out his observations to Kellett. Failing to hear any reply from his leader' if there was any, 'Paszko' went into the attack firing at a Do 17 until it burst into flames. On their return to Northolt, the Poles were made operational later that evening.

On the following day, August 31, Kellett was again leading a patrol to the east of Biggin Hill. At around 6.25 PM Kellett spotted a formation of bombers with their escort crossing his flight path. At the head of Red Section, Kellett manoeuvred the squadron, keeping the sun at his back, and attacked the formation gaining complete surprise. Singling out an Me 109 he gave it a burst seeing the fighter swerve to the side before its nose pitched up into a stall. Diving away to the left it was seen to burst into flames.

During the afternoon of September 5, the Luftwaffe launched an attack against the oil storage tanks at Thameshaven. Number 303 Squadron had been scrambled at 3.05 PM and encountered the bombers, mostly Ju 88s. Noticing the heavy fighter presence, Kellett leading Red Section, attacked the latter. As they were about to attack the Me 109s, 303 Squadron were bounced by more Me 109s of the high escort and a turning dogfight developed. Picking out an Me 109, Kellett gave it a few deflection shots following these up with a longer burst. The Me 109 burst into flames spewing its oil over Kellett's Hurricane in the process. Looking around for further targets, Kellett gave another Me 109 several deflection shots seeing his fire strike home along its engine cowling. Kellett had by now exhausted his ammunition as he watched the Me 109 dive vertically out of the fight. Kellett himself now became a target as another Me 109 attacked his Hurricane. Taking evasive action Kellett managed to extricate himself from the fight and return to Northolt. The first Me 109 shot down by Kellett had been that of Oblt Lammers of 1/JG 3 (Udet). Lammers was posted missing.[3]

Action came to 303 Squadron on the morning of September 6. The squadron was scrambled at 8.40 AM to intercept a large formation approaching Kent. This formation was intercepted over Sevenoaks and was described by Kellett as; 'The largest he had ever seen' The formation stretching some twenty miles in width. However, 303 Squadron were to arrive on the scene too late. Only two Hurricanes got through to the bombers, Kellett and Karubin. The rest of the squadron was badly bounced by Me 109s while they were still in the climb. Two of 303 Squadron's Hurricanes managed to get in good bursts at the bombers. Kellett was one. Seeing hits along the engine cowling of one bomber, his fire causing black smoke to issue from the bomber. Kellett turned to deliver another attack but, this was thwarted by an Me 109. The manoeuvre caused Kellett to make a steep diving turn to avoid the attentions of the Me 109. However, Kellett did not get away unscathed. His Hurricane had been hit. As he manoeuvred his Hurricane he found there was little response from the controls. Kellett was forced to make a heavy landing near Biggin Hill. On landing Kellett found that he had also been slightly wounded in the affray. Even worse, the squadron had lost seven Hurricanes.

The squadron was back in the air early the following day. Before 5.00 AM the squadron was patrolling at 20,000 feet when they met an enemy formation. Above and to the rear were the fighter escort consisting of Me 109s and 110s. The Poles attacked the bomber formation from out of the sun. Kellett's words best describe the scene; 'We gave them all we'd got, opening fire at 450 yards and only breaking away when we could see the enemy completely filling the gunsight. That means we finished the attack at point-blank range. We went in practically in one straight line, all of us blazing away'.[4] It was reported that almost a quarter of the bombing force were either destroyed or damaged during this attack. Of course attacks like this one rarely go without payment. On this occasion, 303 Squadron lost four Hurricanes with two pilots wounded.

Kellett led a formation of nine Hurricanes away from Northolt at 2.20 PM, September 15. Vectored towards Gravesend, they sighted a large formation of Do 17s approaching from the southeast. Ignoring the fighters Kellett, leading Blue Section, led the Poles in an attack on the bomber formation. Kellett closed in to attack a Do 17 at close range. Firing in short bursts he saw results as his fire struck the bomber in both fuselage and engines. Before he had time to see the outcome of his attack, Kellett's Hurricane came under attack by three Me 110s and was forced to take severe avoiding action. Kellett's Hurricane, V 7465, had taken a few hits. Not to be put off by slight damage, Kellett had managed to evade his pursuers in some convenient cloud cover. He now turned back into the fray. Kellett attacked a Me110. This was a Me110 of 13/LG 1. Kellett got in at least two good bursts and saw the starboard engine hit prior to the wing erupting in flames. The pilot, Lt Ernst Gorisch, was killed and Uffz Gerigk, the rear gunner, was posted missing. Once again the price was high and 303 Squadron were to lose three Hurricanes and one pilot.

September 26 brought a visit from the King. As if on cue for a demonstration, the scramble bell sounded at 4.00 PM and 303 Squadron, in company with some Hurricanes from 229 Squadron, were off. At first the formation was vectored towards Guilford then they were turned towards Portsmouth. A raid was plotted approaching the Spitfire works at Woolston. However, the formation arrived on the scene too late to catch the bombers. Neither did they attack as a wing, as had been the intention. The wing had become spread out in the climb. Kellett led the rest of the formation in an attack against the fighter escort. Kellett picked out the leader of the formation for his attack. His fire struck home and the Me 109 burst into flames with the pilot losing control before his aircraft crashed into the sea. During this action, Kellett received a call to abort the mission. Luckily, Kellett refused to listen. The call, although carrying the proper call sign, was a German diversion. In the middle of the fight, flying at full throttle, the throttle lever of Kellett's Hurricane, V 6681, became jammed fully open. When Kellett managed to get it to work properly, he was too far away to do anything further. The throttle incident brings to mind the recollections of Tom Neil when flying with 249 Squadron earlier in the year.

On September 27, Kellett led 'A' Flight in Hurricane P 3901. On this occasion he was to make a claim for one Me 109 as a probable. On October 1, 1940, Kellett was awarded the DFC, the citation for this award reading; 'Squadron Leader Kellett has built up and trained his personnel to such a fine fighting pitch that no fewer than 113 enemy aircraft have been destroyed in one month, with few casualties to his own squadron'. Kellett was once again to lead the Poles into the attack on October 5 over Lympne; 303 Squadron tangled with the high escort of Me 109s and110s at 11.40am. The Me 110s, in order to defend themselves, had formed into a defensive circle. Some 7,000 feet above the Me 110s were the usual Me 109s at around 25,000 feet.

As they dropped down towards the Hurricanes, a massive dogfight was set in motion only to end in total confusion. Each force gradually withdrew, as if by mutual consent. Kellett could only make a claim for one Me 109 as damaged.

Following his award of the DFC, Kellett was awarded the DSO, October 25, 1940. This was followed, December 24, by the award of the polish Virtuti Militari (5th class). Later in the same month, Kellett was posted away from 303 Squadron. His new posting taking him to Cranage, Cheshire. There he was once again to form a squadron, this time Number 96 Squadron. This squadron was to become primarily a night fighter squadron flying a mixture of Boulton Paul Defiant's and Hurricanes.

In March of 1941 Kellett was once more on the move. Kellett was placed in command of the North Weald Wing. The Wing taking regular part in offensive sweeps over the Continent. Later in this year Kellett was taken off operational flying and sent to the Air Ministry in London where he later became the Member for training. From 1943 through to the end of the war in 1945, Kellett worked on instructional duties. First at the Army Staff College and later at the RAF Staff College finishing his career with the RAF on attachment to the Turkish Air Force in Ankara. In 1945 Kellett was released from RAF service with the rank of Wing Commander.

Back in civilian life, Kellet made a return to the Stock Exchange. In June of 1946 the Royal Auxiliary Air Force was reformed. Kellett rejoined in July of the same year, dropping his rank to Squadron Leader (Aux AF) in order to do so. Kellett became the Commanding Officer of 615 Squadron. The squadron was at that time being equipped with the Spitfire Mk XIV and the F 21. In order to help in the encouragement of recruits, Kellett along with his adjutant Flight Lieutenant F.B. Sowrey, bought an old Walrus amphibious aircraft for the grand total of £150. This they flew from its old home in Ireland back to England. The old Walrus was put to use giving groundcrew air experience, a service that they could not enjoy otherwise. The old Walrus was also employed in transporting the ground personnel to their summer camps up and down the coast.

Seeing the first of the new age jet aircraft, the Gloster Meteor, into the Royal Auxiliary Air Force, Kellett retired the following year. In November of 1998 Ronald Gustave Kellett died.

Kellett Notes
1. Shores: *Aces High*, P 198.
2. Wng Cmdr Tom F. Neil: *Gun Button To Fire*.
3. Ramsey: *The Battle of Britain Then and Now*, P 263. States that these events occurred at 10.30 AM.
4. Grp Cpt Peter Townsend, *Duel of Eagles*, P 391.

Neville Charles Langham-Hobart, 77792
Pilot Officer

Neville Charles Langham-Hobart was born in Tynemouth in the first quarter of 1912. He was one of two children born to Frank and Hilda Daisy, formerly Strutton, Langham-Hobart, the family home at this time being Number 3, Newborough Crescent in the Jesmond area of the City of Newcastle upon Tyne. He was later to be educated at the Royal Grammar School in the City of Newcastle upon Tyne. Little is known of his life at this time.

In August of 1939, Langham-Hobart joined the Auxiliary Air Force. Travelling to Usworth in County Durham where he was an airman under training as a pilot. However, his training was cut short by the outbreak of the Second World War. In September of 1939 Langham-Hobart was called to full time service. His first posting was to Peterborough where he was to resume his training at Number 7 Flying Training School (FTS). During March 1940 Langaham Hobart was posted to his first fighter squadron, Number 611 (West Lancashire) Squadron. As its title implies, 611 was an Auxiliary Air Force Squadron. The squadron was flying the Spitfire from its base at Digby a few miles to the south of Lincoln. It is not clear if Langham-Hobart was just not up to flying the Spitfire or if there was some other reason for posting him. Either way he was soon on the move again for his next stop was to be Sutton Bridge.

Langham-Hobart arrived at Sutton Bridge April 28, 1940, to convert onto the Hawker Hurricane. Completion of his conversion was carried out without mishap and Langham-Hobart was posted on to Number 73 Squadron, arriving on the squadron May 11. Langham-Hobart's posting can be seen as being thrown in at the deep end. With little training, only enough to be acquainted with the Hurricane, Langham-Hobart was sent to France to take his place on a front line squadron.

One of the first RAF Hurricane squadrons to be posted to France, 73 Squadron was part of the Air Component of the Advanced Air Striking Force and was based only a short distance from the Franco-German border at Rouvres. It was from around this time that Langham-Hobart came to be known as plain Hobart or by his nickname, 'Hangman' Hobart, an anagram of his hyphenated name.

The squadron was at a full strength of twelve Hurricanes when it set out on an offensive patrol, May 19, 1940. A formation of enemy aircraft was sighted, consisting mainly of He 111s with a smaller number of Ju 88s, 73 Squadron attacked. Above and behind the bomber force was a formation of Me110s stacked up in two layers. The fighter escort was left as the Hurricanes moved in to attack the bombers. Two of the bombers were already diving earthwards, trailing smoke, before the escorting fighters became aware of what was happening. When the escorting fighters did become aware of what was happening, a dogfight broke out from which two Hurricanes were seen to fall. One of these being the Hurricane of Langham-Hobart.

One of the pilots on 73 Squadron, Sgt L. Pilkington, kept a diary at the time and recorded his observations of the above. 'Two pilots force landed today P/O 'Hangman' Hobart and Thompson'. Langham-Hobart had been able to guide his stricken Hurricane down and made a reasonable wheels up, rough belly landing. The landing was responsible for causing his only injuries, two bruised and swollen knees, the aftermath of colliding with the dashboard of his Hurricane. Later that same evening Langham-Hobart returned to his unit at Rouvres only a little bit worse for wear. As 73 Squadron had been one of the first fighter squadrons in France, they were one of the last to leave. Leaving after the fall of Dunkirk. Departing from France, June 17, they flew back to England and were reformed at Church Fenton. There they were to rest and rebuild the squadron.

Number 73 Squadron were to remain in the north for a while, not moving south again until early September. September 5, 1940, was their first operational day in the south, during the Battle of Britain. While based at Church Fenton, August 15, one flight of 73 Squadron had been involved in the air fighting near Bridlington when Luftflotte Five made its attack against the North East. On their first day in battle, 73 Squadron did not come out of it very well. In a vicious dogfight, 73 Squadron were to lose three of their Hurricanes with a further three damaged but repairable. One of those shot down was the Commanding Officer M.W.S. Robinson, who was unhurt.

September 7 saw the Luftwaffe launch a large raid against London. While the bombers carried out their attacks, the Me 110s of the fighter escort formed circles over Croydon as they waited to escort their charges back home. After being scrambled into action, 73 Squadron became involved in a turning dogfight with the waiting Me 110s. One of the Me110s found itself detached from the defensive circle and was singled out by Langham-Hobart. This Me 110 was a Do version, known in the Luftwaffe as a 'Dora'. Due to its extended range, the 'Dora' was being used more frequently in escort duties over the south. This particular aircraft was numbered 3334 (A2+NH) and was operated by 11/ZG 2. This aircraft was to crash at Park Corner Farm near Hornchurch. It crew of Lt Schonemann and Uffz Meschede were both killed, the latter when his parachute failed to deploy due to bailing out too low.

Number 73 Squadron were to be moved further north, firstly to Debden then on to Castle Camps, Cambridge. Number 73 Squadron had suffered a catastrophic day on the afternoon of September 14. The squadron lost six of its Hurricanes in one afternoon. Spitfires shot down two of these, due to bad controlling. September 23 saw a large formation building up over France. This plot was followed as it moved to the English coast where it fanned out as it crossed the coast of Kent. Some two hundred aircraft in all, with the largest majority being fighter aircraft. The intention appeared to be to draw the fighters of the RAF into a battle with the escorting fighters. Once again 73 Squadron were to fare badly at the hands of the Me 109s, losing four of their Hurricanes. One of those that fell was Hurricane L 2036, the Hurricane flown by Langham-Hobart. In a turning dogfight with Me 109s, Langham-Hobart's Hurricane had been badly hit and set on fire.

Langham-Hobart had decided that his Hurricane was still flyable as he decided to ditch it. The fire obviously became worse as he got nearer the ground, however, Langham-Hobart managed to ditch his Hurricane near Lightship 93 in the Thames Estuary. Langham-Hobart was eventually rescued by the Royal Navy and when brought ashore was admitted to the Royal Navy Hospital at Chatham. At a later date Langham-Hobart was transferred to the Queen Victoria Hospital at East Grinstead, there to become one of Sir Archibald McIndoe's 'Guinea Pigs'. These men, many of them rebuilt both mentally as well as physically, later formed their own club—The Guinea Pig Club. The sole criteria for membership being that a member had to have been badly burned and given their life back by McIndoe.

On March 7, 1941, Langham-Hobart was promoted to the rank of Flying Officer and posted to the Ministry of Aircraft Production. He was later posted to Canada where he took a special navigation course and was to instruct on the subject. The rest of Langham-Hobart's career involved postings with a navigational background. On one of these he was posted to HQ 13 Fighter Group, Newcastle where he became Navigation Officer. More posts were to follow all with a navigation theme before Langham-Hobart was released from the RAF in September of 1945 with the rank of Squadron Leader. Langham-Hobart died in his home of Ponteland, Northumberland in September of 1994. He was cremated at the West Road Crematorium, Newcastle upon Tyne.

JOHN LONSDALE, 81682
PILOT OFFICER

John Lonsdale was born at Stockton-on-Tees in 1914. He was the son of Robert and Esther Lonsdale. It is believed that in the year 1937 John Lonsdale joined the Auxiliary Air Force as a tradesman. Certainly, John Lonsdale was a member of Number 608 (North Riding) Squadron which was then based at Thornaby only a few short miles to the south of Stockton-on-Tees. At this time the squadron was a fighter unit flying the Hawker Demon. From March 20, 1939, the squadron was redesignated as a general reconnaissance unit. To carry out their new role, the squadron relinquished their Demons and took on charge the Avro Anson—a twin-engine reconnaissance aircraft. Shortly after this date, in May 1939, John Lonsdale made the decision to change his role within the Auxiliary Air Force. He applied for pilot training and, on being accepted, he remustered as an airman under training as a pilot.

In all probability Lonsdale began his pilot training with 608 Squadron. However, on August 24, 1939, 608 (North Riding) Auxiliary Air Force Squadron was embodied into the RAF. Lonsdale was called to full time service on the same date. Little is known of his movements at this time.[1] However, it is known that by June 29, 1940, Lonsdale had completed his training schedule and had been commissioned with the rank of Pilot Officer. The following month Lonsdale was posted to his first fighter squadron this was to be Number 3 Squadron.

Number 3 Squadron were equipped with the Hawker Hurricane.

This aircraft had replaced the squadron's Gloster Gladiators in April of 1938. Little action came the way of 3 Squadron during what came to be known as the 'phoney war'. However, with the German Blitzkrieg of May 1940, 3 Squadron were sent to France as one of the squadrons sent to reinforce the hard pushed Air Component of the Advanced Air Striking Force (AASF). As with most other squadrons, Number 3 Squadron were to suffer severely at the hands of the more battle experienced Luftwaffe. The remains of 3 Squadron were returned to England and posted to Wick in Scotland to re-equip and rebuild the squadron. It was while Number 3 Squadron were based at Wick that they were joined by P/O John Lonsdale in July of 1940.

Apart from building the squadron strength, Number 3 Squadron carried out practices and trained its new pilots, such as Lonsdale, in the art of aerial combat. Number 3 Squadron were also responsible for the air defence of the naval base at Scapa Flow and its approaches. Squadrons based at Wick saw little action. There was no mass raid to contend with in the area and the only likely targets being the sporadic raiders. These were usually of the hit and run type. Other visitors being the high altitude reconnaissance flights that were mainly flown from Norway. The latter flying mainly in the early hours of the day, using their high altitude to avoid the defending fighters. They were not, therefore, the easiest of targets. Accidents, and there were more than a few, were the main cause of casualties at Wick.

The monotony for Number 3 Squadron was broken on the morning of July 25, 1940. A He 111 of Wekusta 1 was carrying out a reconnaissance flight in the vicinity of Scapa Flow. A patrol consisting of F/O Denys A.E. Jones and P/O John Lonsdale was sent off to locate the enemy aircraft. The pair successfully located the lone He 111 and carried out their attacks. The He 111 coded (T5+AL), was shot down and crashed into the sea off Pentland Firth at around 8.30 AM. The crew of the He 111, Uffz Bauck, Gefr Muller and two other NCOs were killed. The pilot, Franken, had managed to survive the initial crash and make use of his dinghy. He was rescued, and taken prisoner by a Royal Navy destroyer that picked him up a few miles off Rora Head. Lonsdale was awarded a half share in the kill.[2]

Unfortunately for Number 3 Squadron, they were forced to sit out the rest of the Battle of Britain in relative seclusion in various bases in Scotland. Consequently the squadron was to see very little action at all during this period. Practices and patrols were the order of the day mixed in with other flying duties.

By October of 1940, Number 3 Squadron had moved further south to Turnhouse, Edinburgh. On October 1, 1940, Lonsdale was flying on a routine patrol, probably a cross-country flight, when he came to grief. Flying Hurricane P 3261, Lonsdale was flying over Lanarkshire, to the south of Glasgow, when he experienced what he thought was engine trouble. Lonsdale came to the conclusion that the Hurricane could not continue; neither did he want to abandon his Hurricane. He therefore decided to make a forced landing. This he did without injury to himself but with more than a little damage to the Hurricane, which was more than slightly bent.

The maintenance crew duly arrived on site to recover the Hurricane. They carried out an inspection to discover the cause of the engine failure. After examining the controls and cockpit, the maintenance crew came the conclusion that the fault lay with Lonsdale. Lonsdale had somehow mishandled the fuel cock in the cockpit, causing fuel starvation which in turn caused the apparent engine failure.[3] No doubt Lonsdale was more than a little embarrassed on his return to Turnhouse. Hurricane P 3261 was the fourth from last aircraft built in the first production batch 500 built by Gloster Aircraft Co Ltd at their Brockworth factory.

Things were to pick up for Lonsdale at a later date, however. On June 29, 1941, Lonsdale was promoted to the rank of Flying Officer and, one year later he was promoted to the rank of Flight Lieutenant, June 29, 1942. John Lonsdale was to remain with Number 3 Squadron for the rest of his flying career. Number 3 Squadron were to keep their trusty Hurricanes but were to move on to other variants. Firstly they were equipped with the Mk 2B, the fighter-bomber variant. These were to give way in turn to the Mk 2C, the cannon armed variant. Number 3 Squadron being the first squadron to be equipped with this variant of the Hurricane. Operations at this time were being carried out at low level against ground targets on the Continent. With their cannon armed variants Number 3 Squadron went on the fighter sweeps against ground targets as well as anti shipping missions.

On November 26, 1942, John Lonsdale was killed in action, presumably on a fighter sortie. He was twenty-eight years old. His body was returned to his home in the Norton area of Stockton-on-

Tees where it was buried in Durham Road Cemetery. John Lonsdale is buried in section C1 C of E row B grave number 24. He left a widow, Doris Ledgerwood Lonsdale.

LONSDALE NOTES

1. An uncaptioned photograph of Lonsdale's training days survives. This is shown in *The Battle of Britain: Then and Now Mk V*, P xxii. Pilot's names are given and it is thought that John Lonsdale sits second from the left, front row.

2. Ramsey: *Battle of Britain Then and Now* states that the He 111 was shot down 'off Pentland Firth'. However, Pentland Firth is the channel between the northernmost tip of Scotland and the Orkney Islands. Rora Head, given as the point where the pilot was picked up is not marked on the map. However, Rora lies over seventy miles to the south of the crash site. Mason states that this He 111 was shot down, '… near Wick', P 193.

3. Ramsey: *The Battle of Britain Then and Now* states that this Hurricane was, 'a write off,' P 491. Mason states that it was, 'damaged', P 427. The latter would appear, due to the controlled landing of the Hurricane, to be the more likely.

Ernest Mayne, 46324
Warrant Officer

There are many myths that surround the Battle of Britain. Many of these have been preached so often that they are now passed off as truth. One of these myths is that the pilots who fought in the Battle of Britain were young men: boys even. As with everything in history, if someone sets up a theory along will come someone else to knock it down. Ernest Mayne is one of those pilots who fought the Battle of Britain who seem to have been born to break myths. Ernest Mayne was born when Queen Victoria was still on the throne. At least he was born in the last year of her reign. Ernest Mayne was born January 2, 1901. He was the son of a fitter, also named Ernest, who worked in local industry, and his wife Isabella Mayne. At the time of Ernest Mayne's birth the family lived in Number 23, Fifth Avenue, Byker, an area known for its hard working industrial connections in the east end of the City of Newcastle upon Tyne.

Like many young men of Newcastle, Ernest Mayne marched out of the City of Newcastle and went to fight in the Great War of 1914/18. Mayne flew with what was then, the RFC. The RAF did not come into being until May of 1918. When the RFC became the newly formed RAF Ernest Mayne was transferred to its ranks. It is thought that during the mid war years of early military flying, Ernest Mayne flew on the North-West Frontier. The RAF was carrying out policing duties there.

Little more is known of Mayne during this time. However, it is known that he was still in the ranks of the RAF during 1935. At this

Ernest Mayne circa 1935. Pilot to the left is "Sailor" Malan.

date he was part of what was known as the 'Demons Flight'. This flight being equipped, as its title suggests, with the Hawker Demon. This Flight was part of three flights that were moved out to Malta for policing duties in the Middle East. At a later date, the three Flights were formed into one squadron. This squadron was given the Number 74. A squadron that had first flown with great distinction during the First World War: and known as the 'Tigers'; now it was reborn. The rebirth of 74 Squadron became official as from November 14, 1935. Ernest Mayne was one of the squadron's pilots. At this time 74 Squadron were based at Halfar, Malta and, as its earlier name suggests, it was flying the Demon. The Hawker Demon was to remain as 74 Squadron's compliment until April of 1937. Originally earmarked to take on charge the Gloster Gladiator, a sudden change of policy made 74 Squadron the last in the RAF to be equipped with the Gloster Gauntlet.

February 13, 1939 brought further change, for the better. On this day, 74 Squadron took on charge its first Spitfire. Along with it came a Fairey Battle equipped with a Spitfire blind flying panel for training purposes. Ernest Mayne, from around this time, was known to all as 'Tubby'. From photographs, the name was not misplaced. Ernest Mayne was bulky to the point where it defied logic how he could fit into a Spitfire cockpit; the cockpit of the Spitfire was known for its tight fit.

Mayne was an experienced pilot, used to flying in all weathers. During this period, Mayne was often picked to fly Spitfires through thick, heavy cloud in an attempt to find a way around the persistent problem of the windscreen icing up, a fault common in early Spitfires. Fellow pilot, P/O H.M. Stephen was later to say of Mayne; 'If ever there was a difficult or dirty job to do, invariably Mayne got it'.[1] It took an experienced pilot to sort out the difficult jobs, especially on a new fighter such as the Spitfire. At this time Mayne was classed as a very experienced pilot. Mayne's logbook showed over eighteen hundred flying hours at this time.[2]

It was on September 6, 1939, that 74 Squadron were involved in what became known as 'The Battle of Barking Creek'. It was presumed by ground defences that the City of London was about to come under attack from enemy forces. Both flights of 74 Squadron were scrambled into action at 6.55 AM. Also in the air were aircraft from 56, 65, 54 and 151 Squadrons. After what can only be described as a major blunder, 74 Squadron shot down two Hurricanes of 56 Squadron. One of these pilots being killed in the action. Mayne's logbook merely states that he was on 'operations'. The flight being of fifty minutes duration. On the same date as the above, Mayne along with the rest of 'B' flight, carried out some aerial filming. This was for the flying sequences in a feature film; *The Lion Has Wings*, The stars of the film being Ralph Richardson and Merle Oberon. For Mayne, his contribution to Hollywood was two flights. One of twenty-five minutes and the other of thirty-five minutes duration. The first flight took place on September 6, while the second took place on September 20, both flights being carried out from Rochford.

On September 21, 1939, Mayne began a long association with Spitfire K 9871, coded ZP-O. Much of Mayne's flying time over the next few months was taken up with various air tests and practices. A mixture of high flying, formation flying, low flying and anti aircraft co-operation flights interspersed with the odd patrol. Number 74 Squadron were moved to Southend, October 22, 1939, for a few weeks detachment. The mixture of practices and attacks was to continue throughout the winter months. On December 16, 1939, Mayne was to fly his Spitfire from Southend back to Hornchurch. During take off Mayne somehow managed to injure his hand, an injury that was to keep Mayne away from flying until January 9, 1940, then it was back to the endless patrols.

From late May 1940, 74 Squadron were involved in covering the evacuation of Dunkirk, the squadron being moved from Leconfield to Hornchurch so that they were in flying distance. May 26 saw the 'Tigers' on their first patrol of the day over the Dunkirk beaches. A Henschel 126, a high wing, lightweight, reconnaissance aircraft, was spotted. The He 126 was flying was flying at low level, on a spotting mission, when it was attacked by a section of Spitfires led by Pilot Officer H.M. Stephen. P/O D.G. Cobden and Mayne being the other two in the section. The He 126 was shot down and all three shared the kill. Stephen was later to describe the episode; 'This was my first engagement and that explosion was pretty horrifying. I wasn't expecting it and it came as a terrible surprise'.[3] This was the first day of the withdrawal of the troops from the beaches. May 27 was to see the 'Tigers' once more make a claim for enemy aircraft destroyed. On this occasion the honours went to 'Paddy' Treacy and Ernie Mayne. Both making claims for Me109s destroyed.

During the early skirmishes over the English Channel in July, 74 Squadron were often in the action from their base at Manston. It was during a scramble at this time that Mayne was said to have suffered his most personal loss. As an ex-member of the RFC Mayne had continued to wear his RFC badge in his RAF cap. In part this was pride in his old unit, however, his old badge had become a talisman. During the scramble from Manston, Mayne had left his cap in the heat of the moment. On his return, it was to find that someone had relieved him of his cap along with his treasured cap badge. Ernie Mayne was said to be heartbroken at the loss. As far as can be ascertained, Mayne never saw his cap badge again.

Events soon forced Mayne's personal loss behind him. August was to be a busy month for Mayne and 74 Squadron. A heavy schedule of patrols was flown from both Hornchurch and Manston. Two, three and even four patrols per day were classed as the norm. However, most were fruitless and 74 Squadron failed to engage the enemy on many, if not most occasions during this period. The first actions against the enemy were to come on August 11, 1940. On this day Mayne was in the air on four occasions encountering the enemy on each occasion. On two of these encounters Mayne was to claim, in his logbook, that he shot down a Me109 and damaged another in each of the two patrols. He merely states that he was, '… in action against Me 109s', in the other two.

The events of August 11, began at around 7.49 AM. This was a probing attack in the area of Dover, which was met by 74 Squadron with success. On returning to base, 74 Squadron were scrambled once again at 9.50 AM. Several small groups of Me 109s were spotted once again in the area of Dover. The Me 109s on this occasion being on a 'free hunt'. 'Sailor' Malan was at the head of the squadron on this occasion, but unfortunately his radio was hit by a single bullet, rendering it useless. He could neither send nor receive messages. The result was that some of the squadron failed to engage the enemy at all. This did not affect Ernie Mayne so much as he was flying with his leader. Between them, 'Sailor' Malan and Ernie Mayne accounted for four Me 109s damaged and shared the honours.

Number 74 Squadron had only a short time in which to rearm and refuel their aircraft before they were once more called into the air, the squadron being airborne by 11.30 AM. The action on this occasion was over a convoy codenamed 'Booty' which was off Clacton. The squadron could only manage to get eleven Spitfires airborne on this occasion. At the head of the squadron was P/O 'Johnny' Freeborn in the absence of 'Sailor' Malan. A number of Do 17s escorted by a force of Me 110s were putting the convoy under attack.[4] On seeing the Spitfires; the Me 110s employed their usual defensive tactic of forming a circle. Freeborn ignored the defensive tactics and led the 'Tigers' straight through the centre in an attempt to break them up. Mayne is reported to have claimed an Me 110 as damaged during this action.[5]

Number 74 Squadron were once again scrambled at 1.56 PM. In the lead once more was 'Sailor' Malan as he led the squadron, now reduced to eight Spitfires, to the area of Harwich and Margate. Ten Ju 87s were spotted, while above them were some twenty Me 109s flying at around 10,000 feet. Mayne engaged the Me 109s of the fighter escort and, in a turning dogfight, found himself at 28,000 feet. There, while in the middle of the action, Mayne passed out due to oxygen starvation. Mayne's Spitfire, K 9871, then fell into a power dive at full throttle. His Spitfire had dived through 20,000 feet before Mayne regained consciousness.

Managing to pull his Spitfire from its power dive, and probably straining every part of it in the process, Mayne found himself approaching the French coast. Ahead of him were, what he took, to be his comrades on 74 Squadron returning home. Approaching from the rear, Mayne was to find to his cost that the 'friendly' formation was made up of Me109s returning to France. Mayne had to make a swift departure, and some avoiding action, to make his escape from the German formation and return to Manston. Cossey[6] states that this was Mayne's last combat due to injury from his rapid descent, August 11. He states that Mayne's eardrums had burst and this had caused him to be taken off operational flying. The squadron was not flying on August 12, but Mayne was flying on August 13, albeit on a ferry flight. There is no doubt that Mayne was taken off operational flying. However, there may have been another reason. It has been suggested by Ira Jones[7] that the powers that be had eventually caught up with Mayne, removing him from flying due to his age. At this time Mayne was thirty-nine and a bit long in the tooth to be hurling a Spitfire around the sky.

Mayne's usual Spitfire, K 9871 was handed over to Polish pilot P/O H. 'Sneezy' Szczesny who flew it on patrol August 13 and was forced to force land it. Thereafter, K 9871 was issued to a variety of Operational Training Units and squadrons. On December 21, 1943, K 9871 crashed on take off flying from Ouston in Northumberland. After being used for maintenance for a short period, it was finally struck off charge October 15, 1945. Mayne was to spend his last few days on 74 Squadron ferrying Spitfires between bases. When 74 Squadron moved to Kirton-in-Lindsey for a 'rest', it was without Mayne. Ernie Mayne was posted to Sutton Bridge to begin life as a flying instructor.

At Sutton Bridge, Mayne was to join 56 OTU. The instructional duties revolved around the Hawker Hurricane. Mayne's summary of assessments as an instructor placed him above average as both an instructor and a navigator as well as, not surprisingly given his experience, in air gunnery. On August 21, 1941, Mayne was commissioned and was awarded the AFC January 1, 1942. Mayne was further promoted to the rank of Flight Lieutenant, August 21, 1942. Mayne was to attend a course at the Central Gunnery School at Sutton Bridge from August 6 to September 2, 1942. While there he achieved an assessment of above average in gunnery, both in the air and air to ground. As an instructor he was described as exceptional and departed with an overall 'A' pass.

Mayne remained on flying duties and spent most of 1944 ferrying various people in a Miles Master. A departure from this routine was made May 24, 1944 when he treated himself to a local flight in a Spitfire. In May 1945 Mayne became Station Gunnery Officer at his old station of Manston. Mayne finally left the RAF, December 4, 1945 with the rank of Squadron Leader. His overall total of flying hours was 2, 595 hours and ten minutes.

With the end of hostilities Mayne settled in Kent and became a market gardener. Mayne also resumed his association with his old station of Manston. Ernie Mayne was instrumental in obtaining a Spitfire Mk XV1, TB 752 for Manston in 1956. When higher authority decided, at a later date, to scrap the Spitfire they did not reckon on the North East Battle of Britain fighting spirit of Ernie Mayne. He fought for, and won, the right for the Spitfire to remain at Manston. Today, the Spitfire and Hurricane Memorial Building at Manston still retains its Spitfire thanks to the efforts of Ernie Mayne. At the age of 77, Ernie Mayne died on March 24, 1978, at his home in Birchington on the Isle of Thanet in Kent; an area that Mayne had defended so often against the might of the Luftwaffe.

After his death, Mayne's widow, Mrs Pauline Mayne, presented her late husband's logbook to the Spitfire and Hurricane Memorial Building at Manston. The small museum set aside a special corner devoted to Squadron Leader Ernest 'Tubby' Mayne. The corner consists of a large, life size, oil painting of Mayne in full dress uniform. A selection of photographs and various pieces associated with the career of Ernie Mayne. Pride of place is given to the 'Tubby' Mayne's logbook, which remains on permanent display. A plaque is also on display, which informs the reader that, 'Tubby' Mayne was the oldest pilot on the British side, to have contested the Battle of Britain. However, his age at the time of the 'Battle' is given, inaccurately, as 42: he was 39 years old at the time.

Ernest Mayne may not have been one of the most distinguished pilots amongst 'the few' but he certainly was the oldest and, therefore, has a unique place in the Battle of Britain history. He was also, with over two thousand flying hours behind him, mostly on fighter aircraft, one of the most experienced men to fly in the Battle of Britain. It is rather odd, and telling, that Ernest 'Tubby' Mayne is remembered and respected as a 'war hero' in an area far away from the place of his birth. In his hometown of Newcastle upon Tyne, Mayne is unknown or worse, forgotten.

Mayne Notes

1. Correspondence between Sqdn Ldr H.M. Stephen and the Spitfire and Hurricane Memorial Hall, Manston.
2. Entry from Mayne's log book which is held by the Spitfire and Hurricane Memorial Hall, Manston.
3. Cossey: *Tigers*, P 67.
4. This was a convoy coded 'Booty' which was sailing about twelve miles off Clacton. Mason states that this convoy was placed under attack by Do 17s with an escort of Me 110s. Cossey in *Tigers*, P 75–76, and Wood and Dempster, *The Narrow Margin*, P 277, state that this attack was carried out by around forty Me 110s.
5. Cossey, P 76, claims that Mayne shot down one enemy aircraft in this action and damaged an Me 110. Mayne's logbook states only that he was in action against Me 109s, claiming one shot down and one damaged.
6. Cossey P 76, states that this was Mayne's last combat due to damage caused to his ears by the rapid descent, this led to Mayne being grounded.
7. Ira 'Taffy' Jones had originally served on 74 Squadron during the Great War. He was to keep in touch with the squadron throughout and after World War Two, as a result he new many of the pilots. Jones was later to write the first official squadron history of 74 Squadron, *Tiger Squadron*.

JAMES HENRY GORDON MCARTHUR, DFC, 37925
FLIGHT LIEUTENANT

Born in Tynemouth, February 12, 1913, his mother's former name had been Grant-Gordon, the Gordon part was handed down to her son, James Henry Gordon McArthur. McArthur was one of the North East pilots to be granted the status of 'ace'. In earlier times, McArthur had been educated at Rutherford College in the City of Newcastle upon Tyne. A technical career was the direction that McArthur wished to take. He was to combine this with an interest in aviation, an interest he had from an early age. In later years Mc Arthur was to be employed by British Continental Airways. McArthur was to fly with British Continental as a first officer.

As well as flying on the commercial routes, McArthur became involved in flying on record attempts. In 1935 he accompanied T. Campbell Black on his record flight from London to Cairo. While flying as co-pilot, McArthur also doubled up as radio operator. At a later date McArthur attempted another record. On this occasion it was to be the Cape. However, after a mishap, McArthur was forced to take to his parachute. During this period McArthur was based at Croydon, a developing airport on the southern side of London. After his escape by parachute, McArthur became the youngest member of the Caterpillar Club. The membership of this club being made up exclusively of those who had escaped from their aircraft by parachute. McArthur was also to hold the London to Baghdad record.

In 1936 McArthur decided on a career change. Moving from civil aviation he applied to join the RAF. Applying for a short service commission, McArthur was accepted. Initially McArthur was sent to Number 9 Flying Training School (FTS) at Thornaby on Tees near Middlesborough, arriving at his new base July 18, 1936. On completion of his training McArthur was posted to Aldergrove in Northern Ireland where he was to join the station flight on January 14, 1937. His experience in aviation was soon recognized and McArthur was posted to the Royal Aircraft Establishment at Farnborough, taking up his duties there from October 1, 1938, as a test pilot.

McArthur appears to have remained at Farnborough until he joined Number 238 Squadron on its formation in May of 1940. It would appear, that it was from around this time, that McArthur, because of his stocky build, acquired the nickname 'Butch'. During this period the squadron was based at Middle Wallop to the south of Andover. There it was to remain throughout the early part of the Battle of Britain. McArthur does not appear to have enjoyed much success during his stay with 238 Squadron. At a later date he was posted to 609 Squadron, also based at Middle Wallop. His move the short distance across the airfield was to take up the post of 'B' Flight commander from August 1, 1940. Where 238 Squadron had been equipped with the Hurricane, 609, an Auxiliary Air Force Squadron, was equipped with the Spitfire.

August 8, 1940 saw the convoy coded 'Peewit' passing through the English Channel, having set sail the previous day from the Thames Estuary. As it passed almost under the nose of the enemy, it was not surprising that they came out in force with a determined effort to destroy it. Large numbers of Ju 87s put the convoy under heavy attack, sinking around three ships. The Ju 87s were escorted by a formation of Me 109s. Number 609 Squadron joined in the battle between Weymouth and the Needles, taking on the Ju 87s. McArthur was to make a claim for one Ju 87 destroyed and another as probable.[1] A further formation of Me 110s arrived in the area over Portland. The formation was flying well ahead of the bomber force at an altitude of 23,000 feet. Number 609 Squadron, well placed for an attack, flew over the top of the Me 110s and attacked down the far side. This manoeuvre had the effect of denying the Me 110s the use of their heavy forward firing armament. The Me 110s had been slow to react to the bounce by 609 Squadron, as a result only two of 609 Squadron's Spitfires engaged the enemy. These were the Spitfires of P/O J.C.

Dundas and McArthur. McArthur, on this occasion, found himself cornered by an Me 110 and was forced to take severe avoiding action in order to extricate himself. This consisted of putting his Spitfire into a spin and spinning down some 15,000 feet. Later, McArthur was to admit that this manoeuvre had made him feel; '...rather unwell'.

The Luftwaffe carried out an attack, August 12, in a build up to the day that came to be known as 'Adler Tag'. This attack consisted of attacking the radar stations along the southern coast. An attempt to blind the RAF defences. Among the first to be attacked was Ventnor radar station. After being ordered off, 609 Squadron arrived on the scene too late to attack the bombers. However, their escort of Me 109s were still loitering in the area. A dogfight broke out over the needles with the Me 109s of JG 53. In the resulting melee, 609 Squadron was to lose three of its Spitfires and McArthur was to make a claim for an Me 110 as a probable.

The following morning was fairly quiet due to the poor weather conditions. However, with the afternoon came a large force of Ju 87s escorted by an equally large force of Me 109s, their task being to destroy the airfield of Middle Wallop. Number 609 Squadron were not at Middle Wallop at this time but at their forward base of at Warmwell. From there they were ordered into the air to intercept the incoming raid. Fortunately, the bomber force appeared to have got rather lost on this occasion. They had failed to find Middle Wallop and were in the act of attempting to find Warmwell. Others had already given up hope and turned for France. The fighter escort was running short of fuel by this time and were also considering a return to France. It was at this point that 609 Squadron came onto the scene and fell on the bomber force. McArthur had singled out an Me 109, but in a turning dogfight, which was inconclusive, he could only make a claim for one damaged.

August 15, 1940, the acknowledged date for the height of the Battle of Britain saw McArthur once more in action. On this occasion he was to claim two Me 110s as destroyed. One of these aircraft, an Me 110c of the Stab Flight 11/ZG 76 was to crash at West Wellow Farm near Romsey at 5.55 PM. Its crew of Uffz R. Rohrich and Uffz T. Neymeyer were both killed. McArthur had only a third share in this kill, sharing with F/O R.A. Barton of 249 Squadron and F/O A.R. Edge of 609 Squadron.

August 25, 1940, was to see McArthur making another claim. Number 609 Squadron had encountered a formation of Me 110s, McArthur had singled one out and was carrying out a determined attack continuing to press home his attack until the Me 110 crashed into the ground. An eyewitness was later to state what he saw as; '... a twin engined Me in a shallow descent with a British fighter hammering away at him until it hit the ground. The aircraft could have made a reasonable belly landing but it hit a rise in the ground and burst into flames'. McArthur was to make a further claim on this day for another Me 110 as destroyed. This aircraft was to crash at Priory Farm, East Holme at 6.00 PM. The crew of Uffz S. Becker and Obergefr W. Wopzel were both captured as well as being wounded.[2]

A large enemy force was en route to London, September 7, 1940. All of 10 Groups squadrons were in the air to meet the large force and were severely pushed. A call was hastily made to 11 Group for reinforcements. McArthur was leading the squadron on that day and already had them in the air when the call came through. Heading at full speed towards London, they were to arrive too late to attack the bombers before their bombs fell. The bombers were already leaving the area by a prearranged route that would take them over the southwest of the city. There, their fighter escort was waiting. Arriving on the scene too late, 609 Squadron were also at a height disadvantage as well as still being in the climb. McArthur's combat report sets out the story; '... I led the squadron into a quarter attack on a large number of twin engined and twin tailed bombers which I think must have been Do 17s. I went for the nearest bomber and opened fire at about 400 yards, meanwhile experiencing very heavy return cross-fire from the bomber formation. After about twelve seconds smoke started to come from the port motor and it left the formation. I broke away as there were many 110s and 109s behind. The bomber with one motor still pouring out thick smoke continued to lose height, so I waited until it got down to about 3,000 feet and then dived vertically on to it and fired off the rest of my ammunition (about 3 to 4 seconds). It kept going down seemingly under some sort of control, until it hit the water about ten miles out from the centre of the Thames Estuary'. This aircraft was reported later as a Do 17. Altogether 609 Squadron gained six confirmed kills in this action.

September 15 saw the Luftwaffe launch one of its largest raids to date in the Battle of Britain. Number 609 Squadron scrambled and in position, attacked the bombers along their flank as they flew across south London. McArthur was to make a claim for one Do 17 as damaged and one Me 110 destroyed. The fighter escort were flying at a much higher altitude during this raid. McArthur was attempting to meet the enemy on their terms, flying at a disadvantage. While still in the climb, McArthur's Spitfire dived away from the battle and fell into a steep dive. McArthur had suffered oxygen failure at high altitude, not an uncommon occurrence in the early marks of the Spitfire. With his Spitfire in a vertical power dive, heading for the ground at high speed, McArthur regained consciousness in time to save his Spitfire. However, the damage had been done. McArthur suffered severe internal ear damage due to the pressure change. Medical tests were later to prove that this damage was to be permanent. At the end of September, McArthur handed over command of 'B' Flight to F/O J.C. Dundas. Not only was the Battle of Britain over for McArthur but, so were his fighter days. McArthur lost his operational category, as he was not allowed to fly above 5,000 feet.

On October 21, 1940, McArthur was awarded the DFC. The citation for this award reads; 'This officer has led his flight and squadron with skill and determination. His gallant leadership has been reflected in the high standard of morale in his flight. He has destroyed at least seven enemy aircraft'.[3] On September1, 1941, McArthur was promoted to the rank of Squadron Leader and on January 1, 1944, he was further promoted to the rank of Wing Commander.

In 1947 McArthur was released from the RAF but was later to join the Royal Canadian Air Force. Eventually he was to gain the UN Korean War Medal and the Canadian Forces Decoration. In May 1961, while in the USA, McArthur was killed in a flying accident in Las Vegas.

McArthur Notes

1. Mason: *Battle Over Britain* gives these two aircraft in his lists.
2. Ramsey: *The Battle of Britain Then and Now*, P 598, does not mention McArthur. He gives this kill to two other pilots, P/O N.le C. Agazarian and P/O G.N. Gaunt. Both of these pilots were also on 609 Squadron. Shores, *Aces High*, gives this as McArthur's eighth victory.
3. Shores: *Aces High*, P 214, credits McArthur with eight confirmed victories.

John William McLaughlin, 146149
Sergeant

John William McLaughlin was born in 1920, the son of John William and Mary Ellen McLaughlin. The family home at this time was Number 88 Dibley Street in the Newcastle upon Tyne east end suburb of Byker. The young McLaughlin was an athletic young man who excelled in most sports. He became, what is known as an all-round sportsman. He played football for Gateshead AFC, being a goalkeeper. He also represented his county in water polo and was a member of the East-End ASC. A strong swimmer, he represented his county in the Northern Counties Amateur Championship. His youth and all-round fitness would play a big part in his survival in the future.

In 1939, with the war clouds gathering over Europe, McLaughlin like many of his contemporaries, decide to play his part in the defence of his country. The first step for McLaughlin was to join his local branch of the RAFVR, joining as an airman under training as a pilot, his part-time training beginning in July of 1939. Part-time training was brought to a halt for McLaughlin in September of 1939 when he was called to full time service. Training was to be carried out at Number 10 Flying Training School (FTS) at Ternhill near Sallop. After completion of his training and gaining his 'wings', McLaughlin was next posted to Number 6 Operational Training Unit (OTU) Sutton Bridge in Lincolnshire. Training began there August 17, 1940. McLaughlin was to be converted to the Hawker Hurricane.

Like almost all of the other fledgling pilots at that time,

McLaughlin was taught how to fly in formation, carry out aerobatics and generally get used to the handling of the Hurricane. He was not, however, taught to fight with the machine he would be asked to go to war with. This training was supposed to come later but, only if there was time. Usually there was none. McLaughlin was relatively lucky with his first posting. His new fighter squadron Number 238, was equipped with the Hurricane and was based at St Eval to the north of New Quay in the relative safety of west Cornwall. However, due to increasing pressure on the front line squadrons, more squadrons were needed to reinforce those already on the front line. Number 238 Squadron, therefore, was soon to find itself based within the battle zone at Middle Wallop.

Number 238 Squadron were in action from Middle Wallop from at least September 11. While on September 15 the squadron was to lose four of its Hurricanes in the heavy fighting over south London. September 26, 1940 saw the squadron lose a further three Hurricanes to the guns of the Me 110s of ZG 26 and a further three Hurricanes were to fall on September 28, again to the Me 110s and 109s. It is not clear if McLaughlin took part in any of these actions. However, due to the attrition within the squadron it is more than likely that he did, even if only to gain valuable experience. McLaughlin was certainly in action on October 5, 1940.

October 5, 1940, was an almost perfect day, weather wise, for the Luftwaffe's offensive. Bright periods intermixed with plenty of cloud to provide valuable cover from the enemy. The Luftwaffe was by now mounting swift, light raids allowing the fighters more time to deal with their British counterparts. Junkers Ju 88s were detailed to make an attack in the area of Southampton. Behind them were the fighter escort of Me 109s. Further behind and above were yet more Me 109s, some of their number carrying bombs to make swift attacks. Number 238 Squadron had been scrambled and were in position well in time, high over Dorset where they took on the fighter escort of Me 109s and 110s. On this occasion McLaughlin was flying in the lead group as Red 3 in Hurricane P 3611 coded VK-L. In the ensuing dogfight, McLaughlin found himself cornered and cut off from the rest. From somewhere an Me 109 appeared and found himself a target. McLaughlin's Hurricane was set ablaze at around 2.25 PM.

Of this period, McLaughlin was later to say that because he was real 'rookie' he felt very frightened waiting around for the scramble. This feeling was to alter when he came face to face with the enemy in the air. 'We knew we were going to be in a big fight'.[1] However, once the actual fighting got under way, the concentration took over and self preservation took came to the forefront. On the afternoon of October 5, McLaughlin was flying at high altitude when his Hurricane fell victim to the Me 109s of the high escort. During the combat, the wings of McLaughlin's Hurricane were blown off. Whether his cockpit hood was damaged or he was just a bit slow in getting it open, the result was the same. McLaughlin was to suffer severe burns. He could never remember how he escaped from his blazing Hurricane. All that remains in his memory was the sensation of falling over and over and that the ground came into view before his parachute eventually opened. With multiple burns and probably other injuries as well McLaughlin was admitted to Shaftsbury Hospital.[2]

The local press in McLaughlin's hometown of Newcastle was to give him a write up under the title of 'miracle boy'. The term 'miracle boy' was bestowed on him as he had made a remarkable recovery from very serious injuries which left him, according to the press story, '... dangerously ill for some weeks. No doubt his prowess in the sporting field came to McLaughlin's aid and his all round fitness helped him pull through. After his initial recovery McLaughlin was transferred to the Queen Victoria Hospital at East Grinstead. It was at this hospital that the rebuilding of lives of so many aircrew who, like McLaughlin, had suffered serious burns, was undertaken by the renowned plastic surgeon Sir Archibald McIndoe. These men suffered not only the rebuilding of their physical lives but their mental lives as well. Such was the spirit of these men that they formed their own society. This came to be known as the 'Guinea Pig Club'. The club taking its name from the fact that these men termed themselves as 'Guinea Pigs', no one having done this kind of work before.

The injuries suffered by McLaughlin October 5, 1940, not only ended McLaughlin's part in the Battle of Britain. It also ended his days as a pilot. He was later promoted to the rank of Warrant Officer and then commissioned with the rank of Pilot Officer, April 22, 1943. Later he was to be further promoted to the rank of Flying Officer,

October 22, 1943 and, finally to Flight Lieutenant April 22, 1945. McLaughlin was released from the RAF in 1946 with the rank of Flight Lieutenant. He was later to move to Australia, where he died June 16, 2001.

McLaughlin Notes

1. Interview in a TV documentary for the anniversary of the Battle of Britain, 2000.
2. Ramsey: *The Battle of Britain Then and Now*, states that there was only one Hurricane from 238 Squadron shot down on this day. However, rather oddly, he states that this was Squadron Leader J.R. Maclachlen. Not only did he get the name wrong but he promoted him as well. McLaughlin was a Sergeant at the time.

JOSEPH PEARSON MORRISON, 754728
SERGEANT

Joseph Pearson Morrison was born probably in January of 1915. Certainly his baptism took place on February 28 of that year, in the parish church of St Stephens, Elswick, a suburb of the west-end of Newcastle upon Tyne. Joseph Pearson was the only son and probably the only child born to Joseph Morrison, a soldier, and his wife Mabel (formerly Richardson). Home, at this time for the family Morrison, was 31, Tullock Street in Elswick. Apart from this nothing is known of the early life of Morrison. He must have worked somewhere, as it was not until the middle of 1939 that Morrison was to join the RAFVR as an airman under training as a pilot.

Like his contemporaries, Morrison was called to full time service, September 1, 1939. For continuation of his flying training Morrison was posted to Number 6 Operational Training Unit (OTU) at Sutton Bridge in Lincolnshire, arriving there August 3, 1940. Number 6 OTU was a Hurricane conversion unit. As such it presented Morrison with his first chance of flying a modern generation aeroplane. Put more simply, an aeroplane with a retracting undercarriage and variable flaps. It was not to be a very auspicious introduction to the new generation of fighter aircraft. Only a couple of days into the course Morrison was to suffer a slight accident. His Hurricane, L 1741, suffered an undercarriage failure. It is not clear if the accident was due to Morrison's mishandling of the controls or if the accident was just straightforward mechanical failure. It is more than likely; due to the fact that this was so early in his training that Morrison just forgot

Joseph P. Morrison.

to lower the undercarriage. Either way, Morrison's confidence must have been slightly damaged, even though he was not.

It can be safely presumed that the rest of Morrison's training went according to plan and to the satisfaction of the RAF. September 7, 1940, with only a months training on the Hurricane behind him, and the Battle of Britain nearing its height, Morrison was posted to 43 Squadron. Number 43 Squadron; the 'Fighting Cocks' was based at this time at Tangmere. Well in the front line of the Battle of Britain, Tangmere was not the best place for a 'rookie' pilot to be. The squadron had been scrambled that same morning but had returned only thirty minutes later.

The afternoon of September 7 turned out to be unusually quiet for a forward fighter airfield. Tangmere was after all on the battlefront. Morrison had been posted to 43 Squadron mainly for further training. This was begun on the afternoon of September 7. Morrison and another North East pilot Sgt G.C.C. Palliser, also recently arrived on the squadron, were sent out to get some dogfighting practice. Things were destined not to remain quiet for long. The Luftwaffe had changed its target area to take in London. Tangmere was more or less directly in the path of the Luftwaffe. At 4.40 PM 43 Squadron scrambled nine aircraft, all they could manage due to unserviceability, At the head of the formation was Flt Lt Caesar Hull. Number 43 Squadron were to engage around sixty bombers and as many Me 109s. Heavily outnumbered, 43 Squadron were to take a beating at the hands of the Luftwaffe. The worst was yet to come, however. Both Caesar Hull and Dick Reynell, a Hawker test pilot seconded to the RAF, were killed. Already under strength, 43 Squadron had suffered its worst day in the Battle of Britain. Later that evening, 43 Squadron were withdrawn from the battle and ordered to move north to reform and rest.

Number 43 Squadron left Tangmere the next day, September 8, and moved north to Usworth in County Durham. The squadron was now classed as a training unit. It was possibly with the latter in mind that Morrison had been posted to 43 Squadron. Over the next eight or nine days Morrison received his battle training in the skies over County Durham. Firing his guns at aerial flag targets and ground or sea targets, this would in all probability have been the first experience Morrison had of firing his guns. It would also have been the first time that he had used the fighter for the purpose it had been designed for, fighting. He had never been taught how to fight with an aeroplane. After nine days of flying in mock combat conditions it was thought that Morrison was ready for the real thing. To become a fully-fledged fighter pilot, Morrison had to be posted to a fighter squadron. To meet this end he was posted to Number 46 Squadron. Morrison arrived on his new squadron, September 17, 1940. Number 46 Squadron being based at Stapleford Tawney, Essex was well placed, just to the north east of London, for the coming action. The squadrons in this area being charged mainly with the defence of London.

Number 46 Squadron was relatively new in the RAF. It had only been reformed a month before Morrison joined it. The squadron originally had flown the Gloster Gladiator before being re-equipped with the Hawker Hurricane. From May 1940, the squadron had been engaged in the battle of Norway, the only Hurricane squadron in this battle. When things became impossible, the airfields under threat by the advancing Germans, rather than leave their Hurricanes the squadron was embarked on the aircraft carrier *HMS Glorious*. While travelling home from Norway, the *Glorious* was sunk by the twin sister surface raiders, *Scharnhorst* and *Gneisenau*. Not only were all the aircraft lost but, forty-four pilots as well. In one action a whole squadron had been decimated. The squadron was later reformed under the leadership of Squadron Leader J.R. MacLachlan. Now with its new aircraft and aircrews, the squadron was to fight in the Battle of Britain.

The day after Morrison arrived on the squadron, it was in action over the Essex coast where it promptly lost three of its Hurricanes to the high flying Me 109s. Although all three pilots survived, they were out of action and, therefore, lost to the squadron. The squadron seemed to play little part in the Battle of Britain over the next few days. Number 46 Squadron were once again in action on October 15. Flying over the Thames Estuary they were bounced by Me 109s losing a further three Hurricanes with two of the pilots killed. Their action so far would not have been seen as a morale booster for the pilots. With rising casualties the pressure moved to the new pilots like Morrison.

By now adverse weather conditions was beginning to slow down the German offensive. October 22, 1940, was one such day. Fog covered much of the area and it was not until the afternoon that the Luftwaffe began to develop its attacks. Attacks were carried out but these were against convoys off Dover rather than the normal target of London. At around 4.00 PM a further raid was plotted heading in the direction of Dover. Convoy 'Fruit' was in this area and called for help when it became obvious that it was the intended target. Among the squadron scrambled into action was 46 Squadron. Morrison was in

Hurricane R 4074 during this action. Hurricane R 4074 was the first aircraft built in the second production batch of one hundred. These aircraft being built by Gloster Aircraft Company Ltd at their Brockworth works during 1940. At high altitude a dogfight broke out over Dungeness. Both JG 26 and JG 27 were carrying out the escort duties on this day. At 4.50 PM a Hurricane dived earthwards out of the fight. This was Hurricane R 4074, which crashed near Newchurch Church. Its pilot, Morrison did not survive the crash.

The remains of Morrison were returned to the North East and buried in St Andrews and Jesmond Cemetery, to the north of the City of Newcastle. He is buried in section 'O' of the unconsecrated section, grave number 277. His grave is part of a family plot and has no CWGC headstone. The grey headstone bears the names of the family, all of whom are buried there. Beneath Morrison's name is the legend; 'Per Adua Adastra'. The motto of the RAF. The local press at the time of his death fail to mention the passing of this pilot. Neither was there any death notice.

Today, the cemetery in which Morrison lies can best be described as 'shabby'. The grave is covered with ferns that seem to pass for grass in this cemetery. As the only son and probably the only child, there are no survivors in this family. The result is that the grave has been allowed to fall into a state of wilderness. This is not helped by a tree, from the next grave, which has been allowed to cover the bottom third of Morrison's. Sergeant Joseph Pearson Morrison is one of today's forgotten men of the Battle of Britain.

GEORGE CHARLES CALDER PALLISER, 64891
SERGEANT

George Palliser was born January 11, 1919 in West Hartlepool. His education was carried out at Brougham School before he moved on to the local technical school. Palliser had always been interested in aeroplanes. Often he would cycle miles into the country just to see one. His technical school training helped him along the road to a technical career. Palliser was later to become an engineering apprentice. As the end of his apprenticeship came ever nearer, together with the war clouds that were forming over Europe, Palliser put his interest in aeroplanes and his technical background together and joined the RAFVR in June of 1939.

Training for Palliser began with Number 3 Initial Training Wing (ITW) at Hastings. With the square bashing over, Palliser moved on to Number 11 Elementary Flying Training School (EFTS) at Perth where he arrived December 5, 1939. Basic training was followed by a period at Little Rissington, Gloucestershire, with Number 6 Flying Training School (FTS) before his move to Number 6 Operational Training Unit (OTU) at Sutton Bridge where he began his conversion training July of 1940. With all of his training now behind him Palliser was posted to his first fighter squadron, 17 Squadron, which was then based at Debden. Arriving at Debden August 3, Palliser's stay with 17 Squadron was to be brief. He was posted on to 43 Squadron at Tangmere, August 18. It is possible that Palliser's stay with 43 Squadron was only for training purposes. He took part in some dogfighting practice with Sgt J.P. Morrison, September 7 and, moved north to Usworth with the squadron, September 8. However, six days after his move north, Palliser was posted once more. On this occasion it was to 249 Squadron, then based at North Weald, where he arrived September 14, 1940. Palliser, because of his baby face, was to be known on the squadron as 'Titch'.

Palliser did not seem overly enthusiastic with his new squadron. He was to record at the time; 'Hell... this is a rotten dump... officers worse than the last lot...'[1] Number 249 Squadron had taken over from 56 Squadron. On the latter's departure, they had left most of their Hurricanes for the new incoming squadron. Among those Hurricanes left was P 3615. This Hurricane was still bearing its previous squadron's code letters, US-G. This was the Hurricane assigned to Palliser. He was to fly it September 15, when the squadron was scrambled in the afternoon. Sighting a formation of bombers, the squadron went in to the attack.

However, as so often happens to new pilots during their first encounter with the enemy, Palliser became separated from the rest. Now on his own Palliser looked around for a target. It was not long in presenting itself. Palliser noticed a Do 17 flying at 9,000 feet dodging between patches of cloud. Attacking the Do 17 from about 350 yards, Palliser gave the Do 17 a three-second burst. The effect was immediate. Pieces began to fly off, followed by the crew evacuating the aircraft. It was now around 1.55 PM and Palliser was now lost and with his fuel so low his engine was intermittently cutting out. The safest thing to do was to get down as quickly as possible. This Palliser did using the first available field. Shouting to a young man in the field Palliser enquired where he was. On being reassured that he was in England and told of his exact location Palliser got out of his Hurricane. The Hurricane was out of everything, fuel ammunition and oxygen and, to cap it all, his radio was not working. The latter was due to debris from the doomed Do 17 that had broken the radio aerial. After getting in contact with his nearest airfield, Hornchurch, a lorry duly arrived with a fifty-gallon drum of fuel and a groundcrew. At around 7.00 PM took off from the field and returned to North Weald.[2]

It is well worthy of note that on this occasion Palliser was not carrying a map, one of the reasons that he was lost. This was due to the fact that sergeant pilots had to follow rather than lead. Only officers at this time were required to carry maps. A further social note: officers were usually billeted off the airfield, often living some miles from the airfield itself. Sergeant pilots, on the other hand, lived in any accommodation that was available. Usually this was of the bell-tent variety which was usually quite near to their parked aircraft. This was the accommodation available to Palliser and the NCO aircrew of 249 Squadron. This was soon to change, however. A near miss with a German bomb caused shrapnel to pass through a tent shared by Palliser. The NCO pilots decided to move to a nearby hut, even though it was not yet finished. They rigged up some corrugated sheeting for extra protection and took possession. At least they felt safer than they had in the bell-tent.

On both September 21 and 25, Palliser was credited with damaging Do 17s. Two days later the squadron was scrambled at 8.50 AM and vectored towards an incoming force of Me 110s over the coast of Kent. Palliser was flying with Red Section. The Me 110s took to their usual form of defence, forming defensive circles. Palliser dived through the circle of some twenty to twenty-five Me 110s and became separated from the rest of the section in the process.

On looking around, Palliser noticed an Me 110 and managed to deliver two good bursts into the fighter while still in the turn. This Me 110 was seen to dive away with smoke streaming from its starboard engine eventually crashing into the sea some six miles south of Redhill. Picking out another Me 110 Palliser chased it round in a steep turn. With the port engine issuing black smoke and no return fire from the Me 110 it dived away towards the southwest. Trying his luck on a third Me 110 Palliser ran out of ammunition and was forced to break off his attack when he became the target for the rear gunner. On his return to base it was found that a shell had gone through the Hurricane's rudder. Palliser's second victim, during this skirmish, appears to be the Me 110D-3 of the Staff Flight of ZG 76. Coded M8+XE, this was the Me 110 of Oblt Wilfred Von Barkhorn and Uffz Bartmus. While Von Barkhorn was rescued by a fishing boat off Hastings, he was badly burned in the crash, Bartmus was killed.

On October 21, Palliser was credited with the destruction of a Do 17. On the afternoon of October 29, North Weald airfield was attacked by the Me 110s of Erprobungs Gruppe 210.[3] Number 249 Squadron were caught on the hop and were in the act of taking off when the bombs began to fall. Palliser's Hurricane was hit by the flying debris that removed part of the propeller. As he climbed away from the airfield the engine of his Hurricane began to suffer severe vibration. Turning his Hurricane back into the circuit Palliser circled the airfield and landed amid the chaos left by the air raid.

On November 7, 1940, 249 Squadron were ordered to patrol the area of the Thames Estuary. A convoy reported as being under attack by Ju 87s. When the squadron arrived on the scene it was noticeable that a large number of Me 109s were in evidence. Palliser immediately attacked the fighter escort. Singling out an Me 109, with Sgt R. Smithson flying as Red 2 behind him, Palliser engaged the enemy fighter and was credited with its destruction. December 5 saw Palliser once more in the area over the Thames Estuary on a patrol. Flying Hurricane V 6565 he got caught up in a dogfight, with his Hurricane slightly damaged. Finding himself out of fuel, he had once more to make use of a convenient field. On this occasion it was near Stanford Le Hope to the south of Basildon.

With the official version of the Battle of Britain now over, the squadron found itself making more and more offensive patrols. February 4, 1941 was one such patrol, although over a convoy. Palliser was on patrol with P/O A.R.F. Thompson and Squadron Leader R.A. Barton. The formation spotted an Me 110 over a convoy, having already dropped its bombs without much success (evidence of this was noted by the bomb splashes which were visible wide of the target). Squadron Leader Barton led the section in a dive from 10,000 feet to execute a head-on attack. Both Barton and Palliser got in good bursts before the Me 110 tried to make good its escape with use of nearby cloud cover. Barton stayed above, making sure that it did not return, while Palliser and Thompson flew below to cut off any kind of retreat. A large splash was observed by the aircrews, with the convoy confirming that the Me 110 had crashed into the sea. This aircraft was Me 110 (S9+PK) of Erprobungs Gruppe 210 flown by Unffz Gustav Drews.

Palliser was flying as part of the escort to a group of Blenheims, February 10, 1941, en route to attack targets in and around Dunkirk. This raid was classed as Circus 4. Palliser noted that a Hurricane was under attack from an Me 109. Lining up his Hurricane, Palliser brought the enemy aircraft into his sights and gave it a two-seconds burst. The Me109 took violent evasive action but to no avail. Palliser still had the Me 109 in his sights and gave it another two-seconds burst. This time his fire was observed striking the Me 109 around the cockpit area. The Me 109 dropped away in a diving turn, with Palliser giving it another two-seconds burst. On this occasion hits were seen along the fuselage and the engine of the Me 109. To make extra sure Palliser gave the aircraft yet another two-seconds burst. As the Me 109 made no attempt to evade his attacks Palliser judged that the pilot must be dead. On April 24, 1941, Palliser was commissioned. It was, therefore, as Pilot Officer Palliser that he was ordered with the rest of the squadron, to report to London's Euston Station, May 8. From there they were to travel by train to Liverpool were they were to embark on *HMS Furious*, bound for Malta.

On the night of October 6/7, 1941, 249 Squadron's Hurricanes were fitted with bomb racks for an attack on Comiso airfield. The raid was to be carried out by moonlight. Squadron Leader Barton and Palliser carried out a dive-bombing attack. Bombs from the two aircraft fell amongst the dispersed aircraft and also blew up a hangar. Both Hurricanes returned safely to base. After being refuelled and rearmed, they once more set off to carry out another attack on the same airfield, attacking it once more with success. Three nights later they were to repeat the attack with more success. The target was shifted when Palliser flew on the night of November 4, 1941. Palliser was leading with Sergeant Etchells as his Number 2 on a raid to attack targets in Sicily. With the attack successfully accomplished, the Hurricane pair were en route back to base when they were pursued by six Macchi 202s. The pursuit lasting for around fifteen minutes before the pair could finally shake them off. The squadron was ordered to intercept a formation of four Ju 88s, December 4, 1941. Palliser, flying with the Commanding officer, attacked a Ju 88 that was seen to go into the sea.

With the new year of 1942 just started, Palliser was posted away from 249 Squadron to join 504 Squadron as a Flight Commander, the latter squadron being based at Hal Far. Also with the New Year came the award of the DFC that was awarded January 30, 1942. A few months later, April 24, Palliser was promoted to the rank of Flying Officer. A further move came, February 26. On this occasion Palliser was posted to Number 25 Air School at Standerton in South Africa, arriving there to take up his new post of Flying Instructor.

Palliser was to be posted to three further flying training establishments in succession during 1943. From the end of January 1944 until the end of the following May, Palliser was in hospital with an unspecified illness. Palliser left South Africa, May 24, to return to the U.K. For the next two years Palliser was posted to various training establishments as a flying instructor. A move back to South Africa came in October of 1946 when Palliser was posted to a flying school in Southern Rhodesia. Palliser was eventually to leave the RAF, October 1947. Palliser decided to make South Africa his home; however, he was to move to Australia at a later date. He was to settle in Melbourne where he still lives.

Palliser Notes

1. Palliser was interviewed for a TV documentary to commemorate the sixtieth anniversary of the Battle of Britain.
2. Article written about the event by Paddy Porter, related to him by Derek Farndon, an eye witness to the event. "Flypast Magazine", September 1990, Page 27
3. Mason states that this was Erpro Bungs Gruppe 210. Ramsey states that this raid was carried out by 11 Staffel LG 2, *Battle of Britain Then and Now* P 530.

Vincent Parker, 42356
Pilot Officer

Vincent Parker is listed in most aviation literature as Australian. In one way this is correct. However, Vincent parker was born in County Durham. No exact place names can be connected with his birth. The difficulty lies in the fact that Parker may not have been the name he was born with. According to Wynn,[1] Vincent Parker was born February 11, 1919 in Durham. It is not clear if this is meant to be Durham City or County Durham. What is known for sure is that, at an early age, probably no more than one or two years old, Parker was made an orphan. His uncle and aunt, John William and Edith Parker, then fostered him giving him the name Parker. His new foster parents then emigrated to Queensland, Australia, settling down in the town of Ingham. The young Parker was then educated at Bohleville State School. On completion of his education, Parker appears to have departed from his foster family and moved to Townsville. While there, he is reported to have met up with a magician who took him under his wing as a trainee. Parker, now a trainee magician, appears to have travelled far and wide, on one occasion touring England.

In 1938, Parker was to make a return trip to England. His days as a magician had obviously not come up to expectations or, with a war not too far off, Parker had a twinge of patriotism. Either way Parker applied to join the RAF and was accepted on a short service commission, his training beginning in May of 1939. April 10, 1940, was the day Parker finished his training at Number 11 Flying

Training School (FTS) at Shawbury. Parker was then posted to his first fighter squadron Number 234 Squadron which was based at Leconfield to the north of Beverley. At this time, 234 Squadron was one of the newer squadrons within the RAF. The squadron had formed at Leconfield in October of 1939, flying the twin engine Blenheim. In April of 1940, when Parker joined the squadron, 234 had just re-equipped with the Spitfire. Also new on the squadron was its Commanding Officer, Squadron Leader Edgar (Dickie) Barnett.

Number 234 Squadron were later to move south but were to see little action in the early part of the Battle of Britain. Mainly this was due to the fact that the squadron was based at the relative backwater of St Eval on the north west coast of Cornwall. The main duties of the squadron during this period was to provide air cover for the convoys passing through the approaches to Bristol.

During August the squadron was moved nearer the battle zone when they were posted to Middle Wallop. The squadron was in action from there August 15, 1940. A raid of some forty plus Ju 87s were moving towards the south coast. These Stuka dive-bombers of 1/StG 1 and 11/StG 2 were en route to attack Warmwell airfield. The bomber force was escorted by a number of Me 109s and 110s. However, the raid met with strong opposition and the bombers attacked Portland instead. The Hurricanes of 87 and 213 Squadrons attacked the Me 110s leaving the Spitfires of 234 Squadron to deal with the Me 109s.

A vicious dogfight broke out of the area of Portland. The Spitfires of 234 Squadron being heavily outnumbered by more than four to one. With the action becoming rapidly spent, mainly due to the Spitfires running out of ammunition, the defending fighters made an attempt to return to Middle Wallop. However, only some of them were allowed to carry this out. Some of the Spitfires found that they were cut off from returning home by the large numbers of Me 109s, all avenues of retreat being closed. The Spitfires were forced into a turning, one-sided battle. As the dogfight drifted west, P/O C.H. Hight, a New Zealander, was shot down over Bournemouth. His parachute failing to deploy properly, he fell to his death in Walsford road.

Pilot Officer Richard Hardy was forced out over the English Channel. His Spitfire had been damaged in the fighting and Hardy found himself being forced further and further into the Channel. Eventually, Hardy was forced to make an almost textbook landing near Cherbourg in France.[2] The battle continued to move in a south-westerly direction until, over Swanage, Parker's Spitfire was attacked by an Me 110 at around 5.30 PM. Parker's Spitfire R 6985 became unflyable after the attack and he was forced to take to his parachute not far from the Isle of Wight. Slightly wounded in the attack, Parker was left floating in the English Channel and his hopes of being rescued began to fade. However, rescue did come but, from the wrong side. Parker was picked up by a German launch and taken as a prisoner to Cherbourg. Spitfire R 6985 was relatively new and had first flown July 19, 1940. Passing through Number 6 Maintenance Unit (MU), it had arrived on 234 squadron July 25. On August 15, it was presumed to have crashed into the sea.

After originally being held prisoner in France, Parker moved through the system and was passed on to Germany. He was imprisoned in Dulag Luft at Oberusel near Frankfurt. While there, Parker was reported to be on the 'permanent staff'. Their purpose was to initiate new prisoners into the procedures of 'camp life', Dulag Luft being a temporary holding centre for allied airmen. Parker was still on the 'permanent staff', June 1, 1941. On this date, fourteen of these 'permanent staff' tunnelled their way out of Dulag Luft. Although all were eventually recaptured, a large number of the security forces were kept active looking for them. Parker is generally believed to have been among the escapees.

Parker must have remained a nuisance to the Germans, due to his escape activities. At the end of April beginning of May 1942 Parker was moved on to Oflag 1Vc—the notorious Colditz Castle which lay to the south of Leipzig. Parker arrived at his new home, May 5, 1942. Whilst at Colditz Parker had acquired the nickname 'Bush', presumably because of his Australian background. Parker was to become popular in Colditz because of his expertise with locks. Presumably this expertise had been gained while under training as a magician before the war. Parker was noted as being a great help to other escapees in Colditz. At any one time there appears to have been four lock-pickers in Colditz. One of these was Squadron Leader Brian Paddon. However, Paddon was moved on, June 11, 1942. On the departure of Paddon, Parker took over as official lock-picker.

With a talent for lock picking it was not long before Parker was to make his own attempt at escape. His first recorded escape attempt from Colditz was July 15, 1942. He attempted to trade places with a sergeant Gollan. However, his attempt failed and presumably Parker had to pay for it. Sergeant Gollan left Colditz that day. As his name does not appear among those who escaped, it is presumed that he was taken elsewhere. Parker was to make a further escape attempt, March 26, 1943. On this occasion, along with Royal Navy Lieutenant E.M. Harvey. The pairing made their attempt by exiting a window and dropping by rope to onto the causeway beneath. Once there, Parker picked the lock to gain entry into an air-raid shelter. Parker and Harvey were spotted by a guard who opened fire but missed his target. The pair then hid in the shelter while the guards searched outside. Seemingly, it never occurred to the guards to search inside the shelter. However, the escape plan was flawed. The pair was forced to give themselves up when it was found that there was no second floor to allow them to carry out their escape plan.

Parker was involved in another escape, September 2, 1943, which came to be known as the 'Franz Josef' escape. This was an elaborate scheme involving the impersonation of a guard known to look like the Austrian Emperor Franz Josef. The whole idea was to make a mass break out. Parker was to masquerade as one of the guards, as well as using his usual lock-picking skills. The escape was to be unsuccessfu,l leaving one of the prisoners wounded by a gunshot. Parker was to remain at Colditz Castle until he was released in April of 1945 by the advancing American forces.

On his return to England, Parker was sent on leave to recover from his ordeal in a prisoner of war camp. At a later date he was posted to Number 56 Operational Training Unit (OTU) at Milfield, north of Wooler in Northumberland. The unit had been formed December 14, 1944, to convert pilots to the Hawker Tempest Mk V. The course was to last some nine weeks with the converted pilots usually being sent to Germany. This was to replace pilot losses incurred by the Second Allied Tactical Air Force (TAF).

Parker was not destined to be sent back to Germany, however, nor anywhere else. On Tuesday, January 29, 1946, Parker left Milfield Flying Tempest EJ 859. This was to be a routine training flight. He engaged in some aerobatics to the south of Norham on Tweed. While carrying out a slow roll, Parker's Tempest stalled and crashed into a field at Felkington Farm some six miles to the north of Milfield. Vincent Parker was killed in the accident.

Vincent Parker, English Anzac, one time magician, RAF fighter pilot and prison escapee was laid to rest at Stonefall Cemetery, Harrogate, Yorkshire. At the time of his death, Parker held the rank of Flight Lieutenant. His final resting place is some fifty miles from his place of birth in County Durham. His grave is in section H, row N, grave number 1. Stonefall is a cemetery with burials of mainly Commonwealth servicemen. Vincent Parker's grave is adorned with a CWGC headstone. At the bottom of the stone are the words; 'Only those who know can tell the sorrow of parting without farewell. Mum Dad and Mona'. It is presumed that Mona was his sister.

Parker Notes

1. Wynn: *Men of the Battle of Britain*, P 388.
2. Mason: *Battle Over Britain*, P 204. The photograph, taken by a German, clearly shows that Hardy's Spitfire was in reasonably good condition. Also clear are the markings showing that this was Spitfire N 3277 H-AZ. Also clearly visible are the personal markings of the pilot. A broken Swastika with a two-fingered salute at its centre and the legend (Dirty Dick).

William A. Peacock. Photo: Robert A. Peacock.

WILLIAM ALBERT PEACOCK, 808268
SERGEANT

William Albert Peacock was born, the first of two sons, June 11, 1920. His place of birth being Seaton Carew on the southern edge of Hartlepool in what was then Cleveland. Education for the young Peacock was carried out locally. His first school was to be Seaton Snooks School before moving on to the Henry Smith Secondary School. Presumably Peacock went through some technical training along the way as he was later to work as an instrument artificer when he joined 608 (North Riding) Squadron Auxiliary Air Force. The squadron was at that time based at Thornaby on Tees, to the south of industrial Middlesborough. Peacock appears too have joined the squadron, January 27, 1938. June 9, 1939 saw Peacock leave his part-time duties when he was enlisted into the RAF. Presumably this was in a ground trade as he was later to re-muster as an airman under training as a pilot.

With his square bashing over, Peacock was posted to Number 6 Elementary Flying Training School (E&FTS) at Sywell to the west of Wellingborough. Training began on October 21 and was next posted to Number 8 Flying Training School (FTS) at Montrose in Scotland.[1] Arriving At Montrose, March 6, 1940, Peacock was to gain his 'wings' there before moving on to Hawarden in the Welsh borderland to the west of Chester. Peacock was to spend almost a month at Hawarden, June 29 to mid July. A seemingly leisurely training pace in the days before the Battle of Britain when pilot training was cut to the bare minimum due to pilot shortages. While at Hawarden, Peacock was converted onto the Hawker Hurricane.

On July 18, 1940, Peacock arrived on his first, and as fate dictated, his last fighter squadron. Peacock had been posted to Digby to join Number 46 Squadron. The squadron was at that time reforming after its disaster in the Norwegian campaign.[2] After the squadron's reforming, Peacock at least had the time to learn to fight with the Hurricane before being thrust into the Battle of Britain. While at Digby, Peacock would have been taught at least the very basics of air fighting from the more experienced pilots on the squadron. From September 1, 1940, Number 46 Squadron were to be fully operational. The squadron was then posted to Stapleford Tawney in Essex.

The fighting was long in coming to 46 Squadron. September 3 was to be their first day of action. On this occasion Peacock was flying Hurricane P 3062. A large raid was inbound for North Weald, Hornchurch and Debden. Number 46 Squadron were to patrol the area over Rochford. The raiding force was made up mainly of Do 17s with an escort of Me 110s and 109s.[3] Peacock was to survive his first encounter with the Luftwaffe. However, 46 Squadron were not so fortunate, they were to lose two Hurricanes with a further two damaged. Two of the squadron's pilots were wounded in the fighting while another was killed.

On the following day 46 Squadron were once again in action and, like the day before, were to suffer at the hands of the Luftwaffe fighter escort. A large raid was plotted moving in over the coast at Beachy Head, Dover, Folkestone and Hastings. The bomber force was escorted by a large number, put around three hundred, of Me 109s and 110s. Once again, 46 Squadron were patrolling in the area of Rochford at some 15,000 feet when they were bounced by the Me 109s of the fighter escort. Peacock, flying Hurricane N 2599 on this occasion, appears to have avoided any damage. The same cannot be said for 46 Squadron. They lost a further two Hurricanes with two more damaged. One of the pilots, F/O R.P. Plummer was badly burned but managed to bale out of his Hurricane. Ten days later, however, he was to die of his wounds.

Peacock was in the air twice the following day, September 5. Patrolling the area over Chelmsford at 15,000 feet and later, the squadron were at 20,000 feet over Rochford. Peacock was in Hurricane N 2599. The first flight was to last almost an hour and a half with the second lasting fifty-five minutes. The result was the same on both occasions, nothing seen. September 6 was to be the same as the day before. Two flights, both over Rochford, with nothing seen. September 7 was the day that the Luftwaffe switched its targets to London, however, it coincided with Peacock's day off, he was not flying that day. The following day was to prove to be a bit more hectic.

Several raids were launched by the Luftwaffe, mainly against the airfields in and around Kent. Number 46 Squadron were in the air to meet the enemy and Peacock was flying Hurricane V 7232 as he patrolled over his base. Number 46 Squadron was one of four Hurricane squadrons to engage the enemy on this occasion. Peacock identified the bombers as Do 215s and estimated their number as around thirty. Above and behind was the fighter escort of Me 109s and 110s. Peacock estimated the number in the fighter escort as about fifty. Peacock carried out a beam attack against a Do 215.[4] At around this time, the fighter escort made its presence felt. Peacock entered a dogfight with an Me 109 and made a claim for it destruction.[5] Once again 46 Squadron were to suffer at the hands of the fighter escort. Two Hurricanes being lost with a further two damaged and one pilot, Sub Lieutenant J.C. Carpenter, killed. Carpenter's body was returned home to Wales from where, in accordance with naval tradition, he was buried at sea.

September 9 saw Peacock patrolling once more over Rochford at 15,000 feet. After a flight lasting an hour and a half, he returned to base to record nothing seen. Deteriorating weather conditions added to the gloom on September 11 as all activities were brought to a halt. However, with the afternoon came better weather. This in turn brought out the Luftwaffe. A raid was reported as building up over the Pas de Calais. Shortly after 3.00 PM this raid was followed across the Channel and up the east coast of Kent. There it made a turn to run up the Thames Estuary. On this occasion the fighter escort was large, estimated at around two hundred. Behind them was a further formation of Me 109s on a 'free hunt'. Some of these fighters were to attack the Dover balloon defences. Such a large number of escorting fighters made it extremely difficult to get anywhere near the bombers. If any aircraft was lucky enough to get through the defences, they faced a heavy crossfire from the bomber force.

Peacock was once more flying Hurricane V 7232. It is believed that Peacock was one of the first Hurricanes to fall in the initial attack on the bombers. What is not known is how he met his fate, bomber crossfire or fighter. It is believed that Peacock fell in the vicinity of the Thames Estuary. The last page of Peacock's logbook carries the words; 'Estimated missing'. Today, Peacock is still one of those pilots listed as 'missing'. Peacock is virtually unknown in his hometown of Hartlepool. His only surviving relative, his brother Robert, moved to New York.

William Albert Peacock is remembered on the Runnymede Memorial, panel 18. Peacock had just turned twenty-one and his operational career had lasted only eleven days. Hurricane V 7232 was one of the early aircraft from the fourth batch of five hundred built by Hawker Aviation.

Peacock Notes

1. A photograph exists of Peacock during his training days. Ramsey: *Battle of Britain Then and Now*, P xxii. It is thought that this may be Montrose. None of the pilots have their 'wings' badge. Also in the shot is John Lonsdale second left, front.
2. Number 46 Squadrons Hurricanes were aboard the aircraft carrier *HMS Glorious* en route for Scapa Flow. At 4.45 PM, June 8, 1940, the *Glorious* was sighted by the German surface raiders, *Scharnhorst* and *Gneisenau*. Opening fire at arrange of 27 miles, the aircraft on the deck of the glorious stood little chance as the opening salvos straddled the ship. *Glorious*, along with its escort destroyers, *Ardent* and *Acasta* were sunk. Few survived to tell the tale.
3. Peacock identified the bombers as Do 215s. Dornier 215s were little used in the Battle of Britain. They were used as reconnaissance aircraft and not as bombers. Outwardly, the Do 215 looked the same as the Do 17 with one exception, the former had in-line engines rather than the radial engines used on the Do 17.
4. As above. Author, should I copy Note #3's text here?
5. Individual aircraft has not been identified. The record of its demise is in Peacock's logbook. A copy of this appears in *Battle of Britain Then and Now, Mk V*, P xxii.

OSWALD ST JOHN PIGG, 39678
FLYING OFFICER

Although Oswald St John Pigg was born in South Shields, the town was not his home. Oswald St John Pigg was one of two sons born to the Reverend John James Pigg and his wife, Mabel Tyson, formerly Riddell. Pigg junior was born January 17, 1918 and, February 14, was baptized in the church where his father was curate. This was the church of St John the Baptist in Grainger Street in the heart of the City of Newcastle upon Tyne.[1] It must have been with some pride that Pigg senior gifted his son with the name of St John, the first church in which he had become curate some nine years before. Home for the Pigg family at that time was Number 32, Breamish Street, Jarrow, on the south side of the river Tyne. This area is now known as 'Catherine Cookson Country', however, the family Pigg lived at the other end of the social scale from the north-country author. A vicar's life was one of the people yet apart from the people. It is more than likely that the young Pigg knew little of life outside the vicarage. His life would be almost a sheltered one. This middle-class existence was to be carried through into his school life. Pigg junior was later to become a pupil at the Royal Grammar School in Newcastle, entering the school in April 1926. Presumably Pigg junior stayed as a boarder at the Royal Grammar School. His father moved from Newcastle Cathedral to take up his new post of Prison Chaplain at Durham Prison in 1929.

It would appear that Pigg was to join the RAF straight from school. A fellow pupil, Philip Markham,[2] was later to state that, Pigg and he

(Markham) shared a common interest in all things to do with aviation they, therefore, became good friends. Mr Markham also stated that Pigg left school in January 1936, to join the RAF. It is known that Pigg applied to join the RAF and that he was awarded a Short Service Commission in March of the following year, 1937. His flying training was begun at Number 10 Flying Training School (TFS) Ternhill. After his training, Pigg was posted to his first fighter squadron, Number 72, then based at Church Fenton.

Number 72 Squadron had been reformed at RAF Church Fenton, January 1937. The squadron, in this form, was still classed as a new one when Pigg joined it, November 27, 1937. The squadron was at that time flying the Gloster Gladiator. Number 72 Squadron being the first fighter squadron to be equipped with this new little fighter. Number 72 Squadron was to spend most of its time in the north of the country moving between various bases, Church Fenton, Acklington and Drem. In May of 1939, Number 72 Squadron were to give up their Gladiator's for the new-age fighter, the Spitfire.

The transition from Gladiator to Spitfire was not an easy one. The Gladiator, although a frontline fighter in the late1930s, still relied on technology dating from the First World War. The gladiator was a biplane braced with wires and armed with four machine guns and carrying a fixed undercarriage. It was the latter that was to cause so much grief on the squadrons that were to convert to fighters with retractable undercarriages. A common mistake was for the pilot, concentrating on making a good landing in a fighter with a limited forward view, to forget to lower the undercarriage. The Spitfire, unless the pilot was warned in time, would then come to earth on its belly causing an amount of damage mostly to its under surface as well as the propeller. On July 13, 1939, this is what happened to Pigg. Attempting a night landing at Church Fenton, Pigg, it would appear, forgot to lower the undercarriage of his Spitfire. A thump and much grinding of mettle overtook the approaching growl of the Merlin. The crash crews and fire engine found Spitfire K 9923 embedded in a hedge: Sitting on the cockpit door was an abashed looking pilot. Even more embarrassing was the fact that Pigg was a training officer in charge of the link trainer.[3]

Photographs of Pigg are few and far between during his fairly short life. He appears in a group photograph of 72 Squadron taken at

Church Fenton. Among others in the group are James B. Nicholson who was later to win the VC during the Battle of Britain while serving on 249 Squadron. The photograph used in the book *The Battle of Britain Then And Now* shows a young man who appears to be on the reserved and retiring side. The photograph was taken in what appears to be a large formal garden. This may have been taken in the garden of his father's house; the prison chaplain's house at HMP Durham.

Tasked as part of the air defence of Great Britain, the Spitfire squadrons were to remain in Britain while many of the Hurricane squadrons went to war in France. However, with the fall of France and the retreat towards the Channel port of Dunkirk, many of the Spitfire squadrons were to be moved south to supply air cover for the retreat from Dunkirk. One of these was 72 Squadron. The squadron being based at Gravesend for this purpose.

Air fighting and patrols were to be frequent over Dunkirk. June 2, 1940, Number 72 Squadron took off at 6.40 AM in company with 609 Squadron and set course for the area over Dunkirk. On this occasion the two squadrons were to maintain air cover over a hospital ship that was lying just off the harbour. Red Section was flying at 12,000 feet with Yellow Section keeping station to the seaward side. Blue Section were flying some 1,000 feet higher to protect their comrades from being bounced by the high flying Me 109s. At around 6.55 AM, Red 2, Pigg, spotted a formation of Ju 87s approaching. Yellow Section was ordered to guard their rear while Red Section moved in to the attack. Squadron Leader R. B. Lees, the Australian Commanding officer, called Red Section into line astern and proceeded to attack the enemy formation.

Lees was to pick out the leader of the formation, while Pigg was to attack the number two in the formation. Getting in some good bursts, Pigg saw the enemy aircraft crash in flames. The third Ju 87 I the formation was a bit more determined than usual. He turned towards Pigg and carried out his own attack. The Ju 87 carried out a head-on pass on Pigg's Spitfire, the latter being lucky to escape injury. At this time, Spitfires were only still being fitted with new bulletproof windscreens. Pigg's Spitfire did not fare so well in the attack. There was damage to the port starboard wing as well as the port aileron and the air-pressure system. Pigg could only point his Spitfire in the direction of home and hope. His Spitfire was difficult to handle and his guns were out of action, making his own defence impossible. Fellow squadron pilot Douglas Winter made a pass against the Ju 87 but overshot the target.

It was only now, as he flew back across the Channel, that Pigg realized that his troubles were only about to begin. The gunfire from the Ju 87 had robbed Pigg of all aileron control—making flying an uncomfortable experience. As he neared his base, however, it became apparent that his Spitfire was without flaps or brakes. To make matters worse, the undercarriage could not be lowered, either. Pigg also noted that he had been wounded in the leg, so rudder control was also difficult. Pigg opted for a belly landing on the grass surface of his base at Gravesend. Managing to carry out a copybook, wheels up landing. Pigg had not only saved himself but had brought a much-needed Spitfire back home. Although severely damaged, it could be repaired.[4] This Spitfire was K 9924. Having first flown April 4, 1939, it was part of the squadrons original compliment. It remained in flying condition until struck off charge in August of 1944.

Later in June, with the evacuation over, 72 Squadron were ordered back to the north for a 'rest'. Their base was now Acklington. Routine convoy patrols were interspersed with the training of new pilots and working the squadron back up to full strength. Apart from the convoy patrols, the lone sporadic raider provided the mainstay of the action at this time. The 'rest' period for the squadron came to an unexpected end August 15, 1940. On this day, a large force numbering around sixty He 111s with a fighter escort of twenty Me 110s, were to put the North East under attack. Flying from their base at Stavanger, Norway, the bombers of I and III Gruppen KG 26 were to attack Dishforth airfield in northern Yorkshire. The escort of Me 110Ds of I Gruppe ZG 76, were to see them safely there and back again. Some say that the attacking force made a mistake with the navigation and got 'lost'. This is open to question.[5] What is known for sure is that radar picked up the raid some fifty miles or so north east of the Farne Islands. Their element of surprise went with their discovery. From now on the bomber force was on borrowed time.

Shortly after 12.15 PM, 72 Squadron were ordered into the air, initially to patrol their base as the controllers attempted to work out the possible target. Moving north, eleven Spitfires of 72 Squadron, led by Flight Lieutenant Edward (Ted) Graham, had sighted the enemy force at around 12.30 PM and dived into action. Graham had split his force into two sections. Graham led one section towards the bombers while Flight Lieutenant Desmond Sheen led the other to attack the fighter escort. On this occasion Pigg was to make a claim for one of the Me 110s shot down according to one source.[6] In all the pilots of 72 Squadron were to claim eleven aircraft as destroyed. In the cold light of day, however, much of this was pure mistake. Only three enemy aircraft were shot down at this time.

For 72 Squadron's pilots at Acklington, things could not get quieter after the action of August 15. Just over a week later, in time for some of the heaviest fighting of the Battle of Britain, 72 Squadron were deemed ready to return to the fray. The squadron moving south to take up station at Biggin Hill then, because of the bombing, it flew from Croydon. However, reality proved a hard taskmaster. On August 31, 1940, during a late afternoon patrol, 72 Squadron were in combat with Me 109s over Dungeness. The squadron losing two aircraft and one pilot with another pilot severely wounded.

September 1 saw the squadron once again in the air. A large formation of enemy aircraft was plotted crossing the coast over Dover. To further confuse the defences, the formation divided into two. As usual the bomber force was escorted by a large number of Me 109s. Number 72 Squadron were to attack the fighter escort. At 11.15 AM high over Beachy Head, Spitfire P 9458 dived out of the combat area trailing smoke. Its pilot was F/O Pigg, who failed to recover his Spitfire from its dive. Pigg's Spitfire eventually crashed into a field at Elvey Farm, Pluckley.[7] However; the story of Oswald St John Pigg was not to end there. Official casualty records show that Pigg was killed a day after he actually was, his death given as September 2, 1940.

Evidence of this discrepancy was to come to light many years later.[8] Officialdom was to state that Pigg was killed September 2. Further evidence was to show that a Spitfire had crashed at Elvey Farm, Pluckley September 1, and that the fate of the pilot was 'unknown'. He was not in the cockpit. A further report, from the Local Casualty Clearance Station notes that '… the ashes of F/O Pigg were collected from Elvey Farm, Pluckley'. It would appear from this evidence, that F/O Pigg's ashes only were recovered from the burnt out wreck that was his Spitfire. This would account for the fate of the pilot being 'unknown'. It can only be hoped that Pigg was killed in the initial attack rather than being burned to death.

The Reverend John James Pigg was at this time, Chaplain at Durham Prison. The remains of Pigg was, therefore, sent to his home in County Durham. Oswald St John Pigg was laid to rest in St Oswald's Burial Ground, Durham City, October 10, 1940. The parish registers give no address for the deceased it is merely left blank. A CWGC headstone marks his gravesite in row 1, grave number 90. Later in the war, his father was to become vicar at Chatton near Wooler in the north of Northumberland. The death of Oswald St John Pigg is remembered in two places, the above burial ground in Durham City and the war memorial in the Northumberland village of Chatton.

Over the years, the grave of F/O Pigg became somewhat neglected and overgrown. The headstone had taken on an unusual angle. Thanks to the local enthusiast, Mr Wentworth Appleby, who alerted the local RAFA to the fact; this was put right in time for the sixtieth anniversary of the Battle of Britain. The local RAFA also placed a new cross on the grave and returned the site to a more acceptable, and tidy state. Also in later years, a dig was carried out on Elvey Farm by a local wreck recovery group. This yielded a small amount of engine pieces and some head armour from the crashed Spitfire. These pieces were deposited in the Kent Battle of Britain Museum where they can be seen today. However, thanks to the bureaucracy of the MOD, the gravestone of F/O Oswald St John Pigg, which bears his name and rank, still bears the wrong date of his death.

PIGG NOTES

1. Personal correspondence from Board of Finance, Diocesan Secretary. This states that 'It would seem unlikely that Oswald Pigg would have been born in South Shields'. It goes on to state that it would be 'unheard of' for a Clergyman to hold a licence in one diocese and live in another. Parish records for St John's Church show that this was not the case. Oswald St John Pigg's address is clearly visible, showing that he lived in Jarrow, near South Shields.
2. Letter from Mr Philip Markham to Ramsey, *Battle of Britain Then and Now*, editor's notes.

3. Personal correspondence with Mr Cyril Nugent, a former member of 72 Squadron.
4. Osprey Aviation: *Aircraft of the Aces—Spitfire*, photograph of Pigg's Spitfire, P 14.
5. This attack on the North East, August 15, is often understated. Wood & Dempster, *The Narrow Margin* describe it as '… the most interesting of the day'. Southern authors also have difficulties with it. Both Mason, *Battle over Britain* and Bungay, *The Most Dangerous Enemy* describe the second Me 110 shot down in this attack as crashing in Durham: a mere sixty miles from the event. Bungay and others, give the targets as Dishforth and Usworth, some even throw in Newcastle and Sunderland. The only target named on the official statements from KG 26 are Dishforth.
6. Wynn states that Pigg made a claim for a Bf 109 on this date. *Men of the Battle of Britain*, P 404. This was an impossibility due to the distance involved.
7. Pluckley Farm, Kent, was to become famous as Pa Larkin's farm in the Television adaptation of the *Darling Buds of May*.
8. Ramsey: *The Battle of Britain Then And Now*, P 404.

Alan Leslie Ricalton. Photo: Michael Carrie & William Ricalton.

ALAN LESLIE RICALTON, 70872
FLYING OFFICER

Alan Leslie Ricalton was born January 21, 1914 at Hazelrigg, Northumberland. He was the second son of William Ricalton, a colliery winding engineman, and his wife, Margaret Jane, formerly Darling. Home for the family Ricalton at this time was Number 4, Strawberry Terrace in Hazelrigg. Later the family were to move into nearby Gosforth where they lived at 52, Salters Road. In March of 1938, Ricalton was commissioned in the Reserve of Air Force Officers. After initiation, Ricalton was posted to Number 8 Flying Training School (FTS) at Montrose, Angus in Scotland. Arriving there April 9, 1938 he began his flying training that was to last until October when he was passed as suitable for bomber aircraft. Ricalton was next posted to his first squadron, Number 142 Squadron, arriving at its base at Andover October 29, 1938. In January of 1939, Ricalton was offered a Short Service Commission. On Acceptance, he relinquished his commission in the Reserve of Air Force Officers.

Number 142 Squadron was equipped with the Fairey Battle. A single engined, three-seat light bomber destined to become outdated almost before the war had started. With the outbreak of hostilities in 1939, 142 Squadron were soon on the move to France as part of the Advanced Air Striking Force (AASF). Taking up station at Bery-au-Bac, much of the Squadron's time, in this early part of the war, was taken up with training. This consisted of a mixture of night flying training intermixed with practice flights for observers and air-gunners. Operations were soon mounted, however, the squadron being mainly active in leaflet dropping operations known as 'Nickel' raids. Ricalton was to fly on one of theses raids, on the night of April 20, 1940. The target for the 'raid' being the town of Coblenz.

On May 10, 1940, the 'phoney war' came to a sudden end. At 4.35 AM, He 111s attacked 142 Squadrons airfield, giving the squadron a rude awakening. Although there was a fair amount of damage to the surrounding airfield, none of the Battles of 142 Squadron were damaged to a great extent. As 142 had been the first of the squadrons attacked, they were given the honour of being the first bomber squadron in the AASF to attack the rapidly advancing German columns. As the war built up, so did the attacks against the enemy.

Ricalton was in action May 15, attacking a target near Montheme. On the night of May 23, Ricalton flew in a formation that attacked targets around Florenville. However, on this occasion Ricalton was unable to locate the target due to increasing cloud cover. Dropping his bombs onto a convenient ant-aircraft battery, he then made his way home. Further targets were to include a Chateau near Ribemont, thought to be an enemy HQ. At this time, 142 Squadron were to move detachments to Echemines, the squadrons advanced landing ground, for night operations. As June wore on it became increasingly apparent that 142 Squadron would soon be forced to depart France. As it was, the squadron was forced to move from one airfield to the next to stay ahead of the advancing German forces. Finally, June 15 saw the squadron withdrawn from France. The Battles, those that were left, flew out of France. The groundcrews departed as best they could, mainly from the port of Brest. Number 142 Squadron were once again united at RAF Waddington in Lincolnshire. A rumour began at this time, and increasingly grew, that the squadron was to exchange their outdated Battles in favour of the newer Wellington bomber. At this time, however, the pressure was on Fighter Command. They needed fighter pilots. Ricalton was to one of those pilots who were to volunteer for fighter pilot training. To meet this end, Ricalton was sent on a conversion course to convert to the Spitfire. His next squadron was equipped with this type.

The next squadron Ricalton was posted to was Number 74 Squadron; the 'Tigers' were based at that time at Kirton-in-Lindsey. Ricalton was to arrive on the squadron, August 21, 1940. It was during this time that 74 Squadron suffered minor sabotage problems. Some pilots had reported difficulty in raising and lowering the undercarriage. When the groundcrew inspected the Spitfires concerned, they found that the split pins were missing from the selector levers of some of the aircraft. This was reported to the Commanding Officer, 'Sailor' Malan, who agreed that it looked deliberate. It was also during this period that Malan was to write his 'Ten Rules of Air Fighting'. These were later to be spread throughout Fighter Command. The days at Kirton-in-Lindsey were given over to practice and more practice as Malan trained his men, especially the new pilots, in air fighting techniques in preparation for the fighting that was sure to come. September 9, 1940 was the day that the squadron moved to Coltishall in Norfolk.

Action for the squadron was not far off, and came on September 11. On this occasion 74 Squadron were to provide eight Spitfires as part of Duxford's 'Big Wing'. During the action, the squadron put up what was described as a 'hectic fight'. It was obviously successful as well, 74 Squadron sustaining no losses. Due to the increasing bad weather, the squadron was grounded until September 14. On this day 74 Squadron were to find themselves in a series of minor engagements off the coast of East Anglia. Blue Section was scrambled with Mungo Park in the lead. The patrol intercepted two Me 110s flying at around twenty-three thousand feet. The old attacking technique was still in evidence as Park ordered his section into line astern before leading them into the attack. Opening fire at a range of two hundred yards, Park noticed fire from the starboard engine of the Me 110. However, the Me 110 was to disappear into cloud cover at five thousand feet. Blue 2, Ricalton, managed to squeeze off a burst at the second Me 110. Hits were observed, but Ricalton could only claim the Me 110 as damaged.

Apart from the infrequent bursts of action and routine patrols, practice and training was to be the order of the day. This inactivity did not sit well with the pilots. Many thought of themselves patrolling the rural 'backwaters' of East Anglia while their comrades, in the south, were making contact with the enemy on a daily basis. Fighter Command had deemed it necessary that 74 Squadron should stay at Coltishall. Malan saw it as equally necessary to keep his men well trained. Practice had to be as realistic as possible. However, realism could have hidden dangers. That some of the pilots were maybe a little too enthusiastic can be seen by the number of air crashes that occurred during this time.[1]

October 14, 1940 was the day that the pilots of 74 Squadron had been waiting for. The news came through that they were to be sent to the south. Number 74 Squadron were to replace 72 Squadron at Biggin Hill. The following day saw the squadron move to Biggin Hill and, a quote from the squadron records reflects the euphoria felt on the squadron. 'Should now get back into our stride'.[2] Since their last visit, Biggin Hill had paid dearly. Many of the hangars and service buildings had been flattened by the bombs of the Luftwaffe. Aircrew were to be accommodated out with the airfield, taking over an old country house formerly belonging to Waldren Smithers, MP.

While there was much change at Biggin Hill, some things did not change. One of the latter was the fact that the Luftwaffe still bombed the airfield on a regular basis. Only their tactics had changed. In order to avoid being bounced, the Jagdwaffe were flying at higher altitudes. This was also a tactic designed to bring RAF Fighter Command squadrons into battle at their disadvantage. At this time the main target was the destruction of RAF Fighter Command. This had not escaped the notice of the commander of 11 Group, Sir Keith Park. He had fears that the new tactics, employed by the Luftwaffe, could be reverting back to the mass attacks that had been used throughout August. He warned his controllers to bear in mind the climb rate of the defending fighters so that they would not be caught at a disadvantage in the climb. Park ordered the Spitfire squadrons to engage the high flying Me 109s and leave the bombers to the Hurricanes. In particular, he singled out the Spitfire squadrons from Biggin Hill and Hornchurch to engage the enemy's '… high fighter screen…'

October 17, 1940 was a day of 'snatch raids' carried out by the Luftwaffe. At 3.00 PM, 74 Squadron were scrambled to intercept such a raid. This one was approaching at around twenty-six thousand feet. Ever mindful of using the sun and altitude to best effect, Malan led his squadron away from the incoming raid. Climbing and ever watchful of his rear, Malan climbed his squadron to its operational height before turning in the direction of the enemy.

Malan's attention was drawn to the direction of the Thames Estuary there, he could see AA bursts. Approaching the area, 74 Squadron surprised a group of Me 109s numbering around sixty, in the area over Gravesend and Maidstone. Battle was joined around 3.30 PM. It is probable that these Me 109s were of JG 53, who were known to have been in the area at this time. Three of their number were to fall to the guns of 74 Squadron, one of these being Oblt Rupp, Staffel Kapitan of 3/JG 53. His Me 109 was to belly-land on Manston airfield. It is not known if Ricalton was to claim any of these aircraft. Within ten minutes of the start of the engagement, Ricalton was seen to fall. This was witnessed by none other than Malan himself who was later to state; 'Flying Officer Ricalton is missing, and I think he was killed, as I saw his Spitfire go down'. We must presume, from such a seasoned eyewitness, that the hits on Ricalton's Spitfire must have been quite decisive, either hits on the cockpit area or an explosion.

Spitfire Mk2, P 7360, had first flown August 26, 1940. It was one of the Mk2s that 74 Squadron had taken on charge September 10 as a replacement for their ageing Mk Is. Spitfire P 7360, crashed near Hollingbourne, Kent at 3.40 PM. Mason states that Ricalton's Spitfire crashed near Southborough, some ten miles from Hollingbourne. However, that Ricalton crashed near Hollingbourne there is little doubt. The press in Ricalton's home town of Newcastle, reported merely that he had been killed in, '... an accident'.[3]

The remains of Ricalton were buried in Sittingbourne Cemetery old ground; section 'W' grave number 142. His grave is marked by a CWGC headstone bearing the usual name, rank and date. At the bottom of the headstone, is he legend, '"Ricky" He Died For Us'. As is to be expected, the grave of Ricalton, which lies among other fallen airmen, is immaculately kept. At the opposing end of the scale, the War Memorial, in Ricalton's hometown of Gosforth, bears no names of those fallen in either of the World Wars. The Church of St Nicholas, on the east side of the town, carries a 'Roll of Honour' dedicated to the honour of the men of both wars from the town. Sadly, the name of Ricalton does not appear there either. It would appear that Alan Leslie Ricalton, one of the band known in history as 'Churchill's Few', is truly one of the forgotten few of the North East. All that remains to mark the passing of Alan Leslie Ricalton are a handful of photographs and his Omega service watch, now in the hands of his remaining family.

RICALTON NOTES
1. Cossey: *Tigers*, P 78.
2. Number 74 Squadron diaries.
3. "Newcastle Journal" October 22, 1940, P 6. The report also carries a photograph of Ricalton.

Marmaduke Ridley at Leconfield, 1940. Believed to be the only surviving photograph of Ridley, it was taken by fellow pilot William L.B. Walker.

Marmaduke Ridley, 565201
Sergeant

Marmaduke Ridley was born in the latter part of September 1915, his baptism taking place in the church of St James in Benwell, October 6, 1915. Marmaduke was the elder son of Marmaduke Ridley and Isabella Grove, formerly Brown. Marmaduke senior was employed as a fitter in a nearby engineering company. The family home at this time being Number 43, Hugh Gardens, now demolished, in the Newcastle western suburb of Benwell. The area of Benwell was an industrial centre of west end Newcastle. As a result, many of the residents of Benwell worked locally in industry. Education for the young Marmaduke Ridley was at Atkinson Road Technical School in Benwell, a school known for giving its pupils extra training for the surrounding industries. These were mainly Parsons Engineering and Vickers Engineering, many of the pupils being bound for one or the other.

Although Marmaduke Ridley was destined to work in engineering, he had other ideas in mind rather than the local works. For Ridley there was only one on his mind: that was to be the RAF. On leaving school Ridley found himself at Halton, Buckinghamshire, where he was to be one of the so-called 'Trenchards Brats'. Ridley began his training with the RAF January 1, 1931. He proceeded through his training until he passed out at the end of December 1934. Ridley was now a fully trained aero fitter on engines. Nothing is known of his service life after training. However, like many 'Brats' Ridley was not satisfied with being a fitter in the RAF and harboured ambitions to be a pilot. Ridley applied for, and was accepted for flying training. His training days now appear to be lost. The first we hear of him as a pilot, was when he joined 616 (South Yorkshire) Squadron, one of the newer Auxiliary Air Force Squadrons.

Number 616 Squadron had been formed November 1, 1938. Like most other Auxiliary Air Force Squadrons, 616 had been a bomber squadron. However, only ten days after its formation, 616 Squadron was transferred to RAF Fighter Command. Originally the squadron was equipped with the Gloster Gauntlet. These aircraft were already dated and, by the end of 1939, 616 Squadron had been re-equipped with the Spitfire. At this time, the squadron did not have enough experienced pilots in its ranks. To boost its experienced numbers in its ranks and, provide experienced pilots to train its less experienced pilots on the Spitfire, a group of pilots from other squadrons joined the ranks of 616. Among these men was Marmaduke Ridley.

With the start of the new year of 1940, 616 Squadron were posted to Leconfield. This was to be the squadron's war station. With the Blitzkrieg launched in France, the home based fighter squadrons were placed on alert. As the German forces pushed the British forces back towards the Channel port of Dunkirk, the squadrons of RAF Fighter Command were rotated through the airfields in the south. When 74 Squadron were withdrawn from the south, May 26, 616 Squadron took their place flying from Rochford.

Number 616 Squadron had as yet seen no action and, had only flown Spitfires for a few short months. Lack of experience was to come to light, May 28. The squadron was caught unawares and bounced by upwards of thirty Me 109s. The squadron C.O., Squadron Leader M. Robinson, was among those who had their aircraft severely damaged. Managing to get his crippled Spitfire back across the Channel, Robinson made a forced landing at Manston. Also hit during this action was the Spitfire of Marmaduke Ridley. Ridley had been taken by surprise by the diving Me 109s. His Spitfire was raked by gunfire from the enemy aircraft and he was lucky to escape with his life. Ridley's Spitfire did not come out o f the action as well as its pilot. Among other things that had been hit was the cockpit and, most of the instruments were put out of action. Ridley was slightly wounded in the head and his Spitfire was flyable, just. However, it was enough to get Ridley back across the Channel. Later, while on sick leave, Ridley was asked by a friend how he managed to get back without his instruments. Back came the matter of fact answer, 'I followed the ships'.[1]

June 6, 1940 saw the return of 616 Squadron to its home base at Leconfield. Over the next few weeks the squadron's duties were to revert back to convoy patrols and the interception of lone raiders. Only limited success was to be recorded for the latter. Ridley was in action, August 1, over the North Sea. While carrying out a patrol, in company with P/O W.L.B. Walker, Ridley had spotted a lone Ju 88 over a convoy. He managed to engage the Ju 88 and drive it away from the convoy. Ridley had the satisfaction of getting in some good bursts, the result being black smoke coming from one of the Ju 88s engines. The combat was to remain inconclusive, however. Although the Ju 88 was last seen trailing smoke and disappearing in the direction of home, Ridley's Spitfire, K 9829, had also been damaged in the action. On arrival back at Leconfield, K 9829 was found to have damage in the radio equipment and one of the engine bearers. It was around this time that, what appears to be the only surviving photograph of Ridley, was taken by a fellow pilot.[2]

At this time Leconfield had no concrete runway. When it rained, the airfield took on the resemblance of a large pond, so badly was it waterlogged. Even this was not enough to dampen the spirits of the pilots of 616 Squadron, who always seemed to find a way to take off. August 6, 1940 saw the Luftwaffe once more attacking the coastal shipping. A section was ordered off, the C. O., Squadron Leader Robinson, with Flt Lt R.O. Hellyer and Ridley. The section was vectored towards a small convoy. When they got there they found that the convoy was under attack from a Ju 88. As with the action of August 1, this combat was to be inconclusive. The Ju 88 was driven away from the convoy; however, it left its mark on the Spitfires. This Ju 88 appears to have been a fairly belligerent one. All three of the Spitfires were damaged in the attack by return gunfire.

The next action for 616 Squadron was to come on the afternoon of August 15. This was the southern arm of a two-pronged attack against the North East of England by the aircraft of Luftflotte Five. This arm of the attack being launched by Ju 88s of KG 30 flying from their base at Aalbourg, Denmark. The full squadron was scrambled at 1.07 PM and met this attack over Flamborough Head, Yorkshire.

Attacking from 20,000 feet, the pilots of 616 Squadron were to make claims for no less than eight Ju 88s destroyed. However, it is not known if Ridley took part in this action. A few days after the successful defence, 616 Squadron were ordered south, to Kenley.

On August 22, Winston Churchill paid a visit to Kenly. During this visit, as if on cue, 616 Squadron was scrambled. The pilots believing that it was a demonstration for the Prime Minister. However, they were vectored over Dover where they were bounced by Me 109s. One Spitfire, that of F/O H.S.L. Dundas, was set alight and fell onto 'Adam & Eve' Hill near Elham.[3] At first it was thought that Dundas had been shot down by AA ground fire, however, P/O L.H. 'Buck' Casson returned to Kenley with bullet damage to the rear of his Spitfire.

Number 616 Squadron were scrambled into action no less than three times, August 24. Each occasion was to turn out the same; they failed to engage the enemy. The following day, August 25, looked as if it was going to be quiet. There was no action at all until the evening. Number 616 Squadron were scrambled at around 6.15 PM to investigate an incoming raid in the area over Canterbury. This raid consisted of fifteen plus Do 17s with a fighter escort of twenty plus Me 109s.

Ridley singled out one of the Do 17s and placed it under attack. However, the hunter became the hunted when Ridley was attacked by the Me 109s of the fighter escort. Ridley was caught up in a turning dogfight over Canterbury. Managing to extricate himself, Ridley turned once more to the bombers. Attacking with good, sort bursts Ridley observed pieces falling away from the Do 17. Once again, Ridley was driven away from the bomber force by the defending Me 109s. After the skirmish over Canterbury, Ridley could only make a claim for one bomber damaged. In return, the squadron had lost two Spitfires and their pilots.

The pattern of raids on the following day turned out much the same as August 25. Biggin Hill and Kenley were singled out for attacks. The bombers approached their targets from the Thames Estuary a tactic formed by the Luftwaffe in order to gain an element of surprise but also, to avoid flying over Kent where they suffered at the hands of the ground defences. At 11.05 AM, 'B' Flight were scrambled into action to intercept an He 111. The latter managed to give the fighters the slip. Flight Lieutenant D.E. Gillam ordered

Yellow Section to return to Kenley leaving Blue Section to patrol Dover looking for an errant barrage balloon. Arriving over Dover, Blue Section were badly bounced by almost one hundred Me 109s. Yellow Section, hearing the shout for help, returned hastily to the fray and were caught up in the fight. Finding themselves caught up in the action, heavily outnumbered, they were forced to fight on the defensive while waiting for the reinforcements.

Five aircraft of 'A' Flight were then scrambled and vectored towards Dover in order to give aid to 'B' Flight. While still in the battle climb, 'A' Flight were also bounced by a heavy force of Me 109s. One pilot, P/O W.L.B. Walker, was a rookie pilot at the time. He was scrambled as part of 'A' Flight. In the lead was F/O E.F. 'Teddy' St Aubyn with Ridley as his number two. Walker was told to stay close to the other two. The first that Walker knew anything was amiss was when he heard the shouting over the R/T. When he turned to look, St Aubyn and Ridley were nowhere to be seen. Gunfire then hit Walker's Spitfire, forcing him to vacate it rather quickly. Walker was wounded in the foot and it was not until later that he was to learn that the squadron had lost seven Spitfires to the Me 109s. St Aubyn was burned and Ridley was dead.

Confusion reigned during the battle and the passing of time has not changed this. If anything, it is worse. So many Spitfires fell from the sky it has remained a problem to find what pilot was flying which Spitfire. Some writers have recorded that Ridley was flying Spitfire R 6633 while others claim that he was flying R 6758.[4] One other writer confidently states that P/O Walker took over R 6633 that morning, however, this may well not be the case.[5] Walker was later to state; 'My log book records that I was flying R 6633 but this has been queried on occasion and it is just possible that I recorded the number wrongly as I wrote up my log book after some months in hospital'.

'With regards to the number of the Spitfire I flew on August 26th 1940, it is, I believe more than likely that the squadron records were incorrect'.[6] Walker admits that he flew at least eight different Spitfires during the month of August. It is not surprising that he made a slight error, especially as he made his logbook entry at a later date.

Whichever Spitfire Ridley flew in this his last flight, it fell away from the fighting, burning as it went. Ridley's Spitfire was to crash into the area near Dungeness where it burned itself out. It is thought by some that his victor was Hptmn Josef Foezoe, Staffel Kapitan of 4/JG 51. However, this same pilot is thought to have shot down F/O G.E. Moberley at the same time. This would appear a bit fanciful. By the time he made one pass, his dive would have carried him some distance away. One of the others at a different time, yes. Two together, I would not think so.

Unlike most of his countrymen, Ridley was not brought home to the North East. His burial was to take place in Hawkinge. This would account for why no death notice appeared in the local press. No report appeared either. Ridley was buried in Folkestone New Cemetery, Kent. He lies in plot 'O' grave number 23. As usual, his grave carries a CWGC headstone and his grave is kept in pristine condition. In his hometown of Newcastle, Marmaduke Ridley is a forgotten man. A former pilot sums Ridley up: 'Sgt Ridley is not forgotten by me... Ridley was a most likeable chap although rather quiet...' he was '... a brave and courageous young man'.[7]

Ridley Notes

1. Conversation with Miss B. Cracknell, a personal friend of the Ridley family.
2. Photograph taken at RAF Leconfield by William Walker.
3. D. Knight: *Harvest of Messerschmitts*, Dundas fell on Adam & Eve Hill, P 102. Ramsey: *The Battle of Britain then and Now*, Dundas' Spitfire crashed at Runninghill Elham, P 374.
4. Ramsey, states that Ridley was flying Spitfire R 6633. Shacklady, *Spitfire: The History*, states that this aircraft was flown by P/O R Marples, P 84. Ridley was flying Spitfire R 6758, P 85. In the heat of battle, Ridley may have been in any. However, R 6758 is reported to have force-landed at Adisham, some twenty-five miles from where Ridley's Spitfire was reported to have crashed.
5. D. Sarkar: *The Battle of Britain A Last Look Back*.
6. Personal correspondence with Flight Lieutenant William L.B. Walker.
7. Personal correspondence with Flight Lieutenant William L.B. Walker.

ROBERT DURHAM RUTTER, 42574
PILOT OFFICER

Robert Durham Rutter was born in Newcastle upon Tyne, although it is thought that he lived in the Gosforth area, which at that time was in Northumberland. He was born August 3, 1919. His mother's maiden name was known to have been Thompson. At an early age, probably along with his family, the young Rutter moved to Belgium. It was in Belgium that Rutter received his education. He attended the College of St Michel and the Athenium, in the town of Brussels. When still only nineteen, Rutter decided on a career with the RAF. Applying for flying duties, Rutter was accepted on a short service commission. Rutter's flying training began in mid 1939. On this date he began training with the Elementary and Reserve Flying Training School (E&RFTS) at Ansty. On leaving Ansty, Rutter continued his training at Number 14 Flying Training School (FTS) at Kinloss, arriving there September 1, 1939. Next stop for Rutter was Number 6 Operational Training Unit (OTU) at Sutton Bridge. Rutter's training continued there from February 28, 1940. At Sutton Bridge Rutter was converted onto the Hawker Hurricane.

On May 11, 1940, the new, yet still raw pilot was posted to his first fighter squadron. This was to be 73 Squadron. At this time 73 Squadron were based in Belgium as part of the Advanced Air Striking Force (AASF). The squadron at this time being based at Rouvres a few miles to the north of the First World War battlefield of Ypres. Number 73 Squadron were often to be in the thickest of the fighting. When the British forces began their retreat towards the Channel port of

Dunkirk, 73 Squadron were moved further to the south to help with the air cover.

June 1 saw the squadron flying an offensive patrol in the vicinity of Malmaison airfield. The patrol had come under severe and accurate fire from the ground defences when Rutter saw a patrol of Me 109s. Bringing his observations to the attention of the rest of the patrol, Rutter prepared to move into the attack. Nine Me 109s made up the German patrol and two of them decided to single out Rutter. However, Rutter managed to make good his escape. The squadron had become separated during this time, each trying to gain the better of his individual target as well as trying to evade the attentions of the Me 109s.

Rutter had broken upwards, seeking refuge in the cloud cover above. Descending once more, he spotted an Me 109 putting another Hurricane under attack. Closing in, Rutter opened fire at close range. The Me 109 was seen to flip over and break away downwards, trailing black smoke. From Gaye to LeMans and on to Nantes, Number 73 Squadron fell back, though still fighting. The groundcrews still managed to maintain the fighting unit somehow, under difficult conditions. Finally, June 18, 73 squadron were forced to retreat to England. For his actions in France, Rutter was mentioned in despatches.

Through July and into August, 73 Squadron rested and trained its pilots, old and new, at Church Fenton in the relative quiet of Yorkshire. August 15, 1940 saw 'B' Flight of 73 Squadron scrambled at 1.07 PM. They were to intercept an incoming attack in the area of Flamborough Head. There, they intercepted a formation of Ju 88s, managing to destroy three. Number 73 Squadron were to remain in the north until early September. The squadron were then posted back to the south, taking up station at Debden. No doubt the squadron was elated to be back in the action. However, the happiness was to be short lived. Within four hours of their arrival at Debden, 73 Squadron were in action against the enemy, an action that cost the squadron three of their Hurricanes destroyed and a further three damaged.

This action took place on the afternoon of September 5. Scrambled at around 3.00 PM, 73 Squadron were attacking a formation of Ju 88s to the north of London. Inexperienced, the squadron were bounced by Me 109s. Rutter had lined up a Ju 88 and was about to put it under attack when he was bounced from the rear by an Me 109. Cannon and machine-gun fire raked Rutter's Hurricane. Rutter was wounded in the ankle, his Hurricane was damaged to the extent that he had to take to his parachute. Rutter's Hurricane, P 3110 coded TP-G, was from the middle of a batch of five-hundred built by Gloster Aircraft Co at their Brockworth factory. This Hurricane took part in the action over Flamborough Head, August 15. A photograph exists of this Hurricane flown by Sergeant John Griffiths. Rutter was picked up and admitted to Bilericay Hospital. Hurricane 'G' crashed near Steals Farm near Stock to the north of Billericay.[1] In more recent years, the Essex Historical Aircraft Society have unearthed parts of Rutter's Hurricane. These were engine parts and pieces of airframe from the cockpit area.[2]

Later in the Battle of Britain, 73 Squadron were to evolve into a night-fighter unit. Rutter was to remain with 73 Squadron until March 3, 1941. From then, Rutter was posted to 17 Squadron. Some three months later, Rutter was posted on to the Defence Flight at Takoradi where he stayed for the next sixteen months. At the end of this period Rutter was posted back to the UK. Rutter was next posted to Number 56 Operational Training Unit (OTU), then based at Tealing, Dundee. While serving there, Rutter was Chief Flying Instructor from January 13. Later in the year he was to leave and take a course at the Fighter Leaders School (FLS). On completion of his course, Rutter was next posted to 195 Squadron, based at Fairlop, December 3, 1943. With his new squadron, Rutter became a Flight Commander. Number 195 Squadron disbanded, February 1944. After his short stay with 195 Squadron, Rutter was posted to 183 Squadron then based at Tangmere.

The next posting for Rutter came on April 9, 1944. On this date Rutter was posted to take command of 263 (Fellowship of the Bellows) Squadron at Harrowbeer. This squadron had just relinquished their Westland Whirlwind fighters in favour of the Hawker Typhoon. From their base at Harrowbeer, Rutter led the squadron to France, August 6, 1944. September 1, 1944 saw Rutter decorated with the DFC as well as the French Croix de Guere.

Rutter was later to join the Directing Staff at the School of Air Support at Old Sarum, arriving there January 3, 1945. A year later, February 5, Rutter was admitted to hospital with Tuberculosis. He was to remain in hospital until the end of the year. Although Rutter had been granted a permanent commission with the RAF in 1946, he was invalided out of the service in 1947, retaining the rank of Squadron Leader. Robert Durham Rutter died in October of 1998.

Rutter Notes
1. Ramsey: *Battle of Britain Then and Now,* names the crash site as Seamens Lane, Stock, P 419.
2. A photograph appears in the above, P 419, of the recovery group making a 'dig' on Rutter's Hurricane.

STUART NIGEL ROSE, 81920
PILOT OFFICER

Stuart Nigel Rose was born in the Elswick area of the City of Newcastle upon Tyne, June 21, 1918. His mother's maiden name was known to be Birrell. Little is known of the early life of Rose and, it is presumed that at least he, if not his family, moved to the south. Rose was a trainee Quantity Surveyor at the time he joined the RAFVR. This he did in March of 1939. As he joined in the Southampton area, it is presumed that this was the area to which he had moved. His service number indicated that he was in the catchment area for 615 (County of Surrey) Squadron.[1] His initial training was to be carried out at Hamble. Rose was then called to full-time service in September of 1939. His first posting was to the Initial Training Wing (ITW) at Cambridge, arriving there November 22, 1939. In the early part of the following year, Rose was posted to Number 14 Flying Training School (FTS) at Kinloss, Scotland. Rose was to spend the winter months, February 3 to April 19, 1940, at the Scottish airfield. His next posting was to take Rose back south, to Cranfield near Bedford. Rose completed his training June 17, 1940 and was commissioned. The following day, Rose was posted to his first fighter squadron, Number 602 (City of Glasgow) Squadron, Auxiliary Air Force. Rose was to find himself once more on the way back to Scotland.

Number 602 Squadron were at this time based at Drem, a few miles from Edinburgh. Number 602 Squadron had been the first Auxiliary Squadron to be formed, beginning its life at Renfrew, September 12, 1925. Another first for the squadron was that it had the distinction of being the first Auxiliary Air Force Squadron to be equipped with the new generation fighter, the Spitfire. The squadron divided its time between its satellite bases of Dyce and Montrose before settling at Drem. While at Drem, the squadron's duties included the air defence of the Firth of Forth, this area being visited sporadically by the Luftwaffe on both reconnaissance flights and hit and run attacks.

During this period 602 Squadron was at readiness from before first light. Although scrambled on many occasions a lot of the alerts turned out to be false alarms. One such occasion occurred, July 25, 1940. From readiness the squadron was scrambled into action at 4.15 PM only to find it had been a false alarm. During this period most of the damage on the squadron's aircraft was self inflicted rather than caused by the enemy. On return to one of the satellite airfields, the Spitfire of Rose hit a marker flag on its approach. This in turn released a parachute flare container that failed to detach and battered the underside of the Spitfire, causing considerable damage. August 1, 1940, while attempting a night landing, the Spitfire of Flt Lt J.D. Urie hit the ground on landing and tore off a wing due to heavy mist conditions. On the same night, another Spitfire, flown by P/O H.W. Moody, overshot the flarepath in the same conditions as above.[2]

On August 12, 602 Squadron were ordered south, stopping en route at Church Fenton in order to refuel. The squadron was soon on its way again to its new base, the Tangmere satellite base of Wethampnett. The pace of life was to be lived at a much faster pace in the south. August 15 saw Westhampnett put under attack by Ju 87s. The following day, Rose received his baptism of fire when the base was once more put under attack by the Ju 87s. Number 602 Squadron tangling with the Ju 87s of II/StG77 over Bognor.

Number 602 Squadron were in the air no less than three times on August 22. However, the result was to be the same on each patrol; no contact with the enemy. August 25, 1940, was to bring no let up as 602 Squadron flew two patrols. At 4.00 PM the squadron was scrambled into action to intercept a formation of a hundred plus bombers that was heading towards the Weymouth area. The squadron was in the air in plenty time to make the best of a height advantage. Unable to get at the bombers due to fighter interference from almost two hundred escorting fighters, 602 Squadron used their high altitude to good effect against the fighter escort. Number 602 Squadron swooped down on the Me 110s over Dorchester and Portland.

Rose singled out an Me 110 and pressed home his attack until he witnessed black smoke and coolant pouring from one of the Me 110s engines. Rose was to make a claim for this Me 110 as destroyed. Rose turned his attention to another Me 110, which took evasive action by entering into a steep dive as it tried to make good its escape. Not to be outdone easily, Rose followed it down. He was to notice that in his own headlong dive, his Spitfire recorded a speed in excess of 420 MPH. However, the Me 110 was to win the day on this occasion; it got away. Rose was forced to make a landing at Hamble, as he thought he was suffering from a fuel shortage. Later, the ground crew found that his Spitfire had suffered a fuel gauge failure. It was also found that, one of the gun covers on his Spitfires port wing had blown off. This had been caused by his high-speed pursuit of the Me 110.

The Luftwaffe carried out further attacks in the area of the Solent, August 26. Number 602 Squadron went into action along with 43 Squadron. As the fighters approached the bomber force, many were seen to jettison their bomb loads in an attempt to avoid the fray and make a run for home. This was to present a dangerous problem for the fighter pilots, especially those that had already carried out their attacks. As they manoeuvred beneath the fleeing bombers, they had to avoid the falling bombs. A number of He 111s were brought down. Two of them fell to the guns of 602 Squadron. The Luftwaffe's rescue service was out in force in their He 59s. One of these He 59s was observed to be 'spotting'. Although the aircraft was carrying clearly defined Red Cross markings, it was shot down. This aircraft was He 59 (935. of Seenotflugdo 2. It was shot down by Spitfires of 602 Squadron some twenty miles south of St Catherines Point. The crew of two were killed. It was to be stated that this aircraft was shot down on '… the Prime Ministers personal orders'.[3]

Rose was next to be in action, September 4. Shortly after lunchtime, 'A' Flight was ordered off and encountered a group of Me 110s over Beachy Head. In the ensuing dogfight, Rose fired at about eight separate Me 110s. One of 7these was observed to be trailing white smoke as it dived away; however, he could only claim it as damaged. During September 5, Rose carried out two patrols, attempting to engage Me 109s on each. However, on both occasions the enemy departed the scene without a fight.

September 7, 1940 saw the Luftwaffe turn towards London Number 602 Squadron got caught up in a running dogfight to the south of the capital as the enemy turned for home. Number 602 Squadron lost two Spitfires with a further two damaged. One of the pilots was later to die of wounds, while another was missing. Rose attacked an Me 110 which he was later to claim as destroyed. Number 602 Squadron were probably at their lowest point during this period. The squadron was under pressure and they were down to eight serviceable Spitfires. When the order was made to scramble, September 11, 602 Squadron had to join forces with 213 Squadron to make a fighting unit.

The two squadrons were airborne just after 3.00 PM in answer to intercept a large raid on London. The Me 110s had formed defensive circles over Croydon as they awaited their charges en route south. Number 602 Squadron plunged into the fighting and a running dogfight broke out which was to be carried out all the way to the south coast. Rose saw an Me 110 which filled his sights and he manouevred into position. Momentarily distracted by the thrill of the chase, Rose failed to see another Me 110 approaching from his rear. The first he knew that it was there was the sound of gunfire hitting his Spitfire. Spitfire L 1027 was to suffer severe damage in this encounter. Rose was slightly wounded in the arm. With most of the flying controls out of action Rose managed to land his Spitfire safely.[4]

Rose was out of action for a few weeks and did not fly again until October 7, 1940. Between then and the 29th of the month Rose made a number of flights, mostly at high altitude, without making any contact with the enemy, even though they were seen on a number of occasions. On October 29, the squadron was ordered into the air to intercept a number of Me 109 fighter-bombers. Number 602 Squadron found themselves well placed to take advantage of the situation. They had a height advantage and, at 27,000 feet were well above and behind the enemy formation of fifty plus. Rose singled out an Me 109 and attacked, seeing white smoke pour from the enemy aircraft before it dived away. Making an attack on another Me 109, Rose saw his gunfire hitting the Me 109 along the side of its fuselage and around the cockpit. However, he could only make a claim for a probable, as no one saw the fighter hit the ground.

Later rose was to be part of what could have been an unfortunate incident. He observed two aircraft flying together at quite a distance. Rose opened fire at the rearmost aircraft at maximum range. He was fortunate in that he missed. The rear aircraft on this occasion was a Spitfire that had just been attacking the front aircraft, an Me 109. The return flight was to be a bumpy one for Rose; his Spitfire was fired on twice by the 'friendly' ground forces. On both occasions they failed to find their target.

As November moved into its first week, the weather began to take control of the air fighting. November 6, 1940, began by hampering the operations. With the afternoon the weather began to get better and the skies began to clear. A lone Ju 88 took the opportunity to make use of the good spell and attacked Westhampnett. Number 602 Squadron managed to get two of their aircraft airborne at 5.06 PM. One of these was Rose. The two aircraft, Squadron Leader J.D. Urie with Rose as his number two, soon caught up with the marauding Ju 88 and attacked it. After delivering a number of attacks without seeing any result, the Ju 88 made an attempt at escape through a break in the cloud cover. Rose followed the aircraft through the cloud and found the enemy aircraft below cloud level. Rose then turned to carry out a beam attack. However, Rose was to misjudge the angle of attack and he overshot the target. Not believing his luck, the pilot of the Ju 88 pulled back up into the cloud and must have made good his escape as he was not seen again. Rose was to make a claim for a damaged Ju 88. November was to carry on as it had started. When the weather allowed, 602 Squadron were on patrol. However, due mainly to the bad weather, these patrols were inconclusive when the enemy was hardly ever sighted.

December 6, 1940 saw Rose suffer a slight mishap. Flying at some 5,000 feet over Chichester, Rose found himself flying a Spitfire without an engine. The engine deciding to cut and refusing all attempts to restart. With a bit of skillful flying, Rose managed to return his Spitfire to base without further mishap. Now that the official Battle of Britain had run its course, paranoia appears to have taken over. As well as Rose's Spitfire, other Spitfires on the base had proved to have niggling failings. These mishaps put together, led some members of the squadron to believe that sabotage was to blame. The tour of duty in the south was now at an end for 602 Squadron and they were ordered back to Prestwick December 17. Among the lighter moments at this time, was the use of 602 Squadron by the film makers, 20th Century Fox, in the flying sequences of their film *A Yank In The RAF*. A return to the south came later when 602 Squadron flew on offensive patrols from Kenley.

Rose was later posted on to 54 Squadron, arriving at their base, September 2, 1941. He was to remain with 54 Squadron until the end of his flying tour which came in November. Rose was now posted to a training unit to pass on his skills. Rose was posted to Number 57 Operational Training Unit (OTU) at Hawarden. He was later promoted to the rank of Flight Lieutenant and posted once more to the Central Flying School (CFS) at Hullavington, arriving there November 11, 1942. Rose remained at the Central Flying School until February of the following year. He was then posted back to 57 OTU, the training unit now being based at Eshott in Northumberland.

The remainder of Rose's flying career was spent as an instructor at various bases throughout the UK. These being interspersed with various courses to further update his abilities. From 1944 to 1945, Rose was posted to the Middle East. While there he was based at the Bombing and Gunnery School (BGS) at El Ballah. In December of 1945, Rose returned to the UK where he was released from the RAF in February of 1946 with the rank of Squadron Leader. After a break of nine years, Rose finally qualified as a Chartered Quantity Surveyor. Now retired, Stuart Nigel Rose lives in the south of England.

ROSE NOTES

1. Shores: *Aces High, Vol 2*, P 17.
2. Ramsey: *The Battle of Britain Then and Now*, P 337.
3. Hunt: *21 Squadrons*.
4. Shacklady states that this Spitfire, with Rose in it, was shot down 21 September. Ramsey states that this aircraft was shot down on 11 September after being damaged. Mason, states that this Spitfire was shot down 9 September and the Spitfire was destroyed. Records show that this Spitfire was later to fly with Number 53 OTU until it was struck off charge in October of 1941 after being damaged in a crash landing the previous July.

John Sample, DFC, 90278
Squadron Leader

John Sample was born in Longhirst, Northumberland, in the early part of 1913. His baptism taking place, February 27, of that year, in the local village church of St John's. John Sample was the first son of Thomas Norman, a ship owner, and his wife, Kate Isabel Sample. The family home at this time was Longhirst Grange, a farmhouse situated to the west of Longhirst village and some two miles north of the market town of Morpeth. Education for John Sample was private until old enough to attend public school. This was to be Aysgarth School. A school situated in the Pennine district of west Yorkshire. It is thought that John Sample may have later attended Lansing School in the south of the country.

There was also to be an association with the neighbouring village of Bothal. It was at Bothal that the Sample family had been land agents to the Dukes of Portland since 1828. This business was handed down through the family and, on occasion, father was the land agent with the son as the joint agent. It was John Sample's uncle, William Collings Sample, who held the position of land agent at this time. William Collings Sample became joint agent with his father before becoming agent in 1906. It came as no surprise, therefore, when John Sample went into business with his uncle. As a joint agent, John Sample was a member of the Land Agents Society and the Surveyors Institute.

The young John Sample must have spent a great deal of time at Bothal. Not only was the Castle his place of work but also the home of

607 Squadron summer camp 1937 sports day. Rear left – John Sample, Peter Dixon, Reddington. Middle row, Left – M.M. Irving, J.M. Bazin, G. White, Lance Smith, Will Gore, James A. Vick, (?), Leslie Runciman Squadron C.O. Photo: Nicholas Craig.

his uncle. His uncle was to live there until his death in 1950, and his aunt Hilda also died there in 1964. The best documentation to be found on the Sample family was written by a local author, Roland Bibby. Although all the land agents are listed, there is one omission, the name of John Sample. Considering John Sample was a joint agent this omission is rather odd.[1]

Born in the countryside, it is not unexpected that John was adept at countryside pursuits and fieldsports. John was to become a keen rifleman as well as an accomplished revolver shot. In later life he was to represent an Air Force team at Bisley. While it was common for young men of the day to drive around in fast cars, it was to the skies that John looked for his added excitement. New shapes were taking flight with new exciting noises. John found that he had to travel down to the next county, County Durham, if he wanted to join these men who were taking to the skies in exciting new machinery. To meet this end, John joined the Auxiliary Air Force. Young men like himself were swelling the ranks of the local Auxiliary squadrons. These squadrons were to be termed, by the press, the 'weekend fliers'. John

Sample was to join Number 607 (County of Durham) Squadron Auxiliary Air Force as a Pilot Officer.

It was at RAF Usworth that John Sample was to begin his association with flying. A Gypsy Moth and an Avro 504 provided the means to learn to fly. A succession of biplanes were to pass through the squadron as part of their equipment. The standard aircraft on the squadron, until 1936, was the Westland Wapiti. This aircraft was replaced with the Hawker Demon. Part of the training in the Auxiliary Air Force was the summer camps at host airfields. John Sample can be seen in the official photographs. In less official photographs, he appears more in the background. At some squadron functions, he appears to keep his face away from the camera. However, he was a fighter pilot and appears to be more confident when carrying out this role. A photograph exists of the young fighter pilot as he flies his Hawker Demon K 3800 over the County Durham countryside. Altogether, he presents the image of a shy man. At the other end of the scale, however, he appears to have been talented musically. He is known to have been adept at playing the concertina, accordion and the flute. He also made and played a set of Northumbrian Pipes[2]. In fact, he was so good with the latter, that he played with Jack Armstrong, later to become official piper to the Duke of Northumberland. As well as taking part, and winning, local piping competitions, he made at least one broadcast on BBC radio.

Back on the squadron, things took another turn in. With the war not too far off, 607 Squadron were re-equipped with the Gloster Gladiator. With this aircraft, still World War One technology, John Sample and his fellow pilots trained for war. Life for John Sample at this time was still a mixture with his life divided between flying as a fighter pilot and working as a land agent. However, things were about to change in the very near future.

In early 1939, John Sample was promoted to Flight Commander, taking command of 'B' Flight. The squadron, at summer camp at Abbotsinch, Glasgow, were hastily recalled. Within a short time, the squadron and its men were embodied into the RAF. Number 607 Squadron took on the duties of a full time fighter squadron. September 10, 1939 saw the squadron moved to Acklington in Northumberland, there, to take up their war station. This was to be on a temporary basis. Usworth was to undergo work on its runways. The main opposition that could be expected at Acklington were lone raiders and aircraft on mine-laying missions along the English coast.

Most of the time spent at Acklington was taken up with training duties. However, the afternoon of October 17, 1939, was to bring a change to the routine. At 12.45 PM, Blue Section of 'B' Flight were ordered away from Acklington. This section consisted of Flying Officer G.D. Craig, and Pilot Officer W.H.R. (Nits) Whitty, Sample leading. On the return leg of their patrol, a Do 18 was spotted flying at around 1,500 feet. The section went into the attack diving from 8,000 feet. Each of the aircraft made three attacks from the rear, but damage appeared to be negligible, being limited to pieces flying off and fuel being observed escaping. With fuel low and ammunition expended, Blue Section made its way back to Acklington. The Do 18 was last seen by the trio, trailing smoke as it headed out to sea. All was not over, however. The Do 18 had been wounded more than had been thought. Some fifty miles out to sea, it made a landing alongside the Destroyer *HMS Juno*. The German crew were all taken prisoner.[3] Number 607 Squadron had drawn its first blood. Craig was later to write; 'Probably Johnnie's work'.[4]

More changes were on the way for the squadron, however. Numbers 1, 73, 85 and 87 Squadrons were sent to France as part of the Air Component of the Advanced Air Striking Force (AASF). Rumours were rife within the ranks of 607 Squadron, that it would follow suit. November 13, 1939 saw the rumours come about and 607 Squadron packed its bags and moved south. A mixture of airliners and Gladiators made their way south, making a detour over Sunderland as a farewell. Sample must also have looked down with feeling as he passed over his house, some five miles south of Acklington. After a two-day stay at Croydon, due to bad weather, the squadron made the short hop across the Channel, landing at Merville.

A move was soon to come for the squadron. This was due to the heavy mud conditions at Merville. The squadron was moved to Vitry-en-Artois. There, the mud was replaced by the frozen variety that left potholes. This was to be the worst winter on record. One or two photographs have survived from this time. They show Sample in the complete 'Irving' flying clothing and topped off with a wool hat. During this period, most of the time was spent on training as well as flying patrols, some of these of the cross-Channel variety as they escorted troops home on leave. A visit to Seclin, by King George VI also relieved the monotony. Squadron Leader Lance Smith, the Commanding Officer of 607 Squadron, and Sample were presented to the Monarch.

In April, 607 Squadron were re-equipped with the Hawker Hurricane. The changeover taking place at Abbeville. The change coming none to soon. May 10, 1940 saw the German *Blitzkrieg* break through into Belgium and France. Number 607 Squadron were one of the first squadrons to be on the receiving end of the German attack. Many of the aircrew were still in bed and had a rude awakening. Shortly after 5.15 AM, Sample led his section into the air. A formation of He 111s were reported in the vicinity of Douai. The formation were soon spotted; Sample, ever cautious, made a visual sighting to make sure of his target. Having ensured that they were German, Sample led his section into the attack. Lining up behind a He111, Sample opened fire. After only three bursts, Sample was forced to break off his attack. The windscreen of Sample's Hurricane had become covered with oil from the enemy bomber. Sample was forced to return to base.

The afternoon was to bring no respite from the attacks. Sample was once more in action. On this occasion, Sample spotted a formation of He 111s in the vicinity of Albert. These aircraft turned out to be He 111s of 1/KG 1. Ordering his formation into line astern, Sample moved into the attack, lining up one of the bombers. The formation had been flying in a 'V' formation. One of the bombers had lagged behind the rest and Sample used this to his advantage. The first burst of the Hurricane's gunfire encouraged the bomber to look for shelter among the rest of the formation. However, it was too late and Sample moved in for another attack. Sample noticed pieces coming away from the bomber during this second attack. He could also see his fire passing through the bombers wings and fuselage. The port engine had also been hit; white smoke was pouring back from it. The wounded bomber now began to turn away from the formation in an effort to make a run for home. However, all was not yet over.

Sample lined the stricken bomber up to make yet another attack. As he did so he was caught in a hail of gunfire. This was the crossfire from the rest of the formation. In a short time, the hunter had become the hunted as the German bullets found their mark on Sample's Hurricane. Black smoke came back towards the cockpit and Sample found that his own engine oil now covered the windscreen of his Hurricane. Unable to see anything outside, Sample decided to vacate his Hurricane as he would not be able to see to carry out a landing.

Sample now took to his parachute, managing to vacate his Hurricane without injury. His landing was not so fortunate. Landing on the British side of the lines, Sample managed to badly sprain both of his ankles in the landing. Hurricane P 2615 came to earth some distance away. Delivered back to base, Sample was taken off flying duties and was forced to wear carpet slippers for the duration of his stay in France.

Grounded Sample may have been, but he was still of use to the squadron. Daily the losses mounted and 607 Squadron, in particular, were severely hit. The severity of the fighting at this time can be measured in the fact that 607 Squadron lost two of its Commanding Officers over a relatively short period. Squadron Leader Lance E. Smith, a long term friend of Sample's and one of the squadron originals, only just back from leave, was shot down and killed. Another pilot drafted in to the squadron, Squadron Leader George M. Fidler, took command only to be shot down and taken prisoner. Sample, the most senior pilot remaining, took command of what was left of the squadron, for its last days in France. May 21, 1940 saw the retreat of 607 Squadron as it was withdrawn back to England. The squadron personnel finding their way back as best they could.

In late May 1940, Sample was posted away from 607 Squadron. Although still with the rank of Flight Lieutenant, Sample took command of 504 (County of Nottingham) Squadron, another Auxiliary Air Force Squadron. Number 504 was another squadron that had suffered heavy losses in the French campaign. The squadron being reduced to four serviceable Hurricanes. Also gone was their most of their equipment and probably their morale as well.

Sample was to join his new squadron at Wick in Caithness. The main task of the squadron at this time, apart from the reforming and rebuilding, was the air defence of the Royal Naval base at Scapa Flow. To be further away from the forth coming Battle of Britain was almost an impossibility. After a short stay at Wick, the squadron was moved even further north to Castletown, an airfield still under construction. However, the move had the effect of increasing their patrol area around Scapa Flow.

The time at Castletown was spent mainly in building up the squadron strength in both pilots and aircraft. Practices were flown both day and night. Convoy patrols also fell to the lot of the 504 Squadron pilots. In June of 1940, Sample received recognition for his services in France. He was awarded the DFC, June 4. The citation for the award reads;

> 'Flight Lieutenant John Sample (902781). This officer was for most of the time in command of a squadron which he led extremely well. He shot down two enemy aircraft during May 1940, but then was shot down himself and forced to jump. He was a great inspiration to his squadron'.[5]

Sample was promoted to the rank of Squadron Leader, September 1, 1940. Number 504 Squadron was now deemed fully rested and fit enough to return to the fray. Number 504 Squadron flew south, September 5, their destination was to be Hendon and they were in time for some of the heaviest fighting so far. Two days later the squadron lost one of its aircraft and another was damaged, one pilot being seriously wounded. Over the next few days, 504 Squadron seemed to avoid the heavy casualties, only a couple of minor accidents marring their record. However, as September 15 dawned, the heaviest day of the fighting was about to begin. John Sample and 504 Squadron were to be in the thick of it. This was the day marked down in history as Battle of Britain Day.

Number 504 Squadron were scrambled at 11.15 AM and deployed to patrol the area of Maidstone at 15,000 feet. An incoming bomber force was heading for the London area. The bomber force was somewhat staggered when encountered by 504 Squadron. Sample noticed this and led his squadron into the attack. One of the Do 17s had dropped back from the rest. This bomber had already been attacked by a number of fighters, probably as many as four at that time. However, it was still flying, so Sample attacked it. One of Sample's pilots, sergeant R.T. 'Basher' Holmes, was next to carry out an attack on this bomber. After an initial short burst, he ran out of ammunition. In the heat of the moment he collided with the bomber. The Do 17 was eventually to crash into Victoria Railway Station, writing itself into history in the process.[6]

Later, Sample was to write a description of the above attack. 'I found myself below another Dornier which had white smoke coming from it. It was being attacked by two other Hurricanes and a Spitfire, and was travelling north and turning slightly to the right. As I could not see anything else to attack at that moment I climbed above him and did a diving attack. Coming into the attack, I noticed what appeared to be a red light shining in the rear of the gunner's cockpit, but when I got closer I realized I was looking right through the gunner's cockpit into the pilot's and observer's cockpit beyond. The 'red light' was a fire. I gave it a quick burst and as I passed over him on the right I looked through the big glass nose of the Dornier. It was like a furnace inside.' Sample was also to observe the results of the Dornier collision with Sergeant Holmes. Once again, he described it later. 'The bomber did a forward somersault and then went into a spin... his wings broke off outboard of the engines, so that all that was left as the blazing aircraft fell was half a fuselage and the wing roots with the engines on their ends'.[7]

Later that same day, Sample was once more to lead his squadron into the air. On this occasion they were flying from North Weald. The squadron had been scrambled at 2.00 PM and vectored to patrol Hornchurch at 15,000 feet. Another large bomber force was seemingly en route for London. One of the bombers, a Do 17, had developed engine trouble. Alone, it had turned and was attempting to return to France. Sample spotted the bomber and began an attack. Sample's combat report is simple and matter of fact. He was flying Hurricane P 3429 coded TM-R at the head of Red Section within 'A' Flight. The squadron, on this occasion was flying in company with 249 Squadron when they attacked a formation of about twenty Do 215s, later identified as Do 17s, in the area of Gravesend at 2.35 PM. This formation was flying in a north-westerly direction, on an approach to London. Sample attacked the nearest 'Vic' in the enemy formation. The formation then broke up after his attack. He then spotted a lone Do 17 which was using the cloud cover to make good its escape. Sample carried out four attacks against this bomber. On each occasion, Sample states, he began his fire at a range of 200 yards closing in to 75 yards. Firing in short, two-second bursts.[8]

This Do 17 was flown by Leutnant Herbert Michaelis of 4/KG 3. The aircraft finally succumbed to the attack by Sample and crashed into a copse adjacent to Barnehurst Golf Course. The nose of the Do 17 had been shattered in the attack by Sample. One of the Hurricane's bullets had torn a hole in a pouch of Michaelis's life jacket. This allowed the yellow dye, used for air/sea rescue purposes, to escape, much of it into the eyes of the unfortunate Michaelis. When the noise and the muck had died down, the onlookers, a number of which had gathered, heard the more familiar note of a Merlin engine. From behind the smoke, the victorious Hurricane was seen to carry out a victory roll over the defeated bomber.

Sample then came across an He 111. This aircraft had come under heavy attack from a mixture of Hurricanes and Spitfires. Some twelve fighters in all. This He 111 was flown by Uffz Lange, II/KG 53 and was, at the time of attack, attempting to make a forced landing at West Malling. Sample again takes up the story:

> 'I climbed up again to look for some more trouble and found it in the shape of an He 111 which was being attacked by three Hurricanes and a couple of Spitfires. I had a few cracks at the thing before it made a perfect landing on an RAF aerodrome. Then the Heinkels undercarriage collapsed, and the pilot pulled up after skidding fifty yards in a cloud of dust'.[9]

The fighters had continued to attack this bomber even after it had landed. This was much to the annoyance of the station diarist who was to record the incident: 'Heavy firing from 8 or 9 Hurricanes and Spitfires made the aerodrome unhealthy...' Uffz Lange was one of two crew killed in this incident. The others were captured.

After the attacks of September 15, the area became quieter. Sample was ordered to move his squadron westwards to Filton. From there they would provide air cover for the approaches to Bristol. Enemy aircraft had made an attack on the Bristol Aeroplane Company's works, September 25, claiming a success. They came again two days later to be met and routed by the Hurricanes of 504 Squadron. The squadron was presented with a barrel of beer and a parcel of cigarettes from the grateful people of Bristol. Filton was a major factory in the aviation industry at this time. Sample was also leading his squadron when it beat off an attack against the Westland Aircraft works at Yeovil. The Bristol workers had a whip-round and donated

£39 to the squadron. This was passed on to the RAF Benevolent Fund. However, a gift of some 2,000 cigarettes found their grateful way to aircrew and ground crew alike.

In early 1941, Sample led his squadron to their new base at Exeter. From here the squadron now flew on the offensive. The main task now was to escort the daylight bomber offensives against targets in the Cherbourg Peninsular. Also on the list were random targets such as enemy airfields or transports that could be duly strafed. It was in March of this year that Sample was posted away from the squadron. His new posting took him to Group HQ. There, Sample was to spend some time as a controller. When Sample returned to flying, it was with an aircraft that was a world away from the Hurricane.

In September Sample was given the job of forming a new squadron to be based at Charmy Down. This was to be Number 137 Squadron. Only the second squadron in the RAF to be equipped with the Westland Whirlwind. A twin engine aircraft with an attitude. The Whirlwind was to be used mainly in the ground attack role. With the squadron formed by September 21, Sample went to work on his pilots. In fact he worked them so well that the first Flight was declared fully operational within a month. The first squadron operation was to come October 24, 1941. This was an attack on the Landernam railway sidings, which was a noted success.

October 28 saw Sample back at work with the second Flight. He left Charmy Down in company with two other pilots to carry out simulated fighter attacks. Sample ordered Sgt J.F. Luing to carry out an attack from the rear. This done, Sample ordered Luing to go round again and have another go. As Luing turned to make his second attack he noticed that the other two aircraft appeared to have collided. Sgt M.J. Peskett's aircraft, the third aircraft of the formation, had collided with Sample's aircraft, or vice versa. The result of the collision was that Sample's Whirlwind was seriously damaged. The tail unit had gone and, with all lateral control gone, Sample's Whirlwind P 7053, fell into a vicious spin. Sample appeared to take a long time to try and evacuate his stricken aircraft. This has led to suggestions that the cockpit area of his Whirlwind may have been damaged. Sample himself may have suffered injury.

The Whirlwind descended in a vertical spin that terminated when it crashed into a cowshed on Manor Farm, Englishcombe. Sample eventually freed himself but he was too low for his parachute to deploy properly. The result was that he collided with the farmhouse roof of Manor Farm and was killed.

It has been suggested that John Sample was originally buried in Bath. However, this is erroneous. The body of John Sample was buried, not in the village of his birth, but in the neighbouring village of Bothal. His grave lies within a family plot in the parish church of St Andrew's and has no CWGC headstone. Today, John Sample is almost forgotten. His exploits known only to a decreasing number of men who knew him and others who care to seek out the information. His name is carried on the war memorial in Longhirst village—the only name from World War Two. His moss-stained headstone bears his name and rank along with his DFC and age. The parish registers carry the incorrect age of 29 years.

Apart from the above, John Sample's name is remembered on a trophy. The John Sample trophy is still awarded in bagpipe circles. Mrs Kate Isabel Sample awarded this trophy in 1949 to the Northumbrian Pipers Society in memory of her son. Time has also attempted to rid us of the memory of John Sample. The house in which he was born, Longhirst Grange, fell victim to the march of progress in the 1970s. Longhirst Grange was demolished to make way for opencast mining. However, in fighter pilot circles, John Sample was known as a quiet, almost retiring personality but a courageous and grand leader of men. John Sample was never granted the status of 'ace'; however, in the words of one of his former pilots: 'When he led us into a schwarm of Messerschmitts nobody hung back'.[10] There can be no better epitaph. The fact remains, however, john Sample deserves better recognition than he has enjoyed so far.

SAMPLE NOTES

1. Roland Bibby: *Bothal Observed*. Section on Sample family.

2. Conversation with Mr Lance Robinson, former friend of John Sample.

3. Ramsey: *The Blitz Then and Now Vol 1*, shows a photograph of this aircraft and attributes its demise to someone else, P 34. The same volume states that the German airmen were all missing.

4. Entry from George Dudley Craig's logbook.

5. Cull, *Twenty-one Squadrons* credits Sample with only one victory.

6. This is one of the most familiar photographs from the Battle of Britain. A 'Fox Photographer' was on site and took the picture as the Dornier fell. It has appeared in many books on the Battle of Britain. A 'moving' version can also be seen. This is used in the Battle of Britain section of the film *Reach For The Sky*.
7. As part of a 'morale booster', many airmen and women, were broadcast on the BBC. This was later published in book form under the title: *Winged Words*, published in 1941. The section by John Sample, has been used more than a few times by various writers. Sample's account appears on pages 107–109.
8. Combat report of John Sample.
9. *Winged Words*, section by John Sample.
10. Personal letter from Flt Lt R.T Holmes to Mr Bryan Stoneham.

RICHARD SMITHSON, 46174
SERGEANT

Richard Smithson was born in 1918, one of three sons born to Johnson and Susan Marion Smithson. The family home being in South Hetton, a mining community to the south of Hetton-Le-Hole in the County Durham coalfield. The family Smithson living at Hawthorn Cottages. Education for the young Smithson was carried out at South Hetton Council Schools. Like his father before him, Richard Smithson was expected to work at the local colliery when he left school. This he did, but it is not known in what capacity.

However, RAF life supplanted colliery life and Richard Smithson joined the ranks as an aircraft hand in August of 1935. At a later date, Smithson was to volunteer for flying training. He was accepted and began his flying training at Number 10 Flying Training School (FTS) at RAF Ternhill. After a succession of training aircraft Smithson was eventually converted onto the Hawker Hurricane. After completion of this part of his training, Smithson was posted to a front line fighter squadron. All fighter training at this time had to be carried out by the fighter squadrons themselves. No special training units were in operation with which to acquaint the pilots with the service aircraft they were about to fly. No speciality training on firing the guns. That would come later. The first time many of these pilots would fire a gun would come when they faced the enemy. It was into this life that Smithson found himself posted to Number 249 Squadron.

Originally, Number 249 Squadron had been formed at the end of the First World War. The squadron being formed from a selection of various seaplane flights, Number 400, 401 and 450, coming together made up 249 Squadron at their new base at Dundee. Not only was the squadron made up of various Flights, it was also formed with a variety of aircraft. Among them were the Short S 184, Fairey Hamble Babies and Sopwith Babies. With these aircraft the squadron was tasked to carry out coastal patrols and anti-submarine duties. The original squadron was not to last long. October 8, of the same year saw the disbandment of the squadron. It was not thought of again until 1940. With the fall of France, new squadrons were being formed and old ones were being reborn. One of the latter was Number 249 Squadron.

Number 249 Squadron was officially reformed, May 16, 1940. Its new base was to be Church Fenton in Yorkshire. The officer given the task of reforming the squadron was Squadron Leader John Grandy. Grandy had been formerly with Number 13 Flying Training School (FTS) at RAF Drem. Prior to this, Grandy had been a flying instructor with the London University Air Squadron. The tone of attitude, set out by Grandy, can be noted from his own words. 'One of my first moves was to fly to Cranwell. At that time I had some experience of our University Air Squadrons and had formed a high opinion of the calibre of undergraduates who chose to learn to fly in these splendid volunteer units.'[1] Like so many others at this time, Grandy was in favour of the university graduate above all others. Many, like Grandy, were under the illusion that an academic life is proof positive of leadership qualities. Grandy, and others like, were to learn a lesson during the coming months.

Confusion was to reign for a while on 249 Squadron. When first formed, the squadron was equipped with the Hawker Hurricane. The very next day, the squadron was informed that it was to be equipped with the Spitfire. June 10, 1940, brought the news that once more the squadron was to re-equip with the Hurricane. This time it was to stay as the squadron equipment. The squadron also relocated during this time. Moving east to Leconfield, near Beverley. Flying training was soon under way, with gun firing practice at towed aerial targets, taking place from Acklington, Northumberland. Air to sea gunnery, using a float as a target, was carried out in Filey Bay. Fresh from Number 10 (FTS), Sergeant Smithson was to join 'A' Flight, one of three sergeants in the Flight. Commanding 'A' Flight at this time was Flight Lieutenant Ronald Gustave Kellett.

That training on 249 Squadron was rigorous and hard, there is no doubt. Two sergeant pilots on the squadron failed to meet the limits set by the Commanding Officer and his Flight Commanders. It can be safely presumed that Smithson rose to the challenge, as he was to stay with the squadron.

Training or not, Number 249 Squadron was 'green' and inexperienced. This was to come to light during their first engagement with the enemy. Flying Officer J.R.C. Young led a section, consisting of Pilot Officer T.F. Neil and Sgt Smithson, on a routine patrol on the afternoon of July 4, 1940. A Dornier Do 17 was spotted by Young, who began stalking the bomber. Neil then saw the bomber and 'waggled' his wings to inform the section leader. Unfortunately, Neil's wing 'waggling' brought the section to the attention of the Do17. Young ordered a number one attack in line astern, diving in from the sun. The Do 17 had already begun its bid for freedom, diving to the left towards cloud cover. The number one attack took up valuable time as the Flight formed up and began to attack in formation.

Critical of this manoeuvre, was P.O. Neil. He was later to write:

> 'Going through the nonsensical No 1 attack routine, we reared up like startled pheasant chicks, dropped into line astern, then plummeted down on the Dornier… we shot into a cloud after him and out the other side… He must be somewhere. Absolutely nothing! The Hun had disappeared.'[2]

It is worth bearing in mind that Neil, like Smithson, had just come from (FTS). The more experienced Young, had a few years experience in both civilian flying as well as the RAF. Had the trainee pilots been taught something that their more experienced leader had not? At this time, much of the training had been carried out by experienced 'combat' pilots, their knowledge having been hard earned during the fighting in France. What they had learnt had been passed on to their pupils. However, much of this knowledge had not yet filtered down to the fighter squadrons. The lack of this knowledge would later cost many fighter pilots their lives.

Patrols in the north were mainly uneventful. The squadron diarist was to write, August 6: 'We are all hoping to get a move south.'

Number 249 Squadron got that wish. August 14 saw the whole squadron depart from Church Fenton and proceed south to their new base at Boscombe Down in the Middle Wallop sector.

The Luftwaffe directed a two-pronged attack towards Hampshire and Wiltshire on the afternoon of August 15. The formation was put under repeated attack from around 5.00 PM, various squadrons joining in. However, the attack still got through. Worthy Down, Portland and Andover all received hits. The station siren at Boscombe Down brought three 249 Squadron Hurricanes into action. Climbing away from the airfield, they began to patrol at around 1,000 feet. As the Hurricanes circled the airfield in an anti-clockwise direction, three Ju 87s of 1/StG 1 and II/StG 2, dropped from a convenient cloud cover, directly astern of the patrolling Hurricanes. They dropped their bombs as they flew across the airfield and were gone. All this went unseen by the patrolling Hurricanes. The only saving grace being that the dive-bombers missed their target. Even so, it proved that 249 Squadron were still relatively inexperienced. Later the squadron was ordered to patrol Warmwell airfield. Although 'B' Flight scored success, 'A' Flight failed to make contact with the enemy.

The day of glory, for 249 Squadron, came on the following day. At around 1.05 PM, 'B' Flight was ordered into the air. An enemy formation was putting Gosport under attack. Red Section, led by Flt Lt J.B. Nicholson, were badly bounced by Me 110s. The results being that all the Hurricanes were badly hit. Flt Lt Nicholson, for his part, was awarded the VC, the only Fighter Command pilot in World War Two to be granted the honour. However, the hard fact was, that two aircraft were lost and a pilot was killed in this action.

Number 249 Squadron were moved to North Weald, September 1, 1940. They were to take the place of 56 Squadron, some of the latter squadrons aircraft being left for the incoming 249 Squadron. Even though 249 Squadron had been in the south, the battle area, for over two weeks, their relative inexperience was still evident to many who were more battle hardened. The attitude of the 249 Squadron pilots left their groundcrews with a feeling of pure dismay. When 56 Squadron departed, some of their groundcrew were left, along with the Hurricanes, for the reinforcement of 249 Squadron. One of these, Corporal Eric Clayton noted: '… the groundcrew were dismayed to witness the nonchalant attitude of 249 Squadron pilots when ordered to scramble for combat sorties. They strolled casually out to the aircraft whilst groundcrews stood by them, engines running, waiting with disbelief.'[3]

After a number of uneventful patrols, 249 Squadron were scrambled into action, in company with 46 squadron, at around 1.20 PM, September 5. Large formations of enemy bombers were making their way along the Thames Estuary. The fighter escort of Me 109s, of possibly, 8/JG 2,[4] was ignored in favour of the Do 17s, the fighters diving into the attack over Shellhaven.

One of the plots involved with the attack on the bombers was Smithson. He was flying as Yellow 3 when he attacked a Do 17. Smithson's combat report reads;

> 'Flying as Yellow 3 when we sighted a large formation of e/a flying east towards Gravesend. Enemy bombers were flying at 20,000 feet with fighters above up to 30,000 feet. Breaking away I flew up towards the underside of a Do 215. On coming into range I fired a burst and saw tracer bullets going ahead of the bombers nose. Holding my fire and easing the stick back slightly; I poured a further four-seconds burst and saw tracer bullets raking e/a from nose to tail. Tracer bullets from e/a were passing my starboard mainplane. On braking away I observed large clouds of white smoke pouring from the Do 215. I lost about 1,000 feet, pulled out and carried out the same attack on a second Do 215, and on breaking away observed smoke trailing from the centre of the fuselage, just behind the cockpit.'[4]

It is of interest that Smithson thought that the bombers were Do 215s. The Do 215 was an export version. In its early days mass production for the Luftwaffe was stopped as the engines were needed for other aircraft. The Do 215 was used mainly for reconnaissance duties and, therefore, was not used as a bomber. During this encounter Smithson was flying one of the ex-56 squadron Hurricanes, P 2863. The aircraft still bearing the markings of that squadron. Smithson was to make claims for one DO17 damaged and another probably damaged.

September 7 began with only light raids, the controllers beginning to wonder where the next attacks might come from. There was even some talk that the attacks had stopped to allow for an invasion to begin. However, two decisive decisions had been made: one by the Germans, one by the RAF. Reichsmarschall Goering had decided that RAF Fighter Command was almost beaten. To deliver the coup de grace he had decided on an all out attack on London. This would draw out all the RAF fighters, even from the north, then his Jagdwaffe would take care of them. To make doubly sure, Goering took personal command of the air assault on London and installed himself at Cap Gris Nez. Meanwhile Dowding, noticed that some of the defending fighters were taking too long to get to combat height. Allied to this, the squadrons were not working together efficiently. Squadrons had now to work in pairs. Hurricanes would take on the bombers, Spitfires would account for the fighter escorts. To make the whole thing work properly, controllers had to get the fighters into the air in plenty time to gain advantage.

At 4.15 PM, a mighty force of enemy bombers began to cross the coast between Deal and North Foreland. Numbers of the enemy formation vary but were estimated at around three hundred bombers with a fighter escort of around six hundred Me 109s and 110s. Each rank stepped up higher and behind each other. The mighty force made its way towards its target of East London's dock area. RAF Fighter Command was caught slightly on the hop, mainly by the change of target. Airfields and sector stations were covered. The road leading to the capital was left quite clear. One source[5] likened the raid to one twenty-five years before, when the Zeppelins had attacked London, September 8; 1915. The fighting that took place was fought at break-neck speed. Kellett's 303 Squadron waded in with all they had got. McArthur on 609 Squadron reported very heavy return fire from the bomber formation.

By 4.30 PM, 249 Squadron had cleared the airfield of North Weald and were on their way at full power. Patrolling Maidstone at around 15,000 feet, the radio silence was broken by the controller. 'Hullo, Ganer leader, bandits on your right.' Pilot Officer George Barkley was to report, 'I saw that the rapidly closing bombers were surrounded by black dots, which I knew to be Me 109s. So we were in for it this time'.[6] And so it proved to be for on this occasion their opponents turned out to be the Me 109s of JG 2, the Richthofen

Geschwader. Attempting to attack the bomber force down their southern flank. No sooner had the Hurricanes began to attack than they were surrounded, cornered and cut off by the defending Me 109s.

The Me 109s were using their standard tactic of diving straight through the defending fighters, shooting as they went. Once through the formation, their speed gained in the attack, aided them back to the security of the fighter formations. Smithson, attempting to carry out an attack on a bomber, found himself cut off. Attempting to find a way out, he was forced into a turning dogfight with the Me 109s. Literally fighting for survival, Smithson, unable to get out of the fight, had stayed too long. His Hurricane, seriously outnumbered, was raked by gunfire from an Me 109 while flying over Maidstone. Smithson, wounded in the arm, managed to force-land his Hurricane, V 6574, at Eastchurch, Isle of Sheppy. Number 249 Squadron had lost four Hurricanes with another two damaged.

It is not known who was the victor over Smithson. Among the claims of JG 2 made that day, the unit who attacked 249 Squadron, two claims by Oberfw Gunther Seeger and the legendary Major Helmut Wick, Geschwader Kommadore of JG 2, both of the Stab Flight who made a claim for one. A quote from one old pilot states: 'If you are going to get shot down, then it may as well be by the best.' This may well have been the case for Smithson. Sent home on leave, the local press gave his story under the headline: 'North pilot fought ten raiders.'[7]

Smithson was out of action until shortly after October 12 when he made it back to the squadron. However, things had quietened down somewhat. Sporadic patrols were all that was encountered. An enemy formation was plotted in the area of the Thames Estuary shortly after mid-day, November 7. Number 249 Squadron were airborne and into action. A formation of Ju 87s of 1/StG 1 were attacking a convoy. On this occasion, 249 Squadron attacked the fighter escort of Me 109s. Smithson was flying as Red 2 to Sgt George C.C. Palliser when the latter carried out a close attack on an Me 109. Smithson was to make no claims for this attack. Smithson was again flying as Red 2 to Palliser, November 7, 1940, when 249 Squadron were scrambled shortly after midday. Vectored towards the Thames Estuary, 249 Squadron engaged a formation of Ju 87s of 1/StG3 attacking a convoy. Above them were the ever-present fighter escort. On this occasion the Me 109s of JG 26, JG 51 and JG 53.

As autumn turned into winter, the scrambles and patrols now began to decrease. Mainly this was due to the reduction of air raids, which, in turn was due to the shortening of the days as well as the worsening weather. Many of the pilots found themselves on the move to other units. Among these was Smithson. With fellow pilot Sgt R.J. McNair, Smithson found himself posted to Number 96 Squadron, stationed at Speke. Smithson's new squadron was a night fighter unit operating both the Hawker Hurricane and the Boulton Paul Defiant, the main duties of 96 Squadron being the air defence of Liverpool and its approaches.

It is not recorded what Smithson thought of his new posting. It is doubtful if his thoughts would have been complementary. The Defiant was a large and heavy fighter. Its career during the Battle of Britain had been a disaster. The pilots, who flew the Defiant, were reduced almost to the level of a taxi driver. The main, and only armament of the Defiant was a powered turret fitted with four guns. Much less powerful and manoeuvrable than the Hurricane, the Defiant was described by one pilot: 'Whoever invented the rear gun fighter completely forgot to invent how it could attack anything! You just couldn't attack unless you ran away—and if you ran away how could you possibly call the thing a fighter'? After the Hurricane, Smithson must have found the Defiant a backward step.

Smithson was commissioned, July 17, 1941. Five days later, Pilot Officer Smithson climbed aboard Defiant T 4071 in the early evening of July 22. Smithson was to take his aircraft on an air test. Just over a hundred miles to the south of Speke, at around 6.59 PM, the Defiant flew into the rising ground that forms Eddisbury Hill, above the village of Delemere. The resulting crash caused the death of both of the crew and the Defiant burned itself out. The body of P.O Richard Smithson was returned to his home of South Hetton. Richard Smithson was buried in the holy Trinity Churchyard: grave number 815.

SMITHSON NOTES
1. Cull, *249 Squadron*, P 1.
2. Tom Neil in Cull, *249 Squadron*, P 3.
3. Cull: *249 Squadron*, P 11.

4. Combat fighter report of Richard Smithson.
5. Wood and Dempster: *The Narrow Margin*, P 345.
6. Cull: *249 Squadron*, P 18.
7. "Newcastle Journal" issue of September 8, 1940.

Jack Stokoe, 60512
Sergeant

Jack Stokoe was born February 1, 1921. In his early life Jack Stokoe lived in the mining community of West Cornforth, County Durham. The son of a coal miner, it would seem that Jack Stokoe was born to defy convention. Like many other miners sons, he should have followed his father into the local coalmine. However, Jack Stokoe wanted to be something different. He wanted to be a fighter pilot.

The build up of the RAF during the mid nineteen thirties caused an influx of would be aircrew and, in particular, pilots, into the service. In turn the RAFVR was created in July of 1936. In June of 1939, along with many other like-minded young men, Jack Stokoe decided the RAF offered the best way of life for him and he joined the Volunteer Reserve. His weekend flying was to take place at Number 26 Elementary and Reserve Flying Training School (E&RFTS) at Oxford. It was here that Jack Stokoe got to grips with his first flying machine, training at this time being carried out with the trusty Tiger moth. Also at this stage of their training, the young pilot hopefuls had to get to grips with the basics of flying. This was carried out in the classroom and consisted of tuition in airmanship, navigation, signals and armament among others. The tutorials went hand in hand with the flying training. To fail or fall back on either one would jeopardize the other. Put more bluntly, to shirk the classroom would mean failure in flying. After this, the young hopefuls would be well and truly out.

Life across the English Channel during this period was changing fast. The German Air Force, The Luftwaffe, had joined with the

Wehrmacht to form a new devastating form of warfare known as the Blitzkrieg. This new form of lightning war was to smash its way through the defences of Western Europe, defences which fell one after the other. Jack Stokoe, along with other RAFVR pilots, was called to full time service. In a short period of time, Stokoe found himself posted to Cambridge. In the university town, the young sergeant Stokoe found himself based at Magdalene College with the Initial Training Wing (ITW). Here, training would once more begin as the young fledgling, but still wingless, pilots got to grips with the training aircraft over the next few months.

From Cambridge, Stokoe was sent to the next link in the training chain. This was to be Number 15 Flying Training School (FTS) at Lossiemouth on Speyside in the far north of Scotland. While at Lossiemouth, the fledgling pilots would get to grips with more advanced aircraft. Training had so far been restricted to aircraft with the technology and characteristics of First World War aircraft: the Tiger Moth and Hawker Hart variants. Now the pilots would get to grips with aircraft such as the Miles Master. A monoplane that at least looked as if it was born of the modern age. Stokoe had completed his course by June 8 and was sent to Number 5 Operational Training Unit (OTU) at Aston Down in Gloucestershire. It was here that Stokoe and his contemporaries would gain their much-needed training on single seat fighters.

However, shortage was much in evidence during this period both in aircraft and experienced pilots. There were no real (OTUs) in existence at this time. The training of new pilots, especially in single seat fighters, was provided by the fighter pools. After much reluctance on the part of Air Chief Marshal Dowding, experienced pilots were released from some of the fighter squadrons to act as flying instructors. Eleven and Twelve Group pools were redesignated, in March of 1940, as Numbers 5 and 6 OTUs. However, things were not so simple. While the instructors could be found from among the ranks, mostly of 'resting' pilots, aircraft were still in short supply. Training at the OTUs, therefore, was mainly carried out on the more numerous Hawker Hurricanes. Also lacking in the training programme was the lack of ancillary equipment. Camera-guns were missing from the training units causing a gap in the knowledge of air-to-air combat. Radiotelephony was also missing in most cases leading to lack of communication in the air. The usual training programme took around three to four weeks. However, at the time of Stokoe's training, the need of pilots became extreme. Only eighteen days after the end of his course in Lossiemouth, Stokoe was posted to 263 Squadron based at Drem. His course at 5 OTU must have lasted at the most, allowing for travel and leave, fifteen days. Another shock was awaiting Stokoe at Drem.

Stokoe's first fighter squadron had originally been equipped with the Hurricane. The squadron, when Stokoe arrived, was busy re equipping with the Westland Whirlwind. A twin-engine aircraft that was not well accepted by many fighter pilots. The Whirlwind was underpowered, and was thought by many to have an attitude. The squadron at least did have some of its old Hurricanes still on the airfield. This allowed Stokoe to carry out some much needed practice on the type.

The new sergeant pilot was to hold preference for the single engine aircraft. A short while later, Stokoe was posted to 603 City of Edinburgh Squadron based at Dyce. Stokoe was to join the squadron July 3, 1940, some three days before the more celebrated Richard Hillary. A comparison can be drawn between the two pilots, both reservists, with one a sergeant and the other of the officer class. With training over, Stokoe was posted to a squadron with aircraft he had no experience of, Whirlwinds. He was then posted on to 603 Squadron. Hillary, also just out of training, appears to have picked where he wanted to go. He was to state: 'Next day squadron vacancies were announced. I walked down to the Adjutant's office with Peter Pease and Colin Pinckney. 603 (City of Edinburgh) Squadron had three vacancies. It was out of the battle area (the first battle over Dover had already been fought), but it was a Spitfire squadron and we could all three go together. We put our names down.'[1] After a leisurely two-day trip, Hillary and friends, joined 603 Squadron. Obviously, on Hillary's evidence, while the officer class could chose where they went, the NCO class could not. They were sent.

Number 603 City of Edinburgh Squadron was originally formed at Turnhouse, now Edinburgh Airport, October 14, 1925. On October 15, 1939, 603 squadrons Gladiators were replaced with the Spitfire. The 16th of the same month saw 603 Squadron along with 602 City of

Glasgow Squadron, hit the headlines when they shot down a Heinkel He 111 which subsequently fell into the sea off Port Seaton. On the 28th of the month, once more in company with 602 Squadron, they shot down another He 111. This aircraft was the first enemy aircraft to fall on British soil since the First World War. The He 111 eventually ground to a halt in the Lammermuir Hills south of Haddington. During this period, 603 Squadron's two flights were dispersed between the two airfields of Dyce and Montrose. The two flights amalgamating once more at Turnhouse, August 22, 1940. A few days later, on the 26th, news was broken that the squadron was to fly south. Posted to Hornchurch, the squadron arrived there on the 26th in time to relieve Number 65 Squadron.

While the pilots of 603 Squadron received the news of their move south with some enthusiasm, this was not matched by their new Station Commander, Group Captain C.A. Bouchier. He was to describe the arrival of 603 Squadron on his station. '603 Squadron's C.O., Squadron Leader Denholm, dismounted from his Spitfire with his forage cap stuck on the back of his head. He meandered towards the control tower with his hands stuck in his pockets and his shoulders bent.' His men following behind, were the motliest collection of unmilitary looking men he'd ever seen for a very long time. He was amazed—and then remembered, that Number 603 was an Auxiliary squadron. That explained it, but why, he thought, should they be unloaded on him?[2] Group Captain Bouchier's observations reflected the feelings, of the time, that regular airmen had for the Auxiliaries.

The relatively inexperienced pilots of 603 Squadron began their learning curve with some hard experience, on the afternoon of August 28. At 4.45 PM the squadron was in the air. A large group of fighters had been detected flying at some 25,000 feet in the vicinity of Dover. The group consisted of Me 110s with a fighter escort of Me 109s, the later being of JG 54. Although Sqdn Ldr Denholm managed to claim one Me 109 destroyed and some of the other pilots claimed an amount of probables, the squadron lost three of its Spitfires with a further one damaged. Among those claiming probables, was Stokoe.

The following day the squadron fared little better. Two of the squadrons Spitfires were lost with a further two damaged. One of those who bailed out during this action was Richard Hillary. He was later to state that he found a squadron: 'flying around the sky'. Taking it upon himself to act as tail end Charlie or, as Hillary puts it: 'Arse-end Charlie', to this squadron, he found it an, 'amusing though painful experience'. After being attacked by Me 109s, he could not warn the Hurricanes, as his radio had been shot away.[3] While it may make a good story, the audience was still enduring the war years when this book was published. Hillary fails to point out that he could not have contacted the other squadron as, they were on a different wave-length.

A counterpoint is given to this story by the leader of the Hurricane squadron that was 'flying around the sky'. He was none other than Sqdn Ldr Peter Townsend, C.O. of 85 Squadron and, at that time a highly experienced and battle-hardened pilot. His views on Hillary are expressed in his log book and speak for themselves: 'If this Spitfire pilot can be identified, I would like these facts brought home to him, because his… action contributed to the loss of one of my flight commanders'.[4] The flight commander referred to by Townsend was Flight Lieutenant H.R. Hamilton. His Hurricane crashed on Rye foreshore at 6.15 PM. Jack Stokoe had been one of the pilots who had claimed a probable while flying Spitfire L 1021, coded XT-A.

The latter part of August saw heavy raids against RAF airfields. The 31st of the month saw 603 Squadron heavily engaged in the actions of that day. At around 1.00 PM, a large formation of enemy aircraft attacked Hornchurch. The enemy formation, flying at some 15,000 feet, began its attack at around 1.15 PM. Sixty bombs were dumped across the airfield and, 54 Squadron were caught in the process of taking off. Some of these Spitfires were severely damaged in the attack. The bomber formation was escorted by Me 109s of JG 3 Udet who were to tangle with 603 Squadron. A second attack on Hornchurch was carried out at 6.00 PM. A formation of enemy bombers managed to force their way, by sheer weight of numbers, through the defences and bomb the airfield once more. This raid was not to be so successful. Bombs were to fall near the perimeter track, disabling only two Spitfires.

High over London, 603 Squadron lost another two Spitfires with one further aircraft damaged. Pilot Officer G.K. Gilroy watched his Spitfire as, in its last dive, it crashed into a house at Number 14 Hereford Road, Wanstead. A crowd had gathered to watch the fighting being carried out over their heads. Now, they watched the hapless P.O. Gilroy as he descended towards them. It is not clear if the crowds mistook Gilroy for a German. A crashing fighter had damaged one of their houses and Gilroy was on the receiving end of their anger. After the attack, P.O Gilroy was admitted to King George Hospital, Ilford.[5]

Stokoe had singled himself out an Me 109 and pressed home his attack. This Me 109, *Werke* no 1503, was the Me 109 E of Leutnant Walter Binder of 3 Staffel JG 3 Udet. Stokoe got the better of his German foe and the Me 109 was to end its flight in an English garden between Anne Street and Robert Street in Plumstead at 6.20 PM. Its pilot, Leutnant Walter Binder was killed in the action. Stokoe also attacked an Me 110 during the fighting over London. However, he could only claim a probable. Stokoe gained further success, September 1, when he downed an Me 109.

September 2 began with warm weather. With the dry haze, the Luftwaffe raids began early. Normally reconnaissance aircraft were the first visitors, heralding oncoming attacks. However, it was a large raid of over one hundred, which was plotted over Calais. Their target was to be the airfields of southern England. The enemy formation was stepped up from 12,000 to 20,000 feet with a further high escort awaiting their chance to pounce on the unwary. On this occasion it was 603 Squadron who were the unwary. They were bounced, with fighters of both Air Forces twisting and turning in all directions over Hawkinge. In the area at this time, were the Me 109s of JG 54. It may well have been them who carried out the bounce on 603 Squadron. In the resulting melee, Spitfire X 4250, XT-X came under attack. Its pilot, Jack Stokoe, had his cockpit hood shattered in the conflict at around 8.15 AM. Stokoe returned to Hornchurch none the worse for wear, though probably feeling more than a little lucky.

However, for Jack Stokoe, the day was not yet over. Another large raid, once more intent on attacking the airfields, was plotted over Dungeness. During this time, a new tactic was being introduced by the Jagdwaffe. While some of the fighter escort remained close to the bombers, the top escort remained at high altitude. This tactic was meant to lure the defending fighters towards the bombers and their close escort. With the trap set, the top escort could pounce. Flying at great speed, firing as they went, they could pass through the defending fighters and be gone before the defending fighters new what hit them. Relying on their great speed, built up in the initial dive, the Me 109s could safely recover to the safety of the top escort once more.

Stokoe had opened his attack against a Junkers Ju 88, seeing his bullets striking home. He then turned his attention to another Ju 88, again opening fire. While he was thus occupied, an Me 109, presumably of the top escort, caught Stokoe's Spitfire in his sights.

The first Stokoe knew about his predicament was the clatter of bullets and shells hitting his Spitfire. Stokoe turned to avoid the attack. Too late. The fuel tank of his Spitfire had been hit and now erupted. Stokoe decided the time had come to depart from his Spitfire. Opening the hood of his Spitfire to facilitate his evacuation had the effect of turning his cockpit into a raging inferno, the incoming air acting like a bellows on the fire. However, to depart from the aircraft, it had to be inverted so that gravity could help the pilot to drop out. To invert the Spitfire, Stokoe had once more to force his hands into the raging inferno in order to grab the stick. To make matters worse, in the scramble to get his Spitfire into the air quickly, Stokoe had forgotten his gloves. In the agonizing fractions of a second it took to carry out this manoeuvre, fractions that must have felt like a lifetime, Stokoe watched as the skin was burned from his hands. At last Stokoe fell free of his doomed Spitfire and descended by parachute into a field. As he hit the ground, some of the local Home Guard queried the nationality of the burnt flyer. A few choice words, delivered by Stokoe, proved that he could only be English. Stokoe was then rushed to Leeds Castle Hospital suffering severe burns to face, neck and hands. Stokoe's Spitfire, N 3056 coded XT-B, crashed to earth near Maidstone at 5.25 PM.

Jack Stokoe was out of action until October 19, 1940. When he returned to 603 Squadron, it was still based at Hornchurch, carrying out patrols against a dwindling number of raids by the Luftwaffe. However, Stokoe celebrated his return to the squadron by shooting down an Me 109. He claimed another as damaged November 8 with another destroyed November 17. It was during this period that the Regia Aeronautica, the Italian Air Force, lent its hand to the Luftwaffe formations. Number 603 Squadron was credited with seven of the Italian aircraft shot down, November 23. From December1 to the

12th, 603 Squadron were based at Rochford. With the Luftwaffe air raids becoming even less frequent, 603 Squadron were returned north to Drem to recover their strength.

With the New Year, Jack Stokoe was commissioned, January 26, 1941. Now, as Pilot Officer Stokoe, he was posted to 54 Squadron. At that time, 54 Squadron were based at Stokoe's old base of Hornchurch. Having been away from Hornchurch for just over a month, Stokoe must have felt at home. The squadrons of RAF Fighter Command were now on the offensive. The battle was to be carried out across the English Channel as 54 Squadron was involved in escorting bombers. Known as 'circuses', these raids were designed to bring the fighters of the Luftwaffe to battle.

Number 54 Squadron had replaced 41 Squadron at Hornchurch. In doing so, 54 Squadron had inherited some of 41 Squadron's Spitfires. Stokoe was given Spitfire P 7666, coded KL-Z. This Spitfire was a presentation aircraft, named 'Observer Corps'. Having passed from the Maintenance Unit to 41 Squadron, it became the Commanding Officers aircraft, the C.O. being Squadron Leader D.O. Finlay.[6] March 5, 1941 saw Stokoe shoot down an Me 109 with this aircraft. On April 20, Stokoe attacked, and got the better of, an Me 110. This aircraft was forced down. However, while intent on attacking the Me 110 Stokoe failed to see the Me 109 that had already lined him up in its sights. The end result was that once more Stokoe was shot down in flames. On this occasion, however, he avoided injury and managed to bail out of his Spitfire successfully and landed in the waters of the English Channel. A ship picked up Stokoe and he returned to his squadron safely.

On May 6 1941, Stokoe damaged an Me 109, while on June 7 he shared in the destruction of an Me 109 claiming it as a probable. A further Me 109 was claimed by Stokoe on June 24. This was to be his last with 54 Squadron. Three days later Stokoe was posted to 74 Squadron then based at Gravesend. His stay with the 'Tigers' was to be a short one. He does not even get a mention in any of the squadron histories.

Stokoe was next posted to Number 59 OTU at Crosby-on-Eden, taking up his duties as a flying instructor. However, his stay with 59 OTU was to be equally short. Stokoe was next posted to Number 60 OTU at East Fortune in Scotland, again taking up his duties as a flying instructor. Stokoe was promoted to the rank of Flying Officer, January 15 1942. He then served as an instructor on specialized airborne radar equipment while based at Drem.

After a further succession of various posts, which saw Stokoe awarded the DFC on June 6 1944, Stokoe ended his RAF career as the Station Commander of RAF Great Missington. Stokoe had, by the end of his RAF career, been promoted to the rank of Squadron Leader. Retaining Squadron Leader rank, Stokoe was released from RAF Service on August 21, 1946. However, the flying career of Jack Stokoe was not completely over. He joined the RAFVR in July of 1947. While with the Reserve, Stokoe flew Tiger Moths and Chipmunks with Number 24 Reserve Flying Training School at Rochester. He remained in the reserve until June of 1952. Jack Stokoe died in 1999.

Stokoe Notes

1. Richard Hillary: *The Last Enemy*, P 92.
2. Bruce Robertson: *Spitfire The Story of a Famous Fighter*, P38–39.
3. Hillary, P149–150.
4. Peter Townsend: *Duel of Eagles*, P363.
5. *Battle of Britain Then And Now*: photo P 403.
6. *Battle of Britain Then And Now*: photo P 403. Spitfire is shown with Sqdn Ldr Finlay. A photograph of this Spitfire but in 54 Squadrons colours is shown in *Aircraft of the Aces* P 50. However, the Spitfires number is wrongly given. The aircraft can be identified by its presentation badge, 'Observer Corps'. Many things can change on aircraft; however, the presentation badge is peculiar to one aircraft only, these are not transferable.

Sydney Stokoe, 754855
Sergeant

Sydney Stokoe was born in 1916 the son of Edward and Lizzie A. Stokoe. The family appear to have originated in the Felling area of Gateshead. Later they were to move to the area of Heworth, a town on the south bank of the river Tyne, lying in the shadow of its near neighbour Gateshead. Little else is known of Stokoe's early life. Only one thing is certain: Sydney Stokoe joined the RAFVR in August of 1939 as an airman under training–pilot. His training had hardly begun before war was declared and Stokoe was called to full-time service September 1, 1939.

At the end of his training, Stokoe was passed as suitable to fly twin-engine aircraft. Stokoe was posted to Number 29 Squadron, then based at Digby in Lincolnshire. Number 29 Squadron was destined to be not only Stokoe's first squadron, but also his only squadron. Stokoe's skills as a pilot were to be tested in the night skies over Britain. At that time Number 29 Squadron was a night fighter squadron flying the Bristol Blenheim.

The Bristol Blenheim was originally designed as a bomber. In that role, especially during the early part of the war, it was quite successful. At the time of its birth (it first flew in 1935) the Blenheim had an impressive top speed of 307 MPH. At that time, the bomber had a higher speed than any of the fighters then in service with the RAF. However, by 1939, the newer and faster machines of the emerging German Air Force, the Luftwaffe, could not only match the speed of the Blenheim, they could also carry a greater bomb load. In a short space of time, the Blenheim became obsolescent. Some versions were equipped as a fighter. These versions equipped seven fighter squadrons. However, as a day fighter the Blenheim turned out to be a bit of a failure. It proved to be an easy target for the Me 109s and its appearance resembled the Ju 88 to the point that it was attacked on many occasions by the fighters of the RAF. Later in the war the Blenheim was later to serve as a passable night fighter until the advent of its stable-mate the Bristol Beaufighter and, later, the DeHaviland Mosquito.

Digby, in flat Licolnshire was not exactly at the forefront of the Battle of Britain. However, stalking lone raiders during the hours of darkness became their main trade. With the coming of the new airborne interception equipment, the Blenheims of 29 Squadron were to play havoc with the bombers of the Luftwaffe during the night Blitz.

A notable pilot, who was later to fly with 29 Squadron, after Stokoe had departed, was flight Lieutenant, later Wing Commander Guy Gibson of 'Dam Buster' fame. He was later to write of Digby: 'Here Lincolnshire is at its worst—a vast area of flatness, spreading out towards the East Fenlands of the Wash. Hardly a tree breaks the horizon, hardly a bird sings.[1] A contemporary pilot of Stokoe was Flying Officer J.R.D. 'Bob' Braham. He was later to write that there was a spate of low-flying at Digby during this time, which could have led to accidents.[2] More than one of the Blenheim pilots was to be hauled before the C.O. to be 'carpeted' for their low-flying activities.

On December 19, 1940, Stokoe was flying Blenheim L 6612 on a routine training flight. As so many pilots before him, Stokoe decided to enter into the spirit of a bit of low flying. Approaching Digby airfield from the west at low-level, Stokoe's Blenheim hit a tree in the area of Leadenham some six miles from Digby and near the RAF College of Cranwell. Stokoe and his crew were killed in the accident. Sydney Stokoe was 24 years old.

Stokoe's remains were transported north to his home. There, they were buried in the churchyard of St Mary at Heworth. He shares the family plot with the rest of his family and there is no CWGC headstone. The grave is in the plot 'F' grave number 11. While the adjoining cemetery is well kept, the churchyard suffers from neglect. As no family members survive, the grave of Sydney Stokoe suffers from the same neglect.

STOKOE NOTES
1. Guy Gibson: *Enemy Coast Ahead*, P 118.
2. J.R.D. Braham: *Scramble: Wing Commander*.

JAMES ANDERSON VICK, 90274
SQUADRON LEADER

James Anderson Vick was born in Kings Norton during the third quarter of 1908. He was the son of H. Hampton Vick, an agent. The family were later to settle in the Gosforth area to the north of Newcastle upon Tyne.

With the expansion of the Auxiliary Air Force, Number 607 (County of Durham) Squadron Auxiliary Air Force was formed, March 17, 1930, at the new aerodrome at Usworth. In fact Usworth was so new it still was not open. Usworth, still not fully complete, was to open officially in November of 1932. However, that the new airfield was not open did not daunt its new squadron. A squadron that still had no aircraft. Keenness was high on the list of criteria expected from the new recruits by the Commanding Officer, the Rt Hon later Viscount Leslie Runciman. One man who was to demonstrate this keenness was James A. Vick. There was little to stimulate the men of the North East in the way of aviation during that time so it is not known why Vick picked out a flying career. Vick was to be only the second man to join 607 Squadron for pilot training. The first had been Launcelot Eustice Smith, later to command the squadron before being killed in France.

The main complement of 607 Squadron, during the period, was a Gypsy Moth and a couple of Avro 504s. The gypsy Moth provided the basic training while further training was carried out on the Avro 504. The fledgling pilots were usually given a flight in one of these aircraft as a 'taster' in the hands of the squadron flying instructor, usually a regular RAF pilot. If the embryo pilot survived the test flight, then they were well on their way to a flying career with the squadron.

Vick obviously survived the introductory flight, as well as the interview with the Commanding Officer, Runciman. Number 607 Squadron was to be a light bomber squadron and, from 1933, was to be equipped with the Westland Wapiti. A photograph exists showing Vick in Westland Wapiti K 1150 flying over Chester-le-Street in County Durham. This aircraft was later to be lost in a landing accident at Usworth, September 17, 1936.

A trainee pilot in the Auxiliary Air Force was commissioned after only three solo flights. On gaining his 'wings' he became a Pilot Officer (Aux AF). Vick gained his 'A' licence and was gazetted, September 4, 1933. As part of the Auxiliary Air Force life, a member had to give two nights a week as well as a weekend to his flying duties. Also on the agenda was a summer camp, which tended to last for around two weeks. Here, the pilots could sample life on a full-time airfield as well as mixing with other squadrons. Among those visited were Leuchars in 1935, Manston in 1936 and Rochford in 1937. Vick, a tall and lanky figure, can be seen in the group photographs of 1937 and 1938 as well as the sports day event that was photographed at the 1937 summer camp.

Vick was promoted to Flying Officer, March 4, 1935 and to the rank of Flight Lieutenant, March 3, 1937. Vick is missing from the 1939 group photograph. The summer camp that year being held at Abbotsinch, Glasgow. However, it is known that Vick was still with the squadron after this date. Number 607 Squadron, due to imminent hostilities, had to cut short their summer camp and return to Usworth. There, the squadron was embodied into the RAF. Vick being called to full-time service, August 24, 1939. October 10 saw the whole squadron moved north to Acklington. Once there, the squadron shared the airfield with the newly formed 152 Squadron and 609 Squadron who were still only operational by day.

From early November there had been rumours that the squadron were due to go to France as part of the Air Component. The rumours were to prove true and 607 Squadron left Acklington bound for France. A hotchpotch of civilian airliners of various makes carried the ground crews and support. The Gladiators flew behind. Vick, in charge of the ground party, made the journey from Acklington to

Croydon then, two days later, to Merville, in an Ensign. While 607 Squadron was to face a severe winter in France, Vick was not destined to stay with it. Vick was posted to 609 (West Riding) Squadron, a Spitfire Squadron, December 12, 1939.

Vick was posted to 609 Squadron as a Flight Commander, the squadron at this time was based at Kinloss in Scotland. However, fate decided to play its hand and Vick was involved in a serious car accident as he was travelling to RAF Kinloss.[1] A period in hospital meant that Vick would no longer be going to 609 Squadron. Vick was promoted to the rank of Squadron Leader, March 1, 1940. However, he did not return to flying until June of that year.

During its tour of duty in France, 607 Squadron had taken heavy casualties both in men and aircraft. Two squadron commanders had been lost in a short space of time and most of the aircraft had also been lost. Of the small number of Hurricanes that returned to England, at least four were flown to Croydon and on inspection were immediately scrapped. One of the Hurricanes had over eighty bullet holes counted on its airframe. Number 607 Squadron was reformed at its old base at Usworth in June. The new Commanding Officer was to be James Vick.

Vick must have noticed a big change in the squadron since his last encounter with it. Many of the original pilots were gone. Some dead, others moved to new squadrons, almost all had been friends of Vick. Their places was now taken with a growing number of foreign pilots. It now fell to Vick to get the squadron back in shape. This was done with practices and the ever-present convoy patrols. Number 607 Squadron's big day came on August 15, 1940, the day that Luftflotte Five launched its mass attack against targets in the North East of England. As 607 Squadron played its part, Vick was to miss his moment in history as he was away on leave and could only watch as the enemy passed by Newcastle.

In early September, Vick led 607 Squadron south to its new base at Tangmere. There, the squadron was to take over from a bloodied and battered Number 43 Squadron. The scene was to be a foretaste of what was to come. In their first encounter with the enemy, September 9, 607 Squadron was taught a savage lesson by the Jagdwaffe in the area over Mayfield. The squadron lost six of its Hurricanes, half the squadron. Later in the same month, Vick took a routine medical and failed the eye test; his days as a fighter pilot were over.[2]

Vick was posted away from the squadron in late September. Vick took up his new post as Wing Commander Training with HQ 14 Group, October 12, 1940. He appears to have remained there until early 1942. Early in that year Vick was released from RAF service and seconded to the civilian airline Imperial Airways. Vick was to work in the organization and administration side of the airline. Vick was to remain with the airline, in various parts of the world, until his eventual retirement. James Anderson Vick died in 2002 at the age of 94 years.

VICK NOTES
1. Frank H. Ziegler: *The Story of 609 Squadron*, P 72.
2. Personal correspondence with W.H.R. Whitty.

Douglas Cyril Winter, 43372
Pilot Officer

Douglas Cyril Winter was born in 1914. He was the eldest of two sons born to Douglas Curle and Margaret Winter. The family home at the time was situated in Lyndhurst Street in South Shields. Winter senior was a motor mechanic by trade. It is, therefore, presumed that it was from his father that Douglas took up his interest in mechanics. Education for Douglas Winter was by way of Westoe Secondary School situated in the Westoe area of South Shields. This was followed by a period at South Shields High School from where Douglas Winter gained the higher level of education needed to join the RAF apprenticeship scheme.

Leaving school at fifteen, Winter applied to join the RAF as an apprentice. His application was successful and Winter left South Shields to take up his new post at RAF Halton in September of 1929. After serving his apprenticeship to the satisfaction of the RAF, Winter completed his training in August of 1932 as a fully trained fitter. Little is known of Winter's service life at this time. However, he appears to have had a competitive frame of mind. He was an accomplished athlete and took part in the team that competed for the Kings Cup of 1932. He also appears to have been an accomplished shot, winning medals at Bisley. As a tradesman, his career took Winter to various parts of the UK as well as overseas. It is known that Winter served in both Egypt and Palestine during this early period in his career.

In 1939 the former apprentice turned fitter, decided on a career change. A tradesman's life was one thing; a pilot's life was another.

Winter applied for training as a pilot and was accepted. After training Winter was posted to his first squadron, Number 72. Winter joined 72 Squadron at Church Fenton. Number 72 Squadron had been equipped with the Spitfire Mk I since May of 1939. Shortly after joining 72 Squadron Winter received his commission. Because of his bright blonde hair, Winter had acquired the name that remained with him, 'Snowy'.

Much of the work on 72 Squadron during this time was training. Formation training, cross-country flights and combat training; all was interspersed by the routine convoy patrols. However, things were to change by the end of May. Number 72 Squadron was moved to Gravesend. From there it could take part in the patrols covering the evacuation of Dunkirk. Like most pilots on the squadron, Winter was to receive his baptism of fire over the beaches of Dunkirk. Winter was awed by the sight of the smoke that billowed into the sky over the northern French town. Navigation was not to be a problem at this time along the Channel coast. By the time the fighters had gained height from their bases in southern England, the smoke rising from the besieged town could be clearly seen and acted as a guide.

Number 72 Squadron were in the air by 6.40 AM on the morning of June 2. In company with 609 Squadron, they set off for France. At around 6.55 AM they were in the vicinity of Dunkirk. Junkers 87s were spotted bombing the troops on the beaches. As 72 Squadron turned into the attack, Winter picked out a Ju 87 and delivered an attack. The dive-bomber entered its last dive giving Winter his first taste of victory over the enemy. However, all of the Ju 87s were not so easy overcome. Some of the Ju 87s gave 72 Squadron a rough ride. Not thought of as much of a defensive aircraft, one Ju 87 went on the attack against the Spitfires. It carried out a head-on attack against Flying Officer Pigg, rendering his aircraft hors de combat. Winter witnessed this attack and lined the Ju 87 up for an attack. However, he overshot the target but had the satisfaction of driving the Ju 87 away from Pigg. Number 72 Squadron were to receive a hard time over Dunkirk. As a result they were rotated north to re-equip and train their new pilots. The move north on this occasion took them to Acklington.

Life at Acklington was once again the routine of practices and routine convoy patrols. Only on occasion was life spiced up by the occasional lone intruder. Mainly these aircraft, operating from Norway and Denmark, attacked the shipping that plied up and down the coast. These were mainly of the small coaster or even fishing boat variety. Feelings against these raiders, in the pre-Battle of Britain days, ran high particularly in the area around the northern ports. This was not helped by the local press who frequently ran their stories under the headlines referring to the German aircrews as 'murderers'. The downside was, when any of these airmen were shot down, it was increasingly difficult to find them a burial place. Often they had to be transported well away from the area, often into Yorkshire, so that they could receive a Christian burial.

For the men of 72 Squadron, however, work went on. Routine was broken by a detachment to nearby Woolsington, now Newcastle airport. Night flying training was carried out from Woolsington. On one occasion, the night of June 26, 1940, one of 72 Squadrons Spitfires managed to shoot down a Ju 88 that had been caught in the searchlight beams over Newcastle. This was one of the rare occasions that a Spitfire shot down an enemy under the cover of darkness. The Spitfire on this occasion was flown by New Zealand pilot Flt Lt R.A. Thompson. On June 29, Winter was flying with a Canadian pilot, F/O F.M. Smith when they spotted a Do 17 between Berwick and Holy Island. The pair carried out attacks on the bomber, which was to crash into the sea off Holy Island. Winter was awarded a share in the kill with F/O Smith. Number 72 Squadron caused a bit of a furor on July 1, 1940. An early morning patrol led by Flt Lt 'Ted' Graham with F/O E.J. Wilcox and Sgt J.Steere came across an He 59 of SntKomm 3 a few miles off Sunderland. The He 59 was duly attacked and made a rapid forced landing some eight miles off the coast. The crew, picked up by a Royal Navy cruiser, voiced their opinion that they had been wrongly attacked. The aircraft marked clearly with Red-Cross markings and having no armaments. The attack on the aircraft was later fully justified when orders were released that all enemy aircraft, carrying Red-Cross markings or not, flying near a convoy, which this one had been, became a legitimate target for fighter aircraft.

The pace of life for 72 Squadron moved up a gear on August 15. Aircraft of Luftflotte Five had left their base at Stavanger in Norway. Ahead of them a flight of some two hours duration at the end of which was their target, the RAF station of Dishforth.[1] Number I and III

Gruppen of KG 26 were tasked to carry out the bombing. The fighter escort would be provided by Me 110 Ds of I Gruppe ZG 76. The leading Me 110 was flown by the Gruppenkomandeur Hpt Werner Restemyer. With him was Hpt Hartwich, radio expert of X Flieger Corps, who was to operate special radio equipment to give advance warning of attacking aircraft. In the back seat was Uffz Werner Eichert.[2]

Eleven Spitfires were ordered off from Acklington. Initially they were to patrol base. Shortly after takeoff the Spitfires were put onto a course to intercept an incoming raid some fifty miles northeast of the Farne Islands. Flt Lt 'Ted' Graham led the squadron into the attack. One section attacked the bombers while another section took on the fighter escort. In the first few seconds of the attack, the leading Me 110 D of Hpt Restemyer erupted into a fireball, taking with it the equipment meant to give the enemy formation an advantage. Leading the section against the fighter escort was F/O D.F.B. Sheen; one of his pilots was Winter. Winter was flying Spitfire K 9922 on this day and was to make an optimistic claim for two Me 110s destroyed.[3] Equally optimistic was the claim of 72 Squadron for eleven aircraft destroyed. The hard reality was three.

With their day of glory over and their appetite for action sharpened, 72 Squadron were deemed to be rested and ready for action. Number 72 Squadron were moved south to the Kenley sector within a week. The squadron were to relieve 610 Squadron at Biggin Hill with the latter moving north to Acklington. For Number 72 Squadron the action, from now on, would never be far away.

The squadron's vulnerability to the enemy was brought to light at 5.30 PM August 31. A low-level attack was carried out on Biggin Hill by Erprobungs Gruppe 210. The enemy aircraft managed to drop some thirty bombs across the airfield. Other elements of the enemy force gave the same treatment to Hornchurch. In the aftermath of this attack, 72 Squadron managed to lose two Spitfires. F/O E.J. Wilcox was killed and Flt Lt F.M. Smith was severely burned. Over the next four days 72 Squadron were to receive a severe mauling at the hands of the Luftwaffe. The squadron lost seven aircraft with a further nine damaged. Luckily, only one pilot, F/O Pigg, was killed. During this period 72 Squadron had become short of operational aircraft. Spitfires left by 610 Squadron, still carrying their markings, made up the strength of 72 Squadron. Two of these, flown by Flt Lt 'Ted' Graham and Sqdn Ldr A.R. Collins, had been shot down on September 2.

The afternoon of September 5 saw 72 Squadron moved to Hawkinge. After refuelling they were brought to readiness. The second major raid of the day advancing in the direction of Biggin Hill, this was a large force of some one hundred plus aircraft with an equally large force of Me 109s as fighter escort. Evidence suggests that 72 squadron were bounced while still in the climb. Three of 72 Squadron's aircraft went down. Two of the pilots, Winter and Sgt Malcolm 'Mabel' Gray, were killed while F/O Desmond Sheen was wounded.

On the afternoon of September 5, Winter was flying Spitfire X 4013, an ex-610 Squadron Spitfire. This aircraft was reasonably new having been first flown July 25 1940; it was taken on charge by 610 Squadron, August 27. The records show that it was still with 610 Squadron when it was shot down. However, as explained above, the aircraft of 610 Squadron were left at Biggin Hill.

At around 2.25 PM, Spitfire X 4013 was attacked by Me 109s over the village of Elham. With his Spitfire out of control Winter attempted to get out of his stricken fighter. It is not fully clear how badly Winter's Spitfire was hit. Obviously, bad enough for Winter to try and vacate the aircraft. However, it is not known if he was wounded or if his aircraft was just too low; either way, when he vacated his Spitfire, Winter was to low for his parachute to deploy properly and he fell to his death. Spitfire X 4013 fell into Covert Wood, Elham.

The body of Douglas Cyril Winter returned to the North East and buried in Harton cemetery, South Shields only a short walk from his home in Lyndhurst Street. The local press gave Winter a short write-up and noted that he had left a widow, Marjorie Winter. Winter is buried in Section 'O' grave number 11795. Over the years the gravesite has become neglected and uncared for. However, the occasional passer-by tends to give it a touch up now and again.

Winter Notes
1. German records of KG 26, Bundesarchiv.
2. German records of ZG 76, " " For some reason just about all who have written on this subject omit the rear gunners.
3. Wynn: *Men of The Battle of Britain*, P 550.

BIBLIOGRAPHY

Addison, P. & Crang, J.A., Eds. *The Burning Blue*. Pimlico. 2000.

Beedle, J. *43 Squadron RFC—RAF*. Beaumont Aviation Literature. 1966.

Bowyer, C. *Hurricane at War*. Allen. 1976.

Brandon, L. *Night Flyer*. William Kimber. 1961.

Brickhill, P. *The Great Escape*. Faber. 1951.

Brickhill, P. *Reach For The Sky*. Collins. 1954.

Brookes, A. J. *Fighter Squadron At War 85 Squadron*. Allan. 1980.

Cossey, B. *Tigers: Arms & Armour*. 1992.

Cull, B. *249 At War*. Grub Street. 1997.

Cull, B., Lander, B., & Weiss, H. *Twelve Days In May*. Grub Street 1995.

Deere, A.C. *Nine Lives*. Hodder. 1959.

Deighton, L. *Battle of Britain*. Cape. 1980.

Foreman, J. *Battle of Britain—The Forgotten Months*. Air Research Publications. 1988.

Forrester, L. *Fly For Your Life: The Story of Stanford Tuck*. Muller. 1956.

Franks, N. *Sky Tiger: The Story of Sailor Malan*. Kimber. 1980.

Franks, N. *The Air Battle of Dunkirk*. Kimber. 1983.

Gibson, G.P. VC. *Enemy Coast Ahead*. Michael Joseph. 1946.

Hillary, R. *The Last Enemy*. Macmillan. 1942.

Holmes, R. *Sky Spy*. Airlife 1997.

Hunt, L. *Twenty-One Squadrons: The History of The Royal Auxiliary Air Force*

1925—1957. Crecy Books. 1992.

Johnson, J.E. *Wing Leader.* Chatto & Windus. 1956.

Johnson, J.E.& Lucas, L. *Winged Victory: The Recollections of Two RAF Leaders.* Stanley Paul. 1995.

Jones, I.R.A. *Tiger Squadron.* Allen. 1954.

Knight, D. *Harvest of Messerschmitts.* Warne. 1981.

Mason, F.K. *Battle Over Britain.* Aston Publications. 1990.

Mason, F.K. *The Hawker Hurricane.* Macdonald 1962.

Morgan, E.B. & Shacklady, E. *Spitfire: The History.* Key Publishing. 1987.

Neil, T.F. *Gun Button To Fire.* Kimber. 1987.

Ramsey, W.G., Ed. *The Battle of Britain Then And Now. After the Battle.* 1980.

Rawlings, J. *Fighter Squadrons of The RAF and Their Aircraft.* Crecy Books. 1968.

Rayner, G. *One Hurricane One Raid.* Airlife 1990.

Robertson, B. *Spitfire—The Story of A Famous Fighter.* Harleyford. 1960.

Robinson, A. *RAF Fighter Squadrons in the Battle of Britain.* Arms & Armour 1987.

Shores,C. & Williams, C. *Aces High.* Neville Spearman. 1986.

Shores, C. *Aces High, Vol 2.* Grub Street. 1999.

Sweetman, J. *Tirpitz: Hunting The Beast.* Naval Institute Press. 2000.

Townsend, P. *Duel of Eagles.* Weidenfield & Nicholson. 1970.

Townsend, P. *Time And Chance.* Collins. 1978.

Wallace, G. *RAF Biggin Hill.* Putnam. 1957.

Wood, D. & Dempster, D. *The Narrow Margin.* Hutchinson. 1961.

Wynn, K.G. *Men of the Battle of Britain.* Gliddon Books. 1989.

Ziegler, J. *The Story of 609 Squadron.* Macdonald. 1971.

Explanatory Notes

The squadrons of RAF Fighter Command normally worked with a force of around twelve operational aircraft. A larger number of both aircraft and pilots would be on the strength of the squadrons. This was to cover leave of pilots and maintenance of squadron aircraft. The squadron was divided into two, 'A' Flight and 'B' flight. A flight commander normally of the rank of Flight Lieutenant led each flight. However, during the heavy fighting of the battle of France and the Battle of Britain, a flight could be led by a pilot of any rank and often was, depending on combat experience. Each flight was further subdivided into two sections, which were identified by colours. Red and Yellow Sections formed 'A' Flight with Blue and Green Sections forming 'B' Flight. A section leader in turn led each section while its colour number within the section identified each aircraft: Red leader, Red one, Red two etc. The squadron commander who would take over one or the other of the Flight Commanders positions led the whole of the squadron in the air.

Aircraft were identified by their squadron markings. These were a combination of two letters carried to one side of the RAF roundel. Mostly, this was to the left of the roundel, however, squadrons had their own variations. Its individual code letter identified each individual aircraft within the squadron. Aircraft of 'A' Flight used the first part of the alphabet while the second half was used by 'B' Flight. Aircraft AF * F, would be an aircraft of 'A' Flight of 607 Squadron. However, battle conditions usually threw the theory to the winds; when a scramble was called a pilot quite often grabbed the aircraft nearest.

The structure of the Luftwaffe units is almost a science in itself. The units of the Luftwaffe were divided into Geschwaders. Kampfgeschwader (KG) was the bomber unit while Jagdgeschwader (JG) was the single engine fighter unit. The heavier, twin-engine fighters were formed into Zerstorergeschwader (ZG), the destroyers. In command of the Geschwader was the Geschwaderkommadore who normally held the rank of Oberst. Each Geschwader was divided into usually three Gruppen however some Geschwader had four Gruppen. Numerically, the Gruppe was the equivalent of the RAF fighter Wing, the latter not widely used until 1941. A Gruppenkommandeur normally with the rank of Hauptmann, Captain, commanded a Gruppe. A Stab Flight (staff flight) was also flown with each Gruppe while the Geschwaderkommadore had his own Stab Flight.

Each Gruppe was again divided into three Staffeln, which was the equivalent, numerically, to the RAF squadron and was led by a Staffelkapitan. The Staffel was further divided into three sections of four known as a Schwarm with each Schwarm flying in wide formations, and each aircraft at a different height, which allowed for flexibility of movement without the danger of a mid-air collision. The Schwarm was then further divided, for fighting purposes, into two Rotten a Rotte being two aircraft: a leader and his wingman.

Each aircraft of the bomber units and the Me 110s of the Zerstorergeschwader, carried a four digit code, two letters either side of the nation symbol. The first two, to the left of the cross, identified the unit while the second two identified the Staffel and the individual aircraft: three of the letters were normally painted in black while the individual letter was painted in the Staffel colour. Markings on the fighter aircraft differed slightly in that a bar or wavy line carried to the right of the national cross signified the Staffel: one, two or three. To the left of the national cross was a combination of chevrons denoting the rank of a staff pilot or a number in the Staffel, colour denoting the place of that aircraft within the Staffel. Most fighter aircraft also carried the Gruppe or Geschwader badge, sometimes both, normally mounted near the cockpit. A number of fighters also carried a yellow painted nose. Many have stated that this marked the aircraft of an 'ace' or known pilot, however, it would appear that the yellow nose was for quick identification purposes while in the air.

Ranks of RAF and Equivalent Luftwaffe Personnel*

Wing Commander	Oberstleutnant
Squadron Leader	Major
Flight Lieutenant	Hauptmann
Flying Officer	Oberleutnant
Pilot officer	Leutnant
Warrant Officer	Oberfeldwebel
Flight Sergeant	Feldwebel
Sergeant	Unteroffizier
Corporal	Obergefreiter
Aircraftsman	1st Gefreiter
Aircraftsman	2nd Flieger

* All decorations and ranks in the text refer to the period of 1940. In many cases these changed later in the war."

Printed in the United Kingdom
by Lightning Source UK Ltd.
104924UKS00001B/77